MW00453868

Flirting with Love

The Bradens

Love in Bloom Series

Melissa Foster

MOS

ISBN-13: 978-1-941480-05-2
ISBN-10: 1941480055

This is a work of fiction. The events and characters described herein are imaginary and are not intended to refer to specific places or living persons. The opinions expressed in this manuscript are solely the opinions of the author and do not represent the opinions or thoughts of the publisher. The author has represented and warranted full ownership and/or legal right to publish all the materials in this book.

FLIRTING WITH LOVE
All Rights Reserved.
Copyright © 2014 Melissa Foster
V1.0

This book may not be reproduced, transmitted, or stored in whole or in part by any means, including graphic, electronic, or mechanical without the express written consent of the publisher except in the case of brief quotations embodied in critical articles and reviews.

Cover Design: Natasha Brown

WORLD LITERARY PRESS
PRINTED IN THE UNITED STATES OF AMERICA

A Note to Readers

In FLIRTING WITH LOVE you will meet Ross Braden and Elisabeth Nash. Elisabeth has recently moved to Trusty, Colorado, in search of a better life, and maybe if she's lucky, she'll find the kind of love she's always dreamed of. Elisabeth is from LA, a world away from the small town where Ross grew up and where he runs his veterinary practice. He has a firm rule about dating women in Trusty—and Elisabeth is about to test his strength and dedication to that rule without even trying. Grab a cup of coffee and settle in for a sexy ride.

If this is your first Braden book, then you have a whole series of loyal, sexy, and wickedly naughty Bradens to catch up on, as well as several other hot heroes and heroines. You might enjoy starting with SISTERS IN LOVE, the first of the LOVE IN BLOOM series. The characters from each series (Snow Sisters, The Bradens, The Remingtons, and Seaside Summers) make appearances in future books.

Flirting with Love is the tenth book in The Bradens and the eighteenth book in the Love in Bloom series.

Melissa Foster

For Gracie, 2002–2014
And for Jim and Mikki, whose love of their "coffee dog"
lives on

PRAISE FOR MELISSA FOSTER

"Contemporary romance at its hottest. Each Braden sibling left me craving the next. Sensual, sexy, and satisfying, the Braden series is a captivating blend of the dance between lust, love, and life."
—*Bestselling author Keri Nola, LMHC*
(on The Bradens)

"[LOVERS AT HEART] Foster's tale of stubborn yet persistent love takes us on a heartbreaking and soul-searing journey."
—*Reader's Favorite*

"Smart, uplifting, and beautifully layered.
I couldn't put it down!"
—*National bestselling author Jane Porter*
(on SISTERS IN LOVE)

"Steamy love scenes, emotionally charged drama, and a family-driven story make this the perfect story for any romance reader."
—*Midwest Book Review (on SISTERS IN BLOOM)*

"HAVE NO SHAME is a powerful testimony to love and the progressive, logical evolution of social consciousness, with an outcome that readers will find engrossing, unexpected, and ultimately eye-opening."
—*Midwest Book Review*

"TRACES OF KARA is psychological suspense at its best, weaving a tight-knit plot, unrelenting action, and tense moments that don't let up and ending in a fiery, unpredictable revelation."
—*Midwest Book Review*

"[MEGAN'S WAY] A wonderful, warm, and thought-provoking story...a deep and moving book that speaks to men as well as women, and I urge you all to put it on your reading list."
—*Mensa Bulletin*

"[CHASING AMANDA] Secrets make this tale outstanding."
—*Hagerstown* magazine

"COME BACK TO ME is a hauntingly beautiful love story set against the backdrop of betrayal in a broken world."
—*Bestselling author Sue Harrison*

Chapter One

ROSS BRADEN HANDED Flossie, a frail fifteen-year-old tabby with thinning fur and soulful eyes, to Alice Shalmer. Alice had recently retired from the Trusty, Colorado, library, where she'd been the head librarian for thirty-plus years. She lived on the outskirts of town and had seven cats, but Flossie was her favorite.

Alice clutched the cat against her thin chest and buried her angular nose and pointy chin in her side. "Think I'll get another year out of my old girl?"

No, he didn't, but Alice knew this already. They'd been playing the I-hope-so game for several months already. No need to drive the sadness home.

"I sure hope so." And Ross truly did.

Alice pushed her black frames back up her nose and smiled. With Flossie safely snuggled against her, she left his office, closing the door behind her. It was Friday morning, and as the Trusty town veterinarian, Ross had a long day ahead of him. He didn't mind, as

Fridays were reserved for well checks, giving him a less stressful workday than the rest of the week. And Friday night was just a few hours away. He was already thinking about his options—call one of his brothers and have a beer in town, or drive down to one of the neighboring towns and connect with one of the handful of women he'd dated over the past few months, getting lost in her for a few hours. Ross didn't date women in his hometown, where gossip was as plentiful as the grass was green. He preferred to keep his private life to himself, and driving half an hour in either direction offered him the comfort and privacy that he desired.

"Ross?" Kelsey Trowell poked her head into the exam room where Ross was washing his hands. Her long dark hair was pulled back in a casual ponytail. Kelsey was in her midtwenties and rarely wore makeup. In the standard Trusty attire of jeans, cowgirl boots, and a T-shirt, she looked about eighteen years old. She was smart, efficient, and sweet as molasses. More importantly, she was one of the few women around who wasn't trying to rope a husband, or more specifically, wouldn't try to reel in Ross, one of the last Braden bachelors, making her ideal for her position.

"Yes?"

Knight, one of Ross's three Labradors, walked into the exam room behind Kelsey. She reached down and stroked Knight's thick black fur as he passed.

"I told your two o'clock she could come in at ten. She had a hair appointment that she forgot about and couldn't reschedule."

2

Ross arched a brow and reached for a chart. "We wouldn't want Mrs. Mace to miss her hair appointment, now, would we? That's fine."

Kelsey moved to the side as Sarge, Ross's three-year-old golden Lab, joined Knight, now lounging at Ross's feet. Ross's *boys* were always on his heels.

"Want me to take the boys out of the office so you can bring Tracie Smith back with their new silky terrier? Her daughter, Maddy, is so cute. She hasn't put their new puppy down since they got here. Oh, and your next two appointments are here. Everyone seems to be early today. Should I get them set up in the other exam rooms?"

Ross looked up from the chart he was studying. It was eight forty and Tracie's appointment was at eight forty-five. "No. I need to run upstairs for a second. When I come down, I'll get Tracie and Maddy." He closed the file. "Justin Bieber? Tracie named her puppy Justin Bieber?" Tracie had grown up in Trusty, and she was a few years younger than Ross. Justin Bieber was her family's first puppy.

"Maddy named him." Kelsey lowered her voice. "Leave it to an eight-year-old girl."

Ross took the back stairs two at a time with Sarge and Knight on his heels. His house and the veterinary clinic were connected by a front and back staircase, as well as a door that led directly to his kitchen. The property spanned thirty acres, with an expansive view of the Colorado Mountains. He snagged his cell phone from the bedside table and slanted his eyes at Ranger, the two-year-old golden Lab feigning sleep on his bed.

"Off."

Ranger opened one eye and yawned, then crawled to the edge of the bed and slithered off. For the past six years, Ross had been the veterinarian and trainer for Pup Partners, a service-dog training program run through Denton Prison. Denton, Colorado, was forty miles west of Trusty. He had a hard time letting go of the dogs that didn't make the cut, hence his three boys.

Ranger climbed atop his doggy bed and closed his eyes. Ross headed down the front stairs to the reception area of the clinic with Sarge and Knight in tow. They'd wait for him outside each of the clinic rooms while he met with families throughout the day, but when Ross was in the lobby or his office, his boys remained by his side.

Maddy Smith jumped to her feet and held up her silky terrier with a smile that radiated from her green eyes. "Dr. Braden, look at our puppy! His name is Justin Bieber. I named him. Isn't he so cute?"

Tracie settled a hand on her excited daughter's shoulder and shrugged. "She loved the name." Tracie freed Maddy's fiery red hair from where it was tangled in Justin Bieber's leash.

"It's a great name," Ross said as he petted the adorable puppy, while Mack, a Burnese mountain dog and Ross's nine-o'clock patient, sniffed his legs.

"How's it going, Dr. B.?" Mack's owner, David, nodded.

"It's a fine day so far, David. I'll be ready for Mack in a few minutes. Thanks for waiting."

Kelsey was talking with Janice Treelong by the

registration desk. Janice held her cat in one hand and clutched her young son Michael's hand with the other. Ross was unfazed by the three patients. Fridays were his easy days.

A woman burst through the door with a squealing piglet in her arms. Her shoulders rounded forward as she turned from side to side, struggling to restrain the wiggling animal.

"Can someone please help me? I'm so sorry; something's wrong. I don't know what to do." She leaned over the registration desk, her long blond hair curtaining her face as the piglet slipped from her arms and ran across the desk squealing loudly. Janice's son shrieked, sending her cat into full panic mode. The cat jumped from Janice's arms, then bolted down the hall. Knight turned in the direction of the cat while Sarge tried to climb the desk to get to the piglet, which Kelsey was trying to capture. Ross was drawn to the blonde, but he forced himself to focus on the ensuing mayhem.

"Leave it," Ross said in a calm, deep voice as he took a squirming Justin Bieber from Maddy to keep from having one more loose animal to contend with. Sarge and Knight sank onto their butts, tails wagging with a whimper. As trained service dogs, Sarge and Knight immediately responded to Ross's commands. He was used to animals sparking one another into a frenzy, and he'd long ago honed his calm demeanor, which helped keep the animals from getting too riled.

"Stay." Ross eyed the dogs—then the blonde.

David struggled to keep ahold of Mack's leash as

he also tried to go after the cat.

Janice pointed down the hallway where her cat had disappeared and Ross nodded. "Go ahead."

"Kelsey, piglet," Ross instructed.

"Trying." Kelsey lunged toward the squealing piglet.

With Justin Bieber tucked under one arm, Ross stood between Mack and the registration desk. "David, can you please take Mack into room two?" *Two down, one to go.*

"Can do." David pulled a reluctant Mack down the hall.

Ross handed Justin Bieber to Tracie. "Room three, okay? I'll be in in one minute."

"Sure. Sure." Tracie grabbed Justin Bieber and Maddy's hand, then disappeared down the hall.

"I'm so sorry. I didn't know what to do, and I didn't see a crate to carry him in, and—"

Ross turned to address the woman who had wreaked havoc in his clinic. Correction. The incredibly gorgeous woman with hair so silky it reflected light in at least seven shades of blond and green eyes as bright as springtime buds. Holy Christ, she was beautiful, and *definitely* not from Trusty. There were beautiful women in Trusty, Colorado, but none with skin so flawless and with such luscious curves that they looked like they'd stepped out of a fashion magazine.

"Got it! Room four." Kelsey had the piglet wrapped in the hoodie she kept on the back of her chair. She carried it down the hall to the last open exam room.

"I'm so sorry. I didn't mean to cause so much

trouble. He won't eat, and I've tried everything. I couldn't find a carrier or anything, and—"

"It's okay. We'll take care of him. Relax. Take a deep breath." His day had just gotten a whole hell of a lot better. He drew in a deep breath, too, to curb his rising interest.

She nodded, breathed deeply, then closed her eyes and drew in another few deep breaths. Ross took advantage of those few seconds and slid his eyes down her body. She wasn't wearing anything tight or revealing: a simple white peasant blouse with lacy sleeves and jeans tucked into flat-bottomed, brown boots. She was only a few inches shorter than Ross, five nine or ten, he guessed, and when she opened her eyes and smiled, it sent a jolt of electricity straight to the center of his chest.

"Better," she breathed. "I'm really sorry."

"It's okay. I take it this isn't *your* piglet?"

"No, it's mine. I mean, it is now. I just took over my aunt Cora's farmette, and the pig was hers, so I guess it is mine now." She glanced around the empty waiting room, and even with her thin brows pushed together, she still looked like she was happy. She placed her hand softly on Ross's forearm.

Ross had always kept a professional distance between his clients and his personal life. It had been easy to maintain that aura of professionalism, as he only dated women from outside his hometown. He looked down at her hand on his arm and the side of his mouth quirked up, despite his best efforts to remain unaffected. Suddenly, his easy day just got complicated.

"Cora Aslin, as in Cora from Trusty Pies?" Cora owned a farmette on the other side of Ross's property, and she'd run a pie-making business from her home before passing away unexpectedly a few weeks earlier. She lived on the property adjacent to Ross's. The two properties were separated by a willowy forest. Ross knew her well, and she'd spoken of her niece often. There were no secrets in Trusty, where gossip spread faster than the wind could pick up a whisper. Word around town was that Cora's sister had raised her niece to be a stuck-up California girl. Well, she certainly looked like a Cali girl.

"I'm sorry for your loss," he said. "Cora was a lovely person."

"Yes. I loved her very much, and I miss her." She looked around the waiting room. "I've cleared you out. I'm sorry. I'll just go wait in..." She pointed her thumb down the hallway. "Room four?"

"Yes, four." He held out a hand. "Ross Braden, by the way."

"Elisabeth Nash, sorry." She placed her hand in his and squeezed lightly. It was the same way Cora used to greet him, and he felt a jolt of sadness at the reminder.

"Elizabeth," he repeated.

"E—*liss*—abeth."

Ross arched a brow. "Right. Sorry. E*lis*abeth." Maybe the rumors had her pegged correctly after all.

ELISABETH WAS SITTING on the floor of the exam

8

room singing to the piglet, who had finally calmed down, when Dr. Braden came in. *Dr. Hot and Sexy Ross Braden, able to handle chaos without so much as a flinch.* He looked down at her with inquisitive raven-dark eyes and ran his hand through his thick dark hair, giving her a quick glance at his sexy widow's peak before his hair tumbled back down over his forehead. He crouched beside her, and the room got about fifty degrees hotter.

"Singing to a piglet, that's a new tactic. Usually people hum to them. That's what mother pigs do to calm their babies."

"I wondered why he liked it so much," she whispered. "He fell asleep." She reached for the end of her hair and twisted it, then caught herself and dropped her hand. Growing up with a mother who relied on her looks for everything, Elisabeth had worked hard never to follow that same awful path, but sometimes the nervous habit returned.

For a minute, Ross simply stared at her; then his eyes traveled down her legs to the piglet by her feet. She felt naked beneath his slow gaze.

"Exhausted himself. When was he born?" he asked. His deep voice brushed over her skin like a caress, regardless of the matter-of-fact way he'd asked.

She was surprised at the way her body was reacting to him, warming to his voice, his gaze. She was used to handsome men. In Los Angeles even the garbagemen looked like models, but Ross was effortlessly handsome, with his thick dark brows that angled slightly inward, eyelashes so thick and long they gave his eyes a seductive quality, and scruff. *Why the hell did he have to have scruff?* Scruff amped up a man's sexy quotient by about a zillion degrees. In Elisabeth's experience, the guys who didn't have to work at looking good were the most egotistical, least caring men of all—and the hardest to resist. Not that she had a lot of experience. Much to her mother's chagrin—*You're too picky*—her social calendar had been full of more dogs and cats than men.

"Two weeks ago, maybe two and a half. I'm sorry. Is there a pig doctor around that I should have taken him to? I looked through Aunt Cora's phone book, and under vet there was just your first name and address: *Ross, 15 Staynor Way.* You're practically right next door, so I jumped in my car and brought him over."

"How did you get him to stay still long enough to bring him over?" Ross pushed his hand gently beneath the sleeping piglet and captured it in one strong hand, then rose with it pressed against his body. It awoke and squealed and squirmed. Ross tucked it beneath his arm like a football and moved to the counter.

"I sat in the backseat for about fifteen minutes in your parking lot, just kind of talking to him, until he calmed down enough to grab him and race inside."

"Is he eating?" Ross didn't look at Elisabeth. He was focused on the piglet, feeling its body, its legs, while it squirmed and fought his every touch.

"Not much, and he's so much smaller than the other piglets. I just got scared when he wouldn't stop screaming, or squealing, or whatever you call it." She wasn't sure if it was the seriousness of Ross's gaze on the piglet, or the perfect bow of his lips, or maybe the way his dress shirt hugged his biceps, but something was making her babble like an idiot, and what made it worse was that she couldn't take her eyes off of him. *I'm a staring, babbling idiot.*

A knock at the door startled her out of her Ross-induced trance.

"Come in, Kelsey," he said without looking at the door.

The receptionist came into the room and closed the door behind her. "I thought you could use some help."

Elisabeth watched the two move in tandem, like they'd been working together forever as Ross took the piglet's temperature and weighed it, which was a feat in and of itself. Elisabeth wondered if they were dating, although Kelsey looked very young and Ross looked to be in his midthirties, which would also not be out of the question by LA standards. Then again, nothing was out of the question by LA standards, which was one of the reasons she'd been overjoyed to come back to Trusty, a town she'd visited only as a child. Trusty had left such a strong impression of wholesomeness and peaceful living in her young mind that she'd built her hopes and dreams around one day returning.

Kelsey slipped out the back door of the exam room and returned a few minutes later with a baby bottle. She handed it to Ross and smiled at Elisabeth.

"I'll get your paperwork together so you can

complete it at home. You can drop it by this week sometime." Kelsey turned back to Ross. "Mrs. Mace called and canceled. Something about her husband not feeling well."

Ross nodded as he secured his hand beneath the piglet, with his palm against the squirming baby's chest, and plugged its mouth with the bottle. The side of his mouth quirked up, softening his serious demeanor.

"Thanks, Kelsey. I hope he's okay."

Alone in the exam room again, Ross leaned his butt against the counter and finally looked at Elisabeth. He didn't say anything at first, just lifted the side of his mouth again in a semi grin that made her insides warm.

"He's the runt, I take it?" The piglet snarfed and grunted as it sucked the bottle. Ross's sleeves were folded up just above his elbow. The muscles in his forearm flexed against the piglet's efforts. He was somehow gentle yet firm with the piglet, and it drew Elisabeth to her feet and closer to him.

"Yes. He's much littler. His name is Kennedy."

That earned her a genuine, full-on smile. "Kennedy?"

"Yeah. I think he's strong even though he's little, kind of like Jackie O, but he's a boy, so I can't call him Jackie. I mean, I guess I could, but..." She shrugged and smiled. "I guess I just liked Kennedy."

"It's a fine name. Well, *Kennedy* needs nourishment. He's squealing because he's not getting enough. This"—he nodded at the bottle—"is goat's milk. Piglets have trouble digesting cow's milk. They need the immunity protection from the mother's milk, but when they can't get enough, supplement with goat's milk or a goat replacement formula."

Goat replacement formula? There is such a thing? "Okay. Where do I get it?"

"They sell it at the feed store right in town, or if you want it straight from the farm, Wynchels', on the other side of town, sells it." He looked up and their eyes caught.

Elisabeth's pulse quickened, and as if Ross could sense the change, he smiled.

"How's the rest of the litter?"

"Good, I think." She pulled her phone from her pocket. "I can bring them in for you to give them a once-over." She texted a note to herself to buy goat's milk.

He took the bottle from the piglet's mouth and set it down. "You don't have to bring them in. I'll come by and check them out. Is there a day or time that works for you?"

Elisabeth wondered if he made house calls for everyone, or if he felt the air heat up every time their eyes connected, too, and would make a special trip just to see her.

"A house call?"

"Sure. With farm animals, it's easier for everyone and less stressful for the animals."

So much for him feeling the heat.

"Um, anytime is good, I guess. I'm still getting settled and trying to figure out Aunt Cora's business and the whole farm thing."

He ran his eyes down her body, deliberately this time. *Okay, maybe he does feel the heat after all.* She felt her insides melt. Oh, yes, Ross Braden definitely had a sexual edgy side that probably landed any woman he wanted beneath him.

"You don't have much experience with animals, do you?" His lips curved up in a sexy smile.

She was still hung up on that seductive stroll of his eyes down her body. His remark startled and mildly offended her.

"I have a lot of experience with dogs and cats. I ran a pet bakery and pet spa in Los Angeles, thank you very much." She pocketed her phone.

"Pet bakery and...Never mind. I meant farm animals." He reached for the door and shook his head. "I'll be right back."

She let out a frustrated breath. *No experience with animals. Please. I love animals.*

He returned with the piglet safe and secure in a cat carrier. "I'll carry him out for you. This is safer than letting him run around your car while you drive, but don't leave him in this once you're back home. It's too small."

Still disgruntled at the way he'd dismissed her business, she snapped, "I would never leave him in there."

If he noticed her attitude, he didn't show it as she followed him out of the exam room. Two Labradors, one black and one tan, were waiting by the exam room door. She pet them as they followed Ross out to the car. She hadn't had any contact with dogs and cats since leaving LA, and she missed them. Petting them helped calm her agitation.

Ross opened the back door and set the crate on the seat, then opened the driver's side door for her.

Surprised by the gesture, she settled into the car. "Thank you for all your help." *Mr. Tall Dark and Confusing.*

Ross rested one arm on the roof of the car and leaned down so they were eye to eye. He wore a pair of tan slacks with a black Trusty Veterinary Clinic polo shirt. She tried not to notice the impressive bulge in his pants just below his leather belt.

"Take my number in case you have any more emergencies." A dog sat on either side of him.

She pulled out her phone and tried to act nonchalant as he rattled off his phone number and she put it into her contact list. She didn't ask if it was his office number or personal number. She couldn't. His eyes were boring a hole right through her. It was a wonder she could process anything at all. Surely he was just being nice, anyway. She was new in town, and he...*Oh God.* He made the smell of animals and antiseptic soap sexy. Elisabeth imagined women probably followed him around just like his dogs. The thought gave her pause and intrigued her at the same time.

Down, girl.

She set her phone on the passenger seat and turned to thank him again. His face was so close she could see every whisker on his square jaw and three sweet lines in his lower lip that she wanted to run her finger over. He smiled, and her mind turned to mush again.

Jesus, what am I? A dog in heat? These types of thoughts surprised her. She wasn't looking for sex, and even if she had been actively searching for a man, she wanted a relationship, not just sex. Anyone could have sex, but it took two people who were really in love to have a meaningful, lasting relationship, and that's what she dreamed of.

"Ross," Kelsey called from the porch of the clinic. "Luke's on the phone for you."

Ross held Elisabeth's gaze for a minute longer. "Welcome to Trusty, Elisabeth. I'll swing by when I'm free."

It took her a minute to breathe—and to remember why he was stopping by. *To check out the piglets.* She needed to get a grip. Maybe he could give her a shot of *Ross repellant*, because she had a life to build and a business to maintain, and a man like Ross would probably chew her up and spit her out.

But, oh, would the chewing up be delicious.

Chapter Two

IT WASN'T THE hungry piglet Ross was thinking about as he drove forty minutes from Denton back to Trusty. It was the beautiful, befuddled blonde who brought that little piggy in to see him who had his entire body revved up ever since. Ross wasn't often taken by a woman's looks. He was more often taken by a woman's personality, but Elisabeth had a wholesome appearance that had definitely struck a chord.

Storm, a six-month-old black Lab and his weekend charge from the Denton Prison Pup Partners program, yawned on the seat beside him. Ross had been Storm's weekend foster handler since the dog first entered the program as an eight-week-old puppy. Ross picked him up on Friday evenings and kept him until late Sunday, when he returned to the Prison Pup program in Denton for the week. Storm was as bonded to Ranger, Sarge, and Knight as he was to Ross. Ross tousled his head at the same time that his stomach growled.

Storm cocked his head to the side and wrinkled his brow. By seven thirty Friday night, Ross needed nourishment as badly as that little piglet had.

"Gotta eat sometime. Might as well get you some socialization while I'm at it."

Ross parked in front of Trusty Diner and leashed Storm. As a vital part of the service-dog training program, the dogs in training went to weekend puppy raisers, or foster homes, on the weekends. During that time, they went everywhere the foster families did, exposing the dogs to people, traffic, stores, and other noises and elements that weren't available at the prison.

The bell rang above the door as Ross and Storm entered the diner.

"Two of my favorite boys," Margie called from behind the counter.

"Settle," Ross said to Storm, in preparation for the flurry of activity that was Margie Holmes. She hurried over in her pink waitress uniform and touched Ross's cheek. Margie had been a waitress at Trusty Diner forever, and she knew the rules about not petting service dogs, but when it came to people, Margie knew no boundaries. She hugged, petted, and squeezed as she wished.

"You know I love you, Ross, but it kills me not to be able to love up that baby of yours."

"I know it does, and thank you. I've already got three boys who didn't make the cut. I'd like to see Storm go to a good home." That was only partially true. Ross loved the six-month-old black Lab as much as he loved his own pups, but truth be told, his bed was getting a little small for any more bodies. Well, other than a warm womanly one, which brought his mind back to Elisabeth. He hadn't dated a woman in town in years. Knowing about gossip was one thing, but being the center of it was a whole other ballgame.

Margie patted her eighties feathered hair. "Yeah, yeah. I hear ya. You here for dinner, hon?"

"Yes, and I'm starved." Ross climbed into a booth. "Go in," he instructed Storm. Storm crawled under the table and lay down. "Good boy."

Margie brought him a tall glass of ice water and a menu. "If you could train men like that, you'd make a fortune."

"You do realize I'm a man, right?" He smiled up at the woman who was as much a hallmark of Trusty as the crisp mountain air.

"Sugar, that's something no red-blooded woman could miss." She winked at him and then went to help another customer.

Forty minutes later Ross stood before the cash register sated and happy, with a belly full of meat loaf and mashed potatoes and Destination Elisabeth on his mind.

"Heard you had a pretty visitor today," Margie said as she rang him up.

Ross handed her his credit card. "How did you know Alice Shalmer came in to see me?"

"Playing coy, are we?" As Margie ran his credit card through the machine, her eyes never left his. "You know I read right through that coy stuff." She leaned in close and whispered, "She's mighty pretty, but she's an LA girl, Ross. Trouble with a capital *T*. Probably only here to sell Cora's place, take the money from Cora's hard work, and run."

"Hm." Ross slipped his card into his wallet and tried not to let Margie's judgment cloud his own. Margie had always been protective of Ross and his siblings. He figured it was because their father left them when Ross was only five, but he'd since learned that Margie was protective of most of the respected residents of Trusty. Even those she gossiped about could win her allegiance if they set their stories straight.

"Have a nice evening, Margie. Dinner was delicious, as always." He looked down at Storm, standing patiently by his side. "Let's go."

Ten minutes later Ross pulled down the driveway that led to Cora's farmette. *Elisabeth's farmette.* Cora had been widowed at the age of forty-five, when her husband died of a heart attack. They didn't have any children, and the town had rallied around her for the next twenty years. When Ross purchased the adjacent property and built his veterinary clinic and home, he too came to her aid, helping her with her animals and small repairs around the farm, checking on her during storms, and making sure she had groceries in the winter. She'd eventually hired a farmhand, and after she died, the farmhand had continued caring for the animals. Ross hadn't realized her niece had moved in and taken over.

He parked behind Elisabeth's Subaru Outback. Not

exactly an uptight LA girl's car. He stepped from his truck with his medical bag in hand.

"Let's go," he said to Storm.

Storm came to his side as Ross surveyed the property. His heart sank at the sight of Cora's old Trusty Pies delivery van. She hadn't used it in years, but it brought back memories of Ross and his brothers hanging out in town, waving as she drove by on her way to the diner or some other destination. If they caught her at one of her stops, she'd cut them each a slice and tell them not to tell anyone else or she'd have no pie left. Now the van was rusted all the way through above the front tire, the two rear tires were flat, and the grass around the van was waist high. He swallowed the sadness of losing his neighbor and turned in the direction of the barn and the chicken coop. Just beyond the barn was the pasture where Cora's cow, Dolly, and two goats, Chip and Dale, grazed. Ross smiled at their names. Cora always did have a good sense of humor.

He crossed the lawn to the two-story farmhouse. The steps creaked as he ascended them to the wide front porch. He heard music coming from beyond the screen door. Ross peered into the wide hallway, straight through the back screen door, where he caught a glimpse of something black that looked suspiciously like part of a woman's ass and leg, but his vision was obscured by the back door, propped halfway open. He stepped off the porch and walked around to the back of the house.

The music wasn't coming from inside; it was

coming from the backyard. He rounded the side of the house and stopped at the sight of Elisabeth wearing a pair of black yoga pants and a skintight tank top. Her hair was pulled into a high ponytail and her body was contorted into some kind of knot with her incredibly hot ass up in the air. *Christ, you are sexy.* Ross's mind immediately went to her long legs wrapped around him, over his shoulders, and—she unknotted herself and turned, catching him leering at her.

"Oh." Her cheeks flushed.

Ross couldn't even pretend he wasn't staring, so he did the only thing he was capable of. He smiled. "Hey."

"Ross. Dr. Braden. I didn't see you standing there." She rose, and Ross wanted to kiss the feet of whoever had developed yoga pants and tank tops. Elisabeth looked like a young Christie Brinkley. She definitely had the California-girl image, and Ross couldn't find a damn thing wrong with that. She grabbed a towel and patted her glistening face, neck, and chest.

Damn. He'd love to be that towel.

"Ross, please," he finally managed.

"Ross," she repeated. "And who's your adorable friend?"

Ross glanced at Storm. "Free dog," he said to the pup and unleashed him. The command let Storm know he was off duty and free to play.

"This is Storm. He's a service dog in training."

She knelt to pet the puppy. "He's beautiful. Six months?"

"Yeah, about that." Ross was about to ask how she

knew so quickly, but then he remembered she'd owned some kind of crazy pet bakery and spa. He couldn't just stand there ogling her, so he made an attempt at small talk. "Yoga?"

"Yeah. It's the only thing that centers me, and you know, new place, starting over. I definitely need centering." She looked down at her clothes. "Please excuse the sweat."

Ross nodded, unsure what else to say, because he was pretty sure, *Babe, I'll center you, and you can put that sweaty body against mine anytime*, wouldn't go over very well. Besides, getting involved with a neighbor was a bad idea. Even a neighbor who looked like she was put on this earth to fulfill his every fantasy.

"Are the pigs in the barn?" He shoved his thumb in the direction of the barn.

"Yeah. I'll go with you."

She fell into step beside him and Storm, and, he noticed, she pet his pup the entire way.

"So, you're training a service dog?" She pulled the elastic from her ponytail and shook her hair free, sending the scent of fruity shampoo into the air.

His new favorite scent.

"I work with the prisoners in Denton and teach them how to train the dogs, and on weekends the dogs go to foster homes to get acclimated with the sights and sounds of the real world." He pulled the barn door open. The sun had dipped low on the horizon, slanting the last of its light across the pasture.

"I'll get the lights."

Ross watched her walk away, then forced himself to tear his eyes away and turn his attention to the piglets. He dated plenty of women, but he'd given up thoughts of settling down until recently. His brother Luke was engaged to Daisy Honey, who had grown up in Trusty, and was now the only family-practice doctor in town, and his younger brother Wes was living with Callie Barnes, a transplant from Denver who had recently taken over Alice's position as head librarian. Both of his brothers had been scoundrels when it came to women. His oldest brother, Pierce, had treated women as if they were expendable, and even he had recently fallen in love. His fiancée, Rebecca Rivera, was from Reno. A far cry from Trusty, but she'd quickly become everything to Pierce.

Ross wasn't a scoundrel. If anything, he was a careful dater. He'd always had plenty of women to choose from, but Ross liked smart women with a strong sense of self, and he preferred natural beauty to manufactured. He had yet to find a woman who suited him long term. Once women found out that he had a trust fund, they were all about the money. But lately, after seeing how happy his brothers were with their newfound loves, he wasn't giving up hope. Ross was more like his sister, Emily, than his last remaining bachelor brother, Jake, a stuntman in LA who Ross couldn't imagine ever settling down. Ross believed in love, no matter how much he scoffed at it to his brothers. A guy had to keep his image up. He'd even like a family. A big one, and he wasn't blind to the fact that he was thirty-five—and only getting older.

The lights illuminated the barn, bringing Ross's mind back to the issue at hand. *Piglets.* The mother pig was on her side with the piglets lying nearby. She stood as soon as he stepped into the pen.

"Careful. Sadie gets a little testy. She doesn't like anyone near her babies."

He nodded, eyes on Sadie, and crouched down low. "Hey there, Sadie. I just want to check out your babies." The hair on the back of her neck stood on end. He'd been around enough sows to know she could charge at any second.

"This is when I usually get out of there," Elisabeth warned.

He held a hand up in her direction and nodded. "Sweet Sadie, it's okay. I'm not going to hurt your babies." Ross eyed Storm. "Settle," he instructed, and Storm sat obediently. Ross brought his attention back to Sadie, but spoke to Elisabeth.

"Pigs can't see up very well, so getting down to eye level helps. Humming, as I mentioned earlier, also helps." He noticed she had a hand on Storm again. *Lucky dog.*

Sadie grunted and Ross hummed, first one tune, then another, until he found the one that calmed her. Eventually, she came to his side, and he continued sweet-talking her.

"I'm just going to make sure your babies are okay." After a few minutes of bonding, Sadie allowed him to check out the piglets. When he was assured that they were well, he thanked Sadie and stepped from the pen.

"I think they're in good shape. Just keep an eye on Kennedy."

"I will. Thank you, and I'm so sorry about your pants. You're covered in mud."

She touched his arm as she had done in the clinic, and Ross wondered if she did that with all men. The thought made his stomach clench. He decided not to think about Elisabeth and other guys.

"That's why they make washing machines." They turned off the lights and walked out of the barn. The sounds of crickets filled the air as darkness settled in around them.

"I love the sounds of night here," she said as they walked back toward the house.

"I'd imagine it's a bit different from Los Angeles."

"Oh, you can't even imagine. LA is very..." She looked up, as if the answers were in the sky. "I don't know. Not as natural, I guess. You know, the difference between city living and country living. Have you always lived here?"

"Never wanted to live anywhere else." He and his family had lived in Weston, Colorado, for the first five years of his life, but he didn't need to go into his family's sordid past at the moment.

"What do I owe you for coming by?" she asked.

"Don't sweat it. It's on my way home."

She smiled. "How about a glass of wine, then?"

The warm night, her amazing yoga body, and that welcoming smile of hers pulled an unexpected answer from him. "Sure, why not."

Sure, why not?

He knew better than to accept a glass of wine from a woman he was attracted to. He reminded himself of the reasons he shouldn't follow her inside. *She's a neighbor. She's already the subject of town gossip. She's from LA, not exactly the land of the wholesome.* Combined with the fact that she was hotter than hell, they were good reasons to keep a little distance. It took only one reason for him to open a bottle of wine and pour them each a glass as they sat down on her patio beneath the stars. He *wanted* to be there. He couldn't remember the last time he wanted to spend an evening getting to know a woman, but there was something so open about Elisabeth that he found her refreshing—despite Margie's comments. Trusty gossip was usually fed by jealousy. Elisabeth's looks alone could spark enough gossip to set the grapevine afire.

Ross watched Elisabeth tuck her feet beneath her on the chair. She was pretty damn relaxed, not nervous like women usually were the first time they had a drink with a guy.

"So, how long are you in town?" Ross wondered if Margie's comment about Elisabeth selling the property was accurate.

"Gosh, I moved everything I own, so I wasn't really planning on leaving."

Good to know.

"Unless I can't make a career here, which, based on the welcome I've received so far, might be a real possibility." She tucked her hair behind her ear and sipped her wine.

"Have people been unfriendly?" He finished his

wine and topped off her glass before pouring himself another, wondering why the thought prickled his protective instincts.

"Not really unfriendly, but...I don't know. I get a cold feeling from some people."

"Trusty is a great place, but people here do take a while to warm up to strangers." They were sitting on her back deck looking out toward the mountains. Ross had the urge to reach out and touch her, to take her in his arms and comfort her with more than just words. He reached for Storm instead.

"I'm not really a stranger. I used to visit my aunt here during the summer. Well, until middle school. She and my mom had a falling-out, and I haven't seen her much since. But we stayed in touch on the phone and through letters."

Letters. Trusty was probably the only place around where people still wrote letters instead of relying on email. "But to people around here you're a stranger, because you didn't grow up here. They'll come around." He felt himself wanting to defend her, and to help her fit in, and knew he was coming around too quickly.

"I hope so, because I've already talked with an architect about renovating the kitchen to accommodate my aunt's pie business—well, my pie business now—a little better. I have no idea how she kept up with orders with just one oven. According to her records, she had at least twenty-five pie orders each week, and once I get my pet-pampering business off the ground, I'll need space for baking pet goodies, too."

"Baking pet goodies?"

"Uh-huh." She smiled and looked at him like everyone knew what *pet baking* meant.

"You're having the kitchen renovated?" She definitely wasn't flipping the property.

"Yes, I talked to—" Her eyes widened. "Emily Braden. Is she your wife?"

He held out his left hand and wiggled his fingers. "No ring, and if I were married, I wouldn't be drinking wine with a beautiful blonde."

She blushed and dropped her eyes to her wineglass. She was cuter than hell, and Ross didn't want to be the one to squash her hopes, or her smile, and tell her that a pet-pampering business in a ranching town like Trusty was about as good as tits on a bull. The town would let her know that soon enough.

"Emily's my sister. She's a green builder and the best around. She designed my house and clinic." Emily had been right out of college, and she didn't have the experience or resources to build his house, as she did now, but she'd hired another passive house builder from across the country and oversaw the process for Ross.

"Oh, I know she's the best. That's why I hired her. This old place probably leaks like a sieve. I figure it'll take a while. I have a dream of eventually living a completely green lifestyle. I hate the idea of leaving a huge carbon footprint." She breathed deeply and stretched her arms out wide, giving Ross an even better view of her fantastic body.

"You know my aunt's van out front?"

"It's seen better days."

"Yeah." She drew her brows together. "As much as I hate to get rid of it, I think I probably should. I'm afraid of snakes and other things living in that tall grass around it. But I think my aunt would be happy to know that I'll use that area for a big ol' garden. I just have to figure out who I should call to come get it, because I don't think it runs anymore."

"I can help you with that." *What the hell am I doing?*

"Oh, you've done so much already." She shook her head.

"It's okay. I'll call Tate McGregor. He owns an auto shop in town. He'll come get it this week, and he knows where and how to dispose of old vehicles."

She nibbled on her lower lip and nodded. "I feel guilty. I used to love riding with her to deliver pies. I thought about fixing it up, but I think it would cost more to do that than to eventually buy another one."

He reached over and touched her arm. Her skin was warm and satiny smooth. He withdrew his hand before he liked it so much that he wouldn't be able to. "I don't have to get Tate to come get it. I was just trying to help."

"It's okay. I can't hold on to it forever, and it is an eyesore. As much as I love the memories, I have plenty of other good memories attached to the house and land. It's actually a good thing. Thank you. I would appreciate help having it removed, because otherwise I might never do it. I could see myself leaving it there for twenty years because I loved my aunt so much."

Hearing how much her aunt had meant to her, and how she valued family memories, made him even more attracted to her. He shouldn't have accepted the offer to have a glass of wine, and as much as he knew it was a bad idea, the last thing he wanted to do was to leave.

She leaned down and petted Storm's head. "Look at how gorgeous this place is. You're so lucky to have grown up here. This is the kind of place I want my children to grow up in. Small town, fresh air. I can only hope for good friends and clean living."

"You make Trusty sound as good as it feels to me. So you gave up everything in LA to come here for a pie-making business?" Ross couldn't imagine leaving his family or his practice behind and starting over.

She ran her finger around the edge of her wineglass, and her eyes softened. "Aunt Cora was my favorite person in the world. She was so loving, and she lived this natural life full of goodness. I think it's because of my aunt that I've always believed in the power of love. I mean, she adored my uncle, and even after he died, you could hear the emotion in her voice. She'd write me letters, and they were always padded with thoughts of how much she missed him, or that she was reminded of something he did recently, and when I was here with her, it was so different from my life with my mom. It's hard to imagine that they were sisters." She breathed deeply and shook her head. "Don't get me wrong. I love my mom, but she's a total California woman. She loves fast living, name-

31

dropping, the whole lot. Where Cora was all about family and knowing as much as she could about everyone, my mom gets off on glamour and glitz. Gosh, come to think of it, when Cora and I talked on the phone, she'd tell me about how this person or that person was feeling, or that someone's granddaughter was pregnant or getting married. My mom never knew what I was doing, much less a neighbor, but she always knew what the celebrities were up to. She's a great mom, but our values are just at the opposite ends of the spectrum."

He liked what he was hearing, and he enjoyed being with Elisabeth, both of which surprised him. Ross wanted to sit with Elisabeth and get to know even more about her, which was not a good idea. He fished for a negative to quell his mounting interest.

"What does she think about you being here?" Was Elisabeth escaping a bad family situation? Was she a rebellious woman who just came across as clean as sunshine? *Oh hell, rebellious could be fun.* Great. He was already rationalizing his way into her pants. In any case, he couldn't deny that she was damn brave to move away from all that she knew and follow her heart to a town she hadn't been back to in probably fifteen years.

She laughed under her breath. "My mom and I have a good relationship, even with our differences in opinion and lifestyles. I tried to love LA. I really did, and in some ways, I *did* love it for a while. Who wouldn't love sunshine and summer all year long? When I was a teenager, I kind of liked the fast-paced lifestyle, but living in a big city where everyone's trying to get ahead can be exhausting. People were too busy to relax or have a glass of wine without an ulterior motive or agenda." She held up her glass. "Or go for a walk without having to rush between appointments. Something about Trusty—and how happy Aunt Cora lived—always stuck with me. Some people have a calling for the Lord. I have always had a calling for life here, even though it's not my hometown."

He scratched the rebellious daughter idea and added, *too good to be true?* He knew about those women, too. They told you what they thought you wanted to hear to lure you in, and then the real person came out and knocked you on your ass a few weeks later. He sat back and squared his shoulders, trying to restore the reserved demeanor he was so good at presenting. It wasn't so easy when his body was urging him to reach out and touch her, stroke her cheek, run his fingers through her silky hair to the nape of her neck and see how sweet her beautiful mouth tasted.

Holy Christ. Get a grip.

He cleared his throat to bring his mind back into focus.

"I could have gone anywhere after vet school, but this is where I wanted to be, and it's where my family is. Do you have brothers or sisters?" Ross thought about Emily, who was four years younger than him. He couldn't imagine her starting over in a new city without the support of their family. He'd worry endlessly about her. Still did, and she was five minutes away.

"No, it's just me and my mom. I sort of missed out in the sibling department, but that's what friends are for, right?"

"Yeah. That's what friends are for." There was nothing platonic about his attraction to Elisabeth. Ross wanted to sit and talk to her, but the more he talked to her, the more he focused on what else he'd like to do to her. "Thank you for the wine, Elisabeth. I don't want to take up your whole night." *My ass, I don't.* Although his radar wasn't picking up on red flags, he didn't need to open up to a woman just to find out she wasn't really who she pretended to be. Been there, done that, in college, which was exactly why he was leaving.

"Oh, okay. Well, it's not like I have anything to do with my night. I'm just working through my aunt's records to understand how she ran the business, and I hope to figure out how to make my pet business work here."

He pet Storm. "Pampering and bakery?"

She smiled and nodded.

Damn, he liked that smile. "Good luck with that." He carried the wine and glasses inside.

"You don't believe in pampering your pups?" she asked as he set the glasses and wine by the sink. He noticed a box on the floor with a framed photograph of Elisabeth and a man. He had his arm around her waist, and Elisabeth was smiling.

Boyfriend. Time to go.

He turned and nearly knocked her over. She

grabbed his arms to keep from stumbling backward. It was one thing to walk away when she was safely ensconced in a chair a foot away, but it took a whole lot more effort when she was holding on to him and gazing into his eyes with an expression so open and pure and the smell of sweet wine on her kissable lips. He wondered if her mouth tasted as sweet as she smelled. His gaze dropped to the pulse at the base of her neck and watched it quicken. Oh yeah, she felt it too. He met her gaze again, and her eyes darkened a smidge.

He'd like to pamper her from head to toe. *With my mouth.*

Which was exactly why it was time to go.

"I'm all for pampering, just not pups." His voice was heady with desire. He cleared his throat and glanced down at Storm. "Let's go."

Her hands slid from his arms and grazed his fingers.

"Thanks, Ross. It was nice to get to know you." She walked him to the front door, and damn if he didn't feel like he was leaving a date and should kiss her goodbye.

Bad idea, he reminded himself. *Neighbor. Gossip. Boyfriend.*

Aw, hell.

He left before he could do something stupid.

Chapter Three

BEFORE SHE MOVED to Trusty, Saturdays were Elisabeth's favorite day of the week. They began with yoga and included visiting the homes of four of her favorite pet-pampering clients. She'd listen to her clients go on and on about their lives. Her clients were wealthy, and most were involved with the entertainment industry—producers, directors, actors—or they were married to someone in the business. They'd ask her about her life, and she never had much to share, but she knew they weren't really interested anyway. They wanted to talk about themselves, which was okay, because she enjoyed hearing their stories, even if she didn't care about the name-dropping aspect as much as they probably hoped she did. Some people enjoyed people watching. Elisabeth enjoyed sharing time with others. Wealthy actors weren't interested in someone who wasn't in the business, so she didn't have to worry about fending off unwanted advances. The time she spent with them helped fill the gap she'd always felt in her life, but the best part of those afternoons was that those fancy actors' pets were some of her favorites. While she listened to her clients talk about themselves, she got to spend a few extra minutes loving up her favorite pets. It was a win-win situation.

Moving to the farmette had filled some of those gaps. She was up at dawn feeding animals and cleaning out stalls, and now that she was mostly unpacked, starting this week she'd spend the mornings baking and the afternoons delivering pies. She'd been lucky; her aunt's clients had agreed to continue with their previous standing orders, and they'd been gracious enough to give her time to get unpacked and settle in before she began baking and delivering the pies on a consistent basis. She found it strange that they'd continue their orders when people weren't that friendly to her, but maybe they were just that addicted to pie. Or, as Ross had mentioned, maybe they just needed time to get to know her. At least they hadn't closed that door completely.

She'd circle back and care for the animals again at night. Most days, she'd been able to fit in her daily yoga before taking on the chores, but some days she'd had to put it off until evening. She preferred doing yoga in the morning and promised herself that once she began baking and delivering the pies, she'd wake early enough to do it before the chores. All in all, she'd found Trusty to be a nice change of pace—and exactly what she'd hoped for, as far as the property and her lifestyle went. It was the people and the larger animals she was trying to figure out.

And Ross. *Definitely* Ross.

After taking care of the deliveries and everything else she had on her plate, Elisabeth stopped at the library and picked up a funny, sexy read, at least according to the nice librarian. She could use a little of both at the moment. She went to the park in the center of town and set out a blanket beneath the afternoon sun.

When the sun began to set, she closed the book feeling rejuvenated. There was nothing like the escape of reading a good book. She bundled her blanket under her arm and headed back to her car thinking of the chores that awaited her. At the far end of the park, she noticed a couple walking arm in arm along a narrow path. Elisabeth sighed. She stopped walking and watched as the woman leaned her head against the man's shoulder. Elisabeth's insides warmed. She loved *love*, and more than that, she believed in it.

One day...

Back at home, she went to the kitchen where the last cardboard box sat against the wall. The side of the box read, PERSONAL STUFF. The flaps were open and bent to the sides. She'd been putting off going through this box because she didn't want to face the contents—or the memories. But she'd seen Ross's eyes linger on it, and it was enough to kick her into motion. She lowered herself to the floor and stared at the box for a long time.

She picked up the framed photograph and ran her

fingers over Robbie's face. She smiled, remembering when the picture had been taken. They were at an outdoor music festival with stars and celebrities all around them. She'd felt out of place among them, but Robbie had been happy as a clam. When his brother took the picture, Elisabeth was laughing at a couple behind him who were doing a sixties-style dance. She set the frame aside and withdrew a folded cotton shirt. It was one of Robbie's. She used to sleep in it. She brought it to her nose and inhaled deeply. It smelled like a shirt. Nothing more. She couldn't imagine how she'd thought it had smelled like him for so many weeks after they broke up. It had been more than a year since the night they'd broken up. She didn't even want to think about that night. She was over him. Over them.

She set aside the shirt and took out a thick stack of envelopes fastened with a thick rubber band and read the return address: *17 Staynor Way, Trusty, Colorado*, written in her aunt's handwriting. She'd saved them all. She held the stack of letters against her chest and peered into the box, thinking of her aunt. Cora had talked to her about coming back to Trusty several times over the past few years, but she'd never pushed her. *You'll know when the time is right,* Cora had told her. Elisabeth had wanted to come back sooner, but after college she'd started her business while she was deciding when she should come back, and that decision had gotten lost in the chaos when her business took off faster than she'd ever imagined. And when Aunt Cora's attorney told her that Cora had left the property to her, she didn't care what it cost. She knew it was time to escape LA and return to Trusty to see if she'd made a big mistake by holding out hope for something more, or if believing in fate and all things love related was the best thing she ever did. She'd been excited to take the risk, and on some level, Aunt Cora must have thought it was the right thing for her, too. She drew in a deep breath and shifted her thoughts back to the box.

There were more pictures of her aunt, her mother, and several of the pets she used to care for. She was in a good mood. She'd had a nice evening getting to know Ross and a lovely day in the sun. Seeing the picture of Robbie sent her back to an unhappy place, and the letters and pictures of Aunt Cora would only make her sad.

I don't need to do this now.

Ross was sending someone named Tate to pick up the van. That was enough cleaning out of memories for now. She'd deal with this box another time. She stuffed the shirt back in the box, along with the letters and the picture, and blew out a breath. Then she pushed to her feet and headed for the door. She had animals to care for.

She brought Chip and Dale into the barn for the evening, fed the animals, and went in search of Dolly. She called for her and walked into the pasture, but Dolly was nowhere in sight. There was a lot of ground to cover, and the sun was descending quickly. She jogged back to the shed and climbed onto her aunt's old silver bicycle. She grabbed the black rubber grips on the straight handlebars and glanced at the old pink bike leaning cockeyed against the shed wall. She'd ridden it as a child, and she couldn't believe her aunt had kept it all these years. She couldn't believe her aunt was gone.

She pushed away her sadness and pedaled through the thick grass parallel to the paddock. The cool evening air stung her eyes as she passed the play equipment for the goats and the big oak tree that looked miniature from the house and enormous as she pedaled by. Still no sign of Dolly. The farther from the house she pedaled, the more her stomach plummeted. She pedaled faster, passing what felt like miles of fencing and empty pasture. *Where are you?* She stopped to catch her breath, gazed into the paddock, and wondered if she'd missed Dolly. Could she have fallen ill? Was she lying in the paddock and Elisabeth had just pedaled by too fast? Looking for a standing cow rather than one lying down?

Her stomach took another nosedive as she pushed her hair from where it had stuck to the bead of sweat above her brow, set her feet on the pedals, and pushed on toward the end of the property.

Her heart leaped at the sight of Dolly grazing in the field near the very end of the property. Dolly lifted her head and looked at Elisabeth with her big round eyes.

"How on earth?" She pedaled closer, then set the bike down in the grass and looked over at the fence. She didn't see any broken areas, and the gate was closed.

"Hi, sweetie. How did you get through the fence?" As Elisabeth approached, Dolly backed away. She needed to get Dolly back into the paddock, and while there was another gate not far from where they were, she'd never been successful in getting Dolly to go anywhere. Not even into the barn. She should have picked up a book on cows from the library instead of a novel.

"Please move, Dolly," she urged. She knew that cows had blind spots and she remembered something about flight patterns, but she didn't remember where Dolly's blind spot was, or what the flight pattern was, exactly. She pushed on Dolly's side. "Come on, baby. Let's go into the paddock."

Dolly swept her head around, then went back to grazing.

Elisabeth sighed and tried again. She pushed, but it was like pushing the side of a barn. After half an hour of pleading with Dolly, she pedaled back to the house as fast as she could, grabbed a hoodie, put one of her doggy treats into the basket—*desperate times, desperate measures*—and pedaled back to Dolly, who had moved about twenty feet in the wrong direction.

Lovely.

She held the doggy treat in her palms. "Come on, Dolly. Let's walk to the fence. I'll give you a treat." She pleaded, begged, held the treat beneath the cow's nose, and finally, she blew out a loud breath and gave up. She should have baked cow treats made with grass. *A doggy treat, what was I thinking?* She walked a few feet away and plopped down into the grass.

43

Who does a person call when they can't get their cow inside the paddock? The police? Animal control?

Ross?

He'll think I'm calling just to see him again.

Elisabeth wondered again whom she could call. She didn't have any friends in town yet, and Ross was her closest neighbor.

I am such a loser. She pulled out her cell and dialed his number. He answered on the second ring.

"Hello?"

"Ross? This is Elisabeth. Your new neighbor?" Like he wouldn't remember having wine with her.

"Ah, yes, my wine and swine neighbor."

She smiled. "Yeah, that would be me, but now I'm the wine, swine, and bovine neighbor. My cow must have sprouted wings, because she's out of the fence and I can't get her back in."

"Wings."

She imagined his thick brows pinched together, a crooked smile on his lips. *Oh, those lips.*

"The gate is closed and I don't have any idea how she got out. Do you think you could help me get her back in? Or tell me how? I don't know who else to call."

Please, please, please.

"I'm in Allure right now, and I've got another client to see, so it'll be a while. Have you tried to move her?" Allure was the next town over, probably a thirty-minute drive.

"Hm, I hadn't thought of that." She rolled her eyes. "Yes, of course I did." Being bitchy wasn't going to help, and she had no one else to call. "I'm sorry. I've been trying, but she just looks at me like I'm crazy."

"I'll try to swing by after I'm done; just don't do anything sudden. You don't want to scare her."

"Thank you, Ross."

Now she was worried about Dolly *and* nervous about seeing Ross. She sank down to the grass to do a little meditating.

A COW THAT sprouted wings. Now, that was the best line he'd heard all year. He doubted Dolly would go too far, no matter how she got out of the fence—and he'd have to check that out, too. An hour and a half later, after seeing his last client and driving back to Trusty, he headed over to Elisabeth's. Chances were pretty good that she'd already corralled Dolly. He knocked on the door, and after a few minutes, he realized that Elisabeth wasn't there.

"Let's go," he called to Storm. He grabbed a flashlight from the back of his truck and checked the barn for Elisabeth. She and Dolly were nowhere in sight. There was a good chance that Elisabeth had walked along the side of the fence nearest the house. He walked to the far side of the fence, where it followed the edge of the forest, and headed out to find them. He checked the fencing for breaks while keeping an eye on the pasture, looking for Elisabeth and Dolly. If this was just an excuse to see him, then she must have really wanted to, because an hour and a half was a long time to wait.

When he neared the end of the property he found a break in the fencing. A large limb had fallen from a tree and taken out a section. He knew what he'd be doing later tonight.

He came around the end of the paddock and crossed to the other side, where he saw Dolly standing in the pasture. He didn't see Elisabeth anywhere. He moved the flashlight across the grass and it reflected off of something. *A bicycle?*

As he made his way across the pasture, he heard Elisabeth singing softly. He stopped and listened for a minute. He couldn't make out the words, but her tone was a happy one. He followed her voice and found her sitting in the deep grass a few feet from Dolly, singing and humming and braiding blades of grass together.

She looked up and smiled. "You came." One hand lifted and twisted a lock of hair.

"You're singing. In the dark." *To a cow. Lucky cow.* He reached for her hand and helped her up.

"Yeah." She drew in a breath and brushed grass from her butt. "I couldn't leave her out here all alone. Without Chip and Dale, she seemed lonely, and I had no success getting her to move toward the gate. I'm sorry for bothering you again, too. You must think I'm a nut."

She had that wrong. He was the nut for taking so long to get there.

Singing in the dark so the cow wouldn't be lonely. Why did he find that so charming?

He drew upon his professional demeanor to force his mind away from heading down *that* road any further. "I found out how she got out. A limb fell on the fence. I can fix it for you tomorrow, but we'll have to do a temporary fix tonight."

"I didn't even check the side near the woods. I'm such an idiot. I was so focused on Dolly. *Ugh.* Thank you, Ross. Really, I'm not usually flighty." She put her hands in the pockets of her very short shorts and smiled again.

Alone in a pasture with a beautiful woman whom he actually enjoyed spending time with. He could think of a million things he'd like to do besides the one thing they had to, and only two good reasons not to. She was a neighbor, and he didn't really know her well enough to trust that she was as good as she seemed, both of which were feeling more and more like lame excuses not to kiss her.

He pushed his lustful thoughts away and focused on the issue that had brought him back to Elisabeth.

"Let's get Dolly safely back into the paddock, and then we'll patch the fence so she can't get out again." He explained what he was doing as he moved Dolly toward the paddock. "Your aunt was really good with Dolly, and she's used to being handled. She's a very gentle cow, but all animals can be spooked, so it's important to approach slowly, and when you want to move a cow forward, you approach from the side, right behind the shoulder." He moved into position, feeling the heat of Elisabeth's gaze.

"A cow's point of balance is the shoulder area, so if you approach ahead of the shoulder area, she'll turn away or back up. Cows see differently than we do. They can see more than three hundred degrees, while we see one hundred eighty degrees. Their blind spot is directly behind them." He pointed behind Dolly. "So if you stand there, she can't see you."

"What's the flight zone?" Elisabeth asked as she walked alongside him.

Flight zones? She was constantly surprising him, and it made it harder for him to keep his distance. "You know about flight zones?"

"No, but I remember the term from an article or something. Maybe a documentary. I can't remember."

"Well, the flight zone is the area surrounding her where she'll move to when she's approached and feels threatened. You want to be aware of her point of balance, and the distance you keep from her body. To keep her moving forward, stay out to the side, like where I am, and at the edge of her flight zone. See how far away I am?" He waved his arm between him and Dolly. "This is about right. If she starts going too fast, then ease off a little until she slows, and if she slows too much or stops, move closer to encourage her to move."

"I approached from the side, but closer to her shoulder, and she let me pet her."

"You have your aunt Cora to thank for that. She spent a lot of time with Dolly." He reached for Elisabeth's hand. "Here, you do this, and I'll get the gate."

"I don't know. What if I send her running the wrong way?"

He smiled to ease her worry and guided her closer to Dolly. "You won't, and if you do, then I'll go get her." He walked beside her until they were closer to the gate. "You're doing great. See? It's not too difficult when you know what to do."

She took over as he opened the gate. "I think I need to study up on husbandry."

"Maybe we need to take a trip over to the library at some point. Callie, the librarian, is my brother Wes's girlfriend." He liked it better when they were side by side, but he allowed himself another greedy glance at her smile, her eyes, her shoulders, her breasts...He turned back toward the paddock and drew in a deep breath. He needed to focus on the cow and fixing the broken wood, not the rising wood in his pants.

"I was there today. Does she have dark hair? Really pretty and sort of quiet?"

He noted that she wasn't afraid to say another woman was pretty. Sometimes women were weird about those things. Chalk another one up to the *What I Like About Elisabeth* list. He wondered how many more surprises she had in that pretty head of hers.

"Yes. That's Callie. She's a sweetheart. You're doing great, Elisabeth." He closed the gate behind Dolly and assessed the broken fence. It was a center break. The railings formed a V-shaped opening. The rails needed to be replaced. It wouldn't be difficult to fix, but Ross wondered what Elisabeth would have done if he hadn't come by.

"I'll walk Dolly up toward the barn. Why don't you ride your bike up to the house; then I'll run out and get wood to fix the fence."

"You don't have to do that, Ross. I'm sure you have better things to do than fix my fence. I appreciate all you've done already."

"Elisabeth, what would you have done if I hadn't come by?"

She shrugged.

"Would you have stayed with Dolly all night?"

She trapped her lower lip in her teeth and fiddled with the edge of her hoodie. "Maybe. I couldn't very well leave her by herself. I would have worried all night that she'd wander off."

He knew she'd have done just that. Ross's phone rang and Jim Trowell's name flashed on the screen. His chest tightened. Jim was Kelsey's grandfather, and his dog was on its last days.

"I've got to take this call, but I'll bring Dolly up to the barn in a few minutes."

"Do you mind if I take Storm with me?" She trapped her lower lip in her teeth and widened her eyes, looking too damn cute for him to even think.

"Sure." He watched her walk away to retrieve her bike with Storm on her heels, and he wondered how long it would take for her to steal Storm's heart.

He turned his attention to the call and spoke to Jim Trowell. Sure enough, Jim's dog, Gracie, wasn't doing well, and Jim wanted Ross to come check her out.

He led Dolly up to the barn and found Elisabeth sitting on the front porch holding a hammer and a box of nails, looking adorable.

"What are you going to do with those?" Ross sat beside her.

"Try to jury-rig the fence so it'll be safe until I can

get it repaired." She knitted her brow and looked at him like he had asked a ridiculous question.

"You can't fix it with a hammer and nails. We have to buy new rails, but first I have to go see a client. Kelsey's grandfather's dog isn't doing very well and I need to stop by."

"Aw, poor thing. What's wrong with it?"

"Old age. I'm afraid she doesn't have much time left." He pushed to his feet. "Why don't I pick up the wood on the way back? Dolly's fine in the barn for the night. I'll come by before dawn and fix the fence."

She rose to her feet and followed him to his truck. "I can call someone to fix the fence."

He arched a brow.

"Okay, maybe they wouldn't come out right away, but you can tell me who to call."

"I'll fix your fence," he said too adamantly. If Ross didn't fix her fence, the only other option was Chet Daily. Chet was Mr. Fix It around Trusty. He fixed fences and barns, and handled other farm and ranch repairs. Chet was known in high school as the virgin slayer—and in the years since, his reputation hadn't changed. There was no way Ross was going to let a guy like Chet go anywhere near sweet, beautiful Elisabeth. "I've got it. Really." He opened the truck door.

"Okay, well, then, can I go with you to see Gracie? I do massages for terminally ill pets."

Massages for pets. He thought about that for a minute. His cousin Rex's fiancée, Jade, did equine massage. Maybe it wasn't too far-fetched of an idea. He dropped his gaze and leaned against the doorframe. "I may have to put her down. You don't want to be there for that."

She stepped closer. "Maybe not, but I can help her feel better. It's only a five-minute massage, but it may really help." She stepped closer. "Please? I promise I won't interfere with what you have to do."

It would be so easy to kiss her. Lean down, kiss her, done.

Done? Yeah, right. Lean down, kiss her, make love to her until dawn.

"Please, Ross?"

He shook his head to clear his head. "You sure you want to do this?"

"I have something to offer her, and I haven't felt very useful lately. I can help ease her pain and help her relax and feel loved; that has to count for something."

"You're really something, Elisabeth. You've got your own issues here to deal with and you're willing to drop it all and help a dog you don't even know."

"You'd do the same thing. Let me just get my house keys."

THIRTY MINUTES LATER they stood in Jim Trowell's sparsely furnished living room. Gracie was sprawled on the futon Jim bought for her. When his son first gave Gracie to him, he hadn't had the heart to teach her that she wasn't a lapdog. Gracie was a mutt. The only heritage they were sure of was that she was part chow. She had a partially blue tongue and until recently, she'd had thick chow fur. Now she was rail thin, her fur was falling out in tufts, and she wasn't eating. She lay on her side with her spindly legs bent at the knee. Her big head was propped on a pillow that Jim must have placed there for her. After examining her, Ross concluded what he'd already known. Gracie was nearing the end of her natural life.

"Go ahead, Elisabeth," he said quietly. Ross approached Jim, who was staring out the living room window into the darkness.

Jim's wife had passed away a few months before Kelsey's father had given him Gracie. Gracie was supposed to be a replacement for the void his wife had left in his life, and she'd filled the space nicely, giving Jim a sense of purpose and someone to love. Thanks to Gracie, Jim had found his way back into the life he let drift away in the weeks after his wife's death. Ross wondered how the white-haired man in his midseventies was going to adapt to losing another loved one.

He placed a hand on Jim's back, and as Jim turned, his eyes went directly to Gracie. Elisabeth was massaging Gracie's leg, holding it between both hands as she squeezed gently, and massaged away the ache. Gracie closed her eyes and Elisabeth began humming a soft tune. Every few seconds, she'd slow her movements and stroke Gracie's fur from between her brows to the base of her head.

"You're okay, sweetie," she said softly, then went back to massaging Gracie's other front leg and then each of her back legs and her hips.

All the while Jim watched in silence, with damp

eyes and a heart so heavy Ross wished he could help him carry it. Elisabeth smiled as she hummed and eased the dog's pain. She looked happy, even though they all knew Gracie wouldn't live much longer, and Ross could see by the way Jim's lips had the slightest upward curve when he watched Elisabeth that seeing her treat Gracie with such respect probably helped Jim as much as it helped the dog.

Elisabeth massaged Gracie's back and neck and rubbed her behind the ears before wrapping her arms gently around Gracie's body and embracing her.

"Thank you for allowing me to pet you, Gracie. You're a beautiful girl." She kissed her on the snout and Gracie opened her eyes.

Ross was sure he saw the dog smile. Gracie had developed diabetes a few years earlier, and she'd gone nearly blind two years ago. As hard as it had been to see her struggle, she'd had a positive attitude, and Jim had chosen to keep her with him, when others might have put her down. About two weeks ago, Jim had called Ross because he'd noticed a difference in Gracie's energy level. Ross had known then that the time was near.

"Jim?" Ross waited until he had Jim's attention. "The blood you saw in her urine is likely from her kidneys going into failure. It's your call." This was the most difficult part of the end of an animal's life, helping the owner make the final decision to continue living without their beloved pet.

Jim nodded and rubbed his eyes with his finger and thumb.

"I know what the right thing to do is, Ross, but I need another day with her." Jim turned pleading eyes to Ross.

"I understand." Ross hadn't become a vet to judge the way animal owners said goodbye to their pets. Some needed it over quickly, while others eked out every moment they could.

Ross and Elisabeth drove away in silence, and when they reached the center of town, Ross reached for her hand. He wanted the connection, and somehow it felt right.

"You okay?"

"Yeah," she said. "I was just thinking about how lucky Gracie is. Jim loves her so much. She must have had a great life with him." She looked down at their hands. "How about you? Are you okay?"

"Sure, of course. I feel bad for Gracie and Jim, but it's all part of life, right?" He squeezed her hand.

"Thanks for letting me go with you."

"Thanks for coming along. I liked having you there with me, and I think Gracie liked having you there, too."

Elisabeth gazed out the window. He could feel her sadness from across the bench seat and wished he knew how to comfort her. He was better with animals than sad women. He turned the conversation away from Gracie with hopes of taking her thoughts to a better place.

"I just remembered that my brother Luke has fencing at his place. Why don't I take you home, and then I'll head over and pick it up. The stores are closed now anyway. I'll swing by in the morning to fix the fence."

"Are you sure? I feel like such a burden."

"You're not, and yes, I'm sure." *Damn sure.* Chet Daily wasn't coming anywhere near her if he could help it.

"Elisabeth, are you going to be okay tonight?" he asked.

She smiled, but it never reached her eyes. "Yeah, but do you mind if I move closer? It's one of those times when a hug would help."

He patted the seat beside him and she unhooked her seat belt, then belted herself in beside him and settled in beneath his arm. Ross didn't think, or hesitate, when he pressed his lips to the side of her head, and it felt natural when she rested her head on his shoulder. They drove like that the rest of the way to her house, and when Ross pulled into the driveway, he did so reluctantly. He'd much rather keep driving, keep holding her.

Elisabeth's house was pitch-dark. She must have forgotten to turn on the porch light when they left. Ross parked in the driveway and helped her out of the truck. He kept a hand on her arm as they walked to the porch.

"You don't have a motion-sensor light?" he asked as he scanned the property. There wasn't much crime in Trusty other than the occasional cow tipping. Trusty crimes cut deeper, like slanderous gossip and sideways glances. Neither of which he wanted to imagine Elisabeth having to endure.

"I guess not." She had her back to him as she tried key after key. "I can't see well enough to find the right one."

Ross stepped behind her and covered her hands with his. His lips grazed her ear and he felt her body shudder. "Let me help you."

"Okay." A whisper.

She turned her head, moving her body a fraction of an inch. Her ass grazed his zipper. Their lips were an inch apart. Desire flooded Ross's body. He couldn't take the wanting any longer. He needed to at least feel her against him, if only for a minute or two. He leaned forward and pressed his thighs to the back of hers, wanting to turn her in his arms and feel the pillows of her breasts brush against his chest.

"It..." She licked her lips.

Jesus, she was sexier than hell.

"It's got a square top."

"What?" His thoughts were tangled, conflicted. He bit back his hunger and tried to focus on the goddamn keys, but her ass was brushing against his hard-on, and her lips were slick where she'd licked them. Holy hell, if he wanted her this much when she wasn't trying to get his attention, he could only imagine what he'd be like if she ever tried.

"The key." She touched his hand again. "It has a square top."

"Right. I've got it." *The hell with it.* He rocked his hips against her ass and unlocked the door. He wanted her to know what she was doing to him. She had to sense his desire, and if she didn't, then at least now she'd feel it, hard as steel, against her. Putting them both in this position was either the stupidest or the smartest thing he'd ever done, and since they'd both stopped breathing, he didn't dare make the call.

He. Had. To. Leave.

He turned her gently toward him and leaned one hand on the door beside her head. He felt her hot breath on his chin and ached to taste her, to breathe in the air from her lungs.

"Ross," she whispered.

He touched his lips to her forehead and pressed her keys into her palm. "I'll fix your fence before the sun's up." Before he could change his mind and take her in his arms, he brushed his lips over her cheek, because he couldn't leave without a little touch, and he whispered, "Sleep well."

Walking away from Elisabeth was the hardest thing he'd done in years.

He watched her go inside and flip the lights on while he started his car.

As he turned the truck around, he amended his thoughts. Driving away from Elisabeth was the hardest thing he'd ever done.

Chapter Four

SUNDAY MORNING ELISABETH got up with Rocky the rooster's call, hoping to catch Ross while he was fixing the fence. Her aunt had named Rocky the first week she'd had him, because he was cocky as hell, the way he went wherever he wanted and refused to come near her. But she'd told Elisabeth that she couldn't exactly go around saying *that* word aloud...and now Elisabeth's mind was on Ross, who was definitely *cocky* last night. *Oh boy, was he ever.* He'd felt so good pressed against her back. She could barely breathe as his lips touched her cheek, but why in the hell hadn't he kissed her? She wanted a relationship, but she also wanted that kiss so badly she could practically taste it. The cold shower she'd taken before bed last night— and the one that morning—hadn't helped much. It was impossible to ignore the heat radiating between them, no matter how much she tried to convince herself that heat like that couldn't lead to a lasting relationship. In truth, she hadn't tried to convince herself of that since she drove away from the clinic the first time, because maybe, just maybe, the passion igniting between them was impossible to ignore because it was really just the icing on the cake? What if beneath that icing lay something much richer, more substantial, like she'd always dreamed of?

She hurried outside and ran to the shed to get the bike. She pedaled along the dewy grass down to the other end of the pasture and felt the weight of disappointment settle like lead in her belly. True to his word, the fence was already fixed—and she'd missed seeing him. She should have just watched for his truck. *I'm so stupid.* She went back to the barn and found that not only had he fixed her fence, but he'd taken care of her morning chores. The animals were fed, the stalls were clean, and when she went to let Dolly and the goats into the pasture, she found a note stuck to Dolly's stall with a nail.

Good morning, sleepyhead. Dolly should be safe now as long as she doesn't sprout wings. Coffee was hot when I brought it. Your neighbor, aka farmhand, RB

She looked around for the coffee and spotted a to-go cup on the table by the door. It was tepid, but it was from Ross, which made it perfect. She pulled out her phone and texted him.

Coffee is perfect. Thank you! Sorry I missed you and I owe you big-time. Xox, E.

Ross texted back. *I like the sound of that.*

How was she supposed to concentrate with that tease on the table? She went inside, and by seven o'clock her counters were covered with flour and sugar, chopped fruits, and other ingredients. The radio was on, and she moved her hips to the music as she worked through her aunt's recipes. These pies would be her debut. Her very first order since her aunt's death. Tomorrow she'd deliver them, and hopefully, if all went well, her pies would be as good as her aunt's and customers would be thrilled to continue ordering. She hoped they'd even spread the word to friends and relatives.

She carefully followed her aunt's recipes, but she had some ideas of her own in store, too. While she was at it, she cooked a batch of doggy cupcakes as a thank-you to Ross for all he'd done for her, but she promised herself she'd wait to deliver them until Monday. She'd already monopolized enough of his time. She wondered again why he hadn't kissed her. She'd thought she'd given off an I-want-you vibe, but then again, she was better at fending men off than sexing them up.

She'd always been proud of being the opposite of her mother in that respect, although she'd let her mother believe she was far more sexually experienced than she really was. That was easier than explaining to a promiscuous mother why, at twenty-seven, she had slept with only two men. She dated often enough that her mother assumed otherwise. The truth was, as Elisabeth's friends were sleeping around, Elisabeth was dreaming of a future in a town she hoped one day to return to, and along with that dream came a husband who had the same values she'd learned from her aunt. She knew in her heart that she was too wholesome for her mother's liking, and that's why her mother had stopped allowing her to spend time with her aunt each summer. *There's a reason women don't live like it's the 1950s,* her mother always said.

She thought of Ross and how she'd answered his question about her relationship with her mother. She hadn't lied, really. She and her mother did have a good relationship. It was just a relationship based on false pretenses. She'd been so hopeful that Trusty held all the right things for her, and now, having met Ross, she was even more excited.

When her phone rang at eight forty-five, she wasn't surprised. Her mother had a standing mani-pedi Sunday mornings at seven thirty. Her manicurist worked only Sundays and Wednesdays, which suited her mother's social calendar well, and by now, they were partially through one foot. Her mother's mouth would be itching to gab and her hands itching to move before being constrained by wet nail polish.

"Hi, Mom."

"Hi, sweetie. How's farm life? Ready to come home yet?"

She pictured her mother's long blond hair, perfectly flatironed, sweeping across the ridge of her shoulders. She'd be dressed in a Chanel suit and expensive heels, red lips carefully painted—all for her mani-pedi appointment. After high school, Elisabeth had given in to her mother's diatribes, and she'd tried to embrace her mother's lifestyle and to buy into her thoughts about relationships—that sexual empowerment equaled social progress and that having multiple partners meant she was climbing some important, invisible ladder. She arrived at college her freshman year with her virginity intact and quickly realized that the minute the guys she'd dated found out, their sole goal became taking it from her. She'd finally given in and slept with a producer's son after six promising dates, but the following week he'd gone away on location and she never heard from him again. Trying to fit in and please her mother had cost her her virginity. She wasn't a prude by any means. She *wanted* to fall in love and have wild, passionate, meaningful sex, but she wanted to have that sex on *her* terms. When she was ready. When she *wanted* to give her heart and body to a man in that way. She realized only too late that her virginity had meant something to her, and she could never get that back. She quickly gave up the feigned interest in fashion and pretentious conversations and let her mother continue to believe she was more like her than her aunt. It wasn't the most honest relationship in that regard, but it made for an easier one with her mother. She was surely born to the wrong Nash sister. And she'd closed herself off even further—until Robbie. She pushed thoughts of him aside and answered her mother.

"I'm not coming home, Mom. We talked about this. I want to make a go of it." She pulled the cupcakes out of the oven and set them aside to cool.

"Oh, I know, sweetie, but you know I have to ask. I miss having you in the same city."

She pictured her mother sitting in a pedicure

chair, her Botoxed forehead as clear and smooth as Elisabeth's. Elisabeth breathed a little easier being away from that pressure. She glanced down at her cutoff shorts and the work boots she'd picked up last week at Target. Her mother would keel over if she knew Elisabeth had shopped at Target, but Elisabeth had enjoyed it. There weren't any *click, click, clicks* of stilettos on marble, and women were holding their children's hands instead of cell phones. Trusty was exactly what she remembered from her summer visits. Well, everything except Ross. He was the best surprise.

"I know, Mom. Guess what I did this morning?" She smiled, knowing her mother was rolling her eyes to go with her sigh. "Oh, Mom. It's not that bad. I fed my baby piglet, Kennedy, with a bottle. Isn't that a hoot?"

"A hoot? You sound like you're from that dinky town. Oh, honey, I hope you know I only kept you here in LA for your own good and that you don't forget all of the cultured things you learned about the world."

Her mother had told her that often, and Elisabeth still didn't know what to make of it. Cultured? She'd learned how to schmooze, live life on a hamster wheel, and that men treated women like trains—ride one after another and never look back.

She breathed deeply. *Don't get caught up in her world. Let it go.* She exhaled a long, calming breath, then drew her shoulders back and set her eyes on the boots she had quickly come to love with a smile.

"I know, Mom."

"Are there even any good-looking men in *Trusty*, Colorado? The name itself has me conjuring up overalls and beer bellies." Before Elisabeth could answer, her mother said, "Oh, sweetie, I have to run. They're ready to do my nails. Love you." She blew two kisses into the phone and ended the call.

A minute later her phone vibrated with another text from Ross. *BTW, careful saying you owe a guy big-time. We guys love big times.*

There were good-looking men in Trusty, and one of them was thinking about her right now. She wasn't missing a darn thing.

Chapter Five

MID-MONDAY MORNING, donning a pretty summer dress and heels, with a TRUSTY PIES cooler and a stomach full of butterflies, Elisabeth went to deliver her first pie order. Aunt Cora had a list of standing orders, and Elisabeth was determined not to lose a single customer. They'd been gracious enough to give her a few weeks to unpack and get settled, and she hoped they wouldn't be disappointed.

Margie Holmes at Trusty Diner was first on her list. Elisabeth had already learned that the diner was the hub of Trusty. Everyone and their brother ate there. She'd gone in for coffee a few times, and she knew who Margie was—she also knew that Margie was quite inquisitive, as she'd asked her a million questions the first time she'd gone in.

The diner smelled like eggs, bacon, and coffee. Every table and booth was taken, and two waitresses called out orders and hustled to deliver them.

Elisabeth stood by the register and waited. The waitresses wore pink uniforms with white aprons, with their names embroidered above their left breasts. She spotted Margie filling up a coffee mug and chatting with an old man. She had a friendly smile that didn't falter as she set the mug on the counter in front of him, then filled two more. A bell rang and the word "up" sailed into the air from a pass-through in the wall that Elisabeth could see led to the kitchen. Margie grabbed the plates, checked them against her order sheet, and smiled through the pickup window.

"Thanks, Sam." She delivered the coffee and food to a table in the corner and was back in an instant. Margie did a quick once-over of Elisabeth's outfit. Her lips curved up in a way that could mean she thought Elisabeth looked pretty—or completely out of place.

Elisabeth felt a little queasy.

"Hi there, sugar," Margie said. "You looking for a seat? Gonna be a few minutes."

"No, actually, I'm Elisabeth Nash from Trusty Pies. I have a pie order for you." How could Margie not recognize her? Everyone else in this town seemed to know exactly who she was.

A couple at a nearby table looked her over as Margie had and gave her one of those stink-eye looks that made her skin crawl. She held her head up high, remembering Ross's words. *To people around here, you're a stranger, because you didn't grow up here. They'll come around.* As much as it stung, he was right. They didn't know her. She took a deep breath and smiled at the couple. All she needed was time for them to get to know her and they'd come around.

She hoped.

Margie's eyes dropped to the cooler by her feet. "I'm sorry. I know who you are, but I missed the cooler." She leaned in close. "Don't let anyone know it got by me. I've got a reputation to uphold. Eagle eyes and elephant ears." She winked and nodded to the door to the kitchen. "Take it right back there, sugar. Sam'll get you all set up."

"Pies coming back," Margie called into the kitchen.

The kitchen smelled like a morning buffet: eggs, buttery toast, bacon, sausage, and pan-fried potatoes. Elisabeth had been so busy baking—and thinking of Ross—that she had totally forgotten to eat breakfast.

"Set 'em on the racks." Sam was a balding, big-bellied man with jowls that jiggled when he turned and beady eyes that weren't smiling.

Elisabeth set the pies on the rack. "I added an extra pie. Raspberry apricot. I thought you might want to try it."

Sam grunted something inaudible.

"It smells so good in here. You must be an amazing cook." She smiled at him, but he never looked up to see it. He grumbled again, and Elisabeth took that as her cue to leave.

The rest of the deliveries didn't go any better. She'd had four stops, each of which began with a once-over and ended with a grunt or something just as reluctant. She drove down to Wynchels' Farm to end her errands on a nicer note and clear her mind from the unpleasant interactions. She needed more goat milk for Kennedy. She'd bought some at the store in town, but she preferred fresh. And the idea of a farmers' market conjured up images of smiling farmers and colorful fruits and vegetables. She smiled at the thought, feeling hopeful for a happier end to her afternoon.

The driveway to Wynchels' Farm was buffered on both sides by trees and wound through acres of orchards before finally ending at a gravel parking lot. Elisabeth parked in the lot and two big dogs ambled over. She loved them up, noting their tangled fur, then followed hand-painted wooden signs that read, STORE IN BARN. The barn was enormous, built of weathered wood, and inside, it smelled of a mixture of fruit and hay. Elisabeth stood in the doorway and inhaled deeply as she drank it all in. She'd always imagined buying fresh fruits and vegetables from a place like this, with row after row of tables topped with baskets of produce, freshly picked, and actually on a farm rather than a farm stand in the middle of a city block. The wall to her left was lined with freezers and glass-front refrigerators, filled top to bottom with fresh bottles of milk, freshly made butter, freshly laid eggs, and homemade jams. A few feet in front of her was a large counter with scales, two cash registers—the old-fashioned type with heavy metal drawers and a pull-down lever on the side. Behind the counter stood a thick-waisted woman wearing overalls. Her straight gray hair was cut just below her ears, and her fingers flew over the register as she moved items from the scale to the other side of the counter.

Elisabeth spent twenty minutes filling a basket with goat's milk, butter, fruits, and vegetables, and by the time she was done, the woman behind the counter had finished helping customers and was busy shucking corn.

"You're Cora's niece," the woman said as her eyes slid down Elisabeth's dress, landing—and remaining—on her heels.

Maybe I should stick to my cutoffs and boots. "Yes, ma'am. Elisabeth."

"Elizabeth, I'm Wren."

"That's a beautiful name. Actually, mine's E-*lis*-abeth." She hadn't had this issue in Los Angeles. Everyone had funky names.

Wren arched a brow, but didn't comment.

Okay, that was it. *Elizabeth* it was. She didn't need to further alienate herself from the community over a letter. She shrugged off the mounting frustration from a day of being looked at like she was an alien and forced a smile.

"I love your setup. Would you ever consider selling some of my fresh fruit pies if I used your fruits?" The idea had just come to her, along with a whisper of hope.

"We don't sell pies." Wren's eyes never left the register as she rang up Elisabeth's purchases.

So much for that idea. "It was just a thought. What hours is the store open?" she asked as she gathered her bags. She picked up a flyer about the county fair from a stack on the counter and stuck one in a bag.

"Honey, this is Trusty, a ranch town. What hours

aren't we open?" She *harrumphed,* with a shake of her head and a mocking smile as she turned back to the corn she was shucking.

Another big, fluffy dog walked lazily into the barn. Elisabeth's heart squeezed. This was her lucky day. She'd found a place to buy fresh dairy, fruits, and vegetables *and* got to put her hands on a few cute pups. It had been hard not to go crazy over Storm, but she hadn't wanted Ross to think she was more interested in his puppy than in caring for her piglets.

"May I pet your dog?"

"Be my guest."

She felt Wren's eyes on her as she set the bags back down and crouched to love up the dog. His fur was so thickly matted that she couldn't bury her fingers beneath it. "What's his name?"

"Barney."

Elisabeth kissed Barney's nose. "Hi, Barney. You're so handsome. I bet you love it here with all this room to roam."

Wren smiled, and it softened the scowl that had drawn her graying brows together. "He likes to chase the rabbits and get all mucked up, that's for sure."

"Do you brush him?" Elisabeth turned her face so Barney could lick her cheek.

Wren's silence drew Elisabeth's eyes. The scowl was back in place. *Oh no.* "I didn't mean that like it probably sounded. I groom dogs."

"Well, if you're looking for business, it's a waste around here. He'll just look like this again ten minutes after you're done."

Elisabeth refrained from going into a speech about how it was bad for the dog's skin and his fur to remain matted.

"I can only imagine. How many dogs do you have?" She'd counted three.

"Six. Didn't have the heart to give the litter away." Wren shook her head again, this time at herself, Elisabeth imagined.

She rose and gathered her bags, formulating an idea on the fly. "Thank you for everything."

Elisabeth skipped going to Ross's to deliver the thank-you cupcakes. She didn't need one more person to look at her like she didn't belong. Granted, both Ross and Kelsey hadn't looked at her like that, but she didn't want to chance it. Even though Ross had looked at her like he wanted to kiss her when he left the other night, she knew how fickle men could be. Wanting a woman one minute and then changing their mind the next. Maybe *sneaky* was a better word. Maybe men know *exactly* what they were doing from square one.

She laughed at herself. Ross didn't seem sneaky at all. A man with a sensual edge? Definitely. Hot, sexy, interested? So damn interested the air between them nearly caught fire when he was around. She pushed thoughts of him aside and set to work making flyers for her idea. If she was going to make a go of her pet bakery and spa, she needed to get the word out. Surely everyone didn't believe that dog grooming was a waste of time.

ROSS WAS CLOSING up shop when his phone vibrated

with a message from his sister.

Mom and I are having dinner at her house. Join us?

He glanced out in the yard at Sarge and Ranger. Knight was standing by his feet, his favorite place. He'd planned on going for a run and taking Knight with him, but that had been a farce. Sure, he wanted a run, but what he really wanted was to run by Elisabeth's house on the pretense of checking on the piglets again. Lame, he knew, but hell. He hadn't been able to stop thinking about her all day. She'd mentioned talking with Emily, and he wouldn't mind pumping his little sister for some information.

He texted her back—*Sure. Be there in twenty minutes*—then went to answer a knock at the front door. Elisabeth stood on the porch with a basket in one hand and a smile that made his stomach do some funky flips.

Ross couldn't help but roll his eyes down the sexy little sundress that accentuated her curves and stopped midthigh. She had on heels that made her legs look a mile long and brought her almost eye to eye with Ross.

"No piglet today?" *Holy Christ, you look hot.*

Knight pushed past Ross and sniffed at the basket.

She knelt to pet him. "Not today. I brought goodies for your pooches as a thank-you for taking care of Kennedy and checking on his littermates. And for helping with Dolly. And the fence. And for the coffee." She sighed and smiled again. "Thanks for being there for just about everything, Ross."

He laughed as he stepped outside and slid his

hands in his pockets to keep from reaching out and touching her. He liked her in those heels, her lips so close to his. "Well, that's really nice of you, but you already shared your wine with me."

"I know." She rose to her full height, and when her hand grazed her dress, some of Knight's fur remained on the fabric.

"Sorry about his shedding." He brushed the fur from her hip.

"Dog fur doesn't bother me." She glanced at his hand, still brushing her hip.

Oops.

Elisabeth held the basket toward him.

"These are pupcakes for your dogs."

"Pupcakes?" He wrinkled his brow as he took the basket from her. "My boys don't need sugar in their diet."

She thrust out a hip. "No dog does, silly. No sugar or unhealthy fats. I use a touch of honey for sweetener, and it has all-natural ingredients like cooked chicken and cornmeal. Trust me, you could eat these, but I don't suggest it. They're frosted with mashed potatoes and decorated with carrots."

"Mashed potatoes and carrots?" His dogs would love that, even if they didn't need it.

"Yeah, see?" She withdrew a small box from the basket and removed a pupcake, complete with swirled icing and tiny flecks of orange. She held it in her palm, and Knight wagged his tail and craned his neck to sniff it.

"Settle."

Knight sat beside him.

"That was really sweet of you, but you didn't need to go to the trouble." He eyed Knight. "You can give it to him if you'd like."

She knelt with another smile that lit up her eyes, and it shattered any chance he had at remaining unaffected. He was trying his best to ignore the fact that she smelled like heaven again, and something sweeter, which could have just been her in general.

Elisabeth popped back up again and reached into the basket. "I have to admit, I'm not completely unselfish." She waved a flyer in front of him. "I was wondering if you'd put these on your counter for your clients."

He tucked the basket under his arm and read the flyer. "Trusty Pet Bakery and Spa?"

"Yes." She bounced on her toes a little, and it made him smile. "I'm still coming up with a name. I'm thinking about something that I can combine with the pie business, like Trusty Pies & Pet Pampering, but first I need to see if I can get this business up and running or not. This name cuts to the chase, so I'll know pretty quickly if it's an epic fail or not." Her tone grew serious. "You're the only vet in town, so I was hoping you'd share my flyers with your clients. I'm also going to hang out at the dog park and visit a few stores tomorrow to spread the word."

Ross sat on the front porch step and patted the space beside him. As she sat down, her hair fell over one shoulder, and a few strands clung to her cheek. He reached up and moved them away with his index finger, causing her to blush like she had last night. If she was a woman who was here to take what she could from Cora's estate and skip town, she was sure going to great lengths to pretend not to be.

"I'm happy to share the flyers, but I think you're barking up the wrong tree trying to get this type of business off the ground here. You know there's a dog groomer in Allure, right? That's not too far from here."

"Yeah, sure. But do you drive to the next town to get your dogs groomed?"

Ross put an arm around Knight's thick neck. "I brush my boys. I like it, actually. It's great bonding time, and I can see firsthand if they have any cuts or issues from playing in the fields."

She thrust her palms out. "See? If only everyone could be like you. I was at Wynchels' Farm this morning—thank you, by the way. I loved the whole setup there. They have six dogs. Did you know that?"

"Sure. I take care of them."

"Of course you do. Sorry." She smiled again. "Anyway, Barney, this big lovable mutt, had matted fur and the others were caked with mud. Wren said that grooming was a waste of time. A *waste* of time, like the dogs aren't worth the twenty minutes it takes to give them even a quick brushing. I would like to know how she'd feel if she wasn't able to brush her hair. Ever."

Knight settled his head between his paws and stretched his nose between them.

"I hate to tell you this, but that's probably going to be the majority of what you're met with. These are farmers and ranchers. Their issues revolve around putting food on the table and making sure the livestock is fed and cared for. They don't have a lot of extra money for pet pampering and doggy cupcakes."

The light in her eyes dimmed. He placed his hand on hers without thinking of the way that touch might stir his attraction even more...which it did.

"Elisabeth, what did you think you were going to do? Come here and start up the same business you had in LA without any reluctance from residents?" He watched her eyes dart away, and he curled his fingers beneath her palm to let her know he understood. She probably felt lonely after discovering Trusty was a town where outsiders were met with careful consideration, trust was earned, and friendships were, too.

"I'm not sure," she said honestly, her eyes trained on their hands. "I guess I've wanted to be in Trusty for so long that I didn't think I wouldn't be able to make it." She met his gaze with a different smile. A determined one. "I'm going to make this work. Even if I can't do exactly the same work I did before, I'll figure it out. Maybe no one will buy pupcakes or pawdicures, but I'm sure a handful will go for pet grooming. I'll adapt."

"I don't doubt that one bit."

"Well, I've already made these flyers, so I don't want to waste them. Hopefully, it won't be a turnoff to see *pet pampering* instead of grooming."

"I hope you're right." *But don't hold your breath.* "Before I forget, I spoke to Tate and he can pick up your aunt's van tomorrow morning. Do you still want him to?"

Knight yawned and Ross stroked his neck.

"Wow, that was quick." She drew her brows together. "Yeah, I would. I need to start making things happen. Out with the old ideas, in with the new. Thank you for taking care of that. That was really nice of you."

His phone vibrated, and he read the text from Emily. *Bring dessert.* He had no idea what possessed him to do what he did next, but the words came before he could think them through.

"Do you have dinner plans?"

"Wha—dinner?" She shrugged and touched the ends of her hair, then just as quickly stopped. "No, not really."

"I'm heading to dinner with my mother and Emily. Want to come along?"

Her eyes grew serious.

"No pressure. Not a date, just a...neighborly dinner."

Her gaze softened again. "Oh, darn," she teased, as they both rose to their feet.

And there they were again, standing so close he could see flecks of yellow in her eyes. *Oh, darn* didn't even begin to touch on his thoughts.

"Are you sure I won't be intruding?"

Ross smiled at her consideration. "My sister told me to bring dessert."

She sucked in a breath. He liked that reaction, a whole hell of a lot. "Ah, so Cali girl has a dirty mind. I hate to disappoint you, but I'm not that kind of guy."

79

He knew she wouldn't expect him to tease her about having a dirty mind, or by saying he wasn't that kind of guy in as serious of a tone as he could muster, but he couldn't help himself. He was a man, after all, and Elisabeth was tugging at every sensual nerve in his body. He let the words settle in, and her cheeks pinked up again. Watching her squirm only turned him on even more. Damn, he liked that way more than he should.

"Oh. Um." Great, and there she was thinking he was making a sexy double entendre.

He stepped a little closer and heard her draw in a breath and hold it. "Elisabeth, it's dinner with my mother and sister. No pressure. No expectations. Oh, and I'd like to buy one of your pies to bring along with us for dessert."

He might not have expectations, but he sure as hell wanted to be with her. Who knows? Maybe they'd have their own private dessert later in the evening.

Chapter Six

ROSS'S MOTHER'S HOUSE was built at the top of a ridge overlooking the Colorado Mountains. The large cedar and stone house had many large windows, a wide front porch, and was surrounded by acres of green grass and gardens bursting with colorful flowers.

Ross put a hand on Elisabeth's arm as they climbed the porch stairs. As if her nerves weren't already on fire. *No pressure. No expectations.* Yeah, she was *so* hoping for a deep relationship, not just a physical one, and his big hand on her arm amplified her secret desires. She carried a strawberry-apricot pie she'd made that morning, and Ross carried a bouquet of flowers he'd bought for his mother along the way. His thoughtfulness made her like him even more.

He reached for the doorknob and hesitated. "Have you actually met Emily?"

"Not in person yet. We've just spoken over the phone."

He smiled, and his eyes lit with mischief as he pushed open the door.

"Ross?" A woman's voice came from the kitchen, followed by fast footsteps. Elisabeth recognized Emily from her Facebook page as she ran into Ross's arms. She looked tiny against him. Her long brown hair was a shade darker than Ross's and curtained her face as she hugged him tight. "I'm so glad you made it."

Ross held her up with one arm, and when he slid her feet to the floor, he turned toward Elisabeth. "Em, this is Elisabeth Nash."

Emily's brows knitted together. She looked from Elisabeth to Ross, and a slow smile lifted her lips. "How did I miss you standing there? I'm so sorry. Hi. I'm Emily." She hugged Elisabeth, and as she drew back, recognition widened her eyes. "Elisabeth Nash? Cora's niece?"

"The one and only. We spoke on the phone."

Emily reached for the pie and looped her arm through Elisabeth's with a wide smile, then dragged her toward the kitchen. Elisabeth's nervousness disappeared.

"How do you know Ross?"

"He kind of saved my piglet from starving, and we're neighbors." She glanced back at Ross, who had a satisfied grin on his lips as he followed them down the hall.

"Mom, this is Elisabeth, with an *S*. She came with Ross."

Emily had been so welcoming that she immediately put Elisabeth at ease. Hearing the consideration she'd given her name made Elisabeth feel even more comfortable, and like she wasn't some form of an alien. She wondered if all of the Bradens were as warm as she and Ross.

Their mother had her back to Elisabeth. She had hair the color of Emily's, like Dove chocolate, and it hung below her shoulders. When she turned, it was easy to see where Emily's and Ross's looks came from. They shared her full lips and welcoming smile.

"Elisabeth, I'm so sorry to hear about your aunt. Cora was a lovely woman, and I miss her dearly." Their mother hugged her. "I'm Catherine, by the way, and it's a pleasure to see you. I haven't seen you since you were probably ten or eleven."

"You knew me then?" She didn't remember Catherine.

"Yes. I'm not surprised that you don't remember me. I met you a few times over the summers." Catherine touched Elisabeth's hair. "You still have the most beautiful hair."

"Thank you." She glanced at Ross as he folded his mother into his arms.

"Hi, Mom. These flowers are for you."

His mother touched his cheek. "You're so thoughtful. Thank you, Ross." She took the flowers as Ross grabbed a vase from a top cabinet in the kitchen.

"I didn't know that you knew Elisabeth," Catherine said.

"We just met, actually. Em said to bring dessert,

and Elisabeth makes pies."

Emily laughed. "Oh, please. You expect me to believe that you brought Elisabeth for her *pie*?"

Ross touched Elisabeth's shoulder and looked at her in a way that made her insides shiver. "I brought Elisabeth because she's just moved into town, and she's my neighbor."

She felt a wave of disappointment. She didn't know why. It wasn't like he'd given her any real reason to hope for more.

"And because I wanted to," Ross added, at the same time he squeezed her shoulder.

Her stomach fluttered and she gave him a curious look, which he caught and answered with a sensual narrowing of his eyes. She remembered how calmly Ross had taken charge of the chaos that ensued when she'd brought the piglet into his office, and she wondered if he was always so calm and in control or if he let loose in the bedroom.

Holy crap. What am I doing?

She wondered if anyone else felt the air between them catch fire.

Catherine tried unsuccessfully to stifle a smile that pulled the edges of her lips up.

Oh God. They can!

She had a flash of worry that maybe she was being too flirtatious, or her lascivious thoughts were dragging her into a life like her mother's, but every time she looked at Ross, she felt good all over. Not just hot in all the right places, but interested in what he said, what he did. She liked him. She really, really liked him, and the only way she could try any harder to hide her attraction was to leave—and there was no way she was going anywhere.

"Well, Elisabeth," Catherine said, "I hope you like chicken Parmesan. It's one of Ross's favorites. Ross, honey, can you grab the salad and an extra place setting for Elisabeth?"

"Sure, Mom."

They followed Catherine to the deck, where a table was set for three. Ross put the salad down, set her place at the table—while his eyes held her gaze—and pulled out a chair for Elisabeth.

"Oh, thank you." She didn't expect this kind of treatment from Ross, but he'd been such a gentleman with her since they'd met that maybe she should have. She liked feeling like she was special to him, and being there with his family, with him treating her the way he was, she felt more and more as though the evening was a date, regardless of what he'd said.

"How about my chair?" Emily stood by her chair and smiled at Ross.

"Of course." He pulled out her chair. "Here you go, princess."

Catherine sat down with a shake of her head and a smile that told of the love she had for them. "So, Elisabeth, I heard that Cora left you her property and you're taking over her pie business. How are things going? Are you settling in okay?"

"I love it. It's different from the pet bakery and spa that I ran in LA, but I do enjoy it. I just wish I had paid more attention to how my aunt cared for the animals, instead of just playing with them, but I'll get the hang of it. My business included baking, but for pets, not people." She smiled at how weird that sounded. "I know that sounds funny, but I think animals like to get treats that are just as delicious as we think cookies and cupcakes are. I mean, who doesn't like a special treat made just for them for their birthday?" *Now I sound crazy.* She glanced at Emily and Catherine, who were listening intently—and without that *are-you-serious* look in their eyes. That gave her confidence, and she continued explaining. "I also did massages, pedicures, and grooming for cats and dogs, but I have a lot to learn about piglets, cows, and goats." She placed her napkin in her lap, hyperaware of how close Ross's chair was to hers and the way he was looking at her, like he was hanging on every word she said.

"My brother knows a little bit about animals. I'm sure he can help you. For a pie, I mean." Emily wiggled her shoulders with the joke.

"Or wine," Elisabeth added, earning her a quiver-inducing smile from Ross.

Emily and Catherine exchanged a glance accompanied by raised eyebrows and smiles. Elisabeth read it loud and clear as, *Interesting.*

"Not to put pressure on you, but you said you wanted to renovate your kitchen. I'd love to know what you have in mind. I could come out next week so you can show me what you're thinking."

"Christ, Em, nothing like putting her on the spot." Ross shot her a narrow-eyed stare.

"It's fine, Ross. I've actually been meaning to call

her again. I just haven't made the time yet. Does next Tuesday work?" Emily was the first woman in Trusty who had made her feel welcome, and she couldn't imagine working with anyone else.

"Perfectly. Your place is on my way home from the office. Can I swing by around five?" Emily asked.

They made plans for Tuesday afternoon. Dinner conversation came easily. They laughed and talked, and Ross told them how he'd found Elisabeth singing in the field with Dolly.

He kept a steady gaze on Elisabeth as he relayed the story. "She was adorable, sitting there in the long grass, singing about sunshine and rainy days..."

She didn't know what to make of him, but the more he talked, the more intimate his references to her became, and the more intimate the references, the more sensual his glances. He was treating her like they were dating—had been dating for a while—and as much as she wished that were true, the fact that he hadn't even ever tried to kiss her made her worry that maybe she was just reading too much into everything.

Catherine asked Elisabeth about her mother, life in Los Angeles, and about her new business. She seemed sincerely interested in Elisabeth's responses, and Elisabeth enjoyed talking with her. She missed having regular conversations that didn't revolve around name-dropping. After they finished eating, Elisabeth, Emily, and Catherine cleared the table while Ross did the dishes.

"Elisabeth, you know I'm just teasing you about Ross, right?" Emily asked. "He's a good guy. A really good guy."

"Oh, it's not like that. We're just friends." *I think.*

Emily grabbed the condiments. "Just friends, really?"

"Emily, stop prying," Catherine said. "It doesn't matter what they are. It's nice that she came with Ross."

"All I'm saying is that Ross hasn't brought a woman to a family dinner in years." Emily carried the condiments into the kitchen, leaving Elisabeth slack jawed.

Years? And he brought me for a no-pressure dinner?

They finished clearing the table, and while Emily and Catherine enjoyed a glass of wine on the deck, Elisabeth went to the kitchen to see Ross. She found him looking insanely sexy, elbow deep in a sudsy sink.

"Your sister has great ideas about my kitchen renovations."

"She's a good egg. You have to excuse the teasing." He set a plate on the drying rack. "My whole family teases each other."

"I like it, actually. It's obvious how much you guys care about each other."

Ross smiled and handed her a plate. "Thanks for coming in to hang out with me."

She picked up a dish towel and dried the plate. "Do you always do your mom's dishes?"

He shrugged. "She cooked, cleaned, and did my laundry for years. It's the least I can do."

Flowers, dishes, and appreciation? She'd thought it was impossible for Ross to get sexier than before, but he'd just skyrocketed in the hotness department.

His phone vibrated.

"Can you do me a favor, please, and grab that?"

"Sure." She looked around for his phone and he thrust his hip out. "Oh. Um." She pointed at his pocket and smiled. "You want me to..."

"Yes, please?"

"O-kay." She slid her fingers into his pocket.

"Nothing in there is going to bite," he whispered, which made her freeze. He laughed, a soft, smooth sound full of innuendo.

She grabbed the phone as quickly as she could and held it out toward him.

He shifted his eyes to his wet hands.

"You want me to read it?" She felt her eyes widen. "What if it's something personal?"

Emily came into the kitchen and eyed the two of them. "What's up?"

"Never mind. I'm sorry," Ross said to her. "Em, can you read my text? My hands are soaked."

"Sure." Emily took the phone and flashed a wicked grin. "Last night was amazing. When can we—"

"Emily!" He grabbed her arm with one wet hand, and she doubled over with laugher.

Elisabeth stooped to wipe the water Ross had dripped on the floor, trying to hide the pang of jealousy she felt tear through her.

"Oh please. I was just kidding. I'm sorry," Emily said. "I couldn't resist. You leave yourself so open to my torture, Ross. It's from Wes. He wants to know where you are."

"Idiot," he said with a smile as he wiped his hands on his jeans, then texted Wes back.

Emily carried the pie out to the deck, and Ross reached down and pulled Elisabeth back up to her feet.

"Sorry. I can wipe that up." His eyes were soft and...seductive. "I didn't think about the whole front pocket thing. I'm sorry. I didn't mean to make you uncomfortable."

"It's okay." She wondered if he really had thought about it. She didn't know what to make of the mixed messages he was sending.

"I'd never ask you to read a text if I was worried it might be something inappropriate."

"It's okay. No need to explain."

He stepped closer, leaving only a sliver of space between them, and touched his hand to her hip, sending them down the sizzling trail once again.

"I don't *do* inappropriate."

She swallowed hard at the hungry look in his eyes.

"Unless you want me to," he added with a seductive whisper and a devilish grin.

The drive home was like sitting in an oxygenless vortex beside a man who made her engine run so hot she could barely breathe. Maybe she didn't need oxygen after all. Ross was calm as the night, driving the truck with one elbow out the window, his hair rustling a little in the wind. She wondered if he could hear her thundering heart, or if he noticed that she was barely breathing. If he did, he didn't let on.

He pulled into her driveway and cut the engine.

For a moment there was only the stillness of the truck, the darkness, and the heat between them. Elisabeth's pulse quickened as he stepped from the car and came around to open her door.

"Thanks for coming with me tonight." He took her hand and helped her from the truck. "I hope you didn't find us too obnoxious."

"I had a great time. Thanks for taking me." She stood inside the open truck door, her back to the cab and Ross a whisper away. Their hands were still intertwined. Just kiss him. *Lean forward. Kiss. Enjoy.*

God, now she sounded like her mother.

But she didn't feel like her mother. The more she got to know Ross, the more clearly she saw him. He was compassionate, generous, and family was obviously important to him. He sure didn't seem like the type of guy who was just out for hot sex, or he would have made a move already, wouldn't he? When she looked at Ross, she felt something tingly and warm in her chest. She wasn't on the hunt for a man, and she wasn't on a scavenger hunt for true love, either. When true love finally found her, she'd know.

One kiss will tell me if this is real or not. I know it will.

She couldn't bring herself to lean a little closer and press her lips to his. Making that move still seemed a little too close to her mother's behavior. She could wait, even if her body was revved up like an electric beater on high speed. Couldn't she?

She moved to get her mind off of his lips. He kept hold of her hand as he closed the door. The silence was deafening. Maybe she should lean closer to him, give him a hint she was interested. Hadn't they both been hinting all night? *Oh God.* This was torture. She needed to get her mind off of kissing him.

"Do you think I could borrow your dogs tomorrow when I go to the dog park?" Leaves rustled in the trees, and she tried to concentrate on that instead of on how much she liked holding his hand.

"Borrow my dogs? They're not cups of sugar."

She smiled at his answer. "I know. I just figured that they would enjoy playing with other dogs while I was there, and it would give me pups to play with while I was meeting people."

"Ah, like candy for children?" He walked beside her up the porch steps.

"No. Maybe sort of, but I love playing with dogs."

"Which begs the question, why don't you have one?"

She tried to formulate a coherent answer, but her words came out stilted and breathless. "Time. I only have so much. One day..." *I'm making no sense.*

He was silent as he walked her to the door, and his eyes filled with serious contemplation, making her even more nervous. She fumbled with the keys. Ross leaned a hip against the house and watched her with an easy gaze.

"You're nervous." His eyes never left her.

"A little," she admitted.

"No need. No expectations, remember? I'm just being a good neighbor." He pushed from the wall, and a rush of heat filled the space between them.

A good neighbor? A good neighbor lets you borrow sugar. They don't turn your insides all fluttery and stand there looking badass and sensitive at the same time, which, by the way, is totally unfair.

He took the keys from her and unlocked the door, then pushed it open.

"You can take the boys to the park if you want to, but they're a handful, so don't feel like you have to take all three."

"I have big hands."

His eyes went nearly black, and his mouth lifted into a grin, tipping off Elisabeth to what she'd implied. *Oh Lord.* He stood in the doorway with her keys in one hand and his sultry eyes locked on her. When he leaned in close, she was ready for a kiss. So damn ready she couldn't breathe. She closed her eyes and he pressed his lips to her cheek; then she felt the keys in her palm and his hand curling her fingers around them. She opened her eyes and he was looking at her with a wanton look in his eyes.

What. The. Hell?

"G'night, Lissa."

Lissa. It was the nickname her aunt Cora had given her. No one else had ever used it, and she loved hearing it come from Ross's lips almost as much as she liked the feel of his lips against her cheek.

And now he was leaving. As her brain screamed, *Don't let him go! Run to the truck, grab him by the collar, and kiss the hell out of him,* she envisioned her mother lusting after some wealthy man. She forced away the thought, but the desire lingered.

And sizzled all the way to her toes.

Chapter Seven

WHEN THE PROGRAM director had first approached Ross about joining the service-dog training program six years earlier, he'd been skeptical about handing eight-week-old puppies to convicts. At the time, he hadn't had any experience working with convicted felons, and his love of animals outweighed any love he'd known other than the love he had for his family. But he'd heard about other prison systems with similar programs, and the dogs and inmates seemed to establish bonds just as well as people outside of the gated walls did. The program itself was providing a valuable service, and the dogs were well cared for. He'd given it a shot. It was Tuesday, and as he parked at Denton Prison, he thought about the program. In the years since he began working with it, he'd seen the hardest of men soften and love the dogs so deeply it made his throat swell to think he'd almost nixed the idea completely. Ross wasn't a risk taker in general, but he'd taken a chance by getting involved in the Pup Partners program, and it was one of the most rewarding programs he'd ever taken part in. He'd been taking risks in his personal life lately, too.

Ross had spent his life avoiding gossip like the plague, but he couldn't put distance between himself and Elisabeth. He'd tried to remain purely platonic at dinner at his mother's house, but he was drawn to Elisabeth like cats to catnip—and boy, did he want to devour her. He nearly did when they'd said good night, but he'd somehow managed to fight the urge. He sensed that once he gave in, that was going to be it. Every time he saw her, his stomach did weird things, and she aroused the hell out of him with the slightest of touches. What would it be like when their lips actually met? When his hands explored the curvy plains of her body?

Fuck.

He was hard again.

He knew it was a bad idea to date a woman who was already the focus of so much gossip, but it was getting more and more difficult to keep his desires to himself. He didn't need to get tangled up in the shitty Trusty grapevine. Even knowing this didn't dissuade his body from craving her and his mind from returning to her.

He flicked on rock music, which he hated, and drew upon the women who were sure to erase any sexual thoughts from his mind. *Rosie O'Donnell. Barbara Walters. Hillary Clinton.* The training session would be a good distraction from his thoughts of

Elisabeth. A few deep breaths later he was ready to handle the dog training without an embarrassing hard-on.

The waiting list for the program was more than five hundred prisoners long, and there were strict guidelines they had to meet in order to be accepted into the program, the most important of which were no history of a sex-related crime and no history of abuse or cruelty to animals. There were other guidelines, of course, such as maturity and education level, term of incarceration, and prisoners must not have had an infraction within ninety days of being accepted into the program, and of course, during the program. Ross was comfortable with the guidelines as a means for weeding out the candidates who would not put the dog's needs ahead of their own, and the fact that prisoners were selected by a committee usually helped ease his mind, but every now and then a prisoner—in the program, they were referred to as handlers because they handled and trained the dogs— would come through that worried Ross. Trout Granger was one of those handlers, and Storm was the dog he trained. Because of that, Ross had chosen Storm as his weekend charge. This allowed him to monitor Storm's progress and watch for signs of trouble. So far, he had no reason to be concerned.

Trout hulked over the six-month-old black Lab. At six five and three hundred pounds, Trout looked like the killer he was—or had been. Ross wasn't sure how to define the inmates after they'd been in the system as long as Trout. Timothy Michael Granger, aka Trout, had been just eighteen years old when he was arrested for cutting his mother's ex-boyfriend's throat—ten years after the man had killed his mother. He'd called the police from the man's apartment and waited for the police to arrive ten minutes after committing the crime. He'd served fifteen years of a life sentence. Trout had graduated as his high school's valedictorian even after being in the foster system for ten years. At the time of the murder, he'd had a scholarship for a full ride to college, and the day after he turned eighteen, he threw it all away. Trout wasn't from Trusty, but his academic background was similar to Ross's until the day he killed a man. Ross's love and loyalty to his family was all-consuming, but he knew he didn't have it in him to kill another human being, and he wondered what had made Trout cross that line and why he'd waited ten years to do it.

At six three, two hundred ten pounds, with a body sculpted by good genetics and exercise, Ross had a strong presence, but he had no doubt the man standing before him could snap his neck in a hot second—and maybe never think about him again.

Storm sat at Trout's feet, wearing his red SERVICE DOG IN TRAINING, DO NOT PET vest. Ross was always impressed when the handlers began their training in the correct position with their dog. Storm was doing well. Last week he'd been antsy and had a hard time settling down. *Progress.*

"Any problems to report?" Ross asked.

Trout's jaw swished from side to side. His deadpan stare didn't change, and he didn't make a sound. Ross knew from their previous interactions that Trout was a man of very few words, and those words were only the necessary words for training Storm: *heel, settle, leave it, good boy, free dog.* That's as far as they'd gotten. Ross watched for the shake or nod of Trout's Frankenstein-sized bald head, upon which the words *Honor Thy Mother* were tattooed in black. They went nicely with his colorful tattoo sleeves. Like a hat might top off an outfit.

Trout shook his head.

"Good. He's eating okay? Sleeping in his crate?" Ross eyed Storm, who was looking up at Trout with the trust and adoration of a child to a father. Ross said a silent prayer that Trout would never lose his temper with Storm, though he hadn't seen even a flash of emotion one way or another from him. In fact, the guards said he rarely spoke to anyone.

One curt nod; then he eyed the dog, and that shift in his gaze gave Ross pause.

"Sleeping trouble?"

He looked down at Storm. "Stay." Trout's commands were delivered in a low voice, barely audible from across the room. That same voice used in combination with the deadpan stare would surely send any man running for the hills. But Trout had found his pitch with Storm, who obediently followed every command.

He stepped closer to Ross—a wall of muscle and silence.

"What is it, Trout?" Trout wore the standard gray uniform—a pullover shirt and matching pants—and smelled of industrial soap and sweat, not exactly a pleasant combination.

Trout leaned down closer to Ross and spoke softly, as if he didn't want Storm to hear him. "Storm had trouble sleeping last night."

He had a gravelly, deep voice, thick with concern at the moment. His grave concern meant that Trout had connected with Storm on an emotional level, which was one of the goals of the program. Ross was surprised to hear something from Trout other than the few words they used in training, and the worry in his normally ice-cold eyes softened Ross's view of him.

"That happens. Was he sick? How's he been acting today?" He moved to the side and eyed Storm, whose eyes were bright. Storm cocked his head and panted.

"Fine today. Fine yesterday. He whined and cried, and I tried covering the crate and talking to him."

"And?"

"And." He looked around at the empty room, then turned back to Ross. "The other inmates were bitching, so I crawled into the crate and put an arm over him."

"You crawled into the crate? You fit in the crate?"

Trout cracked a crooked smile, and dimples appeared in his cheeks, taking his hulking-monster image down a notch, to that of a gentle giant. *A murdering giant.* This was the first real emotion he'd seen from Trout. It struck Ross that the man he'd been most concerned about might turn out to be the most compassionate.

"Shoulders, chest. What should I have done, Doc? I

couldn't just let him cry with all the other guys hollering like they were." Trout stayed in a special wing of the prison, where only prisoners with dogs were allowed.

"That's a good question. We've had handlers who have done what you did, but it's rare, and we don't encourage it, because the dogs have to learn to self-soothe. You tried covering the crate, and that didn't work?"

Trout shook his head real slow. "He was sad, I think."

"Sad?"

Trout nodded. "Sad."

He wasn't about to argue with the three-hundred-pound man. "I'd like to check him out and make sure he's okay; then why don't you see how he does tonight? Expect him to do well. Do whatever you normally do. If you're still having trouble, we can figure it out. But it might have just been a onetime thing."

"I don't mind lyin' with him. Is that allowed?"

After the first few weeks, dogs didn't typically have issues at night. Technically, the inmates were allowed to lie with the dogs in the program, but Ross didn't want to promote anything that would hinder the love for Storm's crate that Storm needed to adhere to in order to pass the program. Then again, Trout was talking, and that was a different type of progress.

"I'm worried about the size of the crate, Trout. You could crush him if you roll over onto him."

Trout narrowed his eyes and nodded. "I won't."

"Let's play it by ear. If it happens tonight, try talking to him. And if you have to, put just your hand in the crate. Okay?"

"Sure, Doc. That's a good idea."

They completed the training for the day, and Ross met with Walt Norton, the prison program director for Pup Partners, before he left. He let him know what was going on with Trout and Storm and asked him to keep an eye on them. Walt was in his midsixties with hollow cheeks and deep-set dark eyes, giving him a serious look, even when he smiled.

"I'll keep an eye on them. The program is making a difference for Trout. He's no longer sitting by himself in the cafeteria. He's sitting with other inmates, and he's answering questions instead of grunting. An inmate asked him why he was sitting with them, and the guard heard him tell the guy that it was good for the dog."

A vital part of the dogs' training was that they remained with their handler around the clock. They learned how to sit without begging when their handlers ate and how to react to other people and dogs, just as they would be expected to behave outside of the prison.

Walt shook his head. "Good for the dog. He's a stone-cold killer. Hasn't done more than grunt or nod since he arrived fifteen years ago, and a dog pulls him out of his shell. Go figure."

On the way back to Trusty, Ross thought about Trout. Not for the first time, he wondered if Trout had adapted to prison by remaining silent as purely a survival technique, or if he was a relatively silent man before his incarceration. He'd tried talking to Trout when he'd first entered the program, but it was apparent after the first three questions that he wasn't going to get far. Ross knew the power of a pet's love could change a person, and he was glad to see that Trout wasn't too far gone to feel an inkling of compassion.

Fitting in anywhere was tricky business. The thought brought his mind back to Elisabeth—*Lissa*—where it had been all morning. When the nickname first slipped from his lips, he hadn't expected it. But he'd felt so close to her that the intimacy of it felt right, which was just another thing that confused the hell out of him. How could he feel intimate with a woman he'd never even kissed? All morning he'd relived every look, the feel of her hand, the want in her eyes when he'd left her at her door. He'd reminded himself all day that she was living in Trusty and just how bad of an idea it would be to get involved. He knew the risks of dating her if they dated a few times and then realized what he felt wasn't really as substantive and consuming as it felt. He knew he could end up making her reputation worse and make himself the object of town gossip, not to mention that it could ruin their relationship as neighbors, but that didn't stop his body from reacting to the very thought of her—or the rebellious side of him he never realized he had to rear its powerful head.

Fuck the gossip.

BACK HOME, ROSS parked behind his younger brother Wes's truck and glanced at the husbandry book he'd brought home from work for Elisabeth. He left it in the cab of the truck and followed a trail of blood to the grass, where he found Wes standing with his bloodhound Sweets in his arms. Wes owned a dude ranch just outside of town, and he had a penchant for dangerous activities such as mountain climbing and skydiving, and he was always getting injured. God only knew what he'd done now.

"Ross, I need ya, man." Wes had a deep gash across his forehead.

"What happened?" Ross did a quick visual assessment of Sweets, who looked to be bleeding from her paws. Sweets was the only bloodhound Ross had ever met with no sense of smell, and she was perfectly named, as she was the sweetest dog on earth.

As if to prove Ross's thoughts, Sweets licked Wes's cheek.

"Fell while climbing a rock face," Wes explained, which made no sense given that Wes would never have Sweets do such a thing, but the amount of blood dripping from the gash on Wes's head told Ross that he was referring to himself.

Ross nodded toward the clinic entrance and they went inside. He flicked on the lights as he led Wes into an exam room.

"I came by last night to have a beer with you, but you were on your date with Elisabeth Nash." With Sweets securely pressed against his chest, Wes sat on the exam table with a smart-ass smirk on his face.

Goddamn Braden grapevine, a direct descendant of the Trusty grapevine. Ross slanted his eyes at Wes. "Mom or Emily?"

"Em, of course. Dating a Trusty girl? That's new."

"It wasn't a date." But it had taken a minute-by-minute effort to keep himself from asking her on one.

"That's not what Em thinks. She said—"

Ross stopped him with a heated stare, then began checking Sweets's paws. "I don't see a cut or contusion on her paws. What happened?"

"Oh, it's not Sweets. Just me. She walked in *my* blood." Wes's jeans were smeared with bloody paw prints, and he'd obviously tried to use his shirtsleeve to stop the bleeding, as it was also soaked with fresh blood.

Ross leaned back against the counter and breathed deeply, thankful that Sweets was not hurt and mildly concerned over Wes's cut. Wes was always getting cuts and breaking bones, and this one didn't look like it would need anything more than a few stitches, but why the hell was he in Ross's office if his dog wasn't hurt, and why did Sweets look traumatized?

"Then why are you holding her like she's injured?"

Wes kissed Sweets's head and spoke just above a whisper. "She got scared when I passed out."

"Passed out? Wes, you should be in Daisy's office, not mine." Daisy was their brother Luke's fiancée and the Trusty family-practice doctor.

"If I go to Daisy, she's going to tell Callie, and then I'm up shit's creek, because..." He held up his bandaged hand, which had been tucked beneath Sweets's body.

Ross laughed. "Same rock face?"

"Three days ago. I told her I wouldn't go again, and I wasn't going to, but—"

Ross held up his hand. "Don't even tell me. I don't want to know." He took Sweets from Wes's arms and loved her up, then set her on the floor, where she wagged her tail and whined at Wes.

"Get down here and sit on the chair. Jesus, Sweets is like a wife." Ross nodded toward the chair and Wes did as instructed. Sweets settled her head in his lap. "How do you think you'll keep this from Callie?"

"I won't. I won't lie to her."

Ross arched a brow.

"It wasn't a lie. I had no intention of climbing that goddamn rock face. It's on the north side of the mountain and I was going to scout out a new trail for a hike with next week's group at the ranch, and..." Wes shrugged, and his mouth lifted into an apologetic smile.

"So, you're going to tell her."

"Yes. Of course. You can't lie to a woman. They have built-in sensors for that."

Good to know. "Then you should definitely be at Daisy's."

Wes sighed heavily. "No way, bro. If Daisy tells Callie *before* me, I'm dead meat. It's as good as lying to tell her after someone else does, and I can't tell her over the phone." Wes pointed to his eyes, which suddenly looked *very* apologetic. "She needs to see me."

"Idiot." Ross cleaned his wound and waited for the numbing medicine to work.

Wes looked around for a minute. "Where are the boys?"

"On a playdate." He thought about when Elisabeth had come by to get the dogs earlier that morning. He'd opened the door, and for a hot minute their eyes had connected and the air between them sizzled and popped. It had taken all of Ross's focus not to greet her with a kiss, and he could tell by the nervous way she smiled and the way her words were breathy and soft that she was having just as hard of a time keeping her distance from him.

"A...Whatever. You gonna tell me about Elisabeth? From what I hear, she's here for the money, which you have, so be careful." Wes leaned down and kissed Sweets's head. Each of the Bradens had hefty trust funds, passed down for generations.

"She's not here for the money, and we're not dating." She'd moved all her stuff, she was talking about renovating the kitchen, and she was trying her best to fit into the community. None of those were signs of a woman interested in taking what she could and leaving town. The hell with waiting. He began suturing, ignoring Wes's flinching.

"Fuck, Ross." Wes fisted his hand.

"Man up, and if Callie asks, I tried to get you to call her."

"Yeah, I know the drill."

After Ross was done, Wes cleaned up as best he

could, which wasn't very well at all. He leaned against the counter. "Wanna grab a beer?"

"You've got a fiancée to come clean to," Ross reminded him.

On the way to the front door, Wes asked, "How do you know Elisabeth's not here for the money if you're not dating her?"

"She's hiring Emily to renovate Cora's kitchen."

"Probably to flip it," Wes suggested.

"Not to flip it." Why was he explaining Elisabeth's plans to Wes? "Next time you want to grab a beer, text the word *beer*. I could have used one after I dropped her off."

"Didn't get any? No wonder you're pissy."

Ross opened the door. "Out."

ELISABETH HAD BAKED all morning for tomorrow's deliveries; then she'd calculated her current income and went back to check it against her aunt's records. Orders were slowing down a little. Not much, and she might not have noticed had she not compared the figures, but seeing a downturn of even a handful of pies in the three weeks since she'd moved to Trusty and taken over the business wasn't exactly uplifting. She'd have to make more of an effort to sell and maintain that business along with her pet business.

She had a great afternoon at the dog park with Ranger, Knight, and Sarge, doing more playing than marketing of her business. It had been a few weeks since she'd had any real doggy time, and she missed having dogs and cats in her life on a daily basis. Farm animals were wonderful, but give her a pup or kitty and she was in heaven. She'd handed out flyers about her business and talked to every dog owner, but most changed the subject the minute it came to grooming or dog care, giving her no time to really try to explain or to market her business.

She'd then gone to Missy's Dog Grooming in Allure to introduce herself and see if she'd be interested in a reciprocal referral relationship, but Missy had done her best to dissuade Elisabeth from trying to build a grooming business. She obviously didn't want competition, which told Elisabeth that maybe there wasn't much of a market for dog grooming in Trusty after all. By the time Elisabeth drove back to Trusty, she was barely holding on to a thread of hope. She needed a better plan.

A better plan. Was she fooling herself? Had she wanted to be in Trusty so badly that she tricked herself into believing it was as wholesome and as welcoming as Aunt Cora? Was the wholesomeness she'd felt nothing more than the love of her dear aunt? Did her mind fabricate the rest? Tears welled in her eyes as she neared Ross's house.

No. No, no, no. Do not cry.

Knight, who had refused to sit in the back of her car with the other dogs, huffed a breath and rested his big black head on her lap, like he knew she needed company. She stroked his fur. Of course he knew. Dogs understood her so well.

"I'm not giving up. No way. I've wanted to be here too long to fold under pressure." Her words were stronger than her conviction at the moment.

She drove down Ross's driveway, passing a guy in a truck who waved and smiled on his way out. Just when she was at her wit's end about how unfriendly the people here were, one guy in a truck gave her a reason to smile. She waved and almost managed a smile, until she drove closer to the house and saw Ross standing on the porch with a serious look on his face. She hoped she hadn't kept his dogs too long.

She parked the car and stroked Knight's head. It was worth Ross being a little upset. All three dogs had already wound their way into her heart and filled her lonely spots with love. When she looked up again, Ross was opening her door, and when he smiled, it softened the tension she'd seen only moments earlier. Elisabeth breathed a little easier, though for some reason she felt on the verge of tears again.

Elisabeth was strong-willed, but she had a sensitive soul. It had always been a bone of contention with her mother, who was one of those steel-willed women who could shrug anything off.

Ross leaned down. "Hey there, Lis. Did the boys behave?"

Lis. God, she loved that. *I shouldn't love it. He's just being nice.* He probably knew her business would fail. Then what? She'd sold her place in LA, and she didn't want to go back there anyway. She wanted to be here. Forever. *Only here.* Despite the unfriendly people and the trouble she was having getting her business off the ground. This is where she'd always wanted to be. She couldn't have been that wrong. Aunt Cora couldn't have been that wrong in leaving the business and property to her.

Knight lifted his eyes to Ross but kept his head in her lap. Elisabeth was thankful for the weight of him. It kept her securely in the car instead of jumping into Ross's arms for a hug on the worst day of the last few weeks.

It was all she could do to form an answer. "They were perfect." She swallowed the urge to unload her heartache on him and stepped from the car, moving swiftly to open the hatchback for Sarge and Ranger.

"I somehow doubt that. Ranger can be a little rascally."

Knight followed them around to the hatchback, where Sarge and Ranger were lavishing Elisabeth's face with kisses. She stood with a hand buried in each of their fluffy necks, soaking up their unconditional love.

"Come on, guys, give her a little breathing room," Ross said.

"No, it's okay, really." She sat between the dogs, one arm over each, her legs hanging out of the hatchback.

"You don't mind dog slobber?" Ross smiled, and it pierced her heart.

"Nope. I need it." *And a hug and about a jug of wine.*

Ross patted his thigh, and Sarge stepped from the car, giving up his spot to Ross. "Hard day at the dog park?"

"I'm fine," she lied, and turned away.

Ross lifted her chin and brought her eyes back toward his. "Hey. Did something happen?" His voice was serious, his eyes concerned.

"No. Nothing like that. I think you might be right about people around here not seeing any value in pampering their pets, or even grooming them." She felt her lower lip tremble and turned away again. She'd come all this way, and she loved her job. She'd never imagined that a job that pulled in six figures a year in Los Angeles couldn't pull in at least half that in Trusty. She'd never been so wrong in her life, and she hated the idea of not doing something with dogs and cats. She loved baking, and her aunt's business was a fine one, if she could keep it going, which she'd work her ass off to ensure, but she wanted her pet business, too, so badly that even the thought of not having it felt like a beating.

Her eyes welled with tears again.

Damn it. She stepped from the car and turned her back to Ross.

"Well, I'd better get going." She hurried Ranger out of the car, intending to leave, but Sarge and Ranger circled her legs, whining and licking her hands. Knight joined them, and it was all she could do not to crumple to the ground and take comfort in them for another hour or two. She felt a tear slip down her cheek. *Oh God. No, no, no.*

She felt Ross's strong hands on her shoulders, his chest pressed against her back, and—*Oh God*—his five-o'clock shadow met her cheek, which for some reason pulled even more tears from her overflowing eyes.

"Hey. Whatever it is, it can't be that bad." He turned her in his arms, and Elisabeth buried her face in his shirt.

She didn't look up at him, and she didn't think about how embarrassing it was to be bawling in front of her hot neighbor as she clutched his damp shirt, wet with her tears. She was thankful for the comfort of his arms around her and the feel of his heart beating against her cheek. She inhaled one deep breath after another, trying to pull herself together and getting a nose of Ross's potent masculinity.

So. Sniff. Sniff. *Unfair.* Could he stop being attractive just for a second while she wallowed in her unhappiness?

He stroked her back and rested his cheek on the top of her head. *Why?* Why wasn't he pushing her away, or telling her to buck up and deal with it? Why wasn't he rushing her to leave, or worried about his expensive dress shirt? Any LA man would have done all those things. This warmth, this allowing her to steal his calmness, take refuge in the comfort of him, those were things her aunt would have done, and they were things Elisabeth had connected to Trusty. In her mind, this is what Trusty was—comforting, safe, open arms at the ready.

She'd been wrong.

This wasn't Trusty at all.

This was Ross Braden.

Knight nosed his way in between Elisabeth and Ross's thighs, which made her laugh a little through her tears. She pushed back, still clutching Ross's shirt, and glanced up at him. God only knew how awful she looked with wet, puffy eyes and probably a pink nose. Ross was looking at her like all he wanted to do was take away her sadness. He looked at her with the same deep concern as when he'd fed her hungry piglet. For a guy who was used to comforting animals, he was doing more than okay with her. He gently cupped her cheeks. His hands were strong, sure, and warm. She closed her eyes as he wiped her tears with the pads of his thumbs. Comfort had never felt so good.

When she opened her eyes again, Ross had a different look in his eyes, one that caused her body to flash hot despite her sadness. She had the urge to go up on her tiptoes and press a soft kiss to his beautiful lips—but maybe she was making that look up, too. Maybe her mind had romanticized not only Trusty, but Ross.

Oh God.

"Walk with me." Ross took her hand like he'd been her best friend forever.

The funny thing was, Elisabeth didn't really have a best friend. She had friends back in LA, but not close friends. She'd always felt a little out of her element around LA girls, which was probably why she'd surrounded herself with animals. Animals didn't judge people. They appreciated love and gave it back in spades. They didn't care if you were the type of woman who slept around or the type who held out hope for true, heart-stopping love, because they were programmed to be loyal and they believed in heart-stopping love, too. Something told her that she wasn't barking up the wrong tree with her attraction to Ross. She had the feeling he was just as loyal and his love would be just as unconditional as any pet's. *Just as wonderful as I've always dreamed love would be.*

Talk about jumping the gun. She tried to push the thought away, but it lingered, chasing away the unhappiness she'd felt.

They walked toward the setting sun. His property went on for acres and acres of pastureland, and in the distance, the Colorado Mountains stood sentinel over this tiny piece of paradise. The sun peeked between the tall mountaintops, threading the last bit of daylight across the horizon. The dogs fell into step behind them, rustling through the thick grass. With every step, a little of Elisabeth's stress fell away. Ross was quiet, looking thoughtfully into the distance, and that was probably a good thing. She felt a little silly for having cried like a baby, and though her tears had stopped, she felt on the verge of them again. Whether they were from being overwhelmed by reality or by Ross's kindness, she wasn't sure.

They walked through the grass and entered a sparse forest. Elisabeth had no idea where they were going, but she would go anywhere with Ross. She worried about her animals needing to be fed, but surely another few minutes wouldn't hurt.

Leaves and twigs cracked beneath their feet. The dogs sniffed at the earth and at just about every hole they passed. It was darker, cooler under the cover of the trees, and as the sun dipped lower, crickets began to sing. The last bit of sunlight streamed through the forest as they broke through the other side, arriving on the far side of her aunt's property.

My property. She hadn't realized their land connected. The dreamer in her whispered, *This is fate.* Then reality of the day's events tumbled forth and stole the idea before it could take hold.

"We should make sure the animals are okay." It wasn't a question. She'd found that Ross didn't really ask questions. He offered them up, waited a minute, and if she didn't answer, he moved on. She liked that about him, and she liked that he thought of her animals and had headed there while still holding her hand, offering her the walk she hadn't realized she so badly needed.

Elisabeth had always thought of herself as being totally in tune with her mind and body, but now she wondered how she'd missed the need for this brief respite—and how Ross had seen it.

He stopped at the barn doors and placed his hands on her shoulders. With dusk at his back, he looked powerful and safe. He gazed down at her looking very handsome and in control, and when he spoke with his strong, sensual tone, her mind and body were in perfect sync. She knew just what she needed and what she wanted. *Ross.*

"Feel better, Lis?" He slid his hands across her shoulders and settled them at the curve of her neck. His thumbs grazed the underside of her jaw. It was erotic and sweet at the same time, and it made her legs go weak.

"I'll check on Dolly and the goats. Are you okay to check on the piglets and chickens?"

No. I want to kiss you, and lie in the grass beside you with your arms around me and let the stars carry us through until morning. I want to look into your eyes and know what you're thinking—the sexy stuff and beyond. I want to feel our hearts beating as one and make the rest of the world disappear. And when the morning comes, I want to face it with you.

"Lis?"

She blinked away her thoughts, and his concerned face came back into focus.

"Yeah…Of course."

His hands slid higher on her jaw, cupping it gently, and he pressed a kiss to her forehead. "Whatever's going on, it's all going to be okay."

Just like that, with no warning and no pretense, he waylaid her worries. How in the hell did he do that? Since he simply walked toward the paddock afterward, she assumed he once again had no expectations. While she was daydreaming about Ross, he seemed to be able to simply move on, without expecting any sort of repayment for his kindness. Not even a single kiss. Maybe she'd waited so long for true love that she was just fabricating everything in her mind. Maybe this was just another neighborly thing he routinely did. Make women feel like they hadn't given up everything they'd worked so hard to build for nothing.

She tried not to let hope carry her forward. After the day she'd had, she should know better, but when

Ross paused at the gate and looked back to check on her with compassion in his eyes, her next breath carried hope so thick she knew it had not only come in, but rearranged her insides as if redecorating a room. It had claimed her and there wasn't a damn thing she could do about it.

And she wasn't sure she'd try to escape even if she could.

Chapter Eight

THERE WERE ONLY a few things that threw Ross for a loop, and women's tears had always been one of them. An animal suffering at the hands of cruelty was another, and third on his list of things that knocked him off balance was the idea of his mother being treated so poorly by his father before his father had left them. He didn't allow himself to think of that often, but even those painful memories weren't as cutting as seeing Elisabeth standing before him silently weeping. Walking with her was about all he'd been able to do. Give him an animal and he knew exactly what to do. Women? They were a different story. And Elisabeth? She'd tugged at his heart from the moment he'd laid eyes on her, which probably made him pathetic, but what power did he have over his heart?

Exactly none.

No matter how much he tried to ignore the pull that drew him to her night and day, he was unable.

He'd begun to wonder if his belief in love was a fantasy built in opposition to his father's leaving. He'd wondered if he'd ever feel as drawn to a woman as Luke and Wes were to their girlfriends, or Pierce was to Rebecca. Now he knew it wasn't only a dream. He was every bit as attracted to Elisabeth, taken with her personality, infatuated with her goodness—hell, he wanted to climb beneath her skin and become one with her.

He walked far out in the pasture and checked on Dolly, and he found Chip and Dale, always nearby, playing king of the mountain on the play equipment Cora had put in the yard for them. *Give a goat a boulder and they're happy*, he'd told her. *Yes*, she'd said. *But give them play equipment and they know they're loved.* Who was he to argue with that logic?

He stroked Dolly's back, taking his time, trying to work through his feelings. He didn't know how long he stood with Dolly, twenty minutes, thirty? Still he remained, thinking of the way Elisabeth had clung to him. The feel of her heart beating against his chest. Hell if it hadn't taken every ounce of restraint to restrict his lips to her forehead, where he'd breathed in her scent and lingered a moment longer than he should have. He had no business kissing her forehead at all, much less lingering, but if it hadn't been her forehead, it would have been those luscious lips, and he wouldn't have stopped there.

He turned back toward the barn and saw her standing in the moonlight, kicking at the dirt with the toe of her boot, her fingers in her pockets, elbows out.

She looked adorable in cutoffs that barely covered her ass. Then again, he had a feeling that Elisabeth could make a potato sack look sexy. Her hair curtained her face, and his dogs stood beside her.

All three of them.

His dogs usually stuck to *him* like glue.

Why on earth had it taken him this long to realize they weren't with him?

The answer was kicking up tufts of dirt about a hundred feet away.

He pushed away his desires as best he could, and after taking care of the animals, they walked in silence back to her car in his driveway.

Sarge and Ranger ran ahead to the back of her car. Knight stuck to her like metal to magnet. Ross and Knight had a lot in common.

"Did Kennedy take the bottle okay?" he asked to cut through his need to touch her.

"Yeah. He's the cutest little thing."

"I brought you home something." He went to his truck and retrieved the book on cows that he'd brought her. "I didn't have time to get to the library, but this is one of mine. I think it'll have just about everything you'll need, and I'm here if you run into any more problems."

She took the book and clutched it to her chest. When she smiled up at him, the urge to kiss her was so strong that he had to shift his eyes away. He focused on the dogs and cleared his throat to try to clear the mounting desire from his body.

"I think you made a few friends today."

"That would make me a lucky girl. Thanks for letting me take them to the park. I've really missed spending time with dogs and cats." She rubbed her arms against the dropping temperature.

Ross draped an arm over her shoulder and she leaned against him in that casual way friends did. That little nudge shouldn't have sent fire through his veins, and when she gazed up at him, he shouldn't have felt like an inferno, but he would be shocked if he didn't have smoke pouring out of his ears.

"Thanks for being there for me, Ross."

"Want to talk about it?" That was better than what he wanted to ask. *Want me to kiss you until you can't feel anything but a full-body shudder?*

"I just need to figure out a new plan." She pressed her palm to his abs and leaned against him as she rose up on her toes and kissed his cheek.

In the space of a breath, he debated turning in to her lips and taking her in a greedy kiss, but in that split second, she said, "I really needed a friend. Thank you." It stopped him cold.

A friend.

Fuck.

How could he have totally misread her?

Chapter Nine

HOT, BOTHERED, AND upset with herself for being a wimp, Elisabeth paced her kitchen. If she'd been any other woman, she'd have pressed her lips to Ross's and shown him exactly how much she appreciated him. The problem was, she didn't just appreciate him. She *liked* him. *A lot.* She'd been attracted to plenty of men, but liking *who they were* was a whole different ballgame. And Ross...Ross made her body go ten different types of crazy.

She had to do something with all that sexual energy before she marched over to his house to see what else he could make her body do.

Focus, Elisabeth.

With a sigh, she thought about the predicament that had sent her tears flowing earlier in the evening. She went upstairs and slipped on her favorite fuzzy slippers and pulled on her favorite hoodie. She needed comfort as she pondered her quandary. She went back down to the living room and paced the hardwood floor. If she was going to fit in to this place, she had to show them just how much it meant to her. There was no way she was giving up on her dreams—any of them. There was more than one way to make her mark, and she'd just have to adapt. When she first opened her business in LA, she'd done all the same things she did in Trusty, only it was easier. In LA pampering pets went hand in hand with owning them, at least in the higher-income areas. There weren't really higher-income areas in Trusty. She'd already checked that out. There were no elite developments, and there was no bad side of town, or any sort of divide at all, which was probably one of the reasons she'd always loved it there. When she and her aunt had gone into town, everyone said hello and took the time to chat with them. Why was she such a pariah now?

I'm not Aunt Cora. I'm not a real Trusty girl.

She rubbed her temples and glanced out the window in the direction of Ross's house. It was pitch-black outside, but if she squinted, she could make out a faint light in the distance. Her mind drifted to his protective arm around her shoulder, the feel of his thumbs wiping away her tears.

Focus. Focus. Focus.

She forced his image from her mind, and in an effort to get her brain off of Ross and onto finding a solution to her problem, she ran through a list of questions that her mother asked her before she'd moved away. *What do you like about that rinky-dink town?* The sense of community and the easy pace of life. *What makes you think you'll ever fit in there?* She hadn't answered her mother honestly when she'd told her that it was because she'd fit in so well when she was younger. She hadn't actually *tried* to fit in, or if she had, she didn't remember it. She had no idea why she felt like she'd fit in. She sure wasn't raised by a farm woman. She wasn't ever in 4-H, and she had no idea how to country dance, though she did love dancing in general. The more she thought about it, the clearer the answer became. It wasn't so much that she knew she'd fit in; it was that she wanted to fit in. It was the feel of being here that made her sense that it was where she belonged. The crisp, clean air, the way her aunt woke up wanting to bake the best pies she could for the customers and friends she couldn't wait to see again, the way her aunt had always made time for friends and had only kind words to say about everyone.

The complete opposite of how I grew up.

Was she just running from becoming her mother?

No. Trusty was the foundation for all of her dreams. Every time she thought of a future, it included Trusty. She'd wanted to come back after graduating from college, but her mother had talked her out of it, and then she'd thrown herself into establishing her business. She hated that it had taken Aunt Cora's death to bring her back, but she also felt that Aunt Cora left her the property for a reason. She wouldn't have left everything she owned to Elisabeth if she didn't think Elisabeth was supposed to be here.

This will be my community, too. I'm an outsider—

Ross was right about that—but in my heart, I belong here. I'll earn the community's trust.

And she knew just the way to do it. She needed to give back to the community whose memory had pulled her through more handsy dates and stressful years than she cared to think about. She'd always been a Trusty girl at heart. She'd just have to show them that she really was one. That she deserved to be accepted, even if she wasn't born there, because despite the rough beginning, she loved the small town as if it were her own.

She glanced out the window at the faint light in the distance, thinking about showing Ross how much she wanted him.

Behave.

She settled in on the couch, put her feet up on the coffee table, and set her laptop across her thighs. Elisabeth hadn't redecorated the house. She liked having memories of her younger years and her aunt everywhere. Cora's black-and-white family photos still hung on the walls, her crocheted blankets were draped across the furniture, and a breeze swept through the open window. As Elisabeth set to work creating new flyers, she had a sense that she was on the right track.

At ten twenty, she printed a handful of flyers and was too excited to sit still. She wanted to spread the word! She paced her living room, wishing she had a girlfriend to call and celebrate with. She was certain this was a great idea. Elisabeth glanced out the window. Ross's light was still on. She didn't let her reasonable, careful mind overtake her excitement about her newly developed plan for finding her footing in Trusty. Ross was the closest thing she had to a friend right now—even if she secretly wished for more. Her heart was beating so fast she could barely breathe as she grabbed a bottle of wine, snagged her keys, the flyers she'd printed, and ran out the door—all the while whispering to herself, *Go, go, go!*

Elisabeth knocked on Ross's door with an armful of flyers, a bottle of wine, and a smile on her lips that she had no hope of squelching. Her body hummed with excitement that had her bouncing a little on the porch. Ross opened the door. His eyes swept over her, and the pooches barreled out to greet her. Elisabeth threw caution to the wind and did a little barreling herself, straight into Ross's bare chest, where she went up on her toes, slammed her eyes shut, and pressed her lips to his. She felt his arms circle her as he deepened the kiss. Her lips parted and their tongues collided. A hungry, masculine groan of appreciation rose from his lungs and made her hot all over. Knight nosed his way between them, and Elisabeth dropped back on her heels, wobbling backward a little.

Ross caught her with one strong arm around her waist.

"Hi," she said breathlessly, reeling from the kiss that made her legs go weak and her body go hot. The kiss that made her lips numb and her brain foggy. Exactly the type of kiss she'd always dreamed a kiss should be.

"Hi." His voice was thrillingly seductive and low.

She trapped her lower lip between her teeth, realizing that she'd just forced herself on him.

"I...couldn't help it. I didn't plan on kissing you. I wanted to, but...I was so nervous. Then I was excited about my flyers, and then you answered the door looking at me like that, and shirtless. *Oh God*, you're shirtless—"

He pulled her against him and took her in another kiss that stole brain cells with every swipe of his delicious tongue, until she could barely think past the next luscious stroke.

"You saved me a trip," he said against her lips, then kissed her again, sending pinpricks through her entire body.

It was a kiss like no other. Right out of the movies. That moment, that second, that kiss, was without a doubt the *best* thing she'd ever experienced in her entire life. When they finally came up for air, her senses slowly returned. Ross's body was hot and hard. *Really hard.* He smelled even more virile, and all he wore was a pair of mesh shorts that did nothing to hide his impressive arousal.

"If this is what I get for being your friend, what happens if I try to move into the boyfriend realm?"

"You..." *Oh God. Boyfriend realm? You can have anything you want.* "You get to share my wine and put my flyers on your counter at the clinic." She leaned against his bare chest, then pressed her lips to his collarbone because she simply couldn't resist.

"I like that. The kiss, I mean." He took the bottle

from her arms. "I've already shared your wine and agreed to share your flyers."

"Congratulations. You just gained access to the possible boyfriend realm." She had no idea where her brazen response came from, but she didn't fight it. For the first time in as long as she could remember, she felt like she was on the right track on all fronts. She wasn't worried about what Ross would think of her idea, or the kiss. *Oh God, the kiss. The magnificent kiss.*

He took her hand and led her across the hardwood foyer to a warm and inviting great room with deep sofas and a see-through fireplace that separated the living room from the dining room. Ranger and Sarge walked by and sprawled on their doggy beds by the couch. Knight followed Ross and Elisabeth through the living room to an open kitchen, separated from the rest of the first floor by a beautiful mahogany and stone bar.

"I was just working out. Sorry if I'm a little ripe." He grabbed two wineglasses from a glass-front cabinet. "What are we celebrating with wine and kisses?"

In the face of darkness, it was easy to be bold, but in the illuminated kitchen, reality came bearing a blush. Elisabeth laid the flyers on the counter and covered her face with her hand. "Sorry."

Ross set the glasses down and gathered her in his arms again. He brushed her hair from her shoulder and searched her eyes with his dark brows knitted together, and then he kissed her forehead in the sweet, tender way he had earlier in the evening.

"Don't be sorry unless it was a onetime thing. In that case, you can be sorry, because it was a damn good kiss, and I've been beating myself up for not kissing you earlier."

"You were?" She breathed a little faster.

"I was." His hand slid down to the curve of her back, causing her to shiver all over.

Her stomach fluttered. Knight, who hadn't left her side since she'd arrived, nudged her leg. She reached a hand down and stroked him. "I don't know what it was, but I hope it wasn't a onetime thing. I was just so excited that I wanted to tell you my ideas, which now that I'm standing here, seem kind of silly."

He sealed his mouth over hers, kissing her like she was all he'd ever wanted, holding her body against his so she could feel every inch of his desire. She let her hands wander down his muscular back and back up again. Each time he tightened his grip on her, his muscles bunched beneath her palms. Every stroke of his tongue stole a few more of her brain cells, until it was all she could do to remember to breathe. When their lips parted she longed for them to return.

"If your ideas are anything like your kisses, I want to hear them." Ross's voice was husky, his eyes seductively narrow and dark. He took a step back and took all of her oxygen with him.

She reached for the counter for stability. He handed her a glass of wine, then took her hand and led her to the comfiest couch she'd ever sat on. She sank into the deep cushions and slid her feet beneath her.

He nodded at her slippers. "Those are the most

adorable slippers I've ever seen. If you don't mind, I want to just go rinse off. I'll be down in five minutes."

Can I help? "Okay," she managed. Holy cow. How was she supposed to sit there knowing he was naked in the other room? She imagined him in the shower, washing that hard body, all lathered up...Great. Now she needed a cold shower. She'd been taking so many of them lately, she worried she'd run out of cold water. She hoped that didn't mean she was being too promiscuous. This had to be more than sex. It had to be. She could feel it in her bones. Who was she kidding? She could feel it from the very tip of her scalp to the tips of her toes.

And in all the glorious places in between.

Oh. Lord.

She tried to focus on her surroundings. Knight had settled onto Ranger's doggy bed with him. There were pictures of Ross's family on the end table and pictures of the dogs everywhere. The cream-colored walls were accented with wide, decorative stained-wood trim. The latest issues of *Men's Fitness* and *Veterinary Weekly* were on the uniquely carved coffee table. His house felt homey, comfortable, lived in, even though it was impeccably neat and tidy.

He came downstairs a few minutes later, wearing a pair of low-slung jeans and a T-shirt that hugged his broad chest. There was something sexy and unpretentious about a guy in jeans and bare feet, and she felt her body heat up all over again as Ross smiled and joined her on the couch. He draped an arm over her shoulder in an easy, comfortable fashion.

"I like seeing you on my couch. It's kind of like finding a rose among weeds."

Surprising herself, she settled right in against his side. "Thank you for not kicking me out for showing up unannounced. You could have had a date here. I'm sorry, Ross."

"Stop apologizing. I don't date women in Trusty, so the chances of you finding me with a woman are nearly nil."

Nearly nil? She fiddled with the edge of her hoodie. He didn't date women from Trusty? Why? Did he chew women up and spit them out? Had he gone through all the single women his age from Trusty? He seemed so low-key, and he'd said it so easily—*I don't date women in Trusty.*

Oh God. I'm in Trusty. Is he trying to tell me that the kiss was just that, a kiss, but he's not interested in anything more?

She pushed away the uncomfortable thoughts.

"I've been thinking about what you said, and I think that you might be right about people around here not seeing any value in pampering their dogs, or maybe they just can't afford it."

"Ah, the harsh reality of Trusty, Colorado."

As harsh as a kiss being just a kiss. "I guess. I really want to be here, Ross. I like Trusty, even if the people here don't like me very much yet. Even if I can't have the same business I did in LA, I can still help the animals. I've decided to offer free pet grooming on Saturday mornings. That way people can get to know me and see that I'm not in the business for the money.

I mean, sure I'd like to make a living, but I can do that any number of ways. Aunt Cora's pie business pulls in a decent amount of money, and I have a lot of money saved. I'm a bit of a penny pincher," she admitted. She had faith that she'd figure out a way to gain back the few customers that she'd lost. She had to have faith. If she didn't have faith in herself, how could anyone else?

"You're going to pamper pets for free?"

"Sure. I can spare a few Saturday mornings. Besides, this will give me some time with dogs and cats, which I love. Being with your boys today reminded me of what I was missing."

"You're really something, Lis."

"Not really. I want to be accepted by the community. I've always wanted to be here, and I'm not going to let the fact that I was raised somewhere else hold me back. Maybe I'm a dreamer—*God knows I am*—but that's me."

She looked directly into his eyes and forced her most serious tone. "Hi. I'm Elisabeth Nash and I'm a dreamer. I probably need a twelve-step program, because I believe in fate, and marriage, and all things warm and fuzzy." She made it appear as a tease, but it wasn't a tease at all; it was a testing of the waters. She'd never been more serious about her feelings, in her life.

Ross laughed and pulled her into another delicious kiss. A laugh wasn't what she was hoping for, but the kiss quickly drove any lingering worry from her mind.

They talked, and kissed, and talked some more, and an hour later Ross walked her to her car with three fluffy boys in tow. She leaned against the driver's side door as they talked about how beautiful the moon was, how different the night sounds were in Colorado than in California, and fifty other meaningless topics that made procrastination easy.

Ross ran his hands down her arms and stepped between her legs, bringing them hip to hip.

"I'm really glad you decided to come over," he said with a seductive edge to his voice. He buried one hand beneath her hair and caressed the back of her neck with his thumb.

Wow. She liked that.

"Me too."

"I said I don't date girls from Trusty."

"Yeah, I got that." *Thanks for reminding me, though.* Well, at least the evening was wonderful, and she had the best kisses of her life with a man she really, really liked.

"That was before I met you." He smiled. "Lis, will you go out with me Friday night? No pressure. You'd just be the first girl I've dated in Trusty for, oh, I don't know, maybe ten years."

She swallowed hard. That was a lot of pressure. "Ten years?"

"Yeah. I guess I should warn you. We're already linked in the rumor mill. I got a call from my assistant, Kelsey, earlier this evening, and she said she heard we were dating from Margie, at the diner."

"Really? But how?" That a rumor could spread so

quickly seemed very Mayberry-esque.

"Leave it to Trusty to figure us out before we did. I'm sure Emily said something, or my brother Wes. He asked me about you, too."

"Is that why you haven't dated a woman here in so long?" *Ten years!*

"Yes. I learned years ago that the only way to have a private life is to do so outside of town. So, I'll warn you. Make your decision carefully, because right now we're a question mark in their minds. Once we go on a real date, we're more of an exclamation point."

She looked up at his handsome face, his compassionate eyes, and those lips she couldn't wait to kiss again.

"I'm one of those girls who uses three exclamation points at the end of a sentence."

Chapter Ten

BY THE TIME Friday afternoon rolled around, Elisabeth was a nervous wreck. In her mind, kissing Ross had inflated to something enormous. *She'd* kissed *him*. Would he think she was easy? Would he expect that she'd fall into his bed? Even if she wanted to—which surprised the hell out of her—she didn't want him to expect it. She hadn't seen him since Tuesday afternoon, but they'd exchanged texts, and he'd called last night to confirm their date. She'd held out for true love for so long. How could she know if this was it, or if this was something less? Even his voice made her mind travel down a dirty path—and she no longer even tried to dissuade those lustful thoughts. What on earth was happening to her? How could she hope *he* didn't expect sex when *she* wanted to feel his body against her, to feel him inside her? *Oh. My.*

She'd kept busy all week, baking and delivering pies, taking care of the animals, and trying to secure new baking orders along with pimping out her pet-pampering services. She hung up flyers at every store, farm stand, and the dog park, as well as the post office and anywhere else she found a community bulletin board. Then she went at it by hand, introducing herself to people at the park and giving out flyers to anyone willing to take one.

She'd done her best, and she'd know in less than twenty-four hours if it had helped. On the way home, she stopped at Wynchels' Farm. This time she brought doggy cookies to try to ease into more of a friendship with Wren via her pups, and to soften the marketing of the flyers she brought with her announcing Saturday's free grooming services.

Wren had a pair of reading glasses perched on her nose. She lifted her eyes when Elisabeth walked in. "Howdy."

"Hi, Wren. I brought you a few things." She put a paper bag of puppy cookies on the counter and handed her a few flyers.

Wren pressed her lips into a hard line while she read it. "I told you that grooming them was a waste of time." She set the flyers aside.

"Oh, yes, I know. But I'm new in town, and I have *loads* of free time." *A little white lie never hurt anyone.* "If you bring your dogs by, I can groom them, and it'll cost you nothing."

Wren picked up a clipboard and flipped a paper over, then scanned the one beneath. "That's where you're wrong. It'll cost me time I don't have. It's just me and my husband. A few farmhands. We don't have the staff to take over while I sit and watch you brush my dogs."

Crap. She hadn't thought of that.

"Why don't I come pick them up?" Things kept coming out of her mouth without checking with her brain. She went with it.

Wren raised her brows. "Pick them up?"

"Sure. I'll pick them up, groom them, and then bring them back. It won't cost you a penny or a minute."

Wren leaned one thick arm against the counter, pulled her glasses down to the tip of her nose, and looked over them at Elisabeth.

"Let me get this straight. You're going to pick up my dogs, brush them, bring them back, and there's no hidden charges? What about your gas to come out here?" Wren eyed the paper bag on the counter. "What's in that?"

"Cookies, for the dogs. All-natural ingredients, no sugar, no harmful ingredients."

"Pet cookies?" She opened the bag and took out a cookie in the shape of a dog bone, iced with peanut butter. "It can't hurt my dogs?"

"No, ma'am."

Wren set it back down on the counter as Barney ambled into the barn.

Elisabeth crouched and loved him up as she answered Wren's earlier question. "No hidden fees for the grooming or pickup. Think of it as a favor you're doing for me. When I lived in LA, I had contact with dogs and cats on a daily basis. I loved spending time with them, grooming them, bathing them, pampering them and—" She realized she was rambling and tightened her answer. "There are no hidden costs."

"We get busy around eight. Can you come before that?"

Elisabeth smiled. "How's seven thirty? I can take three at a time in my car. Is there a good time I can bring them back to pick up the others?"

"Noon."

"Noon it is." *Yes!* Baby steps. That's what fitting in was all about, or at least that's what she hoped.

"GIVE IT UP, Emily. I'm not giving you any information." Ross had been on the phone with his sister for ten minutes. She'd been prying him for information about Elisabeth, but he'd never been one to kiss and tell, which annoyed Emily to no end. She adored her brothers, which was evident in everything she did—taking care of their houses when they were out of town, checking up on them, bringing chicken soup for them when they were sick. She was a caring, warm sister, and Ross adored her. But that didn't change his feelings on sharing information on his personal life.

She sighed. "Fine, whatever. Where are you taking her tonight?"

"Em," he said sternly, and reached down to pet Storm. He'd picked him up earlier in the evening and Trout had said that he was sleeping a little better but wasn't back to his normal sleeping habits yet.

"I thought I could slip it in." She laughed. "Well,

I'm really happy for you. She seems really nice, even if the word around town is that she's going to take what she can and bolt."

That annoyed him to no end. Elisabeth was struggling over how to fit in in a town that had her pegged as a taker. Even he had teetered on doubting her at first, which he now felt horrible about. "Emily, she's going to be working with you to renovate her kitchen. Doesn't that tell you something?"

"Sure. She's either settling in or flipping the property. We're getting together next week, so I'm not sure which yet."

He heard a door slam and Emily breathed harder.

"What are you doing?"

"Looking for my suitcases. I thought I had them in the basement, but they may be in the attic. I'm leaving in a few weeks for Tuscany, and I just realized that I have no idea where my bags are."

He pictured her standing in her living room, tapping her finger on her chin, the way she did when she was deep in thought.

"Well, if you can't find them, you can always borrow mine. I never go anywhere." Ross wasn't big on traveling. He'd never had the urge to travel the world. He had the boys to think about, and the thought of leaving them so he could gallivant around the world wasn't something he liked. They were his family as much as his siblings were. They relied on him to be there and to care for them, and he had no interest in letting them down. Besides, he was content in his surroundings. The only thing he felt was missing was a woman to share his life with, a woman to love. The thought brought his mind back to Elisabeth and their impending date.

"Thanks, Ross."

"I've got to run, sis. Good luck with the luggage. Love you."

"Good luck with the secret date, and I love you, too."

Secret date. Ross had purposely planned a date that could not be misconstrued as *secret*. There was no worse feeling than being talked about behind your back, and he genuinely liked Elisabeth, from her selflessness to the adorable way she teetered between hot and sexy and sweet. The way Ross saw it, he had one of three choices for their first date. Take her to Allure, the next town over, and wait for word to get back to Trusty. *We'd definitely be seen as trying to hide our relationship.* The word *relationship* gave him pause. He hadn't connected himself to that word in a very long time. He took a moment to let it settle into his mind and waited for an uncomfortable wave to knock him over.

It never came.

Huh.

He turned his thoughts back to the options for their date. He could cook her dinner at his house and have a nice, quiet evening together. *I'd feel like I was hiding our relationship.* Or he could do what he hadn't done in ten years—the most appealing option because of how much he liked her—and take her out in Trusty, let people see he was with her and that they had nothing to hide. That was the *only* option in his mind.

Dressed casually in a pair of jeans and a short-sleeved black dress shirt, with the gift he'd bought to give her later in the night, he drove over to Elisabeth's. She answered the door wearing a simple black tank dress that clung to her breasts and hips and stopped midthigh. Her feet were bare and she had a slim, silver toe ring on her third toe, which, for some reason, totally turned him on.

"Hi. Wow, you look so handsome." She flashed her lovely smile.

He placed a hand on her hip and kissed her cheek. "Mm. You smell amazing, like sandalwood and springtime."

"You're good." She casually touched his chest. "It's Michael Kors Sexy Amber. Silly name, but I love the smell. You smell pretty delicious yourself."

"I call it Ode de Labrador." He pulled her against him and kissed her softly on the lips. "Last night you got to steal the first kiss. It's my turn."

"Steal, baby, steal."

He sealed his lips over hers, and every thought he'd had about her smile, her voice, and her luscious mouth coalesced, making their kiss that much sweeter. Kissing Elisabeth, holding her against him, was a million times better than his fantasies. She slid her hands into his back pockets and rocked her hips against his. Holy fuck, she felt good. If they didn't leave soon, they weren't going to leave at all. He reluctantly drew away, pressing a few soft kisses to her lips on the way.

"Ross." A heated whisper. Her eyes were full of desire, telling him she was willing, and God knew she was able.

He cupped the back of her head and brought her cheek to his chest. "I know, Lis. I know." Damn, did he know. He'd never felt anything so powerful in his life as the way he was drawn to everything about her.

"We need to get out of here," he said, more strongly than he meant to. He reached for her hand as she slipped her feet into a pair of strappy sandals and grabbed her purse from a hook by the door.

Once outside, he breathed in the cool evening air as she locked the door. He couldn't help but wrap his arms around her from behind and kiss the back of her neck. They hadn't even gone on a real date yet and it felt like she was *his*. She smelled so damn good, and when she turned in his arms and met his lips with hers, he got harder.

"I love kissing you," she said against his lips, which only made him want her more.

"Me too." Their kisses were heated, urgent. "That's why we have to leave, or I'm going to lay you down on this porch and make love to you."

He heard her breath catch.

"Sorry." Like hell he was sorry, but it was the proper thing to say.

"Don't be."

Holy hell.

They climbed into his truck, and Elisabeth started to pull her seat belt over her shoulder. Ross patted the bench seat beside him.

"I'll never make it with you all the way over there. I promise not to kiss you, but I need you closer. Wait. I don't promise."

She scooted over with a laugh and settled her hand on his thigh. "I used to dream about what it would be like to date a guy with a truck and snuggle up next to him while he drove." She wiggled in beneath his arm.

"You used to dream about it? Don't most girls dream about princes on white horses?" Driving had never felt as good as it did now, with Elisabeth beneath his arm, pressed against his side.

"Probably. Not me. For me it was always about small-town stuff. This town in particular. My aunt Cora got me a subscription to *Farm Girl* magazine when I was seven, and I've kept it going ever since. When I still lived at home, it drove my mom crazy. She used to buy *People* magazine and *Star*, and those other rag mags, and she'd put them all over the house."

"It's so hard for me to imagine anyone outside of those born here wanting to be here so badly. I mean, I love it, but you talk about Trusty like other people talk about Hollywood." Ross glanced at her and caught her looking at him. He kissed her quickly and then turned back toward the road.

"I know how it must sound, but it's true, Ross. I'm not going to pretend it's not. Yes, I was in LA, the land of the beautiful, where life moves so fast, if you blink, you miss the good stuff. Where the sun's always shining, and if you can ignore the threat of earthquakes, then you can have a pretty idealistic, albeit materialistic, life. It just wasn't me. I never felt like I fit in there, regardless of how successful my business was or how long I stayed."

Ross pulled down his brother Luke's driveway.

"How was Storm when you picked him up?"

He loved that she thought of him. "He was fine. Happy to see the boys. Still not sleeping as well as I'd like."

"I wonder why. Maybe he keeps the crate far from his bed."

"I don't buy into that whole thing of the dog needing the crate to be close to the person at night. The cells are small. Storm can see him fine from his crate."

Elisabeth sighed. "That's a little hypocritical coming from a guy who lets his dogs sleep on his bed. How can you not buy into the fact that a dog needs comfort?"

"I'm not saying that. We have to be strict with service dogs. Their owners won't be able to crawl into their crates or move their crates around."

"Okay, I can see how that makes sense. But I still think Trout is probably right and Storm might be lonely. He's here every weekend with the boys, and then he goes back to sleeping without the sounds of other dogs breathing nearby. I just think making sure the crate is close enough that he can hear Trout breathing might help."

Ross couldn't deny that it might make a difference. He squeezed her shoulder. "Okay, I'll suggest that to Trout."

"Where are we?" Elisabeth squinted into the darkness.

"My brother Luke and his fiancée, Daisy, have something that I thought you might enjoy." He parked down by the barn and stepped from the truck, then reached for Elisabeth's hand. They followed a gravel path down to the barn.

Elisabeth turned at the sound of horses whinnying in the pasture. Her eyes widened. "Oh my gosh. Are those Clydesdales?"

"Luke raises gypsy horses. They're like Clydesdales, but their feathers, manes, and tails are much fuller. He's one of the finest breeders in the country. That's Rose and Chelsea, two of his girls." He took her hand and led her into the twelve-stall barn.

"His girls? You have your boys and he has his girls?" she asked with a smile. "Your mother raised you guys right. So many people think of animals as second-class or something. I love that you think of yours as part of your family." She squeezed his hand and inhaled deeply. "Hay, manure, and leather. Sounds gross, but I love the smell of horse barns."

"You really are a farm girl at heart." He pulled her against him. "I'm really glad you agreed to go out with me."

She smiled. "I'm glad you finally asked."

"Finally? Maybe we have time to make up for." He lowered his lips to hers and enjoyed another delicious kiss. They walked to a stall in the back of the barn, where three puppies were sleeping on top of one another.

Elisabeth gasped and shot an elated, wide-eyed look at Ross.

Luke came in the back doors of the barn carrying a puppy in each hand. "Hey there. You must be Elisabeth. I'd hug you hello, but my arms are full. Maybe you could unload me of my burden."

"Oh my God. I'd love to. Ross, look at these babies! They're the sweetest little things." She took a puppy from Luke and rubbed her nose in its neck. "What type of pups are they?"

"They're a special breed of oops and a Friday night." Luke patted Ross's back. "Take this one, bro. Daisy's on her way down."

"Elisabeth, this is my youngest brother, Luke."

She ran her eyes between the two brothers a few times. Ross shared a knowing look with Luke. He was used to the double take. Despite their five-year age difference, they looked so much alike that almost everyone needed a few extra glances to determine that they weren't twins. They both wore their hair shorter on the sides than on top, and their hair was a shade lighter than their siblings'. All of the Braden men stood over six feet, with dark eyes and strong builds, but he and Luke looked strikingly similar compared to their other siblings.

"Hi, Luke." Elisabeth kissed the puppy. "This is possibly my best first date ever. Are you keeping all of the puppies?"

"If I have my say, we are." Daisy breezed into the barn, still dressed from work in a skirt and heels. She tossed her white-blond hair over her shoulder and wrapped her arms around Luke's neck, then planted a kiss on his lips. "Hi, handsome."

"Hey, babe." Luke slid his arm around her waist. "This is Elisabeth. She and Ross are on their first date."

Daisy hugged Elisabeth and kissed the puppy on the head. "Aren't they too sweet for words?"

"I'm in love." Elisabeth laughed.

Ross sidled up to Luke and lowered his voice so Elisabeth couldn't hear him. "I'm jealous of that puppy."

"No shit. Why'd you tell Wes you two weren't dating?" Luke asked quietly.

"We weren't. Now we are." Ross felt a pang of something good in his chest as he said it. It was the first time he'd claimed a connection to a woman in so long that he almost wished Elisabeth would have heard their conversation just so he could see her reaction.

Luke laughed as Ross moved closer to Elisabeth.

"Are you working the county fair this year?" Luke asked.

"Every year, like clockwork."

"Did I tell you that I got a booth at the fair?" Elisabeth asked Ross.

"No. For your pies?" He was happy to hear she was going to the fair, which meant he could see her while he spent the day there, but it also caused his stomach to clench tight. He didn't like how upset she was the other day, or how people must have treated her in order for her to have reacted that way. It was one of the reasons he wanted to take her out in Trusty. To waylay negative judgments, and this way, he could set his eyes on anyone who dared to look at her crosswise.

"Yes, but I think I'll also give out puppy treats and maybe do free grooming, pawdicures, that sort of thing."

She was so damn sweet. "That's a great idea." He'd keep a close eye at the fair, but hopefully by then people would have begun to accept her.

"Pawdicures? I love that," Daisy said. "We'll bring these guys to you when they're older."

Daisy took the puppy from Ross's hands. "I see the way you're looking at my puppies. Don't get any ideas, Ross. You have three dogs already, and a weekend puppy."

"Wrong. I'm looking at Elisabeth."

Elisabeth glanced up and tilted her head with a thoughtful gaze. A smile spread across her lips. Ross didn't think he'd ever met anyone as beautiful as her, and seeing her with a puppy, with her heart practically visible in every stroke of the pup, he could see why she was a pet pamperer. Her love of animals really was a part of her. No one could fake the happiness emanating from her.

They left a little while later and went to the Brewery, a local restaurant and pub. There was only one way to nix rumors, and that was by staring them down. Ross walked into the pub with his arm around Elisabeth. He knew he'd turn a few heads after keeping his dating life private for so long, but he hadn't expected nearly every person in the joint to turn and gawk.

He tightened his grip on Elisabeth's shoulder and felt her body stiffen. He kissed her temple and whispered, "You're with me, Lis. I'll never let anyone bother you." He felt her breathing deeply as the hostess approached.

"Hi, Ross. Are you meeting your brothers?" Maria Cross had gone to school with Wes, and she'd worked at the Brewery for years.

"Not tonight. A table for two, please."

She smiled at Ross and forced a smile for Elisabeth. "You're Cora's niece, right?"

"Yes, Elisabeth," she said confidently.

"Elizabeth, that's right." Maria picked up two menus.

In an effort to make Elisabeth more comfortable, Ross corrected Maria. "Actually, it's E—*lis*—"

Elisabeth touched his arm. "It's okay. Elizabeth is easier."

What the hell? She was changing her name because it was easier for others? Perplexed, Ross refrained from correcting Maria. When she sat them in the center of the room, he asked for a private booth. He wanted people to see them together, but he also wanted Elisabeth all to himself. He struggled with meshing the conflicting feelings and figured a private booth would offer enough of a show, while allowing them a modicum of privacy.

"Of course." Maria led them to a booth at the back of the restaurant, near the billiard room.

"Hey, Ross." Tate McGregor waved from a table

across the room, where he was sitting with three other guys Ross had grown up with. Tate had come by to get Elisabeth's van the other morning. He waved to Elisabeth. "Howdy, Elisabeth."

Ross waved to them, then slid in beside Elisabeth as she lifted a hand and waved to Tate. He pulled her in close. "You okay?"

"Yeah, thanks." She smoothed her dress and shifted her eyes around the room.

"Why didn't you want me to correct her about your name?"

"Because I'll be correcting my name with everyone I meet, and it's just one more thing that sets me apart from belonging here." She smiled, but it never reached her eyes. "It's okay. It's such a small thing. One letter."

He touched her cheek. "It's one beautiful letter, for one beautiful woman. I don't mind correcting people."

"You're so good to me. It's okay, but thank you for offering. Pick your fights, right?"

He kissed her softly.

"Well, look who's out on a Friday night." Christina Stiefel, a slim, large-busted brunette who worked as a receptionist in an accountant's office in town, set her hand on Ross's shoulder.

He shrugged it off, questioning his decision to go out in town.

"Christina, this is Elisabeth Nash. Elisabeth, Christina and I went to school together." He wanted to introduce Elisabeth as his girlfriend, but he realized he'd better clear that with her first.

"Oh, please. We did much more than go to school together." She locked her green eyes on Ross, and his insides went hot. Not in a good way. She and Ross had gone on two dates the summer after Ross graduated from college, which Christina had never forgotten and Ross had worked hard to erase from his memory.

The second date had come to an ugly end. She'd wanted to sleep with Ross and he wasn't interested. She'd turned on him like a vicious snake. She was the reason he hired an accountant in the next town over. The less he saw of her, the better.

Ross tried to play it cool. "We went out twice, many years ago. So long ago, in fact, I can barely remember it." He slid his arm around Elisabeth.

Christina ran her eyes bitchily between them. "Well, nice to see you." She turned on her heels and stalked away.

Elisabeth gave Ross a curious look.

"I'm sorry. She's the epitome of why I don't date women in Trusty, and hardly worth mentioning. Two dates, she wanted to fool around, I thought she was a money-hungry bit—unpleasant person." He cringed at his own venom.

Elisabeth's eyes widened.

"That sounds really bad."

"Not after meeting her, it doesn't. She gave me the stink-eye."

He leaned in and kissed her again.

"I don't mean to be unfair about the women here. They're not all like her, but most are looking to rope a husband, regardless of how little they might have in common with the man they set their sights on. I might be old-fashioned in this regard, but when I get married, I want to know that there's no one else I'd rather spend time with than the woman I'm with." His eyes lingered on Elisabeth. He hadn't wanted to be away from her for a single minute since they met.

"That's what I meant, when I said that I believed in true love and all things warm and fuzzy. I think nowadays couples think love can be bought." She sighed. "But the way I feel is that true love can never be bought, or faked, or even manipulated. It's only got one true form, and it isn't complete until the two people come together, and then..." She shrugged. "God, I sound like a dreamer."

You sound like you crawled out of my head. How can we possibly be so in sync?

"There are worse things than being a dreamer."

There are worse things than being a dreamer? That was the best he could come up with given that he was still a little stunned by what she'd just said.

Ross kept an eye on the people around them as they ate dinner and shared a bottle of wine. He didn't like the whispering that was going on at a few tables, but he knew that there was a good chance it was more about him being out in Trusty with a woman than about the particular woman he was with.

She must have noticed him watching the nearby tables, because she touched his leg, drawing his attention back to her.

"Tell me about your family, Ross. You seem so close to them. Do they all live here in Trusty?"

Even though Ross didn't date women from Trusty, the small towns surrounding Trusty were like feeders from a lake. Families were close, and since the Bradens were one of the wealthiest families around, most people knew of them. It was rare that he was asked about his relationship with his family members by a woman he was dating. He took a second to process his answer.

"I got pretty lucky, as far as families go. I have one older brother, Pierce, who recently got engaged. He lives in Reno with his fiancée, Rebecca, and he owns several resorts around the world. You met Emily and Luke, and I've mentioned Jake, the stuntman who lives in LA, and then there's Wes, who also lives in town with his girlfriend, Callie. Wes owns a dude ranch in the mountains and they spend a lot of time at the cabin there."

"So you have four brothers and a sister? That must have been fun growing up." Elisabeth shifted in her seat so she was facing him and rested her arm across the back of the bench.

"Yeah, we had a lot of fun. Still do. But we tend to be loud and harass each other a lot." She ran her fingers along the side of Ross's neck, making it hard for him to concentrate.

"So you get along with all of them? There's no black sheep of the family?" She scooted closer to him, her knee resting against his.

"No black sheep, but Jake lives on the edge. You'll probably meet him at the fair. He's trying to fly in for a stunt gig Saturday. I used to think Wes lived on the edge, because no risk was too great for him. He's done everything from skydiving to mountain climbing. He's definitely an adrenaline junkie, but he's really settled down a lot since Callie came into his life. But Jake..." He shook his head. "Jake's a good man, a really good man, but between my dad leaving us when I was five, and Jake's first love breaking up with him out of the blue, I think it screwed him up in the relationship department."

"Your dad left, too?" Elisabeth gripped his shoulder. "My father left when I was little."

"Oh, babe, I'm sorry." He wouldn't wish parent abandonment on anyone. The pain of it never really left.

"It's okay. I never knew him. I was only two when he left, and you really can't miss a person who you never knew." Her tone was solemn, but her eyes weren't filled with sadness or longing. She looked just as peaceful as she had a moment before. "Why do you think Jake is messed up as far as relationships go?"

"He's just a big player. I don't think that my father leaving really had anything to do with it. It was probably Fiona, his first love. He thought they were a forever thing, and she broke up with him out of the blue. He's never let anyone get close to him since."

"That's really sad. Maybe he will, eventually."

"Hey, Ross." Charlotte Wellington and her husband ran a hay farm on the outskirts of town. She patted him on the shoulder as she walked past and smiled at Elisabeth.

"Hi, Charlotte. How's Taylor?" Taylor was her two-year-old dog.

Charlotte barely slowed on her way to the front of the restaurant. "Great. His paw healed fine." She waved, then turned to leave.

They left the restaurant a little while later, and Ross drove in the direction of his mother's house, but instead of turning onto her road, he continued up the narrow mountain road to Pike's Peak and backed his truck up to the overlook.

"Where are we?" It was pitch-black, save for the stars above and the lights of the town below.

"You wanted to experience Trusty, so I brought you to make-out point."

Her eyes widened.

"Relax." He laughed a little under his breath. "Come on."

He stepped from the truck and helped Elisabeth out. While she gazed at what Ross considered the most spectacular view in all of Colorado, overlooking his favorite town, he gathered the blankets and the gift he'd brought for her. He spread one blanket out in the bed of the truck, then reached for Elisabeth's hand.

"What exactly are your intentions, Mr. Braden?" She eyed the blankets.

"Don't worry. I'm not going to try to get to home base." *But I won't be disappointed if we end up there.* "I thought you might like to stargaze." He helped her into the truck, and they sat on one of the blankets. He draped the other over her legs so she wouldn't be cold. He wanted to take her in his arms and slide his thigh over hers to keep her warm, but he also wanted to talk to her, get to know more about her. He pushed away the thoughts of touching her and tried to focus on what she was saying instead.

"This is so beautiful. Is this where you used to come and make out with girls in high school?"

"No. That's what the woods were for."

She laughed.

"I'm only half kidding. I've never taken a woman here, well, except for Emily. I brought her here when she graduated from high school, before she went away to college. We sat up half the night and talked about how her life would change, and her hopes, her fears, you know, that kind of stuff."

Elisabeth rested her head on his shoulder, and again that simple touch made him feel like she belonged there. Like she was *his*.

"You seem like such a good big brother. I wish I'd had someone to look out for me like that."

"Em's a smart aleck, but she's also sensitive, and as brave as she is, she was scared to go away to school. She was used to having a house full of boys to protect her, and she was worried about being out there all alone. She did fine, of course. I guess I've always looked after her, and I guess I still do." He wanted to know more about Elisabeth, not talk about Emily. He inhaled the flowery scent of her shampoo, and she shifted her position beside him. He felt the brush of her breast against his side, and it was all he could do to form a sentence. "Lis, how old are you?"

"Twenty-seven."

She gazed up at him, her lips slightly parted, a

smile that reached her eyes, and he was a second away from lowering his lips to hers. *Focus. Talk.* Jesus, it had never been this hard to restrain his desires before. He tried to process what she'd just said. She was three years younger than Luke, his youngest brother.

"Were you nervous when you went to school? For that matter, did you go away to school?"

"I wasn't nervous. I went to UCLA, so it wasn't a big change for me." She ran her finger along the ridge of his kneecap. "How old are you, Ross?"

He pulled her closer and had to feel her skin against his lips. He kissed her temple to tamp down the urgency of his desire. "Probably too old to be with you."

She looked up at him again, this time with her brows pinched together.

"I'm old enough to know what I want in life and young enough to still have time to get it. I'm thirty-five."

She whistled. "You *are* old."

He laughed. "Thanks." He remembered the picture he'd seen in Elisabeth's kitchen of her and a guy. He'd put it out of his mind until now. "Lis, did moving here have anything to do with the guy I saw with you in the picture in your kitchen?"

She dropped her eyes to the blanket across her legs.

His chest tightened as he waited for her to answer.

"I thought you saw that," she said softly.

"Sorry. You don't have to tell me." He couldn't tell if he'd struck a fresh or distant nerve.

"It's okay. No, moving had nothing to do with him. His name is Robbie, and we broke up more than a year ago." She drew in a deep breath and laid her hand on his thigh.

Her fingers moved lightly over his muscles, sending streams of heat straight to his groin. He wanted her hand to move north, to stroke his body, to dig her nails into him while he was buried deep inside her. When she spoke again, he nearly groaned aloud as he tore his eyes from her hand and forced himself to try to focus.

"He's a really nice guy, and we dated for a long time. We were just in different places in our lives." She shrugged and licked her lips.

Jesus, was she trying to drive him insane?

"I thought he was *the one*, and he ended our relationship to focus on getting his PhD."

The one. That pulled him from his fantasy. He processed the information, feeling a little jealous that she'd been in love with someone else.

"I'm sorry." She looked so solemn that he did feel sorry for her, but if she and Robbie hadn't broken up, he might never have met her.

"It's a good thing he ended it. I realized afterward that what we had was this really comfortable relationship. Comfortable, like great friends, but I always dreamed that love was much bigger than that, you know?"

He nodded, knowing exactly what she meant but unable to form a response.

"Well, you're a guy, so maybe you don't know, but

like with you...You take my breath away when we're close. He never did."

His pulse ratcheted up a notch. "I take your breath away?" He leaned closer, holding her gaze.

"Uh-huh."

He kissed her, wanting desperately to touch her, taste every inch of her, feel her hard nipples in his mouth, her body beneath him. He deepened the kiss, then forced himself to draw back.

Eyes still closed, she whispered, "See? Breathless." When she finally opened her eyes, her lids were heavy. She smiled with a lust-laden, faraway look in her beautiful eyes.

"You said you believed in fate, marriage, and all things warm and fuzzy. You're on the cusp of so many changes. I thought you might want a little magic to help you make the more important decisions." He reached behind him and retrieved the gift he'd brought for her.

"Ross. You didn't have to bring me anything. Thank you."

She pressed her lips to his, and he wrapped an arm around her and deepened the kiss, wanting it to go on forever. He'd been with women other men would die for, but not one of them made him feel the way Elisabeth did when they were together.

"Go ahead. Open it."

She opened the box with an excited grin and smiled as she lifted the Magic 8 Ball out of the box. "I haven't seen one of these in years."

"Go ahead. Ask it a question. There are ten

positive answers, five negative, and five neutral." He loved the way her eyes lit up.

"Okay." She drew in a deep breath. "Will I ever really fit in in Trusty?" She shook the black plastic ball in both hands and then held it against her chest with her eyes clenched shut. "I can't look."

"Want me to look?"

With her eyes still shut, she held the ball out to him. Ross wrapped his hands around hers. *Please say yes. Please say yes.*

"Lis, let's look together."

She opened her eyes and nodded. "Okay. I'm nervous."

"That's what makes you so incredible. Don't be nervous. If it gives the wrong answer, I'll heave it over the mountain and smash it to bits."

"No, you will not." She pulled it back toward her chest, but he held on tight. "You gave me this. You can't toss it away."

"Then it sure as hell better give you the right answer, or there'll be hell to pay."

She thrust it out toward him again. "You look first. I can't. I want to, but I can't."

"Okay, here goes." He made a scene of shielding the flat edge of the ball while he read it. *It is decidedly so.* Why on earth a plastic ball made him breathe easier was beyond him, but it did.

"It's safe. You can look." He turned the ball toward her and watched as her eyes widened and she drew in an excited breath.

"Yeah!" She wrapped her arms around his neck

and kissed him again. "Thank you! This is the best gift ever."

"You wouldn't be saying that if the answer was *Don't count on it.*"

"Nope, but it wasn't, and fate and all things sparkly were shining down on me." She looked down at the ball. "Do you believe in fate?"

"I do." He always had, though his brothers would scoff if they heard him admit it.

"Do you believe in all things warm and fuzzy?"

Ross moved closer, so their bodies touched from chest to knee. "I do."

"Ask it a question," she said just above a whisper.

Ross looked out over the town that had never done him wrong. The town that had accepted and saved his family after his father had left them. The town where he felt he belonged and where he hoped to one day raise his own children. The town that he hoped would one day give Elisabeth all that it had given him.

He laced their fingers together, and in the other hand he held the plastic ball.

"Will my wish come true?" He shook the ball and handed it to Elisabeth. "Okay, Lis. Are we tossing it over the ledge or keeping it?"

She peeked at the ball. "As I see it, yes."

"Yes, we toss it?"

"No. That's the answer to your question, but what was your wish?"

"That all your dreams would come true."

When their eyes met, Ross couldn't hold back any

longer. He folded her into his arms and gazed into her wanting eyes. "I'm going to kiss you, and if you want me to stop, you need to tell me, because if you don't, I make no promises."

NOTHING COULD COMPARE to being in Ross's arms, their hearts beating against each other faster than a hummingbird's wings, their tongues dancing together in perfect rhythm. She'd dreamed her whole life of feeling like this, feeling safe and cherished, her heart and mind being in sync. Wanting a man with her entire being. The air was cool, but her body was hot. When Ross rolled her onto her back and lay beside her, one strong leg pulled up over her thighs, his chest against hers, his hand cradling her head, their lips sealed together, she thought she'd died and gone to heaven. He was crazy if he thought she'd tell him to stop, because she could barely think past the hope that their kiss would never end.

Ross drew back, kissed the edges of her lips, then made his way across the center and ran his tongue along her upper lip.

More. Kiss me more.

Her eyes were closed, and she focused on his breathing, the feel of his hand as it slid down her hip to the hem of her dress, then beneath, and he gripped the outside of her thigh. Her breathing came faster at the feel of his strong hand on her bare skin.

He kissed her jaw, the tender spot beneath her earlobe, and then he pressed his scruffy cheek to hers and whispered, "Lissa, you make my mouth water for more of you."

She shivered with anticipation.

"Do you want me to stop?"

Even with her eyes closed, she felt the heat of his stare, heard the desire in his voice. "God no." She reached up and drew his mouth to hers again.

Their mouths came together in a heady mix of want and need. The kiss was hard and rough, spurring sexy noises of desire from them both. Ross's hand slid up her thigh and gripped her hip. He pressed his hard length against her side as he deepened the kiss, and everything intensified. The air grew hotter, her breathing came faster, and her hips had a mind of their own, arching upward, aching for him. His lips slid down her chin, kissing a path to her collarbone. He licked the dip in the center, and she drew in a breath. He dragged his tongue up her neck and settled his teeth on the skin just below her ear, sucking hard enough to make her entire body go white-hot. She was damp with desire. His hand slid from her hip higher, creeping up her ribs, then stopping just below her breasts. She clawed at his back, pulled up the back of his shirt in search of skin.

Oh yes, hard muscles, hot skin. *Heaven.*

His hand moved higher. Finally, his thumb brushed over her breast, sending a shock of need through her.

"Ross, touch me."

He brushed his thumb over her taut nipple, and oh God, she wanted more. So much more. She didn't try to understand the unfamiliar rush of desire and emotions driving her forward, forming words she'd only dreamed of using in this context. She let her mind go blank and opened herself to the moment.

"Please." A heated plea.

He moved down her body, kissing the skin between her breasts. *Yes. Oh, yes.* His hand slid south again, and she held her breath as he hooked his finger into the edge of her lace panties and gazed up into her eyes. She was panting with need as he slid his finger along the seam and swept over her damp center. The pit of her stomach tightened.

"Lissa," he whispered, then lowered his forehead to her belly and stilled. When he lifted his eyes, they were filled with conflict—lust and hesitation.

His finger was barely touching her wetness, and her insides clenched with desire.

"I want this, Ross. I want you." She rocked her hips, urging him to touch her, even though it was fast. Even though they were outside. Even though she'd never been so aggressive before. She wanted this, she wanted him, and she was powerless to do anything but give in to the heat that consumed them.

Thank the Lord he took her hint, and in the next breath his lips met her bare stomach in openmouthed kisses as his fingers explored her slick center. He licked and nipped her belly, moving lower, dragging his teeth over her hips to the area just above her damp curls. She fisted her hand in his hair and urged him lower. He stroked and teased and brought her right up to the edge, then used his mouth and sent her spiraling out of control. One strong hand gripped her hip while the other worked its magic, and his tongue, his glorious tongue, took her up, up, up, again, and she called out his name into the darkness as the orgasm ripped through her again. Nothing had ever felt so good. Or so right.

The sounds of the night came back slowly, crickets, their breathing, and she realized that the moans and mews she heard were coming from her own lungs. Ross moved up her body and she reached for the button of his jeans. His lips met hers, and he tasted of her, salty and sweet. He kissed her harder, thrusting his tongue as he pushed his fingers inside her, until all she tasted was him.

"Lis, are you sure? We can stop."

"Oh my God, no, don't stop." She didn't care that this was new, or that this was their first real date. She wanted to be as close to Ross as she physically could, and she wanted him now. *Fate*. She believed in it, lived by it, and she wasn't about to stop now.

He kissed her again, and when he drew back, she took his cheeks in her hands and honesty tumbled out. "In twenty-seven years I've never wanted anyone like I want you."

"There's one thing I have to know." Ross searched her eyes.

"I've only been with two guys, I'm on the pill, and I'm clean."

He smiled and kissed her. "I'm clean, too, always used condoms. But that wasn't the thing."

"Oh." Embarrassment heated her cheeks.

"You're so damn cute it's painful."

"Is that the thing?" *Hurry. Hurry!*

"No." He kissed her cheek, then her nose, her forehead, and her other cheek. "Will you see only me? Be my girlfriend?"

"Goodness, Ross. I thought...Yes. Of course." She leaned up and kissed him. Relieved that he hadn't tried to put a caveat of some other kind on their intimacy—and she'd probably have agreed to whatever it was because she was out of her mind with need. She couldn't believe now that she'd even thought such a thing. He'd shown her throughout the date that he was willing to risk becoming part of the town gossip for her, and she knew how huge of a deal that was for him.

Heat flashed in his eyes as he shimmied out of his jeans and stripped her of her clothes. She'd never seen such an exquisite creature. His body was lean and defined, muscle after rippling muscle of tanned skin and sinew. He positioned himself over her, and she felt the tip of his arousal against her. Her body ached for more. Ross gazed deeply into her eyes and kissed her softly, pushing the tip of his heat into her, spreading her legs wider with his powerful thighs.

"Lissa, I have a feeling I've been waiting for you my whole life."

He sealed his lips over hers and pushed inside her, until he was buried deep. She sucked in a breath at the magnificent pressure of his girth. He breathed air into her lungs as they began to move as one, slowly at first, then more urgently, each clawing for more. She felt the tease of release. Her insides swelled with anticipation as he thrust harder. His arms slid up her back, and he gripped her shoulders, driving deeper over and over. His heart thundered against her chest, and their eyes met just before hers slammed shut and an explosion of heat and tingling vibrated through her body.

"Oh...God...Ross."

"Lis..."

He buried his face in her neck as he followed her over the edge, grunting and panting until the last shudder rippled through their bodies. Under the cover of night, and beneath the blessing of the moon, Ross laced his fingers with hers and brought them to his lips. Her heart swelled. She closed her eyes and breathed in the cool night air, sending a silent message up to the heavens.

Thank you, Aunt Cora. This is exactly where I'm supposed to be.

Chapter Eleven

THE SUN WAS just beginning to peek over the mountains Saturday morning when Elisabeth came out of the barn with Kennedy in her arms. She'd woken up at four o'clock hot and bothered from a dream about Ross, and by five, she was doing yoga on the back porch. She felt more settled now, after an ice-cold shower and taking care of her morning chores. Her shorts were dirty from feeding the animals, and she probably smelled like hay and mud, but she didn't care. Everything seemed brighter today, more fulfilling, and she knew it was because she and Ross had come together. Something inside her shifted last night when she was in his arms. No, it had happened earlier than that, in the days before, a little more with every look, every touch, and every flirtation. Last night when they'd walked into the Brewery and he'd tightened his grip on her arm. It was a little thing, but she'd seen something much bigger, deeper, in his eyes, and it had filled her in ways nothing ever had.

She sat on a log and watched the sun rise as she fed Kennedy his goat milk. He was eating well and making the cutest little grunting noises as he took the bottle. Her mind drifted back to the evening before, lying beneath the stars, with Ross gazing down at her before they'd made love. Her body shuddered with the memory. She knew he'd felt the earth move, too, and the moment their bodies came together, she was his, and somehow she felt like he was hers, too.

After feeding Kennedy, she went to work putting up the small metal pen she'd found in her aunt's shed. She was nervous and excited about her first day of grooming, and every time she thought of last night, she got dizzy with emotions. She was struggling to clip the metal pieces together on the last two panels when Ross pulled into the driveway.

Her heart raced at the sight of him as he climbed from his truck. Knight, Ranger, and Sarge barreled toward her. Storm remained by his side.

"Free dog." Ross's command sent Storm bounding toward the others.

She dropped to her knees and loved up the dogs. Knight licked her, chin to forehead. Ross walked at a fast clip, reached a hand in the middle of the puppy mayhem, and helped her to her feet. He folded her into his arms and kissed her until she felt the world spin.

"Sorry, but the boys couldn't wait a minute longer to see you." He wore a pair of jeans and a cotton shirt like a second skin, and he looked delicious.

"The boys, huh?" She petted Knight as they walked

toward the metal pen she was putting together.

"I'm just a big ol' boy." Ross draped an arm over her shoulder and pulled her against him. "I came by to see if you needed help with anything before I head out to check on Gracie."

"Gracie? Is she okay?" She watched him connect the metal latches with ease.

He drew his brows together and turned away with a shake of his head. He tested the gate on the pen and changed the subject. "You put this together by yourself?"

She could tell he didn't want to talk about Gracie, and her heart squeezed for him. "Yes. It wasn't hard, and since I don't know Wren's dogs, I figured it was safest to keep them in the pen instead of running loose."

"See why I like you? You worry about animals as much as I do." He reached for her hand and surveyed the grooming station she'd set up in the front yard. "Do you have an awning? It's going to be warm today; you might want shade."

"I didn't see one in Aunt Cora's shed, and I forgot to buy one, but I'll pick one up before next weekend." They stood hand in hand. Ross looked around before finally setting serious eyes on her and leading her toward the porch. "Do you have time to sit for a minute?"

"Always." Her stomach did a nosedive straight into a pool of worry. Maybe she'd misjudged his feelings, even after all he'd said. Maybe he was having second thoughts. They sat on the front porch. Knight plunked his big body down beside her and breathed loudly through his nose as he pressed his head to her thigh.

"Attention hog," Ross teased.

She petted Knight's head, feeling even more nervous. Ross tightened his grip on her hand.

"Lis, about last night."

Don't say it. Please don't say it. She held her breath and trained her eyes on Storm and Sarge playing in the yard.

"I'm sorry for taking it so far. I hope you don't regret it, and I hope you didn't feel like I forced myself on you."

"Wh-why are you sorry?" She couldn't begin to tell him that he hadn't forced himself on her or that she'd never wanted a man more than she wanted him. She was too afraid of the way he'd cushioned the statements. Did he regret it? Didn't he hear everything she'd said last night?

"Because you just moved into town, and that was our first real date. I never sleep with a woman on the first date. It's not the way I..." He put an arm around her and kissed her temple. "I can't even say *not the way I operate*, because I don't *operate*. I'm not a saint by any stretch of the imagination, but I don't usually do that."

"Oh." She wondered if she could slip from his arm and slither along the wooden planks and inside without him noticing. Maybe she could pour herself down the cellar stairs like liquid and just hide there for a month. Or a lifetime.

He lifted her chin and turned her face toward his.

"Do you regret being with me?" He searched her eyes, and she couldn't think past the sound of her heart shattering inside her chest.

"Lis?" A single desperate word.

"Hm?" she managed.

"Shit. Did I totally fuck this up?" His brows drew together as he turned away. "I'm an idiot. A fucking idiot."

"Wait. I'm confused." She gripped his thigh, felt the muscles flex beneath his jeans as he whipped his head back around. "Are you telling me that it was a mistake, or are you asking if I thought it was a mistake?"

"Asking. I'm asking," he said roughly.

"No. I might be the idiot. I thought—oh God—" She covered her face with her hands. "This is so embarrassing." She drew in a deep breath and met his confused stare. "I have never done anything that felt so right in my life, but that doesn't mean that you have to—"

His lips met hers in an urgent kiss. He cupped her cheeks and smiled, a sated, thoughtful smile that told her everything she needed to know before he did.

"I don't do things because I have to. I follow my gut, and with you, I'm following my heart." He kissed her again, and Knight pushed his big black head in between them. Ross glared at him, then turned thoughtful eyes back to her again. "You asked me if I believe in fate, and I told you I did. This. Us. It's fate, Lis. I never thought I'd see the day when I'd think of a woman before my practice, or before my family, and when I got up this morning, my mind went to you—

and it never left."

She knew in that moment that all those years of wanting to return to Trusty, all the years she'd saved herself for the man she'd always hoped existed, hadn't been wasted. Ross was everything she'd ever dreamed of, and more.

Chapter Twelve

LATER THAT MORNING, while Ross examined Gracie, he thought about the paths he'd chosen in life, or rather, the paths that had chosen him. Trusty was a given. Once his oldest brother Pierce went away to school, Ross made the decision that he'd make Trusty his home. More than loving the town in which he had grown up, he wanted to be near family. Ross wasn't the glue that held his family together. In the Braden family, each member had his or her own role in doing that. Pierce, though not physically present on a daily basis, still watched over the family from afar. He was there for Luke when he fell for Daisy and had to face the demons of his past, and he'd been there for each of them over the years. And other than Jake, who lived in Los Angeles and visited often, the rest of the siblings lived nearby and were always getting together or texting, pitching in whenever they were needed. Being there for his family was a given for Ross that he'd never questioned, just like becoming a veterinarian. It had been hard work and taken many years, but not once did he waver in what he wanted. And now he felt the same *given* about Elisabeth.

He wasn't swept up in love like a schoolboy. What he felt was much deeper than infatuation. He thought of her throughout the day and night, wondered how she was doing, worried about what trouble she might encounter in town, and today—he worried about no one showing up for free grooming. If that happened, it would cut him to his core. Elisabeth seemed to take it as part of the process in building a business. But for Ross, it was much more than that. The very town he'd given his all to was turning its back on the woman he felt as though he were born to be with. And he did feel that way. It was like their eyes met and his body and mind filled with recognition. *Oh, it's you. I've been waiting thirty-five years for you*. He hadn't been looking for a relationship, just as he hadn't been looking for a career with his veterinary practice. He'd just *known* it was what he was meant to do. Elisabeth stepped into his arms and into his heart.

He stroked Gracie's neck and took a moment to gather his wits about him. Even though this was a natural part of the life cycle, and he, Jim, and Kelsey all knew Gracie was on borrowed time, knowing her time had come sucked the air from his lungs.

Jim sank onto the edge of the futon.

"It's your call, Jim." Ross set a hand on his shoulder to let him know he wasn't alone.

"She's my coffee dog, Ross. Seven mornings a

week for twelve years she waited by my side, barking, jumping, and causing the loudest ruckus while I stirred my coffee." Jim shook his head, smiled at the memory. "Damn dog." He stroked her head. "All to sit beside my rocking chair on the front porch while I drank the damn coffee."

Ross had heard this story so often he could repeat it verbatim. He smiled, allowing Jim to share his love for Gracie.

"She is a magnificent dog." Jim wrapped an arm around Gracie's neck and rested his cheek on her chest.

Ross waited patiently as Jim made his decision. He turned heavy-lidded eyes toward Ross, and Ross knew that he wasn't ready. He patted his shoulder.

"Take your time, Jim. You have my cell number. I can come back anytime."

On the way back to his truck with Storm, Ross called Kelsey and filled her in. He knew Jim would be calling later in the day, surely by nightfall. When a person loved their pet as much as Jim did, they didn't allow them to suffer.

He stopped at the store and bought an awning and three motion-sensor lights for Elisabeth—one for each porch, front and back, and one for the barn doors. Then he drove over to the diner to pick up lunch for the two of them.

"One of my favorite Bradens," Margie said when he sat at the counter.

"When will I move up the ladder to your favorite?" Ross knew Margie would never designate any of his siblings as the favorite. She was like a favorite aunt for everyone in town, the aunt who spoiled each of them equally. "Settle," he said to Storm, who sat obediently beside his stool.

"When you train a man for me as well as you train those adorable puppies, then you'll be my favorite." She filled a cup of coffee, added cream, and pushed it across the counter to Ross. "I heard about Jim's dog. So heartbreaking."

"How on earth did you hear that quickly?" He sipped the bitter coffee.

"Kelsey. She was here when you called. Poor thing. As soon as she hung up, she burst into tears."

"Christ. I should have anticipated that. What is it with women and tears these days?"

"I have a better question for you. What is going on with a particular woman's niece and one of my favorite Bradens these days?" Margie smiled and patted her hair, like she was *all that*. She was *all that* when it came to Trusty gossip.

"Probably exactly what you think it is," he answered with a smile. He'd never wanted to do so much for, or felt so protective of, a woman than he did with Elisabeth. She made him feel fulfilled, complete. He couldn't fathom how his days felt complete before meeting her, because if he were to lose her now, even after such a short period of time, the void in his life would seem insurmountable.

Margie leaned over the counter and pointed at Ross. "You Braden boys are dropping like flies. Be careful, Ross. If the rumors are true, she's not going to be sticking around."

"If Trusty rumors were true, half this town would be in trouble. Trusty gossip is like water on scarred metal. It finds a weakness and seeps right in, making beautiful things ugly. Seventy-five percent is drawn from jealousy, twenty percent from a disgruntled past with distant relatives, four percent bullshit, and about one percent truth."

"Sounds about right." She laughed.

"The only way Elisabeth's leaving is if she's run out of town, and I'll do my damnedest to ensure that doesn't happen."

"Ross Braden, I do believe you are smitten."

He sipped his drink without answering. Damn right he was smitten.

"Well, there was another rumor circulating around, besides the big news about Ross Braden wooing Cora's niece. I heard about what she did for Gracie." Her gaze softened. "Just tell me one thing. Did she do it to win you over, or did she do it out of the kindness of her heart?"

"She won me over long before she met Gracie."

By the time he left the diner, he hoped he'd planted enough truth to waylay any rumors, and he counted on Margie to see to it that the rumors were slayed. Only time would tell.

He turned in to Elisabeth's driveway a few minutes later. Balloons hung from the mailbox, and a big sign announced, *Free Grooming & Pawdicures Today!* That would surely get people's attention. His heart sank at the sight of the empty driveway.

Balloons hung from the grooming table and chair. Ross cut the engine and watched Elisabeth. She had her back to the truck and was in the pen with the Wynchels' dogs. Each of the three dogs had bows tied to their collars. Their fur was fluffy and clean. She tossed sticks and they retrieved them. He and Storm stepped from the truck, and when he closed the door, she finally turned, with a wide smile on her lips. She flipped her hair over her shoulder and it caught the sunlight. She lifted a hand over her head and waved.

"Free dog," Ross said to Storm.

Storm looked at him, then dashed for Elisabeth. Ross wanted to run to her, too, but he needed a second to diffuse his irritation. Why the hell wasn't anyone there? She was giving away her services for free. He hoped to hell that he'd just missed the crowds.

"How's it going?" He leaned over the dog pen and kissed her.

"I'm having so much fun. Look how happy the dogs are." She reached over the fence and loved up Storm. "Can I groom him?"

"You can do whatever you'd like, but you don't have to. How many people showed up?"

"None." She opened the pen and led Storm over to the grooming station. "But that's okay. It's my first day. I'm sure it'll take some time. I have to take the dogs back soon, and I think Wren was pleased with how the other three dogs looked when I dropped them off and picked up these guys. Aren't they gorgeous?"

"Not as gorgeous as you." He pulled her close and kissed her. "I'm really sorry no one showed up. I think what you're doing is great."

"Thanks." She ran her finger down the center of his chest. "I've missed doing this so much that today was rejuvenating."

"I'm glad. I bought you an awning, but I have a great idea. Since no one is here, why don't we grab our swimsuits and spend the afternoon at the lake? We'll take the boys, have a little lunch, and relax."

"You spoil me." She went up on her tiptoes and kissed him, then sat down to brush Storm.

"I brought lunch from the diner. I wasn't sure what you liked, so I got you a California chicken salad. I figured I couldn't go wrong with California in the name."

"I'm easy. I'll eat just about anything."

He felt his mouth quirk up at that.

She laughed. "Who's the dirty one now?"

"Hey, you said it." He put the awning in the shed, then showed her the motion-sensor lights he'd bought and promised to install them soon.

"I can't believe you bought all this. I'll repay you."

He leaned over her as she brushed Storm. "Okay, but I don't accept money as a form of payment."

THEY ARRIVED AT Wynchels' Farm an hour later. Elisabeth carried a peach pie she'd made using their homegrown peaches. The three pups followed her into the barn as if she were the Pied Piper. She had that way about her. Animals connected with her instantly. *Maybe I'm part animal.* He smiled at the thought. Wren was running the register and helping a line of customers.

Ross walked around the barn with Storm, watching Elisabeth as she waited patiently for Wren to finish with her customers. She'd changed into a sundress and sandals, the straps of an aqua bikini tied around her neck. She looked relaxed and happy. She touched the edge of her hair and twisted it around her finger, then drew in a breath and pushed her hair away, as if someone had tapped her on the shoulder and whispered, *Honey, don't play with your hair.* She'd done that a number of times, and each time there was a millisecond of awareness just before dropping her hand. He wondered why.

"Thanks, Marlene. I'll see you next week," Wren said to her last customer. She closed the cash register and turned her attention to the dogs standing beside Elisabeth.

"Hi, Wren. Thank you for letting me take care of your dogs today. I think they really enjoyed themselves, and I know I did." Two of the dogs stood beside Elisabeth at the counter.

"They're wearing bows." She frowned.

Elisabeth smiled and waved her hand at the dog. "I always do that. It makes them feel special. Oh, and I brought you this." She held the peach pie out for Wren.

Wren's eyes ran between the pie and Elisabeth before she reached tentatively for it.

"It's made with your peaches. I hope you like it."

"You made me a pie after picking up my dogs and grooming them?" Wren set the pie on the counter and crossed her arms over her thick body. "What's your angle?"

Elisabeth's smile faded. "No angle. I enjoyed my time today and wanted to thank you."

"Hm."

Ross walked behind Elisabeth and set his hand on her shoulder. Storm stood by his side. "Hi, Wren. Looks like you're busy today."

"Ross." Wren glanced at Elisabeth, then up at Ross again, and her gaze softened. "I heard about Gracie. Poor Jim. Is he holding up okay?"

"About as well as to be expected."

"I suppose that's all we can hope for. How's your mother doing?"

"She's well. Thanks for asking." Ross gathered Elisabeth's hair and set it over her right shoulder, then leaned down and kissed her cheek. *Planting the truth*, for both Wren *and* Elisabeth. "Ready, Lis?"

"Yeah, sure. Thanks again, Wren. Would you mind if I groomed them again next weekend? I can pick them up."

"You want to...?"

"If you don't mind."

Wren slid a curious gaze to Ross. "Okay."

Elisabeth's voice escalated with her excitement. "Super. Thank you. Enjoy the pie."

After picking up Ross's boys, they drove out to the lake and walked hand in hand through a path in the woods to a secluded area where the lake pooled in between two forests of trees. There was a narrow strip of grass and about twenty feet of waterfront. Years earlier Ross had found the spot when he was taking Knight for a walk. He'd taken the boys there several times since, and he'd never run into anyone else there. Ross stripped off his shirt and spread out the blanket; then they ate lunch and talked while the dogs played.

He caught Elisabeth staring at the tattoo on his arm. "It's a palm tree."

"I know. I'm wondering what it signifies for you."

"What do you think it means?" He watched her cheeks pink up.

"Well, the erect, towering trunk representing the phallus, and the palms are like an explosion, representing the creation of offspring."

"I guess that's not so far off from my reasons, although I like what your description conjures up." Ross looked at his tattoo and remembered when he'd gotten it with Pierce when he was in college. Pierce had teased the hell out of him, but he'd stuck to his guns. "It's a dream symbol, and it symbolizes our ability to rise above conflict and rise above disillusionment. To me, it symbolizes my belief in fate."

"Fate?" Her eyes softened. "I like that, Ross. I have one." She turned halfway around and showed him the tattoo on her lower back. Two delicate flowers whose stems were intertwined. "Me and my future husband. This symbolizes destiny to me."

"Destiny?" He smiled at the likeness in the meanings of their tattoos.

"Yeah. Destiny. Ross, today has been like a dream come true, even though no one showed up for the free grooming. I did get a few new pie orders today. It makes no sense at all for me to feel so hopeful, but I feel really good about everything and just have a feeling things will come together. Or at least I hope they will. Thank you." She sighed and put the trash from her lunch back in the basket, then stood and pulled her dress over her head.

Ross had no idea what she did or said after that. He was mesmerized by the woman who had stolen his heart wearing a crocheted bikini that left nothing to the imagination. Her bathing suit bottom rode low on her hips, the fabric barely covering the sweet part of her he'd tasted in the bed of his truck. He'd loved her body, felt those luscious curves beneath him. It had been his name coming off her lips in the throes of passion, and it should have been enough to hold him over, at least for a few days, but he was already throbbing with need. She came down on her knees beside him, the darkness around her nipples visible through the knitted fabric. Two taut peaks vying to be set free from the restraint of the thin strings. He shifted his eyes away, trying his best to behave, until her warm hand stroked his thigh. Losing the battle, his eyes found hers and his body heated. He had to wrap an arm around her and pull her into a sensual, needful kiss. Her sun-drenched skin was hot against his bare chest. She kissed him eagerly as she climbed onto his lap and straddled him.

"Does anyone ever come here?" she asked in an urgent breath.

"You will, if I have anything to do with it."

She sealed her mouth over his again with a moan of pleasure and leaned forward, pushing him onto his back as she slithered down his body, kissing his collarbone, along the ridge of his pecs, and down the ripples of his abs. Ross gripped her upper arms, intending to take control and shift her beneath him.

She lifted sultry eyes and licked her lips. "My turn." A naughty smile curved her lips.

Holy. Hell.

She pulled his shorts down to his thighs and wrapped her slender fingers around his arousal, then licked him from base to tip. Ross closed his eyes as the air hit his damp skin and opened them again when she took him in her hot, wet mouth, stroking him with her hand as she worked her tongue seductively along his length. She met his gaze as she licked and teased until he was about to come. He pushed up on his elbows and gripped her arms.

"Lis." A hot breathy plea.

With two quick tugs on the strings hanging from her hips, her bikini bottom fell away. He lifted her over his eager arousal, and she sank down, taking him into her velvety heat as their mouths met in a frenzied kiss. He gripped her hips and helped her efforts as she rode him hard and took him in deep. Tearing his lips from hers with a heady groan, he flipped her beneath him and drove in deep again and again. She clutched his back, her nails piercing his skin as she slammed her head back and cried out in ecstasy. The dogs whimpered, inching closer to the blanket.

"Down." All four dogs lay flat on the ground.

Elisabeth lifted her hips and wrapped her legs around his back, angling so each thrust was deeper, more intense.

"Oh God. Ross," she whispered. "Ah....Ah..."

Her body tightened and pulsated around him, and he lost all control. With the next thrust, he followed her over the edge, pumping and grinding until she took every last drop of his desire.

He rolled breathlessly beside her and reached for her hand.

"Holy shit, Lis. I swear I didn't lure you away from your house to make love to you."

She came up on one elbow and traced the muscles on his stomach with her finger. "I know you didn't. I've waited my whole life for you, and it may not seem like it, but I've always been careful. Sexually, I mean, and with you, I don't want to be. What we did in the truck...the things I said, the way I encouraged you. That was all new to me, but it felt right. I trust you."

With the sun at her back, and her blond hair falling in gentle waves around her beautiful face, she looked angelic. He stroked her cheek as she lowered her lips to his for a sweet, tender kiss.

"You don't need to be careful with me. I'll never hurt you, I only want to be with you." He sat up and picked up her bikini bottom, realizing that he was lying completely exposed, his shorts at his thighs, and she was bare save for the crocheted bikini top. He slipped out of his shorts and set them beside her bikini bottom; then he carefully took off her bikini top. In all his years, he'd never made love to a woman and then walked bare into a lake to cleanse her. He'd never met anyone who made him want to do the things he wanted to do for her. In all his years, he'd never met anyone like Elisabeth.

He took her hand in his and led her into the water. The dogs followed.

The water was cool as Ross sank beneath the surface and came up with his arms circling her waist. Her arms and legs wrapped around him as naturally as if he'd been carrying her forever. He took them both deeper, letting the lake wash them clean as the dogs treaded water nearby.

He moved closer to shore so he could stand, still holding her against him. She rested her head on his shoulder and kissed his neck. He loved the feel of her lips on him. He loved the feel of her.

"Lis."

"Mm-hmm?"

He wrapped his arms around her and hugged her close, but no words came. How could he tell her that for the first time in his life, he felt whole? That he'd never realized the life he'd been living was only half a life? How could he tell her that he loved her after knowing her only a few blessed days? His heart took him by surprise, and if he didn't understand it, how could he expect her not to run for the hills?

"I just wanted to make sure you were there."

Chapter Thirteen

ROSS WOKE UP Monday morning to the sound of his vibrating cell phone. He reached for it, then remembered that he had stayed at Elisabeth's, and reached for her instead. His hand fell on empty sheets.

"Lis?" The bathroom light was off. The only sound in the room was the dogs' lazy breaths. He looked at his cell. It was five o'clock, and the text he'd received was from Jim. Gracie was having trouble. It was time.

Ranger and Sarge stretched while Ross pulled on his boxer briefs and brushed his teeth. He'd brought Storm back to Denton late yesterday, and he wasn't surprised to find Knight missing, too. He followed Elisabeth everywhere. Ross and the other two dogs went downstairs in search of Elisabeth. They found her out on the back deck with her arms outstretched, one knee bent toward the rising sun, the other leg stretched behind her, her back and shoulders straight and square. She reminded him of a flower reaching for the sun. Ranger and Sarge made a beeline for Elisabeth. Knight ran in from the yard to greet them.

"Want to join me?" she asked without turning around.

The cool, predawn air washed over his body. Elisabeth walked into his open arms and heated up all that brisk air.

"I just got a text from Jim. I think Gracie's time has come." He felt her body tense.

"Oh, Ross." She breathed deeply, then touched his cheek. "Let me change, and I'll go with you." She grabbed her water bottle and walked inside.

"Lis, this is the end for Gracie. I have to put her down." He didn't want to be there to see an animal's last breath, much less a dog he'd cared for since he'd become a veterinarian. It wasn't something he thought anyone other than the pet's owner should have to endure.

"I want to be there for Gracie, and for Jim." She reached for his hand. "And for you. I'll stay out of your way completely. I promise." Her brows were knitted together, and her pleading eyes made it difficult for Ross to say no.

Forty minutes later they were with Jim, Kelsey, and Gracie. Jim's eyes were puffy, his skin was dull, and his tone was heavy.

"Thanks for coming out, Ross. Elisabeth, I appreciate you coming along. I think your massage helped Gracie make it a little longer."

Elisabeth embraced him. "I'm so sorry that you're losing her."

Kelsey wiped tears from her red-rimmed eyes and Elisabeth hugged her, too.

As she drew away, Kelsey reached for her hand. "Thank you for what you did for Gracie. That was really nice."

Elisabeth smiled in answer and nodded softly.

They all left the room for a minute to give Jim privacy to say goodbye to Gracie.

Ross touched Kelsey's shoulder. "Are you okay?"

"Yeah. I'm sad for Grandpa, though. I hate that he'll be alone again." Kelsey glanced back toward the living room.

"He's been through a lot, but he'll pull through. He's got you and the rest of your family. Just be sure you give him time and space to grieve," Ross suggested.

Elisabeth was standing by the window, and Ross could see the unasked question in Kelsey's eyes about the two of them. He answered with actions rather than words. He draped an arm around Elisabeth and whispered, "Are you okay?"

She shrugged. He could tell she wasn't okay, but she'd wanted to be there for him. That spoke volumes of her inner strength and it meant the world to Ross.

"How about you? Are you okay?" she asked.

Putting a dog down was difficult, even when it was the right thing to do, but Ross had always kept his own feelings at bay during the process. He'd worn the armor of the veterinarian, a mask of strength and understanding. That was harder to pull off with Elisabeth by his side. She was getting to know the real him, and he knew she'd see right through his charade if he gave her an off-the-cuff nod.

"It's sad, but necessary." He felt Kelsey's eyes on them. She'd never seen him with a woman he was dating, and he knew Kelsey well enough to understand that the curiosity in her eyes was driven by her desire to look out for Ross, because she'd heard the town gossip about Elisabeth. After all, that's what friends did for one another, just as he'd do for her if the occasion arose. He could practically see her weeding through the roots of the grapevine and weighing each against the woman she saw before her.

Ross turned his attention back to Elisabeth. "I'm really glad you're here with me. It's okay if you want to wait in here while I take care of Gracie."

ELISABETH HADN'T EXPECTED to have such a hard time with Gracie being put down. She'd never actually been with an animal when it was put to sleep, but she'd given end-of-life massages like the one she'd given Gracie many times. This was very different. She wanted to be there for Ross even though he'd tried to dissuade her from coming with him. She couldn't imagine that even with all the experience he had, he'd be able to do this and come out unscathed.

He stood straight and tall, shoulders back. As strong and manly as they came. Maybe he didn't need her there after all, despite what he'd just said. Kelsey was watching them intently, and it made her a little more nervous.

"I'm okay," she said as confidently as she could,

which sounded pretty weak to her.

Ross nodded, and then they went into the living room, where Jim was sitting with Gracie, one hand on her chest, the other on her paw. Jim nodded as he rose to his feet, giving Ross room to do what he needed to.

"This will be quick," Ross explained. "I'm going to give her an injection, and she'll be unconscious in seconds. She won't feel a thing." He prepared the injection.

Most people might not have noticed the sadness shadowing his eyes. Elisabeth did. She felt the energy in the room change as a breeze swept in through an open window, bringing with it the scent of hay and horses. Gracie's nose twitched, and Jim sank to his knees by her head and stroked her fur. Kelsey stood behind him with one hand on his shoulder. She glanced up at Elisabeth and reached for her hand. In that second, being an outsider didn't matter. Death had a way of doing that to people—making emotions so raw that there was no room for judgment.

Jim blinked away tears.

Ross glanced at Jim again, and a silent sanction passed between the two men. He administered the shot, and true to his word, Gracie's twitching nose became still. Less than a minute later she was gone. Ross checked for a heartbeat, then gave another silent nod. He placed his hand over Jim's for a beat, then picked up his bag, reached for Elisabeth's hand, and led her silently out to the truck.

"Is it okay to just leave them like that?"

Ross started the truck. "It's what he requested.

He'll bury her on the farm." The muscles in his jaw bunched repetitively. He gripped the steering wheel so tightly his knuckles went white.

Elisabeth slid across the seat and buckled up next to him. She placed one arm over his shoulder and rested her head against him.

"You have a hard job," she said honestly.

"Sometimes." He kept his eyes trained on the road.

They rode the rest of the way in silence. There was no need to hash out his feelings—she sensed his heartache in every breath. When they arrived back at her house, he was still reserved. He reached for her and held her for a long time.

"I was really glad you were with me. Thank you." His voice sounded strained.

"But?" She searched his eyes. They were a strange mix of confusion and something else she couldn't read.

"Your being there made me feel much more than I usually do. It was difficult to remain detached from what I was doing."

"Ross, I'm sorry. I didn't mean to—"

He pressed his lips to hers. "I'm not saying it's a bad thing. I just noticed a difference. I hadn't realized how numb I'd become. You opening me up may even be a good thing."

After Ross left to get ready for work, Elisabeth checked on the animals and fed Kennedy. Her mother called, and after listening to her talk about the party she'd gone to that weekend, where she'd met a few A-list actors, Elisabeth was getting antsy to get on with her day.

"Mom, I've really got to get going. I've got a ton of baking to do, but I'm glad you had a good time."

"Oh, honey. I always have a good time. Before you go, just tell me this. How are you really doing out there all alone? Don't you want to come back?"

There was something needy in her mother's tone that made the question feel strange coming from her. "Mom, are you okay? Why do you want me to come back so badly?"

"*Tsk.* I just hate to think about you out there, wasting your assets in that little town. You should be here, with family. Not out there all alone, living a simple life. Honey, I know you loved Cora. She was my sister, and I loved her, too. But you're too smart to live a simple life like she did. You're destined to marry a great man and live a big life."

That's what this was all about. She was jealous that Elisabeth had chosen to follow Cora's life path instead of hers. After the morning she'd had, she didn't have the energy to try to explain to her mother that living a simple life actually allowed her to live a more fulfilling life. She was happier taking care of the animals and being with Ross than she had ever been in LA, and no amount of fame could replace the joy of seeing Kennedy grow, or walking through the pasture, hearing Rocky crow every morning, or waking up in Ross's arms. Unfortunately, there weren't enough words in the English language to convince her mother of those things.

"I know you worry about me, Mom, but I'm happy. I really am."

She ended the call and baked the orders for the next day, then baked a little something for Kelsey and her grandfather. She was still not sure how she'd gotten a handful of new orders over the weekend, but it brought joy to an otherwise difficult morning.

She spent the next few hours delivering pies. The bell above the door at the Trusty Diner announced her presence, and all eyes turned toward her. Her stomach took a nervous dive. She should be used to sideways glances and whispers by now, or at least expect them, but in the joy of baking, she'd somehow managed to forget that part of her day.

"Elisabeth Nash, what have you done to my Sam?" Margie shoved an order pad into her apron pocket, placed her hands on her hips, and ran a scrutinizing gaze down Elisabeth's arm to the cooler she was carrying.

"Sam?" Was something wrong with the pies? She quickly ran through the ingredients in her mind. She hoped he wasn't allergic to something in the raspberry-apricot pie she'd made for him.

"He's added eight raspberry-apricot pies to our order for the week." She sidled up to Elisabeth and spoke in a hushed tone. "Did you put something addictive in that pie?"

Oh, thank goodness! Elisabeth tried to contain her excitement. "No, but maybe I should. I'm so glad he liked it."

"Liked it?" Margie scoffed. "The man took one bite and then hid the pie so no one else could have any. Then he had the nerve to rattle on and on about how delicious it was to the mailman, the bread delivery man, and our dairy supplier, without offering them so much as a bite."

The day just got a hundred times better.

After delivering the rest of the pies, she stopped by Wynchels' Farm to pick up more raspberries and apricots. Three of the dogs bounded toward her as she crossed the parking lot. She loved them up, shaking her head at their thick tangles and the dirt they'd already gotten into.

"You guys must be having tons of fun," she said to them.

"They're never far from fun, that's for sure."

Elisabeth turned at the slow drawl and deep voice. Two men who looked to be in their fifties, wearing cowboy hats, jeans, and boots fell into step beside her.

"Hi," she said with a smile.

"You're Cora's niece? The dog groomer?" the taller of the two men said.

"No, she's a baker. She took over Cora's business," the other man said.

"Actually, I do both. I pamper pets and bake pies." She held out a hand in greeting. "I'm Elisabeth Nash."

The men tipped their hats and ignored her hand.

"Well, I don't know much about pamperin' no pets, but let me know when you come up with a beer pie. That would catch my attention." The taller man laughed at his own joke.

"Heck yeah. I'd buy one every weekend," the other man agreed, before they nodded a goodbye and headed for a truck in the parking lot.

Beer pie. Beer cake. Elisabeth's mind was spinning. When in Rome...

Inside the barn, she gathered the ingredients she needed for the next few days and set them on the counter.

"Harvey loved the pie," Wren said without looking at her.

Harvey loved the pie! "I'm so glad." She handed Wren money to pay for the fruit. "Who's Harvey?"

"My husband. He says no more bows on the dogs." Wren gave her the change.

"No more bows. Got it."

"Can you make me three more?" She glanced up at Elisabeth as she bagged her purchases.

"Three more?" Hope swelled in Elisabeth's chest.

"Pies. To sell."

Elisabeth couldn't stifle the smile that stretched across her lips. "Absolutely. Let me just buy a few more ingredients." She turned to pick up more fruit and had to squelch the urge to do a fist pump.

On her way home, she stopped at the liquor store and the grocery store. The county fair was the weekend after next, and she wanted to come up with the perfect cake to win over the community.

The last stop she made was at Ross's clinic. Kelsey wasn't at her desk when Elisabeth walked in. A plump pug waddled over on a long leash and sniffed Elisabeth's feet. She had brought the cake she'd baked for Kelsey and her grandfather and set it on the desk before bending down to pet the pup.

"What's your dog's name?" she asked the woman

holding the leash.

"Wiggles. When he was younger, he wouldn't sit still." She smiled and tugged lightly on the leash. "Come on, Wiggles."

"It's okay. I don't mind him sniffing me." She rose to her feet as Kelsey came down the hall with Knight on her heels. Knight bounded over to Elisabeth.

"Oh, hi, Elisabeth. Ross is with a client, but you can wait if you'd like." Kelsey sat at her desk and eyed the Bundt cake.

"Actually, I just stopped by to see how you were doing." She loved up Knight and then turned her attention back to Kelsey. "I made this for you and your grandfather." She set a small gift bag on the counter. "I brought you chamomile tea, too. I don't know if you and Jim drink tea, but..."

Kelsey smiled up at her. "Thank you. My grandfather loves cake, and I love tea, so this is perfect. I'm going to see him after work. This was really thoughtful of you."

"I'm really sorry about Gracie. Well, I won't hold you up. I know you're busy." She gave Knight a final few pets and turned to leave.

"Don't you want to see Ross?" Kelsey asked.

"I will, when he's off work. I came to see you." She turned to the woman with the pug. "Enjoy your day with Wiggles."

ROSS WORKED UNTIL after dark. With the county fair right around the corner, there a long list of animals to be seen and paperwork to complete. It didn't matter that he had sent out reminders to his clients sixty days earlier announcing that the fair was coming up and to remember to get their animals checked early. Some clients had taken note, but he found it difficult to teach old farmers new tricks.

Elisabeth had been on his mind all day. They'd exchanged texts during the afternoon, and they made plans for him to stop by after he was done for the day. He did a quick workout, showered, and changed, then loved up the boys and played with them for a few minutes before piling them in the truck and heading over to her place.

Country music filtered through the screen door. Ross knocked, but he knew Elisabeth couldn't hear him over the music. He walked inside with the boys by his side. They found her in the kitchen, which looked like it had exploded. There were baking ingredients on every surface. Bowls, mixing spoons, a mixer, bags of flour, sugar, and other accoutrements, including several empty beer bottles—which surprised him— covered the countertops. Elisabeth's hips swayed seductively to the music. He put a hand down to keep the dogs by his side as he took a moment to drink her in. She wore a simple capped-sleeve dress that was white on top and light pink on bottom. It hung loosely to just a few inches beneath her butt. Her back was to him, and she was belting out the words to the song. She had a lovely singing voice, and as he stood there, he imagined coming home to her every day.

Hell, she had a lovely *everything*.

He came up behind her, intending to wrap his

arms around her waist, but the boys bounded in and she backed into Knight and yelped, dropping a cup of flour on the counter. White powder bloomed into the air, covering his clothing and hers.

"Oh my gosh! Ross. I'm sorry!" She brushed the flour from his clothes.

He laughed and pulled her against him. "I'm not."

"But you're all floury now."

The dogs danced around their legs, sniffing the flour and then sneezing.

"I didn't really want to keep my clothes on anyway." He kissed her again, and she moaned deliciously. "You might have to take off that floury dress, too."

"In your dreams, Mr. Braden."

"I have pretty erotic dreams." He had to take her in another greedy kiss. After finally tearing his lips from hers, he noticed three cakes lined up on the far counter. "Puppy cakes?"

"I can't answer you right now. I'm still thinking about your erotic dreams." She smiled and opened the back door to let the dogs onto the deck.

"Beer cakes. Come, taste." She grabbed a butter knife. "I'm trying new recipes for the county fair. I made one that I call Honey, Nuts 'n' Spice. I made it with honey beer." She cut a piece and fed it to him. "I iced it with honey beer frosting."

"That's delicious." He kissed her. "Like it?"

"My favorite taste. Rossie cake." She kissed him again and then cut a hunk of the next cake.

Rossie. The nickname made him smile. He

definitely didn't think of himself as *Rossie*, but Elisabeth could call him anything she pleased.

Her eyes were wide with excitement as she held the piece of cake up between her fingers. "This is a chocolate Bundt cake made with stout beer and yogurt." She fed it to him and bit her lower lip, waiting for his response.

"Lis, I'm going to need to work out twice a day if you keep feeding me like this. That's delicious, too."

She clapped her hands. "Yay! This is so exciting. These two men made a joke about beer pie today." She cut a hunk out of the third cake. "And I thought, guys like beer. Why not? I'm going to see how they go over at the fair. This next one was a little risky. If you don't like it, please be honest."

The cake was thinner than the others, and it had a rough texture to the top and what looked like chunks of fruit poking out all over.

"I call this oatmeal whiskey surprise. I made it with oatmeal stout beer and a bit of whiskey. I added chunks of apples, too." She went up on her toes, and her eyes grew serious while he chewed.

"Honest answer?" He arched a brow.

She sank back to her heels. "Please."

"Fucking incredible. I may never eat regular food again." He swept her into his arms and kissed her again. "Have you tasted them yet?"

"Not these. I was waiting for you. So you think I should sell them at the fair?"

"Absolutely. People will love these. I'll help you clean up the flour I made you spill." Ross grabbed the trash can. "There's cake in the trash?"

"Those are the ones I made and tasted while I was perfecting my recipes." She smiled and twisted her hair around her finger.

He pulled her close again. "You need to stop being so cute or we'll never do anything but get naked and ravish each other."

"And that's bad because?" She licked her lips and then pushed away from him. "I'm too excited to fool around. I need to plan out my shopping list." She grabbed a pad of paper and began writing.

Ross went to work cleaning the kitchen. "Wow. I've never been turned down for a grocery list before."

"Not turned down, just delayed." She didn't look up from her list, and Ross found her even more attractive standing among the messy kitchen with flour in her hair and all over her pretty dress and a look of sheer concentration on her beautiful face.

"I heard you came by the clinic today." Kelsey had been unable to stop talking about how compassionate and thoughtful Elisabeth was.

"I brought Kelsey a cake and some tea." She brushed flour off of his sleeve.

He wished everyone knew Elisabeth as well as he did. They'd see that she wasn't here only to take what she could get and skip town.

"Are you sure you weren't born in Trusty? Because you're as good-natured and trusting as a person could ever be."

"I think that's the nicest thing you could ever say to me. Maybe my shopping list can wait." She wrapped her arms around his neck and he lifted her easily into his arms. Her legs circled his waist as her lips met his.

Ross's cell rang. He reluctantly pulled back and sighed. "I can check it later."

"What if it's an emergency?"

"Fine." He slid one arm beneath her butt and held her up while he dug his cell out of his pocket and looked at the number. "It's my cousin Rex." He backed her up and set her on the counter, then cringed. "I forgot about the flour. Sorry."

She wiggled her butt. "My boyfriend told me that's what washing machines were for. Answer your call."

Boyfriend. He loved hearing that, but his mind and his heart were already hinting for more.

"Rex, how's it going?" Rex and his fiancée, Jade, lived in Weston.

"Hey, Ross. Things are good. Thanks for asking. I hear Pierce and Rebecca are planning their wedding." Rex's voice was as deep as his body was strong. He worked his father's thoroughbred horse ranch and was the epitome of a brooding cowboy, or at least he had been until Jade came into his life. Rex's love for Jade softened his gruffness.

"Yes, for sometime in the spring. How's Jade?"

"Actually, she's the reason why I'm calling. Are the rumors true? Are you dating Elisabeth Nash?"

"Jesus, Rex. How on earth did you hear about that?" Ross smiled at Elisabeth and lifted her off the counter, then brushed the flour off her butt. He covered the phone and whispered, "Would you mind turning down the radio?"

She danced over to the stereo in the living room and turned it down. Ross caught a glimpse of the picture of Robbie, still in the box on the kitchen floor, and he felt a spear of jealousy tear through him.

"Your mother told Jade that Elisabeth did some kind of pet pampering and she thought it might be a good opportunity for Elisabeth and Jade to trade referrals. Then, of course, Emily and Jade had an hour-long conversation about the two of you." Rex laughed. "Better you than me. That's all I can say about that."

Ross ran his hand through his hair and averted his eyes from the offending picture. Elisabeth was poring over her grocery list at the kitchen table and twirling her hair.

"Leave it to Emily to spread the word."

"Jade wants to talk to Elisabeth about working together. Are you guys free anytime this week? You could come out for a barbeque, or we could come there. Whatever works for you."

"Rex, that's great. Hold on a sec." He lowered the phone. "Lis, Rex's fiancée does equine massage and she wants to get together and see if there's any way you two can combine your efforts. Want to meet them for a drink or dinner?"

She jumped to her feet. "Yes. Oh my gosh. That's great. Please tell him thank you."

He wrapped an arm around her waist and answered Rex. "Sounds good, Rex. We have the county fair next weekend, so things are pretty crazy around here. Are you guys free for dinner tomorrow or Wednesday?"

Ross checked with Elisabeth and they made plans to meet for dinner Wednesday. When he ended the call, Elisabeth flew into his arms. "Thank you!"

"I didn't do anything. You need to thank my mom. She told Jade and then I guess Emily called Jade and they talked about you, or us."

"I kind of like the Trusty grapevine now." She pressed a quick kiss to his lips, then danced around the kitchen as she cleaned up.

"That would be the Braden grapevine."

"Can I have your mom's number so I can call and say thank you?" She began scrubbing the counter.

"Don't you want to talk with Jade first and make sure it's what you want to do?"

"Oh, it doesn't really matter what happens with Jade. The fact that your mom thought about me and recommended that we talk was really nice. I just want to say thank you."

He circled her waist from behind and kissed her cheek. "I think she'd love to hear from you. And you might just make a go of your business after all."

Chapter Fourteen

ROSS AND ELISABETH spent Monday night at his house. The boys had all slept on the floor—at least most of the night. They awoke Tuesday morning with Ranger sprawled across the bottom of the bed. Elisabeth didn't seem to mind. In the morning she crawled down to the end of the bed and hugged Ranger before she even hugged Ross.

They got up early and took care of her animals together, which gave Ross a chance to check out the piglets. Pigs were hearty animals, and even though Kennedy was a runt, he was eating well and growing without issue. Elisabeth was relieved to hear that he'd be just fine, even if small. She'd called Ross's mother before he left for work, and his mother, not realizing Elisabeth had spent the night with Ross, called him a few minutes later to gush about how nice it was of her to call. Tonight Emily was meeting with Elisabeth about the kitchen renovations. They'd gotten along so well at his mother's that he had visions of Emily becoming a staple in Elisabeth's house. He was thinking about his mother's phone call when his phone rang Tuesday afternoon.

Every time he got a call from Walt Norton, the director for the Pup Partners program in Denton, he hoped that nothing had happened to one of the dogs. Luckily, they'd had only one situation where an inmate had to be removed from the program. He'd used the dog to manipulate visitors to bring things to him. What those *things* were, Ross wasn't privy to, and the dog had been unharmed. While Ross believed in the program and had been thrilled with the results for both the inmates and the dogs, the worry lingered in the back of his mind.

"Hi, Walt."

"Hey, Ross. I hope I caught you before you headed this way."

"Is there an issue?" He leaned back in his chair and glanced at the clock.

"I don't think I'd call it an issue. More of a miracle, I think. I got a request earlier today from Trout. He'd like to know if he can get a stuffed animal for Storm. He seems to think the dog is lonely."

Ross leaned back in his chair and thought about Trout and how close he must feel to Storm to be requesting something to make him feel more comfortable. Beneath that hulking exterior was a caring heart—even if he had killed a man. It made Ross wonder even more about the man Trout had been before he'd made the choice to kill.

"It's actually not such a crazy idea. Sure, I can pick one up on my way there. Walt, can you tell me any more about Trout than what I read in his file?"

"Have you Googled him yet?" Walt's voice grew serious.

"Yeah, I did. But what's your take on him?"

"He's either brilliant or an idiot. I'm not one to judge."

Two and a half hours later Ross and Trout were finishing Storm's training and Ross was doing a quick exam on Storm. He opened Storm's mouth and checked his teeth, buying time, and hoping to get Trout talking. Ever since he and Elisabeth made love, he'd been thinking about the future. He'd always wanted to have children, and Trout was a reminder of how wrong things could go for a kid. Ross wanted to understand Trout and the decisions he'd made.

Trout sat with his elbows on his knees, neck bowed, one hand fisted inside the other.

"I brought you the toy you requested for Storm."

Trout turned his head and his hands stilled. "Thanks, Doc."

Ross ran his hands down each of Storm's legs. Touching was good for Storm. Getting used to being handled was key to service-dog training.

"What made you think of a toy? Oh, and I got a toy he couldn't chew through. He can choke on stuffed animals, so you want to be careful with the items you allow in his crate."

"Choke." He nodded.

"There's a button on it that makes a heartbeat

sound, too. It should calm him."

"A heartbeat." He nodded, and his eyes filled with worry. "I don't want him to choke, Doc. You're sure this one is safe?"

He was amazed that Trout was talking to him, but the dog seemed to be a safe subject. "Positive. You had a dog as a kid, right?"

Trout turned his head the other way. He rubbed his palm over his fisted hand. Ross checked Storm's ears, realizing that he'd struck a chord with Trout.

"How'd you come to the decision that Storm was lonely at night?"

Trout's head shifted back in his direction again, his stare cold and vacant. Ross waited him out and held his stare for a full minute before Trout's enormous shoulders rose in a shrug.

"Television show."

Ross nodded. "Good call. My gir—" He caught himself. One rule of thumb was never to talk about your personal acquaintances with the inmates. "My friend mentioned that moving the crate closer to your bed at night might help, too."

Trout nodded.

"What kind of dog did you have as a kid?"

Trout clenched his jaw, remaining silent.

Trying to talk to Trout about his past was proving to be just as difficult as Ross thought it might be. He finished checking each of Storm's paws, then took the toy from his bag and handed it to Trout.

Trout smiled, momentarily flashing those dimples Ross had caught a glimpse of last week. "Thanks, Doc."

"Did you ever give your dog a toy when you were a kid?"

Trout drew his brows together again. His jaw clenched tight, and when he lifted his eyes to Ross again, they were full of rage.

Ross drew his shoulders back and held his stare once again. Instinct told him to treat Trout like a grizzly, look away, walk silently away, but the man in him held him in position.

"Trout?" He didn't know why he felt compelled to try to figure out what had made Trout go from being valedictorian to a murderer, but he needed to understand it. He wanted to understand him.

Trout looked down at Storm. "My dog cried at night. My m—" He looked away, narrowed those angry eyes, and stared down at the floor as he spoke. "Someone said he was lonely. Gave him a toy and he slept fine. Dogs get lonely just like people."

Ross caught the stifled mention of his mother, and in that second, Ross saw Trout not as a murderer, an inmate, or a dog handler, but as a son. A boy who for eight years had a mother who probably loved him, who cared for him, took care of his skinned knees and washed the dirt from his face. The records he'd seen hadn't indicated abuse from Trout's mother. She wasn't a drinker. She didn't do drugs. She was a mother, and this three-hundred-pound man had been her little boy—and she'd been murdered right before his eyes.

A guard came through the door and Trout clenched his jaw tight again.

"We done?" Trout grumbled.

"Trout. What happened to your dog?"

"Carver happened to him." He looked down at Storm. "Let's go." The dog fell into step beside him.

Thomas Carver was the man who'd murdered Trout's mother.

ELISABETH WAS MAKING cookies for Ross's dogs and cookies in anticipation of Emily's visit to discuss the kitchen renovations when her cell phone rang. She hadn't spoken to Ross this afternoon, and she hoped it was him. She tried to ignore the disappointment that washed over her when she didn't recognize the number.

"Hello?"

"Hi. Is this Elisabeth?" a woman asked.

"Yes."

"This is Cherry Macomb. I live on the outskirts of town, and I heard that you pick up dogs for grooming. What do you charge for that?"

Her pulse quickened. "How did you hear about me?" She quickly tried to assess if she could commit to picking up any more dogs, and considered what a reasonable fee for Trusty versus Los Angeles might be.

"My neighbor Sally buys her vegetables from Wynchels' and she said their dogs looked like brand-new dogs. Clean, fluffy, like they'd been to a salon, and Wren told her that you did it. Can I make the same arrangement?"

"Yes, absolutely." She remembered what Wren had said about the bows. "How do you feel about bows?"

"I love them!"

They made arrangements for Elisabeth to pick up Contessa, a two-year-old shih tzu, on her way to the Wynchels'. As soon as she hung up the phone, Emily arrived.

Emily hugged her like they'd been friends forever. She'd come straight from the office and was wearing a nice pair of slacks with a low-cut white blouse and a pair of strappy black sandals. She looked fashionable, comfortable, and pretty, with just a hint of eyeliner and blush.

"Your house smells like a bakery."

"That would be the banana-nut cookies I just made." They headed into the kitchen.

Emily inhaled and sighed. "Do you need a taste tester?"

"They're for you. I love to bake, and your visit was a great excuse."

"Thank you." She reached for a cookie.

"Wait. Those are puppy cookies. It's this tray." She pointed to the banana-nut cookies.

"I almost forgot you had a pet bakery." Emily raised her brows. "No wonder my brother's so into you."

Elisabeth wasn't sure how to respond.

Emily rolled her eyes. "Ross adores animals, and so do you. A match made in heaven."

My feeling exactly. "We do have a lot in common."

Emily surveyed the kitchen and her eyes landed on the beer cakes. "No wonder you said you needed more ovens. You must bake all the time. How can you stay so thin?"

"Oh, those aren't for me." Elisabeth laughed at the thought of eating three cakes by herself. "I was creating new recipes for cakes to sell at the county fair. Ross taste tested them for me. You can actually take one home with you if you want."

"Really? Thank you. We'd better talk about your renovations or you're going to think I came for free food."

They went over Elisabeth's ideas for the kitchen, and Emily took notes on the layout and sketched out ideas for moving counters and adding an island. Two hours later they had moved into the living room, taken their shoes off, and were sitting on the sofa with a sketch of the new layout and a plate of crumbs between them. And Elisabeth had a new friend.

Half an hour after Emily left, Elisabeth heard Ross's truck in the driveway. She went to greet him. His steps were heavy, his eyes serious and pinned on the ground.

She stepped off the porch and hooked her finger in his pocket. "What's wrong?" He shook his head, and her heart sank. "Ross? Did something happen to Storm?"

"No, he's fine, sorry. Just thinking about Trout." He raked his eyes down her body and smiled. "You look beautiful." He leaned down and kissed her. "See? And your kisses wipe my worries away without a trace."

"Fibber. I see that wrinkle on your forehead. What's wrong with Trout?" She took his hand and they sat down on the porch step.

"I just can't figure out how or why a guy who had a free ride to college and was a high school valedictorian would throw his life away." He squeezed Elisabeth's hand. "How does that happen? And more importantly, as a parent, how can you stop it from happening?"

"Didn't you tell me that he killed the man who killed his mother?" She remembered the story Ross had told her, and she knew how much it had bothered him then, but she wondered why his worry had escalated.

"Yes, but I just don't get it. He'd not only made it through ten years in the system, he beat it." He shook his head. "Why on earth after ten years, and all that hard work, would he throw it all away?"

Ross shrugged and rose to his feet. "I don't mean to be a downer. I've been thinking a lot about life and family lately, and when I was at the prison today, I saw him in a whole different light. I've seen him as an inmate all this time, but today I saw him as his mother's son. Surely he wasn't a monster at eight years old. He was a kid, Lis. A little boy who watched his mother die. God only knows what me or any of my brothers would have done if someone killed our mother. It could be any one of us in that jail."

"I wondered if that was what you were worried about. Rossie, you're not a killer." She watched him pace. "You love your mom, but I think something has to go really wrong in someone's brain to actually murder another person. I saw you when you had to put Gracie down. Your eyes were damp, and even if you don't want to admit it, you were upset for a long time afterward. Your body was tense, and you could barely look at me." She touched his arm to stop his pacing. "And if you're worried about when you have children, I highly doubt you could raise a child who would kill another person."

His eyes grew even more serious. "I know that. That's not really what I meant. None of us—not me or any of my brothers—could actually kill a man, but the question running around my mind is this. Does the fact that he avenged his mother's death make him a cold-blooded killer from birth, or did something snap when it happened?"

"I don't know enough about that stuff to answer, but it makes me want to call my mom."

He pulled her into a hug. "Sorry to unload on you. Go ahead and call your mom." He kissed her again. "Did everything go okay with Em?"

"Yeah. I love her. She's like the best friend I've always wanted."

"Really? Well, that gets me a little jealous."

Elisabeth looked into his seductive gaze and felt her heart opening even more to the man who wasn't afraid to show her he was human. He had fears and worries just like she did, and he wasn't embarrassed by them, which made her fall even harder than she realized she could.

Chapter Fifteen

WEDNESDAY EVENING, ELISABETH put on a pair of dangling silver earrings and slipped her feet into a pair of sandals. She looked way too sexy in a royal blue halter-top maxi dress that hugged every inch of her incredible body.

"You look like you stepped out of *People* magazine, and you should have Brad Pitt on your arm." They'd spent the night at Ross's house last night, and he was getting used to waking up with his sexy girlfriend wrapped around him and a dog at his feet. They'd made love that morning, and when Ross was helping her with the animals, they'd made out in the barn like teenagers. She'd left a note next to his keys when she left that morning. *I'll miss you today. Can't wait to be in your arms again.* Even when she wasn't with him, she was present. And every time he was with Elisabeth, he noticed things he hadn't before, like the way she crinkled her nose a little when she was reading, and at night, just before she fell asleep, she twisted the ends of her hair between her finger and thumb, the same way he'd seen her do when she was nervous, only at night she did it with a sleepy smile on her lips.

He folded her into his arms and kissed her neck. "Every guy in the restaurant will have their eyes on you."

"Mm. Jealous?" She arched her neck back, giving him full access to her delicate, tasty skin, which he took full advantage of, trailing kisses up her neck, then sucking hard enough to make Elisabeth gasp a breath.

They were in her bedroom standing by the dresser, and Ross wanted to rip that dress off, lift her onto the dresser, and make love to her until she could barely breathe. But they were supposed to meet Rex and Jade for dinner in thirty minutes.

"Maybe a little jealous," he admitted.

He gathered the skirt of her dress in his fist, then slid his hand beneath, along the back of her thigh, and took a handful of bare ass. He loved when she wore thongs. He was hard just thinking about ripping it off.

"Rossie," she whispered. "The time..."

The seconds were ticking away, but he couldn't stop, not now that he'd touched her. He wanted her too badly.

She spread her legs and he rubbed her through the thin material.

"You're...unfair." She clutched his shirt in her fists and snagged a few chest hairs along with it. "We can't. I'll have to shower again if you come in me."

She panted out a few breaths, and he slid a finger

beneath the damp material and stroked her slick skin.

"Oh God, yes," she relented.

"I'll just make you come," he whispered as he slid his fingers inside her and furtively stroked her until she was so wet he had to have her.

"Ross," she whispered, and spread her legs further. "Oh God. You. I want you."

She tore at the button on his jeans and he had them off in seconds. He pulled her dress over her head and tore her thong from her body—literally shredding the seam. They fell to the bed and he drove into her hard and deep. Their lips met in a passionate, hungry kiss as deep and urgent as his thrusts.

"Jesus, Lis. You're so hot. So wet."

She moaned at his words.

"Come for me, baby."

She wrapped her legs around his waist and lifted her hips. He grabbed her ass and helped her efforts, angling her back so he could push in deeper. Her inner muscles clenched around him as she cried out, a loud, indiscernible sound that shot fire through his body. He started to pull out so he didn't come inside her and she clutched his hips.

"Don't."

"Lis."

"Don't pull out." She pressed on his hips, squeezing her legs tighter around his waist.

Two deep thrusts took him over the edge, and his muscles corded tight as he pumped her full of his love. They were both breathing hard as they rolled onto their sides.

"Lis, you said not to come inside you."

She smiled, eyes still closed. "I couldn't help it. I wanted you in me."

Still in a foggy haze of lust, they forced themselves to get up and showered together. Even if he hadn't been able to see Elisabeth's gorgeous body beneath the spray of the shower, her nipples hard and the sensual look in her eyes, he would still have had a hard time keeping his eyes off of her. There was an energy between them that heated the air and drew him to her like metal to magnet.

"You're like a drug. How am I supposed to shower with you and not want to make love to you again?"

Elisabeth washed up as quickly as she could and smiled at the sight of his formidable erection, eagerly pointing upward again.

"Good, then I can count on a little loving later on." She brushed her fingers along his balls as she stepped out of the shower.

"I'll just stand under the *cold* water for a minute." Holy Christ. Where had she been all his life?

VOODOO WAS A popular restaurant located at the north end of Trusty. The interior was decorated with a plethora of odd paraphernalia ranging from old-fashioned bicycles to trombones that hung on the walls like pictures. The hardwood floor was shiny and dark, as were the tables and booths. Music filtered in from the bar located down a wide hallway in the back of the restaurant. They waited in the lobby for Rex and Jade. At least they hadn't been late. Elisabeth had visions of running in with flushed cheeks and Rex and Jade shaking their heads at them. Her insides were still reeling from the intensity of the orgasm she'd had. She was sure his cousin would know exactly what they'd done.

Ross's hand clutched her waist, and she felt a heavy hand land on her shoulder. She and Ross both turned.

"Hey, cuz." Rex stood eye to eye with Ross, with shoulders as wide as a linebacker, dark eyes that had to be a Braden trait, and thick black hair that hung over the top of his collar. He took his Stetson off and set his boots hip width apart. His thighs strained against a pair of faded Levi's. "I'm sorry we're late. We...uh..." He glanced at Jade, whose cheeks pinked up.

"Had trouble getting out of the house." Jade raised her brows at Elisabeth and flashed a knowing smile.

Elisabeth breathed a sigh of relief, feeling a little less nervous and wondering if there was an aphrodisiac in the Colorado air.

Rex embraced Ross, then opened his arms to Elisabeth. "And you must be Elisabeth. Nice to meet you." He squeezed her tight against his rock-hard chest, then settled a hand on Jade's back.

"This is my fiancée, Jade."

Jade's long hair was as dark as Rex's. She wore skinny jeans tucked into cowgirl boots and a black form-fitting tank top. She was built like Scarlett Johansson, but she was ten times prettier with almond-shaped eyes and higher cheekbones. She and

Rex were the epitome of a beautiful Western couple. Hot cowboy, gorgeous cowgirl, and the way Rex looked at her was the same heated way Ross looked at Elisabeth. The whole scene was so different from LA that she wondered how she'd stayed there for so long. She'd seen more love pass between Ross and his family in just a few weeks than she ever had anywhere else.

Jade hugged Elisabeth. "It's nice to meet you. Emily has told me a lot about you."

"Emily was over last night. She's designing my kitchen renovations."

"She's weaseling her way into Elisabeth's life and eating all her baked goods," Ross teased.

"Sounds like Em," Jade said.

The waitress seated them in a booth. They looked over the menu and ordered a round of drinks.

"Emily said you moved from Los Angeles. Are you still in culture shock?" Jade asked.

"It's definitely different, but I spent time here in the summers when I was younger, so I knew what I was getting into."

Ross pulled her against him. "Well, mostly, anyway."

Elisabeth's insides warmed. She had hoped and dreamed of meeting a man like Ross, but being with him was so much better than those dreams ever were.

"You can't elude fate." Jade gazed up at Rex with eyes full of adoration. "Look at us. Our families feuded for forty years before our love conquered it." She looked at Ross and Elisabeth. "True love can't be stopped, and when it touches you, you're flooded with so much emotion that you don't know whether you're sinking or swimming, or floating. I know this sounds corny, but I swear it's true. I was in love with Rex for fifteen years before we finally got together, and still, to this very day, when I look at him he takes my breath away."

Rex brought a big, strong hand to her cheek and gazed into her eyes. "I'll always breathe for you." He pressed a loving kiss to her lips and Elisabeth felt her insides melt.

She glanced at Ross and saw every bit as much love as she felt in her heart.

Their dinner came, and the conversation shifted to the Braden ranch and Rex's brother Treat's baby, Adriana, who was named for their mother. Rex's mother, Adriana, had passed away when her children were young, and as Rex spoke of her, it was clear his love for her still flourished.

"I want to be next," Jade said.

"Next?" Ross asked.

"A baby. I want to be the next one to have a baby. I'm so ready, and Rexy isn't getting any younger."

"Hey. We've got to get married first." Rex's smile told Elisabeth that a baby was not a bone of contention between them. He shifted his eyes to Ross. "You're coming to Josh and Riley's wedding, aren't you?"

"I wouldn't miss it for the world." Ross turned his attention to Elisabeth. "Josh is Rex's younger brother. He's a fashion designer in New York, and he's marrying Riley Banks, his business partner and childhood crush. The wedding is in New York in the spring. We'll get someone to watch the boys and your animals and make a vacation of it."

Elisabeth felt her eyes widen and tried to quell her excitement. Spring was months away. Ross was planning a future with her. She realized that she hadn't even considered *if* they stayed together. She assumed they would. With the few other men she'd dated, she was constantly battling the things she didn't feel comfortable with about them. With Ross, that hadn't happened even once.

"Elisabeth, you'll love Riley," Jade said. "She's my best friend in the world, and you'll meet all the girls. I can't wait!"

"Do you two have a date for your wedding yet?" Ross arched a brow at Rex.

Rex tightened his grip on Jade. "We're deciding on the location first. I wanted to plan the whole thing and surprise Jade, but so far she's not going for it."

Jade rolled her eyes. "He's the most romantic man on earth, isn't he?"

"I think you should let him," Elisabeth said. "He knows you, and he loves you. Who better to plan your big day?"

Jade's gaze softened. "I hadn't thought of it in those terms. Maybe so. Hm."

"Not to change the subject or anything, although I am..." Elisabeth was itching to ask about the business opportunity Jade wanted to talk about. "Ross said you wanted to talk about my pet-pampering business."

"Yes. Tell me about what you do. I do horse massage, and a lot of my clients have cats and dogs and have asked about my doing massages for them. I can, and I have, but horses are really my specialty—"

"And cowboys," Rex added with a mischievous glint in his eyes.

"Only one cowboy." Jade touched his cheek. "Anyway, I thought maybe we could discuss referrals and maybe share client lists, that sort of thing."

"Gosh, I'd love that *if* I had a client list. Unfortunately, I'm so new to the town that I don't think many people here trust me yet, and they don't seem that interested in grooming their pets. Although I did get a call from someone named Cherry about grooming her shih tzu."

"Cherry Macomb. She's a client of Ross's, but I know of her." Jade laughed. "She acts like she's some kind of movie star and dresses like she's Peg Bundy, but she's really good to her animals."

"Well, I know how to handle film stars, so that's good."

"Why don't we do this," Jade offered. "How about if you come with me to see a few of my clients and talk with them? You can give them your information, and maybe that will get things started for you."

"Really? You haven't seen me work yet. Do you want to watch me do a pet massage or grooming first?" Elisabeth's heart was beating so fast she could barely hear past it.

"I heard about what you did for Gracie, and word has spread as far as Allure about you picking up the

Wynchels' dogs and grooming them. If Ross trusts you, which he obviously does, then I trust you." Jade sipped her drink. "And I'd imagine that all that talk will eventually lead to more business for you."

"Thank you, Jade. You can't imagine how much this means to me." *Is this really happening?*

Ross touched his forehead to hers. "And as far as trust goes, give it time. No one will be able to resist you."

Chapter Sixteen

ROSS AND ELISABETH cuddled on a lounge chair beneath a blanket and watched the sun rise Saturday morning while Storm, Ranger, and Sarge played in the yard. Knight sat beside them, his black fur rising and falling with each sleepy breath. He had become as attached to Elisabeth as Ross had, and since Elisabeth was lying in Ross's arms with one hand stretched out as she stroked Knight's back, he knew she'd become just as attached to Knight. Storm had awoken at five o'clock, and rather than try to go back to sleep, they'd taken all the dogs out and decided to greet the rising sun from the back deck of Ross's house.

"Why do you think Storm was up so early?" Elisabeth asked.

"Who knows. But Trout did say he had trouble sleeping. I'm hoping it's just a fluke. Trout thought he was lonely." He slipped his hand under the back of her camisole. Her skin was warm, despite the chilly morning air. She was wearing a pair of his flannel pajama pants folded down at the waist to make them smaller, and they still nearly fell off her hips.

"Did you suggest moving the crate closer?" Her eyes narrowed.

Ross kissed her. "I did, and I brought him a toy that makes a soothing sound for Storm to sleep with."

"That should help. I think there's comfort in numbers, and dogs get lonely just like we do."

"I have a feeling you'll be one of those mothers who jumps at every cry your babies make."

He felt her smile against his chest.

"Probably, but don't even try to pretend that you'd be any different. You're a big softie. I see how you are with the boys. Don't think for a second that I don't know you're giving them the cookies I give you at the rate of about three a day."

"You noticed that, huh?"

"I notice everything, like the way you take extra time to pet them before bed, until each one finally lays his head down and their eyes get sleepy, and the way you smile when they do something cute like push their noses against each other. You can pretend to be caught up in the fundamentals of taking care of animals, but you have a bigger heart than you let on. The same way you do with me."

"I'll admit I'm caught up in you." There was no denying the way he felt about her. "I'll set up your awning before I go into work this morning. Are you sure you'll be able to pick up all seven dogs for grooming today? All six of Wren's dogs and Cherry's?

Do you want me to ask Luke if Daisy's free, or Callie or Emily?"

She kissed his bare chest. "Oh no, don't bother them. I can do it. I've got it all figured out. I'll put the Wynchels' dogs in the hatchback with the backseat down, and I'll put Contessa's crate up front with me. You're so thoughtful, and you take such good care of me. I wish I could do something to take care of you."

"Babe, you take care of me by just being with me. I've never been happier than when we're together. And you love my boys, and you put up with my sister. It's all good."

She laughed. "I love Emily. She calls me almost every day to talk about the renovations and we end up talking about everything. It's nice to finally have a friend here."

"You have me."

"Yes, and you're the best boyfriend ever. But there's a big difference between a boyfriend and a close girlfriend." She pointed out over the mountains. "Here comes the sun."

"I haven't watched the sunrise in forever, and I may not have ever done it again if we hadn't met."

"Oh, come on. You'd have done it eventually." She leaned up and grinned down at him. "It just wouldn't have been as wonderful without me."

"Damn right about that. Come here." He pulled her into a delicious kiss.

He couldn't think of a better way to start the morning, or a better way to end the day, since they'd been spending every night together.

PICKING UP THE dogs turned out to be more time-consuming than Elisabeth had counted on. At Wynchels', one of the dogs took off after a rabbit, and it had taken her nearly thirty minutes to wrangle him back to the car. And true to Jade's description, Cherry Macomb was a Peg Bundy lookalike from her bouffant hairdo and sky-high heels to her leggings, wide belt, and tight shirt.

"Okay, Tessie, Tessie. Mama will see you soon." Cherry kissed Contessa on the nose and handed her to Elisabeth. "Her full name is Miss Contessa Macomb, but we call her Tessie." Contessa weighed only about fifteen pounds. She had fluffy white fur and a few black spots on her back. She had the sweetest eyes and demeanor. Elisabeth fell instantly in love with the little cuddle muffin.

"I'll take good care of her." She set Tessie in her fluffy red doggy bed in the carrier, and the pup snuggled up to the two stuffed animals Cherry had also put in the crate.

"She hates to be without her babies," Cherry said.

"I love that you pamper her. All of my clients in Los Angeles treated their dogs like you treat Tessie. Don't worry. She's in good hands." Elisabeth went around to the driver's side, and as she climbed into the car, Cherry came to the window.

"Elisabeth, thank you. I'm a little like a three-headed owl around here with the way I treat Tessie."

That might have more to do with your Peg Bundy getup. "Well, so am I, so we make a great pair."

By four o'clock, Elisabeth had groomed and returned three of the Wynchels' dogs, and Tessie. Cherry loved the pink bows she'd put on Tessie's collar, and she said she would mention Elisabeth's service to her friends. There was no greater thank-you than a referral, and Elisabeth carried that happy thought with her as she finished grooming the sixth of the Wynchels' dogs beneath the awning Ross had set up for her. She wondered if he'd found the thank-you note she'd slipped into his truck earlier that morning. She was daydreaming about him when an unfamiliar car drove down her driveway.

Elisabeth recognized the librarian, Callie, as she stepped from the car with the cutest bloodhound on a red leash.

"Hi." Callie waved. "Emily said you were grooming dogs today, and I thought I'd bring Sweets by. I hope I'm not too late. I had to finish my afternoon at the library." She tucked her brown hair behind her ear as she crossed the lawn.

Elisabeth knelt to pet Sweets. "She's beautiful, and you're definitely not too late. You're Ross's brother's girlfriend, right? I'm Elisabeth."

"Yes, Wes's girlfriend. I've heard so much about you, and I kind of put two and two together after Emily told me what you looked like. I helped you at the library, remember?" Callie had on a pair of jeans shorts and a blousy peasant top.

"Yes! You gave me *Wallbanger* to read. Oh my goodness, that's the funniest book. I loved it. Thank you." She took Sweets's leash and they went to her grooming station. "I assume Wes doesn't want her to have bows?"

"You do bows? I want her to have them. Do you have pink?"

Elisabeth liked her already. "I have more shades of pink than blades of grass." She set to work grooming Sweets. "I've never groomed a dog who didn't try to smell everything."

"She has no sense of smell. When Wes found her on a mountain trail, she was really sick. Ross helped save her, actually. She had distemper, and she was all skin and bones." Callie reached out and stroked Sweets's back. "Poor girl. She lost her sense of smell from the distemper, but at least she got through it."

"Well, a sense of smell isn't all it's cut out to be. Sometimes when I'm taking care of the pigs, I wish I didn't have one." She smiled and offered Callie a drink of iced tea.

"Thanks, I'm okay. So how do you like Trusty?"

Callie was easy to talk to, and honesty came easily for Elisabeth. "I've always loved Trusty, since I was a little girl. So, the lifestyle is everything I always knew it would be and hoped for. And I guess it'll just take a little time for everything else to fall into place."

"I'm not from here, either. I'm from Denver, so I know what it feels like to be the new girl in town."

"I didn't know that. I thought both you and Daisy grew up here."

"Daisy did, but I didn't. When I first moved here, I had no idea that people had even noticed me, much less talked about me, but I found out when Wes and I started dating. From what I understand, Wes's settling down kind of shocked the people here. Kind of like with Ross."

"Like Ross?" She had purposely not asked Ross much about his past. He was thirty-five, so he obviously had a past, but it didn't have to affect their relationship. Although now she was curious.

"Well, I don't think Ross was like Wes. Wes was..." Callie furrowed her brow. "He had a busy social life outside of Trusty. I don't think Ross dated a lot, but I know he never dated girls from town either. The Bradens have this thing about dating women where they live or something. I don't know for sure, but I think they don't like to be part of the town gossip."

"Ross mentioned that he didn't date women in Trusty, but I didn't know that about Wes."

"That's why Emily thinks your relationship with Ross is serious." Callie fidgeted with the edges of her shorts, obviously wanting to know more but not wanting to ask.

Sweets licked Elisabeth's leg. She kissed Sweets's head, then went back to grooming her.

"Our relationship is still new, but to be honest, I can't imagine being with anyone else." She held her breath, a little unsure if she should have divulged that much of herself to Callie.

Callie smiled and met her gaze. "That's how it was with me and Wes. I swear the first time I saw him he made my heart stop. He still does."

That was the difference between a boyfriend and having a close woman friend.

"So you totally get it. I'm not crazy to feel that way?"

Callie leaned closer. "Crazy is not following what you feel in your heart. I'm a sucker for happily-ever-afters, and my guilty pleasure is reading romance novels. Ravenously. I thought happily-ever-afters were just for heroines in romance novels, but then..." She rolled her eyes up toward the sky and sighed. "Then Wes came into my life, and it was like we were born for each other. He did all these amazing things, and he really opened my eyes to a whole part of life I'd have missed if we never met. He even picked me up on a white horse for a dance that he put on just for me and my girlfriends."

"No way." Elisabeth could only imagine how romantic that must have been.

"Yup. Even surprised us with dresses and brought my friends' husbands up to his ranch for the dance. It was incredible, and every night since then...it's like just being with him is romantic." She held her hands out when she said *incredible* like the memory was too big for the word.

"Wow, Callie. You're both so lucky. I'm just the opposite. I've *always* believed in love and marriage and that we all have someone we're fated to be with." She finished grooming Sweets and put four little pink bows on her collar. "My whole life, all I wanted was to come back here. I was drawn to this little town as if it were my destiny, or at least as if it were my own hometown, when I'd only spent a few weeks over the years here with my aunt. And now..." She bit her lower lip and drew in a deep breath.

"Now?" Callie's eyes widened.

"Now I wonder if Ross is the reason I've always been drawn here." Elisabeth knew it sounded stupid. *Damn it.* She shouldn't have said it out loud. She covered her face with her hands. "Oh, Callie. I'm so embarrassed. I've known you for all of an hour and I'm gushing like a schoolgirl over your boyfriend's brother. Definitely not the way to appear normal."

Callie pulled Elisabeth's hands down and smiled. "Lucky for you, I think normal is totally boring. And in case you don't know it, Emily is a total romantic, so there's no way she thinks you're crazy, either."

They talked for a while longer, and after Callie left, Elisabeth piled the Wynchels' three dogs into her car. If she kept this up, she'd definitely have to get a larger car, not to mention a few more hours in her day. Toting animals around was time-consuming.

Ross pulled into the driveway behind her car and leaned out of his truck window.

"Leaving?"

"I have to return the Wynchels' dogs. Want to come along?" She went to the window of his truck, and he leaned down and met her halfway for a kiss.

"Where you go, I go." He stepped from the truck and hugged her close. "I found your thank-you note. It made my whole day. How was your day? Did anyone else show up?"

"Callie did, which was a surprise."

They both turned at the sound of wheels on gravel. The red-haired woman who was in Ross's office the day Elisabeth brought Kennedy in came rushing toward them. Her clothes were covered in mud, and she had streaks of dirt on her cheeks and forehead.

"Tracie, what happened?" Ross asked.

"Am I too late? Are you still grooming dogs?" she asked Elisabeth.

"I was just going to take the dogs back to the Wynchels', but I can groom your puppy when I get back."

"I can take the dogs back to Wren. Go ahead and help Tracie," Ross offered.

"I'm so sorry. Justin Bieber got into the bushes by the creek, and he's all muddy and filled with burrs. He's a mess. I tried to give him a bath, as you can see." She pointed to her clothing. "But I couldn't get the burrs out."

Tracie went back to her car to get Justin Bieber, and Elisabeth reached for Ross's hand.

"Are you sure you don't mind?" She hated asking him to do more than he already had, especially after he'd worked all day.

"Of course not."

She touched her forehead to his chest. "Thank you. I owe you."

His mouth quirked up. "That's an even better reason for me to do it."

She swatted his stomach. "Can you please tell Wren that I can't pick up the dogs next weekend because I'll be at the fair? I don't think she'll care one way or the other, but we should let her know."

Ross lifted her chin with his index finger. "Hey, I'm proud of you. You're working so hard, and you aren't getting anything in return."

"Sure I am. I already have one paying client, and I got my fill of pups for the day—until I get to see the boys, of course."

Elisabeth went to work bathing and grooming Justin Bieber. He was a silky terrier, and it took a while to get all of the burrs out of his long locks, but by the time Elisabeth gave him his final brushing, his fur was once again silky and tangle free.

"Wow. He's never looked so handsome," Tracie said. "Maddy will be thrilled."

"Is Maddy your daughter? I saw her at the clinic when I brought my piglet in to see Ross." Elisabeth smiled at the memory of the first time she saw Ross and how everything about him, from his looks, to his voice, to his in-control demeanor, had reeled her in.

"Yeah. She's eight. She's so in love with him. She was too upset to come with me today. She was afraid you'd have to shave him."

"Oh, no. I try not to do that to dogs. They get embarrassed."

Tracie smiled at that and drew her brows together. "So, I guess it's true about you and Ross."

"True?"

"That you two are dating."

"Oh. Yes." *We really are the town gossip.*

"I'm happy for you both. He's such a nice man. I've known him forever. He was a few years ahead of me in school, but if you ask me, he's the best of the Braden men. Not that there's a bad one in the bunch, but he's always such a gentleman." Tracie reached into her purse and pulled her wallet out. "How much do I owe you?"

Elisabeth was still processing Tracie's approval of their dating. "Nothing, it was on the house."

"Oh, no. I can't accept that. You just spent an hour doing something I never could have done." Tracie opened her wallet.

"No, really, Tracie. You came over because you probably saw a flyer, and the flyer announced free grooming on Saturdays, so we're good. I appreciate the chance to meet Justin Bieber, who is such a sweet puppy." She picked him up and snuggled him against her chest.

"Flyer?" She scrunched her nose. "I came over because Janice Treelong said you groom dogs on Saturdays."

"I don't know who that is, but please thank her for me. I do groom, but it's free right now, so we're even." She handed Justin Bieber to Tracie as Ross pulled into the driveway.

"I'll get out of your hair, but I can't thank you enough. Maddy is going to be over the moon!"

"I'll be at the county fair next weekend with puppy treats and probably doing free pawdicures. Feel free to stop by and pick up a treat for Justin Bieber."

"We will. Thank you, Elisabeth."

Ross stepped from his truck and passed Tracie on her way to her car. "He looks like a brand-new dog."

"I know. Elisabeth is amazing," Tracie gushed.

Ross watched her drive away and then swept Elisabeth into his arms. "See? Even Tracie thinks you're amazing. Wren wasn't happy that you weren't going to be available to groom the dogs next weekend. I think she's gotten used to her dogs looking good. I told her that you'd be at the fair and she was welcome to stop by with the dogs."

"She can't. Their store is always open, but I'll get them the following weekend. If I start to get more customers, I'm going to have to rethink the whole pick-up/drop-off thing. It's really time-consuming."

"Maybe you can consider actually charging and making house calls." He pulled a burr from her hair and looked it over. "Even Justin Bieber is leaving his mark on my woman."

She laughed. "I used to make house calls. I could do that again. Or maybe a mobile grooming unit. I could spend a day at the dog park, or the regular park sometimes. But I'd have to charge, of course. I can't work for free forever." Maybe she *could* make a go of this.

"How will you manage both the pie business and the pet business? Wren said your pies sold the first day, and she wants to triple her order for this week."

"Really?" Elisabeth grabbed his hands. "I have no idea how I'll handle it all, but it's a great problem to have. I'll figure it out. Maybe I'll need a regular schedule, because I bake and deliver pies in the mornings and early afternoons. I'll have to come up with something at some point. I can't believe this is really happening!"

"*This* is really happening." He lowered his lips to hers and she melted against him.

"Mm. I waited all day for that, and it was so worth it," Elisabeth said, then went back for another.

Chapter Seventeen

TUESDAY AFTERNOON ROSS was running late. He'd had two emergency patients earlier in the day, making him late for the rest of the afternoon. As he worked through each patient, his mind traveled back to Elisabeth. She was visiting clients with Jade today and he hoped it would go well. She was building the pet business on the fly while trying to increase her pie business. It all seemed so haphazard to him, as if she'd opened her arms and was gathering in anything she could get, and the getting was slow. At the same time, she was determined and confident that she could make it work. If she took on clients in Allure, it would add more travel time, and her days would be even more hectic. She was already up with the sun to care for the animals, fit in her yoga, and do the baking— and then she had deliveries to take care of. When he thought how much time was spent picking up and dropping off dogs on Saturday, it seemed like a waste.

There had to be a way to lessen her load there, at least. It wasn't like his practice, where he set up shop in a town where everyone knew and trusted him. He'd had a full client roster a week after opening his clinic doors. That's what he wanted for her. To be accepted and for people to take stock in, and see the value of, her services and her time.

He was pondering Elisabeth's situation and examining his last patient, a five-year-old cat, before leaving for Denton. When he finished, he went to his office to think.

His office window had a serene view of the mountains. Diplomas hung proudly on the opposite wall, and behind his desk was a row of bookshelves with veterinary medicine and animal books he'd read and collected throughout the years. There was a single framed picture on his desk of his family. It had been taken a few years earlier over the holidays. He and Pierce had their arms over each other's shoulders. Emily was pressed against his other side, one hand around his back, the other around Wes, and beside Wes, Luke and Jake had each other in choke holds. Ross smiled at the memory.

He sat down, and something crinkled beneath his butt. He found an envelope with his first name written on the front in Elisabeth's handwriting. He loved that she left him notes in his truck, on the counters, taped to the bathroom mirror. He wondered when she'd had time to bring this one by. He opened the envelope and read the note. *Picnic under the stars tonight with the boys? XO, Lis.*

He texted Elisabeth. *Picnic sounds perfect. Running late today. I'll come over after I get back from Denton. How are things with Jade?* He hit send, then sent another quick message. *Xox.*

He felt *xox* all the time for Elisabeth, but remembering to type it into a phone was another thing altogether.

He looked at the stack of client files on his desk and another stack of pet food and supply distributors, and slowly, an idea formed. Ross called Walt at the prison and told him he'd be a little late for the training session. He typed a quick memo to the distributors and emailed it to Kelsey, then grabbed his keys and headed for the lobby.

"How's your grandfather holding up?" He stood by the reception desk while Kelsey checked off their inventory on the computer.

"He misses Gracie, but at least he's not barring himself off from the world like he did after Grandma died. He's even talking about getting another dog at some point."

"Good. That's a good sign. Kelsey, I need you to do me a favor. I typed a memo that I'd like distributed to our suppliers today."

Kelsey continued working on the inventory, her eyes trained on the computer. "Okay. Can I do it after I'm done with this? Probably late today or tomorrow morning?"

"I'd rather it went out sooner than later. It's time sensitive."

She eyed him as she saved her work and opened

the email. Ross wasn't usually so demanding, and he wasn't surprised by the curious way she eyed him before scanning the memo. "You're inviting them all to the fair and telling them about Elisabeth's grooming services? They're suppliers. What makes you think they'll come?"

"They're pet owners. They love their pets. What makes you think they won't?" He smiled and walked out the door. It was a start.

On the way to Denton he stopped at Tate McGregor's shop to make sure things were taken care of with Elisabeth's aunt's van.

He was walking into the prison an hour later when a text from Elisabeth came through. *Going great with Jade. Miss you. Love up Storm for me. Xox.*

Trout seemed distracted during the training session. His muscles were tense, and his eyes remained hard, unwilling to meet Ross's gaze. Luckily, Storm was as relaxed as could be, following every command and watching Trout as attentively as Ross expected with the service dogs.

After training, they sat on the bench for a few minutes while Storm was set free to play.

"He's doing great, Trout. You've really done an excellent job with him."

"Mm-hm." Trout circled a fisted hand with his palm. "Toy helped."

"Well, whatever it takes, right?"

Trout turned cold, hard eyes toward Ross. Ross imagined that was probably about the look the man he'd killed had seen just before Trout did him in. Every

246

hair on his body stood on end.

"I've got a problem, Doc."

"Let me hear it." At least he wasn't throttling Ross's throat.

"I can train him, but I can't keep him safe once he's outta here." Trout shifted his eyes back to Storm, who was playing with a ball in the center of the room. "Who's gonna keep him safe?"

"That'll be his new owner's job." Seeing Trout so concerned over Storm was a good feeling, even if his worry translated into a disturbing look.

Trout shook his head and locked his eyes on his hands. "Safety is an illusion."

Ross sensed that they were no longer talking about Storm. "I guess to some degree you're right."

"That's why there's bars, doc." He tilted his face, setting a cold stare on Ross again. "Put danger behind bars, the good ones have a better chance."

Ross leaned forward, elbows on knees, bringing him to the same angle as Trout. Even though Trout hadn't given Ross any reason to fear his strength, Ross had a feeling this was a dangerous dance they were doing, and he let Trout lead. "I suppose."

"You got family?" Trout asked.

It was the jagged line Ross knew better than to cross, and yet he saw it as a way to gain some answers. "Sure."

"I had family once."

"Yes. I know about your mother, and I'm sorry." Ross's muscles clenched just thinking about what the thought of his mother must do to Trout.

"Brother, too."

That brought Ross's eyes to Trout's. "I think I read about him. He was given up for a private adoption at birth, right?"

Trout nodded. "And not all there in the head."

"You knew him, then?" Ross hadn't read anything about a relationship between the two boys in any of the records.

"My mother made sure of it, but no one else knew. She'd take me to the park with my dog near where my brother lived. 'Bout an hour from where we lived." Trout paused and looked away, his eyes going soft when they landed on Storm.

Ross dared not talk. He didn't want to break the spell of whatever had Trout suddenly opening up.

"We were friends. He knew me as Mike. My mother was a smart lady. She knew if he knew my name, she'd be caught by whoever monitors those private adoptions. This way I was just another kid at the playground." He brought his eyes back to Ross. "Sometimes, you gotta do what you think is right, not what everyone else thinks you should do. That's what my mama did. Blood is blood. Never forget that, Doc. Stronger than concrete."

Ross nodded, barely breathing for where this conversation was heading. "He knew your mother, then?"

Trout shook his head. "No. It wasn't like that. He had an image of her in his head, of how great she was to have given him up for a better life." He nodded and flashed those dimples again. "He was right. She was great."

"Trout, where's your brother now?"

He shrugged. "Haven't seen him since the day before...it all went down." Trout turned his head and looked up at Ross. "I know you're wantin' to know what's what. I see it in your eyes. I ain't dumb, Doc, just because I'm in here, or because I choose not to talk to these guys."

"Valedictorians rarely are." Ross sat up straight. He no longer felt threatened by Trout, and he wasn't sure why, but he was pretty sure it had something to do with the fact that Trout was finally opening up and talking to him like anyone else might, making it easier for Ross to see him as something more than just a convicted killer.

Trout let out a breath, half laugh, half grunt, and sat up, too. "His adoptive mother told him his mother was killed. Stupid bitch. He didn't need to know that. He lived in a fantasyland half the time. He could have continued on just fine if..."

He met Ross's gaze. "If I didn't do it, my brother would have, and he wouldn't have survived in here. Spent ten years tryin' to convince him not to, but as I said. He wasn't right. He was obsessed with taking revenge for her death. Once his adoptive mother told him our mother had died, a fucking few clicks later on the Internet told him everything else he wanted to know. He was like a dog with a bone, rattling on and on about how he figured out Carver had killed her and all kinds of shit. By then I had so much anger in me, so much hatred, I wasn't safe either. When I realized I could actually go through with it and kill a man so my brother didn't, I knew something was wrong with me."

Holy hell. He'd killed the man to save his brother from a life in prison. "Trout, aren't you concerned that your brother might hurt someone else?"

He shook his head. "He ain't like that. He's moved on to healthier obsessions. This was a blip on his damaged mind. A ten-year blip that's been washed away. Got a friend on the outside who checks on him, but I told him not to tell me where he is. I don't want him getting wind of what I done. He knows that Carver's dead, and my brother's at peace now. Let it stay that way."

"But you had a promising future, and you killed a man and gave up that future in order to keep your brother from doing the same? Why? Why go so far?"

"Why go so far? As I said, when I realized that I was *capable*, actually willing and able to go through with killing Carver—and make no doubt, I knew I was going to do it—I knew I needed to be behind bars. I wasn't safe out there. I had become Carver. For whatever fucked-up reason, I've got a good brain— and a broken one. You've got to be broken to do what I did. What I planned and carried out. I wasn't drunk, or high, or off my rocker in any other way. I made a choice to kill."

Ross could hardly believe what he was hearing— the confession or the plethora of information Trout was willingly sharing. "I can't imagine deciding to give everything up, but then again, I can't imagine knowing I was going to walk out the door and kill a man."

"That's because you're not fucked up. You got blessed with the good brain and not the broken one." Trout smiled a little; then his face grew serious again. "What'd I really give up? So I'll never cure cancer or build a robot. Kid dreams, Doc. I got a roof over my head, books to read. Know why I waited until I was eighteen to do it?"

Ross shook his head.

"To make sure I was tried as an adult and would have no chance of getting out. Doc, if you can kill a man, you ain't right. I just got lucky in the brains department, but something's gotta be off to do that. Who knows how many people I kept safe." With a shrug, Trout rose to his feet.

Ross followed. "Trout." He didn't know what to say. The man was as much a hero—for seeing the danger he presented to the world and for stepping in to do what his brother might have if he didn't—as he was a criminal.

"Sometimes you gotta listen to that beatin' lump of meat pumping blood in your chest, and you gotta do what you think's right, when everything you've ever been taught tells you otherwise. You gotta let go of what you love so you can move forward knowing that despite it all, you helped someone else live the life they were meant to live. Yeah, I killed a man. A man who killed my mother, my dog, and who probably would have killed my brother had his sorry, demented ass ever tried to get revenge. I'm not proud of it, but when I found the asshole, you know what he had?"

Ross arched a brow, still stunned by the depth of

Trout's confession.

"My mother's ring on his pinky, my dog's collar hanging on the wall like a trophy. Ten years, Doc. Ten years later, he's still got that shit." He turned away, and when he turned back, his eyes were stone cold again.

"Trout, why are you telling me all this?"

"Because, Doc. You're the only person who's seen through my big-ass silence. You didn't shut up or give me a wide berth like everyone else does. You trusted me with Storm, and you had no idea if I'd throttle him, or you, to death. You trusted me. I trust you with my secret." Trout patted his leg. "Storm. Come."

Storm came to his side and sat, his eyes trained on Trout. "Good boy."

Ross watched him walk away and then caught up to him. "Trout, I gotta know. Why'd you ask to be in the program?"

He shrugged. "Selfish, I guess. I'm only human. I need to give and receive love." Trout leaned in closer to Ross. "And no matter how long I'm in this shithole, I ain't gonna do what some of these guys do to fill that need." He rose to his full height again and gazed down at Storm. "Raisin' a dog's the closest thing I got to raisin' a boy. Storm loves me no matter what I've done in my past."

Ross didn't even know how to respond. Was Trout brilliant or an idiot? Ross couldn't make that call any better than Walt could have.

"Oh, Doc. One more thing. I got a rep to uphold."

Ross smiled at that. "You're a silent bastard who'll

rip someone's throat out if they look at you sideways. I've got your back."

Trout's eyes softened, as did the tension around his mouth and across his forehead, and just as quickly as it had appeared, all that softness fell away, replaced with a cold, deadpan stare. He rounded his shoulders and headed for the door, and Ross headed home to Elisabeth, feeling as though he'd learned something about life and love—and how even when he had all the facts, there was no black and white.

Chapter Eighteen

WEDNESDAY AFTERNOON PASSED in a flurry of baking, delivering, and planning. Elisabeth was flying high from both her romantic picnic with Ross the evening before and the great afternoon she'd had with Jade. Three of Jade's clients had already called to schedule grooming and massage appointments for their animals, and now all Elisabeth had to do was come up with a schedule to accommodate the baking *and* the pet pampering. One thing was clear, being a doggy chauffeur was proving to be a big time suck, no matter how much she didn't mind the driving, or how much she loved the time with the dogs.

Her phone rang, pulling her from the kitchen table where she was working on devising a schedule. Her heartbeat quickened when she saw Ross's name on the screen.

"Hi." Why did she always sound breathless when she spoke to him? After their picnic by the lake, they'd spent the night at his house again, and already they were in a routine of taking care of the animals together in the mornings, having breakfast together, and her favorite part of the day, falling asleep in his arms.

"Hey, babe. Just wanted to see how your day was going."

"I woke up with you. How could it be anything but great?"

His voice became seductively gravelly. "It's like you read my mind. I miss you."

"I miss you, too."

"I found your note in my bag. Jesus, Lis, how can a piece of paper make my heart race?"

She smiled, because that was exactly the reaction she'd been hoping for when she left the sexy little promise. *Crave you, miss you, can't wait to kiss every inch of you.*

"I don't know, but I'm glad. Emily called. She's coming by tonight to go over the kitchen designs." She was looking forward to seeing what Emily had come up with.

"Wes called, too. If you're going to be with Em, do you mind if I meet him and Luke for a drink after work?"

"Of course not. Have fun."

"Hey, babe?"

"Yeah?" A feeling settled in the silence as she waited for him to respond. She'd felt it for days, a bubble of oneness that enveloped them every time they were together. Something sacred and precious, born of their emotions and consuming a little more of her every day. She'd fallen for him, and she'd fallen hard.

"I'll see you tonight."

She let out a breath she hadn't realized she was holding. She thought he might say he loved her, and in the silence, she thought she might, too. After they ended the call, Elisabeth sat for a long while, soaking in those emotions and knowing that when the time was right, they'd both know. A knock on the door pulled her from her thoughts. On a sigh, she went to answer the door. A wiry woman with black frames on her pointy nose and an old tabby cat bundled in her arms stood on her porch.

"Hi." Elisabeth opened the door.

"Elisabeth?"

"Yes."

"I'm Alice Shalmer, and this is Flossie. I would have called, but, well, I'm old-school and I believe in visiting when you want to talk to someone." Alice wore a simple blue cotton dress, belted at her waist, with a pair of flats.

She smiled, and Elisabeth stepped to the side and invited her in.

"Jim Trowell is a friend of mine, and not that I think I'm going to lose Flossie anytime soon, but he told me about how you massaged Gracie, and my sweet Flossie could really use a massage. I was wondering if you could fit her in one day."

"Oh, Alice, of course. Come sit down, and I'll do it now." Maybe she should have been miffed at the interruption to her day, but Alice's stopping by was refreshing. *This* was what she'd remembered about Trusty. How many times had people stopped by to see her aunt out of the blue while she was playing in the yard, and her aunt would spend an hour visiting with friends. In the confusion of trying to fit in, she'd almost forgotten how here, relationships didn't rely on email and cell phones. While she was met with resistance for her first few weeks, she felt things changing, and Alice proved that. People were coming around, even if slowly.

She laid Flossie down on the couch and began massaging her back and belly. Flossie yawned, accompanied by a long, lazy stretch. She was obviously used to being stroked and pampered.

"She's really sweet. You must touch her a lot. Cats are usually skittish with me."

Alice's gaze warmed, easing the crow's-feet by her eyes and the worry lines that traveled across her forehead. "She's a little spoiled, I'm afraid. I've had her since she was born. I'm almost embarrassed to say that she long ago claimed my bed pillow as her own."

Elisabeth laughed. "I love that you let her."

"Oh, I had no choice. Every night I'd say, *Bedtime*, and she'd follow me upstairs. While I was brushing my teeth, she settled in." She leaned forward in the armchair where she was sitting. "Do you know that look that cats get, kind of like this." She pursed her lips and drew her brows together.

"The I'm-the-queen look. Cats are so good at that. I'll bet Flossie is a master."

Alice sighed. "Well, she was. No need anymore. It's her pillow, as I said. Now she smiles when I climb into bed."

Elisabeth picked up Flossie when she was done with the massage and nuzzled her against her chin. "Listen to how loudly she's purring. I think she liked it." She handed Flossie to Alice. "I'm glad you came by, Alice. It's a pleasure to meet you."

"Thank you for letting us interrupt your day. It smells heavenly in here. Cora's pies always did smell like home."

Home. She loved that, and not only did it smell like home, it finally felt like home, too. Homes had visitors, friends, and lovers, and finally, hers did.

"Baking with her are some of my fondest memories."

Alice hesitated on the front porch. "I just wanted to say one more thing. You are as lovely a woman as I could imagine for Ross."

Elisabeth was no longer shocked that people knew about her and Ross. Obviously, if word had traveled to Allure, Trusty residents had been the ones to send the gossip there. But she was thrilled to have the approval of longtime residents, even if it seemed like something she shouldn't need or want. She was learning more and more about Trusty every day, and she liked what she saw. The people here watched out for their own. Ross was definitely homegrown, and a strong example of what she'd always believed the people of Trusty to be like, further cementing her desire to be part of the community that she felt more rooted to with every passing day.

Emily pulled into the driveway at six o'clock as Elisabeth was coming out of the barn after feeding Kennedy. Emily stepped from the car wearing a pair of cutoffs and cowgirl boots with a white tank top. Her hair was loose, falling over her shoulders in natural waves. She had an armful of drawings and a smile on her face.

"Hi. Sorry I'm late. I ran home to change." She held an arm out and hugged Elisabeth. "I also brought some goodies, just in case we need them. Can you hold these?" She handed Elisabeth the drawings and pulled a bag from the backseat of her car.

"You didn't have to do that. I have plenty of snacks here."

"Oh, I didn't bring snacks." She pulled out a bottle of ready-made margaritas. "Wes said he was meeting Ross for drinks, so I figured you might want some company."

Elisabeth swallowed against the emotions welling within her. Friendships were so hard to come by. She'd felt like they were becoming close during their daily phone calls, but now she was sure it wasn't just her imagination.

"Come on. Let's go over the drawings." Emily looped her arm into Elisabeth's, the way she had the first time they met. "I might have brought cheese and crackers, too."

Elisabeth cleared off the table so Emily could set the drawings down.

"And a box of chocolate."

"The perfect girls' night."

"I'm an expert at girls' nights. Not so great at the whole date night thing, though. I put together this whole spa day for Callie once and helped Wes plan a fairy tale night. My brothers love to be romantic, but they always need someone to help coordinate, you know? It's easy to help with the romantic stuff. It's just a matter of doing all the things you hope a guy would do for you." Emily sighed.

She poured them each a drink and handed one to Emily. "Well, Ross seems to do well on his own."

Emily sighed. "Yeah. I told you he was pretty great."

Pretty great didn't even begin to touch on what Elisabeth thought of Ross. *Caring. Loving. Empathetic. Masculine. Sexy. The best lover ever.*

They spent the next hour going over the drawings, and Elisabeth loved the ideas Emily had drawn up.

"I kept this all budget friendly. So even though it seems like a lot with three ovens and the island with the extended bar, I think we can still keep it within your original budget. We'll refinish the existing cabinets instead of buying all new ones, and that will save a lot, too."

"I love all of these ideas. How long will the renovations take?"

Emily poured them each a third drink. "My best estimate is about three weeks, but it'll depend on who you hire to do the final work, and we can talk about that." She began rolling up the drawings. "There is one thing, though. I'm leaving for Tuscany in a few weeks, so we should probably get this going, or make a decision to do it after I return."

"Tuscany? Wow, that sounds amazing. Who are you going with?"

Emily pulled another bottle of margaritas from the bag and handed Elisabeth the bag. "I'll fill you in if you put the munchies on a plate."

"I like the way you think." Elisabeth set the food on a platter and added a hunk of fresh bread she'd baked when she'd made the pies that morning.

"Oh, let's not eat bread. Let's eat pizza. I can call Joe's and have them deliver."

They settled into the living room with their drinks, and Emily told her about the trip Wes had given her as a gift for helping with Callie's spa day and fairy tale night.

"I hope there are more single men there than here." Emily sighed.

"You must have guys fawning all over you. You're gorgeous, smart, funny, and an amazing architect."

"Yeah." Emily laughed. "No, really. I never date. Maybe it's because I grew up here, so I know the good, the bad, and the ugly about all the single guys, or maybe they find me intimidating because I have a successful business and five very protective brothers. Hey, maybe they scared them all off." Emily laughed. "All I know is that it kind of sucks, but at least I have girlfriends."

By the time the pizza arrived, they were already tipsy. Emily answered the door.

"Caleb Stowers, look at you all grown up and

driving." Caleb looked about seventeen with a mop of brown hair and wearing a Joe's Pizza T-shirt.

"And you look to be two sheets to the wind." Caleb laughed.

Emily paid for the pizza and handed it to Elisabeth.

"You're the girl dating Dr. Braden. The dog whisperer or something, right?" Caleb said to Elisabeth.

"Dog pamperer maybe, but not dog whisperer." She laughed and held on to Emily when she wobbled a little from the alcohol.

Caleb laughed. "I hope you guys aren't driving tonight."

"We're not," they said in unison and waved as he left.

"Let's call Callie and Daisy. I bet they'd love to come over." Emily carried the pizza into the living room and took out her phone.

"Sounds fun. Oh, and I have the perfect movie we can watch." Elisabeth sank to her knees before the DVD rack and took each movie off the shelf, setting it aside as she assessed the titles.

"Okay, but I don't want to watch some sappy romance."

Twenty minutes later, with two big piles of movies beside her, she finally held a DVD box over her head. "Found it! *Practical Magic.* Totally fun movie about sisters and magic and, well, there is a guy, but it's not sappy."

The screen door opened and Callie and Daisy

came into the living room with another pizza box and a liquor bag.

"Wow, you started without us." Daisy went into the kitchen, and Elisabeth heard the cabinets opening and closing. She came back with two glasses, hugged Elisabeth and Emily, and handed a glass to Callie. "So good to see you guys."

"You have no idea how much I needed this. It's been a crazy week and it's only Wednesday. Who knew working at a library could be stressful?" Callie filled their glasses, then flopped onto the couch.

Daisy raised her hand. "I did. I could never do all that organizing and finding books for people. What if they want books that suck?"

"Oh, they do." Callie laughed. "But my favorite are the old ladies who come in asking, *I think there's a book about relationships. Um. Fifty something.*" Callie rolled her eyes. "As if I'm stupid. They pretend not to know what it's about, and when I hand them *Fifty Shades,* they always say something like, *My daughter told me to read this.*"

They all laughed.

"I would never tell my mother to read that book," Daisy said. "Although she could probably use it to loosen up a little."

"My mother could have written that book," Elisabeth admitted.

"Really?" Callie asked.

"She's the opposite of repressed." Elisabeth opened the pizza and everyone grabbed a piece.

"Well, that's good. At least we know you're not

repressed," Emily said.

Elisabeth froze. She felt her eyes widen. Had someone seen them at the lake?

Daisy elbowed Elisabeth. "She's shittin' you. Emily, you're as bad as Jake."

Emily laughed. She was sitting by the television and put the DVD into the player. "I'm sorry, but that look was priceless."

"Geez. You freaked me out for a second there."

"Ah, so Ross is a hot lover? I wondered...Gentleman in public, bad boy in the bedroom." Daisy raised her eyebrows in quick succession.

Elisabeth felt her cheeks flush, but even though she was embarrassed, she was eating up every second of having real girlfriends and finally feeling like she fit in. The fact that they were all connected to Ross made her cherish their friendships even more.

"You guys going to the county fair?" Emily asked.

"I have a booth. I'm doing pawdicures and selling beer cakes and pies," Elisabeth said proudly.

"Beer cakes? The guys will eat those up. Luke is showing the girls. This is Shaley's big coming out. Do you want help at the booth?" Daisy asked. "I can help except during the showing. I want to see our baby girl's big event."

"Of course! I'd love it. I was a little nervous about doing it by myself," Elisabeth admitted. "Honestly, though, I doubt many people will come by the booth, but the company would be nice."

"I'm sure people will come by. Wes is roping cattle

in the rodeo, so I can help if you want, except I'd like to watch when he does his thing," Callie said. "I swear, he's so freaking hot."

"Please! He *is* my brother," Emily said. "That's the problem. I'm related to all the decent men around here."

"Sorry," Callie said; then she turned to Elisabeth and whispered, "But he is freaking hot."

Elisabeth laughed.

"We'll all help with the booth. It'll be fun," Emily said as they all piled onto the couch. "I can't wait for you to meet Jake. He's doing his stuntman thing at the monster truck rally, or the demolition derby. I don't remember which. He's coming out on the red-eye."

"His stunts scare the pants off of me," Callie said.

"Me too. I can barely watch," Daisy agreed.

"Well, I'm excited to meet him. So your oldest brother isn't coming?" Elisabeth felt like she was already part of their big, glorious family.

"No. He had a big acquisition meeting that he couldn't reschedule. I wish he and Rebecca could come."

Elisabeth started the movie, and Emily jumped to her feet. "Wait."

"What?" Elisabeth asked.

"Rebecca should be here. We need to Skype her." Emily looked around the living room. "Do you have a laptop?"

"Of course. Doesn't everyone?" Elisabeth rose to her feet, and swayed. She had definitely had enough alcohol. She grabbed on to Emily's hand for stability, and they went together to get the laptop from the kitchen.

"Oh. Who's this?" Emily held up the picture of Elisabeth and Robbie.

"Ex. Very long-ago ex." She reached for the picture, and Emily pulled it out of her reach.

"He's cute."

"Yup." She grabbed her laptop.

"Looks nice, too." Emily traced the edge of the frame with her finger and looked at Elisabeth.

"Supernice."

"So? What happened?"

Elisabeth sighed, realizing she wasn't going to avoid this conversation with one-word answers. She took the picture from Emily and stared down at it. "He dumped me to finish his PhD."

"Ouch." Emily scrunched her nose.

"Yeah. It was a long time ago."

"Are you still in touch?" Emily asked.

"Nope. I haven't heard from him in more than a year." She shoved the frame facedown in the box and closed the cardboard flaps. "Come on. Let's go Skype. I don't want to waste our time on that guy."

"You'll love Rebecca. She's so great." Emily lowered her voice to a whisper. "Her mom died, so she needs us."

Elisabeth stopped cold. "Died? Oh my God."

"She had cancer. It's so sad, but Rebecca's doing great, and you know Pierce takes great care of her— even if she doesn't let him do everything. Rebecca's the strongest girl I know." Emily took out her phone and put the call on speakerphone.

"Hi, Em," Rebecca said.

The other girls yelled, "Hi, Rebecca."

Elisabeth's heart swelled. She loved the camaraderie of the girls. She loved them.

"Becca, we're all at Elisabeth's," Emily explained. "She's Ross's girlfriend, and we're having a girls' night. Wanna join us?"

"Oh my God! Yes! I'm so bummed that we won't be there this weekend. I really wanted to come."

"You should have come without him," Emily suggested.

"Yeah, that's what he said, too, but..." Rebecca's voice trailed off.

"But she won't leave her love bunny's side," Daisy said. Callie elbowed her. "What? I meant it nicely. I wouldn't leave Luke for a weekend. I'd miss him too much. Maybe years from now, but at this point? No way do I want to wake up without him."

"I'm so glad you guys called," Rebecca said. "Pierce has a late meeting, so I'm all alone."

"Not anymore," Callie said. "We'll Skype you, and you can watch the movie with us."

They set up Skype, refilled their glasses, and settled into watching the movie squished next to one another on the couch. Emily shifted to her side and stretched her leg over Callie and Daisy; her foot landed beside Elisabeth, and she wiggled it.

"Foot massage?" Emily asked with hopeful eyes.

They all laughed, and so began a round of foot massages and musical chairs—and the best girls' night of Elisabeth's life.

ROSS SAT ACROSS from Wes and Luke in a booth in the back of the bar. Country music blared through the overhead speakers. It had been a few weeks since he and his brothers had gotten together for a drink, and Ross was having a great time, but he missed Elisabeth. He'd texted her an hour earlier, but she still hadn't responded. He checked his cell phone again. Still no text.

"Would you put that damn thing away?" Wes said as he checked his own phone.

"Look who's talking. What the hell happened to you two?" Luke slung an arm over Wes's shoulder. "We used to come here and stay until one o'clock in the morning. It's ten thirty and you're both dying to get home to your women."

"I was just making sure there weren't any texts from Chip about the ranch. We had a big group arriving tonight." Wes shoved his phone in his pocket.

"Yeah, right." Luke laughed. "And what's your excuse, Ross? Checking for animal emergencies?"

"Don't even try to pretend that you didn't go into the men's room to text Daisy, you ass." Ross held his hand out. "Give me your phone."

"No." Luke crossed his arms over his chest.

"Hand it over, big mouth. Five bucks says there are at least two texts to Daisy in the last two hours." Ross narrowed his gaze, and Luke held strong.

For a minute.

"Oh hell. Yeah, so what? If you had Daisy to go

home to, would you rather be here or home in bed with her?" Luke took a swig of his beer.

"I'd rather be with Lis," Ross admitted.

"Says the man who said he'd never settle down," Wes reminded him. "Pierce, too. What the hell? We all bit the bullet except Jake."

"He'll never settle down," Ross said with a shake of his head. "His loss, too."

Wes and Luke exchanged a look that Ross knew damn well meant, *I told you so.*

"So Mr. I'll Never Settle Down has met his match. Happened quickly, too, didn't it?" Luke asked.

"I think I got whiplash." Ross took a pull of his beer.

Wes leaned across the table and asked with a serious tone and a dark stare, "Is this the big L-O-V-E?"

Ross met his stare and took another drink. Yeah, it was love. He had no doubt about it, but he didn't need to admit it to his younger brothers before he told Elisabeth.

Luke and Wes exchanged another glance.

"Shit. You think we don't know?" Luke smacked a hand down on the table. "I was the last one that was going to fall. Remember? Not me. Not Luke Braden. Women were like wine—too sweet not to enjoy a different one every night."

Ross kept a straight face and held his steely gaze.

"You're going to hold out on us? It's us, man. We know. We've been there. We *are* there." Luke ran his hand between him and Wes.

"We're in the thick of it, Ross. Why're you holding

back? Unless..." Wes sat back and crossed his arms over his chest. "Unless you're not sure." He slid another look to Luke.

"True. Or maybe she's not as into him as he is into her," Luke suggested.

They were egging him on, and it was working. Big-time. When the waitress asked if they wanted another round, he slapped a credit card on the table.

"Struck a nerve," Luke said. "The only question is, which one?"

"There's another option. Maybe she seems like she's sweet and all that, but she's really a two-timer and our brother here got wind of—"

Ross reached across the table, grabbed Wes by the collar, and hauled him halfway across the table. "Shut the fuck up before I break your goddamn vocal cords." He shoved him back to his seat.

The waitress brought his card back, and he signed the slip and handed her the receipt, his eyes never leaving Wes, who had a shit-ass grin on his lips.

A cell phone rang and they all reached for their phones.

"Chip, what's up?" Wes lifted his chin at his brothers. "Yeah. Good. Yup. Tomorrow. Okay, bud. See you then." He ended the call and shoved his phone back in his pocket.

"Y'all are assholes." Ross rose to his feet.

"Yeah, so are you," Wes said.

Ross slung an arm over each of his brothers, and they plowed out to the parking lot as they'd done hundreds of times before.

"Daisy's at Elisabeth's house," Luke said as they disengaged from one another.

"So is Callie."

"Really? I thought just Emily was going over to discuss her kitchen plans." The three of them whipped out their keys. "Elisabeth's."

With a nod, they climbed into their trucks and followed Ross to Elisabeth's house.

The house was dark, save for a flash of light from the television in the living room.

"What the hell are they doing?" Wes asked. "You hear that?"

They listened as they ascended the porch steps. Luke went to the window and flagged them over with his hand. The three of them peered into the window at the four girls piled on the couch hugging one another, clutching tissues and wiping their eyes.

"Aw, hell." Ross turned his back to the window.

"Tears." Luke followed suit.

"Fuck." Wes fell into line.

Ross leaned back in and looked in the window just as Emily glanced up and screamed. She fell off the couch, and all the girls started screaming.

"Holy shit." Wes barreled into the house. The girls were huddled together against the wall, still screaming. "It's us. It's us."

"You ass!" Emily threw a pillow at him.

"Wes! What were you thinking? We thought you were Peeping Toms," Callie said with a harsh stare.

Luke wrapped Daisy into his arms. "Peeping Toms in Trusty?" He laughed and Daisy swatted his stomach.

With the others beating on each other, Ross folded Elisabeth into his arms and brushed her tears with his thumb. "I'm sorry we scared you, babe." He pressed his cheek to hers and whispered, "I love you." He hadn't planned on saying it, and he definitely hadn't planned on saying it in front of his brothers as they tried to calm their drunken, upset girlfriends, but he couldn't hold back any longer.

Elisabeth leaned back and blinked her long lashes at him. "You..."

He smiled down at her and nodded. "I do. I love you."

More tears sprang from her eyes. He buried his hand beneath her hair and kissed her. She tasted sugary sweet, and it was a taste he'd never forget.

"Hey!" Emily yelled and slapped Ross on the back. "Look at you two making out while you nearly gave us heart attacks. Thank God we already ended our Skype call with Rebecca. She probably would have called the Trusty police."

Ross reluctantly parted lips with Elisabeth, then turned to face his sister. Her cheeks were flushed, her eyes glassy, and she was swaying on her feet. Ross wrapped an arm around her waist.

"You're either staying here tonight, or I'm driving you home, sis."

Emily banged her forehead against his chest. "I love your girlfriend," Emily gushed.

"Me too. What'll it be? Here or your place?" He glanced at Wes and Luke, holding their girlfriends. Wes and Luke lifted their heads when Ross said, "Me too," and passed him a smile and nod.

"Mine," Emily said. "But we have to clean up. We can't leave Elisssssabeth with this mess." She swayed back and Ross caught her.

"I'll clean up. Wes, can you take Callie and Daisy home? Luke, can you help me deliver cars so everyone has theirs in the morning?"

"Sure." Luke held Daisy against him.

Ross assessed the room. "Pizza, cheese, crackers, chocolate, tears, and margaritas. Looks like we missed a great night, minus the tears."

Elisabeth ran her finger along the back of his neck. "We'll have our own party."

"Promises, promises."

Ross and his brothers got everyone home safely; then Ross stopped at home and picked up the boys. By the time he arrived back at Elisabeth's, she was fast asleep on the couch. Knight jumped onto the couch and snuggled in at her feet while Ranger and Sarge sprawled out on the living room floor. Ross cleaned up the living room and then sat in an armchair and drew in a deep breath. This was where he wanted to be, with Lis and the boys.

He gathered her in his arms, and Knight gave him a look of disapproval as he carried her upstairs. He wondered if she'd remember what he'd said when she woke up. He laid her on the bed and undressed her, down to her skivvies and tank top, then drew the blankets up to her chest. She was so damn beautiful as she licked her lips in her sleep and settled into the mattress with a sleepy sigh. Ross stripped to his briefs and slipped beneath the blankets. Elisabeth instinctively snuggled against him.

He kissed the top of her head. "I love you, Lis." He didn't care if she heard it or not. It felt damn good to say it.

"I love you, too," she said against his chest, and with the next breath she was fast asleep.

Chapter Nineteen

ELISABETH'S HEAD WAS pounding. She must be dying, or someone was surely torturing her. She opened her eyes to the morning light and slammed them immediately shut with a groan. It was Thursday, and she had to take care of the animals and deliver pies. *Oh God. No, no, no.* She rolled onto her side, and when she didn't roll into Ross, she reached an arm across the sheets and felt for him. The bed was empty. She didn't dare call out for him, because even her thoughts echoed in her head, as the night before came back in bits and pieces. She smiled at the memory of the girls' night, then cringed because smiling hurt. The familiar tapping of nails on hardwood came closer. *Click, click, click!* A wet nose pressed against her cheek, followed by a distinct doggy tongue that smelled like one of her puppy cookies. She reached a hand out and stroked the dog's head. She didn't need to open her eyes to know it was Knight. He and Ranger were the only ones who crawled onto the bed, and Ranger did it in stealth mode, pulling himself up by the front paws, whereas Knight came up in one giant leap. As he did now, landing on her feet.

She groaned again and flung her pillow over her head. The bed beside her dipped and the very male, sexy scent of Ross filled her senses. She opened one eye and shoved the pillow to the side, drinking him in. Even through half-open, hungover eyes he looked like the god of hotness.

"My poor girl." Ross spoke quietly. "I brought you some ibuprofen, but I wasn't sure of your cure of choice, so I brought tomato juice, which will help level out your blood sugar levels, or water, your choice."

She pulled the pillow over her head again. "How do people do this?"

"Get through hangovers? I've gotten through many. You just face them head-on."

"I've only had one before, and it wasn't this bad. Can you just shoot me?"

He moved the pillow and kissed her forehead. "No, but I can love you through it."

She opened her eyes and remembered. *I love you.* She smiled, which sent another bolt of pain through her head. "You love me," she whispered.

"So I guess you remember." He smiled down at her and brushed her hair off her shoulders.

"I'll never forget." She pushed up so she was sitting and took a moment to get her bearings. Ross handed her the tablets and she whispered, "Water." She gulped down the medicine and leaned in to his chest. "Can't I just stay here all day?"

"I'm not sure you want all my clients in the bedroom, but I did take care of the animals for you."

She fisted her hands in his shirt. "You're the greatest boyfriend ever. No wonder I love you."

He lifted her chin so he could see her eyes, and he pressed a kiss to her lips.

"My breath has to be nasty." She turned away, and he drew her back again.

"I don't care." He kissed her again. "I want you to know something. I've never said that I loved a single girlfriend before. Not a single one. Just you, babe."

She lowered her eyes. She couldn't say the same, and she wondered if he knew that from their conversation in the truck before they made love.

"It's okay. I know you've said it before. You told me. I just wanted you to know."

She continued clutching his shirt. "Yes, I said it before, but what I had with Robbie wasn't like what we have. I know that now. That wasn't love, Ross. What we have is real and true. What I had with him was friendship."

"Lis, you don't have to explain. We all have pasts. It's okay if you loved him. Some people love many people in their lifetimes. You love me now, and that's what matters." Ross tried to stand, but she held on tight.

"Ross."

He pressed his finger to her lips. "I don't question your love for me, Lis. I believe you. That's what love is, putting aside our insecurities and trusting in our partners. I have to get to work, but if you need me, just text, okay? I'm taking the boys with me to the clinic."

She nodded, gritting through the ache in her head. "Thank you for taking care of me and the animals."

"I always will."

Elisabeth listened as he went out the front door with the boys. She breathed deeply, wondering how on earth she got lucky enough to be with the kindest man on the planet—and how she was going to make it through her deliveries with a killer headache.

Her cell phone vibrated, and she grabbed it from the nightstand and read the text from Emily.

Are you alive?

She texted back. *Barely. You?*

A minute later her response came through. *Did my brother tell you he loves you, or did I dream that?*

She closed her eyes for a beat, reveling in the answer *and* the friendship before texting back. *YES!*

Emily texted back seconds later. *OMG! Yay! Wait...Do you love him? Yes, I'm nosy. Get used to it!*

She didn't hesitate to answer. *LOL. YES!*

Emily didn't text back right away. She showered, dressed, and was fifteen minutes into baking before she received another text from Emily.

Okay, now the whole town knows.

Elisabeth called her.

"Hey," Emily said just above a whisper.

"You sound awful."

"Thanks," Emily said. "Headache."

"Tell me about it. Why did you tell the whole town? They don't exactly like me yet."

"Oh, shut up. We love you and that's all that matters."

That made Elisabeth smile.

"I didn't really tell anyone. I stopped in at the diner for coffee, and I ran into Wes. Sorry it took so long to get back to you."

"You had me worried."

"I'm sorry. You know Margie. She can talk forever, and when Wes showed up, he gave me a hard time about last night. The bugger. Like he's never gotten shitfaced before. I'm happy for you and Ross, but a little jealous. I'm starting to think I'm destined to be single forever. Maybe I should borrow some of Alice's cats." Emily laughed.

Elisabeth finished mixing the beer batter for the cakes she was making and held the phone against her shoulder while she poured it into a bowl. "I think love finds us when we don't even know we're ready, so don't give up. Whether you find your true love here or in Italy, it's bound to happen. You're too amazing for it not to."

"You're so nice, Elisabeth. Daisy and Callie roll their eyes at me and tell me to start dating."

"Well, that would help, but I've never been big on dating, so I don't think that's the answer. The first time I saw Ross, I *knew*. You know how you get a flutter in your chest, and your stomach starts to do little flips? Ross made my entire body wake up and go weak at the same time. He was so in control when I turned his office upside down with my noisy piglet. He didn't even get upset with me, or snappy or anything. He just looked at me and said, *It's okay. Take a deep breath.* I could barely breathe looking at him. He—"

"Okay, okay. Brother. Remember? I get it, so there's probably hope for me yet."

"Sorry. I was gushing." She slid the cakes into the oven. "Are you guys really going to help me at the fair tomorrow?"

"Of course. It'll be fun. What should we bring?"

"Nothing. I'm making beer cakes, puppy cookies, and pies. We should be good. Oh, maybe bottled water? That would be good. Ross is going to put up the awning and help me with the refrigeration unit I rented. I'll set up a grooming station and we'll be all set."

"How are you going to do everything that you do when everyone suddenly wants you to care for their pets? I mean, think about it, Elisabeth, the pet massages, grooming, picking up and dropping off dogs, not to mention baking and delivering pies. My mom said Jade's clients are all talking about you, too, which means your business is likely to really take off."

Just hearing there was a possibility of her business taking off made her pulse speed up. "Not all, just three. I'm not sure. I've been thinking about it and I'll probably have to figure out a way to bring my grooming supplies and do what I did in LA, a mobile grooming van or something. I sold mine before I moved, but eventually I can get another one. That would give me a way to be a little more organized and not have to waste time running back and forth."

"I'm exhausted just listening to all you do. I've got

to go figure out how to get through a meeting with a blinding headache. I'll see you bright and early tomorrow."

They ended the call and Elisabeth eyed the box by the wall. She knelt beside it, feeling much stronger than she had the last time she'd looked at its contents. She withdrew a few pictures of her aunt and closed the top flaps. Packing away Robbie was easy. She had no qualms or emotions about saying goodbye to their past, but packing away the letters from her aunt, and the few knickknacks she'd received from her over the years, was more emotional. But she wasn't shutting her aunt or her aunt's memories away. Aunt Cora was everywhere. This was her house Elisabeth was living in, her furniture, her photographs on the wall. Elisabeth used her aunt's recipes to facilitate the business her aunt had grown from nothing more than an idea and a warm heart. She looked around the kitchen and sighed. It was time to start her own life. To put Robbie away for good and to put the heartache of her aunt's passing behind her.

As she carried the box to the hall closet, she mentally put away the comparisons of her mother to herself, and all the doubt and worry that went along with it. She was in the town she always knew would be her forever place, with a man who was her forever love. How could life get any sweeter?

ROSS HEADED INTO his house to take care of the dogs and work out after work. The house was quiet without Elisabeth there. Knight stuck to his side, following him as he went upstairs to the bedroom, as if he missed Elisabeth, too. He hadn't realized how used to her being there he'd become. He changed into his workout clothes, then texted Elisabeth before going down to his home gym.

Just got home. Doing a quick workout. Then I'll shower and come over. Okay?

He was setting up his weights when she texted back.

Want to stay at your place? My head is better. I can bring dinner. Xox.

Damn, he'd forgotten the *xox.*

He returned her text. *Sounds good. Extra xox from me.*

He'd felt lighter since he'd told Elisabeth he loved her, freer, stronger. He'd always hoped that at some point he'd find the right woman, someone to build a life with. Someone he would love and protect and who he knew would love him for who he was and not for his money. Elisabeth was better than any woman he could have ever dreamed up, and loving her felt damn good. He'd liked taking care of her last night, and this morning, with the exception of how sad she'd looked about him not being the first man she said she loved, but Ross didn't fret over it. He believed her when she said she loved him. He saw it in her eyes and felt it in her touch. He added extra weights to his bench press bar and turned on ESPN, then pushed through a rigorous workout. He was just finishing his last set of sit-ups, drenched in sweat, feeling strong and exhilarated, when he heard the dogs barking. He flicked off the television and headed upstairs.

"Lis?"

"In here."

He found her in the kitchen juggling a casserole dish and a basket of bread with Knight, Ranger, and Sarge rubbing against her legs. Her back was to him, her beautiful back bare to her waist in a white halter dress. Her hair was tied back with a red silky ribbon.

"You took such good care of me that I thought I'd take care of you. I made your favorite. It's probably not as good as your mom's, but..." She spun around, looking radiant. The bottom of her dress was trapped between her leg and Knight and pulled tight across her hips, accentuating her waist. The kitchen smelled delicious, like chicken Parmesan, warm bread, and Elisabeth. But it wasn't his stomach that was growling with hunger. Just the sight of the ribbon gave him all sorts of lascivious thoughts.

"Wow." A breathy whisper as she raked her eyes down his body.

"Wow is right. You look hot." He leaned down and took her in a slow, passionate kiss. She ran her hands along the sides of his back, making him instantly hard. She trapped his lip in her teeth and dragged her tongue along it as they drew apart. When she ran her fingers along the waist of his shorts, he lost all hope of holding back his desires.

"I don't want you to think I love you only for your body or anything, but...I should come over when you're working out more often. You look Photoshopped." She ran her fingers over his muscular stomach, sending a bolt of heat through him.

He pulled the ribbon from her hair and dragged it over her hands. "Photoshopped, huh? Well, then, paybacks are hell, because I have to endure thinking about your hot little body all day every day, and this sexy little ribbon of yours makes me think of a few better uses for it than in your hair." He kissed her neck. Her skin was warm, and she smelled like a fresh summer breeze. He nipped one of her shoulders and kissed his way back along her heated skin to her neck.

"Other uses?" She batted her eyelashes and spoke in a seductive Southern drawl, rocking her hips into his. "Why, Mr. Braden, whatever do you mean?" She took the ribbon from his hand and wound it around her wrist. "It does make a nice bracelet."

Holy hell.

She feigned a loud gasp. "Well, I do declare. Look what that little ribbon did to you!" She looked down at his erection and then back up, wide-eyed and innocent, as she slid her hand beneath his shorts and stroked his hard length.

He sucked in a breath and backed her up against the counter. "I thought you were such a good girl."

"Why, I am a very good girl." She slid her hand lower and cupped his balls, sending a streak of lust through his body.

He lifted her up and set her on the counter, and in one move he tore the dress over her head. Her bare breasts were too beautiful to resist. Two perfect mounds that he had to taste. He lowered his mouth and teased her nipples into hard points, earning him a throaty moan that heightened his arousal.

"Holy fuck, Lis. You're like a centerfold."

She grabbed his head and held his mouth to her breast. "Your centerfold." Her head fell back, her breasts rising and falling with each lustful breath.

In a hot second he dropped his shorts to his ankles and pulled her panties off, then lifted her to the edge of the counter. Her slick center was hot against his arousal. He buried his hand in her hair and fisted it in her silky locks.

"Jesus, I love you so damn much."

"Then stop teasing me." She grabbed his hips and, circling his neck with her arms, she wrapped her legs around his waist, then slid down his body, taking in every inch of him.

"Holy...Good Lord." He covered her mouth with his, taking her in a greedy kiss. He filled his palms with her gorgeous ass and moved her up and down, feeling her heat, her desire, as she buried him deep over and over again.

"I love you, Ross," she said against his lips. "I really love you."

He stepped from his shorts and carried her to the guest bedroom—he'd never make it upstairs. He laid her on the bed and came down over her, his hands on her breasts, his lips kissing every inch of her exposed flesh. He nipped his way back up over her hips, her stomach, ribs, breasts, and finally her mouth, and ran his tongue along the sweet swell of her upper lip. Her breath was hot, needy, but he took his time loving her. He ran his strong hands up her delicate arms and fingered the ribbon on her wrist. He didn't want to do anything she wasn't into. He ran his tongue along the edge of the ribbon. She arched her back, pressing her hips to his.

"I've never done that," she whispered.

"It's okay. We won't." He came back to her lips and kissed her tenderly. He loved her too damn much to do anything she didn't want to, but he loved that she teased him the way she did.

"I want to, with you. I trust you, Rossie."

He touched his forehead to hers. "Lis, we don't have to—"

She leaned up and kissed him. "I want to. I want to do everything with you. I waited my whole life for you."

The love and trust in her voice made his heart swell.

"I'll just hold your wrists. No need for more. If you still want to another time, we can. I need you now, Lis." He settled one hand over each wrist and held them gently above her head. She was completely open to him, his hips between hers, her arms restrained, and her trusting, blue eyes smiling up at him. He nearly lost it.

She lifted her hips, and he slid into her until their hips touched. He rocked his hips, angling up as her body began to quiver. She pressed her wrists against his strength.

"Want me to stop?" he whispered against her cheek.

"Never. More, Rossie. More."

He thrust in deeper and harder, feeling her arms strain against him. He searched her eyes, checking in, making sure they were in sync, and—Oh yeah, they were in sync, all right. He felt her thighs flex, and her eyes slammed shut.

"Ross."

"Come, baby." He pumped faster, taking her right up to the edge. God, he loved to watch her come. Her body tensed around him, and she made the sexiest little noises, which slipped out like promises in the dark. When her body began to ease down from the orgasm, he released her wrists and gathered her in his arms, holding her against him until the last of the tremors vibrated through her.

"Again," she whispered.

He moved his hips faster, pushed in deeper, and she guided his hands to her wrists again.

"Again," she urged.

He took hold of her wrists and rode her hard.

"I'm not going to last."

She made one of those sexy sounds again. "Try," she urged.

Holy fuck, was she kidding? Did she have any idea how close to the edge he was? He slid his hands down to her hips and pressed them into the mattress, then took her quickly up to the peak again. She clawed at his back, pretzeling her legs around his body and lifting her ass so he could go deeper as her body shuddered and pulsated around him and his name sailed from her lips.

"Again," she panted.

"No promises," he groaned, and captured her wrists in his hands, then held them out to her sides as he loved her faster.

"Oh God...Oh God..."

"Come on, baby. Get there, because I'm not going to last. You're so damn sexy you're driving me crazy."

"Come with me." Her eyes flew open. "With me, Ross."

Her invitation sent a surge of heat blazing through him, spurring him into a blind frenzy of need and want and everything in between. He drove in harder, deeper, and released her hands. She clawed at his back, digging her nails into his skin and driving him out of his ever-loving mind. Two more deep thrusts and her hips bucked against his. He stayed in deep, groaning through his own intense release. They remained tangled together, their bodies joined as one, both struggling to regain control of their senses, spent, satiated, and slick with sweat. Ross held her against him until her pulse slowed and her breathing eased.

He lifted up and she tightened her arms around him, holding him in place.

"Don't go," she whispered. "I like being close."

He rested his head on her shoulder and kissed her heated skin. "I'll never leave you." She'd zapped his strength and claimed his heart, and he was the happiest man alive.

Chapter Twenty

THE COUNTY AGRICULTURAL Fairgrounds were located at the edge of town and had been a showcase of all things farm related in the county since the early 1950s. Boasting carnival rides, a petting zoo, live animal competitions, and a variety of foods and entertainment, the county agricultural fair was the largest fair in the state of Colorado. Families came from near and far to enjoy the monster trucks, demolition derby, cattle roping, and of course to see the award-winning animals up close: pigs, goats, sheep, dairy cattle, and horses. Elisabeth had attended a handful of times throughout the years with her aunt, and this year she was excited to be part of the program. She'd always loved the sight of the animal pavilions, and the large barns full of unique handmade items for sale, such as arts and crafts, quilts, wooden furniture, and much more. Fresh-baked goods, locally grown vegetables and fruits, and canned goods were also a big part of the event.

Ross constructed her awning and set up the refrigeration unit she'd rented, then helped her arrange the tables, hang signs, and prepare her grooming station. Elisabeth tied balloons to the table legs and the poles of the awning. Around them, other exhibitors set up their booths, waving and making small talk about the weather and how big the crowds were expected to be. The gates opened while Ross was returning from the exhibitor parking lot, where he'd gone to put away the temporary coolers she'd used to carry the pies.

Elisabeth watched Ross walking back from the parking lot. He looked striking in his jeans and Trusty Veterinary polo shirt that stretched tight across his strong chest. Their eyes caught and her breath hitched. Oh, how she loved him. She'd had no idea what real love was, even though she'd dreamed of it every day of her life, until Ross came into her life, and every second they spent together drove the knowledge deeper.

Ross lifted his hand and waved, flashing his sexy smile that she loved so much.

"I'm not sure I can spend all day watching all those googly eyes." Emily flopped into Elisabeth's chair.

"I'm sorry!"

"I'm kidding. I've actually never seen Ross like this. It's kind of nice, and kind of unfair." Emily was wearing a pair of cutoffs, a tank top, and sandals. She kicked off her sandals and pulled her legs up under her.

"Oh, stop. You'll find your true love. I know you will." Elisabeth reached a hand out to Ross as he came to her side.

"Hey, sis. Seen Jake yet?" Ross kissed Elisabeth's temple.

I love that. I love you.

"Yeah, he's over with the greasy mechanics." Emily pulled at the edge of her tank.

"As I remember, there's a certain greasy mechanic who would love to go out with you." Ross raised his brows.

"Really?" Elisabeth asked.

"Ugh. Don't even go there." Emily glared at Ross. "I'll never do anything for you again if you try to push Tate on me."

"He's a good guy. Nice as hell. You're just too picky for your own good." Ross turned his attention to Elisabeth. "I want to head over and find Jake. Mom's having a breakfast for everyone tomorrow before the fair. I told her we'd come. Is that okay?"

"Of course. I'll make some muffins to bring with us."

Ross kissed her again. "You don't need to do that. You'll be exhausted tonight."

"I want to." She shooed him away with her hands. "Go see Jake before things get crazy. People are already starting to arrive."

He reached into the cooler and pulled out a beer cake. "Can I bring this for Jake?"

"Bring it for *Jake*, yeah, right." Emily rolled her eyes with a teasing smile.

"Of course. Enjoy." She'd made a few extra cakes because most of Ross's brothers and their girlfriends were going to be at the fair.

By noon the grass in front of Elisabeth's booth was trampled flat. Callie and Daisy were tending to customers, selling slices of pie and slices of beer cake, while Emily was handing out puppy cookies and other goodies and selling them to the customers whose dogs Elisabeth was giving pawdicures. She'd been busy since early morning, and she was loving every second of not only the work, but being with the girls.

Emily set up a tip jar beside Elisabeth, which Elisabeth had been excruciatingly embarrassed by, but it solved the more embarrassing position of constantly turning away money that was offered. She'd set up the free pawdicures as a way to meet people and gain new clients, while also getting them over to the table and introducing them to her baked goods. It had worked so well that they'd sold most of her beer cakes already. Emily had also set up a clipboard sign-up sheet, where customers left their names, phone numbers, and email addresses, as well as what they were interested in— pet grooming, pet baked goods, or people baked goods. Emily had such a strong business sense, she'd already begun ticking off ideas, like a weekly Paws & Pies newsletter.

Tracie and Maddy came by with Justin Bieber for a puppy treat. Maddy's long red hair hung loosely to her waist.

"Thank you for cleaning up Justin Bieber. I thought you'd have to shave him bald."

"He's too handsome to shave. Just try to keep him out of the creek."

Tracie bought a bag of doggy cookies. "Thanks again, Elisabeth. I'll call you to schedule another grooming in a few weeks."

When Elisabeth finished with the puppy she was working on, she exhaled loudly. "You guys, I don't think I could have run the booth without you. Thank you so much."

"This has been really fun." Callie pulled her dark hair up and secured it in a high ponytail.

"Yeah. It's been a blast. I have to run to see Shaley and Luke, but I'll try to come back after." Daisy hugged Elisabeth. "Welcome to the sisterhood. Wes told me that Ross said he loves you."

"Really?" Elisabeth felt her cheeks flush.

"Those guys gossip like girls," Daisy explained. "It's all good. Now you're really one of us. One more Braden man enters couplehood."

"Now it's Emmie's turn." Callie put her arm around Emily.

"Speaking of..." Daisy nodded at Tate McGregor heading toward the booth. She leaned in close to Emily and whispered, "You've been spending a lot of time with him lately. Are you holding out on us?"

Emily gave her a shove. "Go see my brother. I am *not* going out with him. I'm working on a project with him."

Elisabeth watched Tate approach. Did every man in Trusty wear low-slung jeans and tight T-shirts? He had a deep tan, shiny black hair, and like most guys around town, a tattoo snaking out from under his sleeve.

"He is cute," Elisabeth whispered.

"We're not dating," Emily snapped. "I'll be back." Emily hurried out of the booth and joined Tate.

Elisabeth watched them walk off together. "You think they're dating?"

"No idea, but I doubt it. She'd be gushing about it if they were." Callie nibbled on a crumb of beer cake. "She needs that trip to Tuscany so badly." A group of women were heading for their booth. "Oh good, customers. Take a break. I'll watch the booth for a few minutes."

"Thanks. Want me to bring you a soda?"

"Iced tea would be great. Thanks." Callie turned to help a customer.

Elisabeth went off in the direction of the snack pavilion. She wandered through the livestock pavilion on the way. The smell of hay and sweaty animals probably turned a lot of people's stomachs, but it made Elisabeth think of Kennedy, Dolly, and the other animals, and how much she loved living in her aunt's house. She sighed and leaned on a stall, thinking of Ross. If it hadn't been for Kennedy, she wondered when they might have met. She was sure they would have. Fate would have seen to it.

A wave of people came through the pavilion, and she weaved her way free of them and into the crowd moving in the direction of the food. The warm summer air carried away the scent of the animals and brought in the aroma of grilling meat, deep-fried foods, and buttery popcorn. The pavilion was packed tighter than a cattle run. Elisabeth was shoulder to shoulder with a man on either side of her. She ordered drinks, paid, snagged some napkins, and turned to leave. A small boy ran in front of her, and she lost her grip on one of the cups. It landed with a thud and cold liquid splashed all over her feet and legs and on the feet of the couple standing beside her. *Great.*

"I'm so sorry," she said as she handed them napkins.

"It's okay." The man raked his eyes down to her chest. His girlfriend glared at her.

Elisabeth had been glared at so much recently that the woman's stare didn't come as a surprise. She hurried toward the entrance and paused at the sight of Ross talking with Tate. A man crossed in front of her and stopped to study a fairground map. Something about the way he was standing was familiar. She glanced at Ross, then back at the man, his familiarity nagging at her. She ran her eyes down his body, and he lifted his head. Elisabeth's breath hitched at his square jaw, the coffee-stain birthmark just below the hairline on his neck. *No.* Her pulse quickened. Her brain told her to move. Get the hell out of there. But she was unable to turn away. *Robbie?* She had to be wrong. What would he be doing here in Trusty? The last time they'd spoken, he was in California, finishing up his all-important PhD.

He lifted his eyes and she held her breath as he surveyed the grounds and slowly turned in her direction.

She spun around, but not before catching a glimpse of his electric-blue eyes.

Ohgodohgodohgod.

She ducked through the crowd to the other side of the pavilion and hurried back to her booth.

"Hey there," Callie said as she handed a customer their change. "Some guy was looking for you. I told him you went for snacks. Robbie something or other."

She sank into the chair and covered her face. *Robbie. Fucking Robbie.* Why would he come all this way?

"Oh my God, what's wrong?"

Elisabeth sprang to her feet and paced the small booth. "Nothing." *Nothing. He's nothing.*

Callie's arm circled her shoulder. "Elisabeth, what is it? You're shaking like a leaf."

She was not only shaking, she felt sick to her stomach. She looked up at Callie and burst into tears. What the hell was wrong with her? She was over him. Done. Totally, without a doubt, done. Why was she so shaken up?

What the hell was Robbie doing here? He didn't belong here. He'd broken up with her and she'd moved on. She had no lingering doubts about him, or them, and definitely no doubts about Ross.

Ross.

Oh God.

She needed to pull herself together.

"It's nothing, really. I just…"

"Who's Robbie?" Callie asked, handing her tissues from her purse.

Elisabeth wiped her eyes. "Thanks." She sniffled and drew in a deep breath. "Oh God, how can this be happening?"

"If I knew what was happening, I might be able to tell you."

She looked at Callie. Sweet Callie who would probably never fall apart over an ex-boyfriend whom she once *thought* she loved. She knew now that what she felt for Robbie wasn't love, but, *oh God*, why was she falling to pieces? Why did her heart ache and her stomach twist into a fist?

"I think I need to find Ross."

ROSS LEANED AGAINST the fence between his brothers Jake and Luke. He'd already seen to a handful of animals and watched Luke show Shaley. Shaley won a blue ribbon. Luke and Daisy were so proud, they were still glowing. Daisy headed back to the booth to help Elisabeth, and Ross was seconds from going to see her himself, but it had been a long time since he'd seen Jake, and he wanted to hang out for a few more minutes first.

"What time's your gig?" Ross asked.

Jake shrugged. "Dunno. Soon." His skin was bronzed, his muscles strong, and his cocky attitude was just as sure as it always was. "Wes said you've got a serious girlfriend."

"Yup." Ross slid him a look that he knew clearly translated to, *Keep your comments to yourself and don't fuck with me.* And he knew from the smirk and arched brow on Jake's face that *his* look translated to, *Yeah, right.*

Jake turned around and leaned his elbows on the fence, kicked one ankle over the other, and glanced at Luke.

"Here it comes," Luke said.

"My only question is, why?" Jake held Ross's gaze.

"Why what?" Ross asked flatly.

"Why tie yourself down? You had it made. You've got a great career. You've always had women all over you, so don't tell me you hit a dry spell. Why give it all up? What do you gain?" Jake watched a blonde walk by wearing Daisy Dukes and cowgirl boots. "Why, oh why, indeed."

"You're an idiot." Ross shifted his eyes away.

Luke chuckled.

"I'm not being funny. I'm really curious. I never thought I'd see the day Pierce and Luke settled down, and I guess of all my brothers, I honestly thought you'd be first." Jake lifted his cowboy hat as a pair of pretty brunettes walked past. "But you held out, man. Why now?"

Ross shared a knowing glance with Luke—*One day he'll understand*—then he settled a hand on Jake's shoulder. "Jake, let me put this into words that you can understand. You know that high you get when you've got two women in your bed?"

"Hell yes." Jake's eyes lit up.

"Remember the feeling when you were in love with Fiona in high school?" He knew he struck a nerve, and he meant to.

Jake's jaw clenched. "Yeah," he said in a deep, gruff

voice.

"Which was better?"

Jake's eyes went cold. His hands fisted by his side, but he made no attempt to answer.

Luke and Ross exchanged a knowing glance and pushed from the fence. Ross patted Jake's back. "I'm going to see my girlfriend, who I'm quite sure makes me feel a thousand times better than any other woman ever could. I'll catch your show, and we can catch up afterward."

Jake nodded and eyed another woman. "You're a buzzkill, man. You had to bring up Fi?"

"Sorry, dude. You asked."

Luke's cell phone rang as he and Ross walked toward Elisabeth's booth. He *uh-huh*ed a few times, then ended the call.

"Bro, you know about some guy named Robbie?" Luke asked.

An icy spear shot through Ross's chest. "Robbie?" Surely Luke didn't mean the only Robbie he could think about. Elisabeth's Robbie.

"Some guy who knows Elisabeth?"

Fuck. "What about him?"

"Looks like he's here, and by the looks of it"— Luke nodded at Elisabeth taking fast, determined steps in their direction—"she saw him. Want me to stay or go?"

"Go."

"Okay, but if he needs taking care of—"

Ross shot him a dark stare. No one needed taking care of, and if anyone did, Ross would handle it.

Luke held his hands up in surrender. "Just having your back, bro."

"Thanks. I'm good." He braced himself. In Ross's experience, *ex*-anythings rarely brought good news, and from the tension streaming across Elisabeth's face, he knew this time was no different.

"Hey, babe." He tried to sound casual, but her eyes were damp and red rimmed, and when she looked up at him, they welled with fresh tears. Worry clutched his gut. He didn't want to think about what those tears might mean. Were they meant for him or caused by Robbie for a whole other reason?

"Elisabeth?" A well-built man with light brown hair and bright blue eyes smiled as he reached a hand toward Elisabeth. *Ross's* Elisabeth.

Elisabeth turned, and when their eyes met, Ross's chest tightened. This was Robbie. He had no doubt that the man dressed in khaki pants and a polo shirt much like his own was her ex. When Robbie touched Elisabeth's hand, it was all Ross could do not to close the gap between him and Elisabeth and put his arm around her. Claim her as his own.

"Robbie." She said his name just above a whisper, the way she might say the name of a friend whom she hadn't seen in a long time—different from the way she said Ross's name, he noticed, which was laced with love.

Then why was her lower lip trembling?

Aw, hell. Here come the tears.

Ross placed a hand on her lower back. "Lis, you okay?"

She glanced at Ross, then back at Robbie, and her breath hitched as she nodded.

Bullshit. He didn't want to embarrass her, so instead he held a hand out to Robbie and hoped to hell Robbie would drop her hand, which he'd been holding for too damn long.

"Ross Braden." He couldn't help but size Robbie up. *Built. Probably works out. I've got a couple inches on him—Get your fucking hand off of my girlfriend.*

"Robbie Prather." He flashed a friendly smile and shifted his eyes back to Ross, finally dropping Elisabeth's hand.

Ross was quite sure his possessive hand on Elisabeth's back had registered, as it was still firmly in place.

"What are you doing here?" Elisabeth asked Robbie.

His eyes shifted back to Elisabeth. "I came to see you."

Chapter Twenty-One

ROSS HAD ABOUT three seconds to make the toughest decision of his life. Should he walk away and give them privacy, opening the door for Robbie to use whatever tactics he might have on tap to get Elisabeth back in his arms, or should he remain where he was, effectively acting as a barrier between Robbie and Elisabeth? He trusted her. Christ, he trusted the hell out of her, and he loved her.

"I'll give you guys some privacy." Ross fought the urge to kiss Elisabeth, further staking claim, and instead he squeezed her hand.

"I...um...." Her eyes grew heavy with an unspoken apology.

"It's okay. Text me when you're done. Do you need me to go run your booth?" *Christ, what the fuck am I doing?*

"The girls are handling it."

Ross nodded, then held a hand out to Robbie.

"Nice to meet you, Robbie. Welcome to Trusty."

Welcome to Trusty, my ass. How about you get the fuck out of Trusty? He walked away, ruing his mother for his goddamn good manners.

Less than a minute later, Luke and Wes were by his side, keeping pace with his fast steps.

"What the hell's going on?" Luke asked.

Ross stormed toward the demolition derby to see Jake, as promised. He needed something to distract him from wanting to turn around and end this nightmare right then.

"Ross, what the fuck?" Wes grabbed his arm.

Ross narrowed his eyes. "Don't."

Wes released him. "Why'd you leave them alone? Callie said Elisabeth fell apart when she got back to the booth, but she never even told her who that asshole was."

"Ex-boyfriend," he grumbled.

"And you left them alone?" Luke grabbed his arm this time, and Ross wrenched it away. "Dude, what are you thinking?"

Ross wanted to get as far away from where Robbie and Elisabeth were as he could, because the closer he was, the easier it would be to walk over and take a stand. Noise from the demolition derby filled the air as they neared the arena. Engines roared, tires squealed, and the crowds cheered.

Ross's mind screamed, *Go back!*

He stopped walking and met Luke's confused and angry stare. "I'm thinking that I trust her, and my standing there will not make her love me any more than she already does. I trust her, Luke. Don't you trust Daisy?"

"Hell yes, but I wouldn't trust some asshole with her."

"The guy's got a PhD. I highly doubt he's going to try anything inappropriate in the middle of a goddamn fair." Ross ran his hand through his hair and paced. Fuck, he hated this.

"So, what's your plan?" Wes crossed his arms over his chest.

Ross stewed. He didn't have a fucking plan.

"It's like throwing her to the wolves." Luke paced alongside Ross. "What if she needs you? What if he lays a hand on her?"

"Their relationship wasn't like that." Which was exactly why he was worried about what Robbie's showing up meant. "They had a good relationship."

"What are you, their advocate?" Wes asked.

"No, I'm not their fucking...Damn it, Wes. The guy's not some cretin, okay? He's an educated guy who treated her great. What the fuck do you want me to do? I love her, and I fucking trust her. There's no other option here. I don't even know what the guy wants, except that he came here to see her."

"What do you think he wants? He tracked her down from LA. How did he even do that?" Luke asked.

Ross slid him an angry stare. *How the hell did he track her down?* Had they been talking this whole time? No. No way.

"There's only one thing he would come all this way to do in person," Wes added.

Ross walked away and Wes yanked him back.

"Open your fucking eyes, Ross. If you love her, you can't leave it up to her to make the right choice." Wes held his challenging stare.

"That's exactly why I'm letting her make the decision. The right choice is whatever she decides, and if you don't know that, then you really are an idiot."

ROSS WALKED AWAY. He left us alone. What did that mean? She'd seen a flash of worry in his eyes, but it was fleeting, and when he'd shaken Robbie's hand, he'd greeted him nicely. What did *that* mean? Elisabeth felt paralyzed, though she wasn't. Her body was trembling. Her insides were on fire, and not in a good way.

"Is there someplace we can go to talk?" Robbie asked.

"Robbie, *what* are you doing here? I haven't heard from you in a year, and suddenly you show up after I move hundreds of miles away? How did you find me?" She hadn't expected the anger that simmered inside her, but damn it, this was *her* town, not his. It wasn't even her town yet, but it was definitely more hers than his.

"I needed to see you, and I knew that if I called, you wouldn't see me. Elisabeth, can we please go someplace to talk? Someplace private?" He touched her upper arm.

Emily jogged over to them with a stern look in her eyes. Robbie dropped his hand, and she looked between them. "Elisabeth, are you okay?"

"Yeah. We're fine." Elisabeth was surprised at her knee-jerk reaction to protect Robbie. Why was she protecting him? Where did her anger go? She wasn't able to hold on to it. Then again, she'd never been able to with Robbie. They hadn't ever had a combative relationship. Their relationship had been comfortable, which was in stark contrast to the relationship she had with Ross. They were so much more than *comfortable*. With Ross she could barely contain her feelings each time she saw him, or the way he made her breathing hitch and her heart race. She wanted to crawl beneath Ross's skin, breathe the same air he did, feel his pain and his joy. She'd never wanted anything even close with Robbie.

Emily stared at Robbie. "You sure?"

"Yes. Really." Elisabeth saw Daisy heading in their direction. *Oh God.* "I'll be back at the booth in a few minutes."

Daisy waited a few feet away. Elisabeth felt the heat of fresh tears over their support.

"Okay." Emily walked away, keeping a threatening stare locked on Robbie until she ran into some guy and had to watch where she was going.

"Sorry," Elisabeth said to Robbie.

Robbie shook his head. "What do they think I'm going to do, kidnap you?"

Elisabeth sank to the grass. She didn't hate Robbie, and she wasn't afraid of him. She was just overwhelmed and confused. She'd cried herself to sleep for weeks after they broke up. She never thought she'd fall in love again, or would ever want to. She'd thought Robbie was *the one*. It took a long time for her to realize how wrong she'd been. And now, with Ross, she realized for sure just how wrong she'd been.

"Robbie, how did you find me?"

He sat beside her and rested his elbows on his knees. He still smelled like football. That was the only thing she could liken his scent to, and it made no sense. It was a leathery scent that reminded her of the weeks when fall was turning to winter, cool and colorful. *Oh God*, she'd forgotten that imagery.

"It wasn't hard. Your mom always did like me." He smiled, bringing back a rush of memories.

In addition to his being a nice guy, he came from the type of family her mother lived to be part of. His father was a world-renowned director, his sisters were A-list actresses, and Robbie was headed in the direction of all the things her mother took stock in—a strong education, wealth, and notoriety. None of that had mattered to Elisabeth. It was his kindness that she'd been attracted to. His desire to help others, and the way he cherished his family.

On the opposite end of the spectrum, Aunt Cora had very strong feelings about love and relationships, and although she never thrust her feelings on Elisabeth, she'd simply told Elisabeth that she didn't think Robbie was her forever love, because he wasn't in the place her heart knew he should be, and she wasn't sure his heart was as pure as Elisabeth thought. Aunt Cora had said that sight unseen, based solely on their conversations. Aunt Cora had also shared a few pearls of wisdom, and in the year since Elisabeth and

Robbie broke up, she'd come to realize that Aunt Cora was right. It became clear that his efforts were a means to an end. He was a nice guy, there was no doubt about that, but much of his reaching out to the community was an effort to lobby for his future, secure his name in their minds, rather than humanitarian outreach from the heart.

"I missed you." His sharp blue eyes softened, but he didn't give her time to react before he spoke again, and it was probably a good thing, because she didn't know how she felt about him missing her. "This reminds me of CaliFest. Remember when we went?"

She smiled at the memory. It was a good one, and it would have been hard to pretend otherwise. Being with Robbie was like being with an old friend. Everything about him was familiar and comfortable, which was nice after being met with such resistance from the people in Trusty. The anger that had snaked into her chest left as quickly as it had appeared.

"Remember how we danced on the lawn with all those sweaty people for like fifteen hours? God, did we stink afterward." She laughed, and felt guilty for it, knowing that Ross had given them this time so graciously, when she knew he must be worried sick. At first she'd wondered what it meant that he left them alone, but now, after having a moment to reflect, she realized that Ross was granting her the space she needed to deal with her past, not walking away from their relationship. How could she have thought otherwise? It was Ross's nature to put her comfort before his own.

Robbie turned and faced her. His jaw was lightly peppered with stubble, and his eyes darkened, grew more serious.

"I don't have much time, Robbie. I have to get back to my booth." She was still waiting to hear what else he wanted.

"I'm here for the night, and I'll be leaving first thing tomorrow morning." He reached into his shirt pocket. "This is where I'm staying."

"Trusty Lodge." It was at the other end of town, near the park.

"I'll say my piece; then I'll leave, and the ball will be in your court."

Gulp.

"After we broke up, I immersed myself in completing my PhD, as you know, and, well, things were never the same after that, Elisabeth."

Ross would have called me Lis.

He turned and looked her in the eye. "Elisabeth, I compare every woman I date to you, every relationship to what we had."

"Robbie—"

"Let me finish, please." He pressed his lips together, then smiled again. "I was stupid to think I had to have a degree in hand before we could take things to the next level."

"Robbie—"

"I want you back, Elisabeth. I want you to come back to Los Angeles with me, start a family. You always said you wanted a big family. I want that, too. You know that." Robbie searched her eyes.

That had been exactly what she wanted, and a year ago she might have gone wherever he asked her to.

"Robbie, don't interrupt me," she said quickly. "You needed your degree, and I understood that. I was happy that you went after what you needed in your life. But I have, too. I need to be here, and you've always known that I wanted to come back here."

He furrowed his brow. "I know. I think we can make it work."

What? This tripped her up for a minute. Did he really think they'd fall back into their old relationship? She glimpsed the line of people and pets by her booth.

She looked at Robbie's bright, hopeful eyes, and she rose to her feet. He did, too, and reached for her hand again.

"Elisabeth, just tell me you'll think about it."

"Robbie, I'm sorry you came all this way. I'm with Ross now, and I'm happy." She began walking toward her booth.

"I'll be at the hotel until tomorrow morning. Just think about it. That's all I'm asking."

That's all? Like it was nothing?

She caught sight of Daisy waving her hands over her head from within the booth, and when she glanced over, Daisy pointed to Wren Wynchel, standing at the booth with a frustrated look in her eyes, Barney and another of the dogs tugging at their leashes beside her.

"I've got to go."

Elisabeth took a few steps away and sensed Robbie staring after her. She knew she was hurting him, and she hated that. It wasn't in her nature to hurt someone else, especially someone she once cared for.

If only walking away was as easy as boxing up their past and stowing it away had been.

Chapter Twenty-Two

ROSS COULD HARDLY concentrate on Jake pulling off one life-threatening stunt after another. He checked his cell for the hundredth time that hour. Still no text from Elisabeth.

"Sun's going down. Why don't you go find her?" Wes suggested. "I can call Callie and see if she's back at her booth."

"No. She'll text when she can. No need to get everyone involved."

Wes arched a brow. "Everyone's already involved."

Ross's phone vibrated and his pulse sped up with hope that it was Elisabeth. It wasn't. It was one of his clients.

"Was it her?" Wes asked.

"No. Mr. Ricker. Problem calving. I've got to go check it out." Ross headed for the parking lot—the opposite direction of where he wanted to go. "Wes,

Elisabeth will need help taking down her booth."

"I'm on it, and, bro, don't worry. She loves you, man. We know that. I'll make sure she's taken care of. Go help the cow."

Ross was halfway across the fairgrounds when he heard Margie Holmes's voice. He'd seen her outside of the diner so rarely that it took him a minute to put the voice together with Margie without her waitress uniform.

"Is that one of my favorite Bradens?" Margie caught up to him.

"Hey, Margie. Sorry, I'm in a hurry." He continued walking at a fast pace, not the least bit interested in small talk, worried about the cow and its calf, and going crazy over Elisabeth.

"Uh-oh. I guess it's true, then."

"What?"

"That the guy who was asking about Elisabeth this morning at the diner and who we saw sitting with her in the grass was her ex-boyfriend." She made a *tsk* sound and shook her head.

Sitting with her in the grass?

"What is it about this town?" Ross picked up his pace.

"We care about you, Ross. It's a shame. We were all just starting to really like her."

Ross stopped cold and closed his eyes to reel in his anger. "Margie, do me a favor. Don't add legs to this gossip, okay? Yes, he was her ex-boyfriend. *Ex* being the operative word. She's with me, and that's all there is to it."

Margie tilted her head and her eyes filled with compassion. "I've known you since you were just a boy, and you've always seen the best in people. It's one of your strongest traits."

What the hell is that supposed to mean?

Margie stepped away. "I'd better go find Alice. We came together, but she went to get a funnel cake. That's something I can afford to skip." She patted her hip and walked away in the direction of the snack pavilion.

He wasn't crazy about interrupting Elisabeth if she was still with Robbie, but he wanted to let her know where he was going to be for the next few hours in case she needed him while he was at the Rickers' farm. There was no way he could answer his cell phone while dealing with a difficult calving. He texted her on his way to the farm. When she didn't text back, he called her. He didn't want to take a chance of her calling while he was busy and misinterpreting why he didn't answer his phone, especially after he'd left her and Robbie alone.

"Ross." She sounded breathless.

"Hey, babe. I'm on my way to the Rickers' farm. So I'll be late tonight. Are you okay?" *Are we still together?*

"Yeah. Just had a slew of people to take care of at the booth."

"You're back at the booth?" Thank God. Then she couldn't have been too hung up on Robbie.

"Yes. Sorry. I walked away from Robbie and right into a barrage of customers. I can't believe it, but Wren showed up with two of her dogs. I have about seven people waiting now, including two guys who said they were suppliers for your clinic, and the fair closes soon, so I can't stay on long, but I really am sorry about Robbie." She was talking fast. He knew she couldn't discuss this in front of customers.

"We'll talk tonight. Go ahead and take care of your customers." Relief swept through him. She was still his Lissa. *Thank God.* "I'll come by when I'm done, and I arranged for Wes to help you break down the booth."

"I know. Callie told me right before you called. Thank you. I'm sorry. I want to talk, but I've got to run."

"Okay." He smiled to himself, picturing her beautiful face conflicted between staying on the phone and helping the people who were waiting for her. "Love you, Lis."

His words met dead airwaves. She'd already ended the call. Even though he knew it was just because she was busy at her booth with a line of people waiting for her, he couldn't help but feel disappointed.

Ross was at the Ricker farm until well after dark. The calving cow had grown tired with her efforts and Ross worried she'd given up. When the calf finally made an appearance, it was with only one leg showing.

Ross knew he had to move quickly. It was a tricky and uncomfortable process for mother, calf, and for Ross, to reach inside the cow and manipulate the calf's leg so the calf could come out without breaking the appendage. After fifteen minutes of patient manipulation, he safely delivered the sweet little calf.

He was relieved when the exhausted mother cow began cleaning off the calf. His muscles were corded tight across his neck and back. The exhausted mother took her tongue to the calf and cleaned the membrane from her slick body. This element of bonding was one of the most beautiful things Ross witnessed in his profession, and it tugged at his heartstrings every time. Despite the blood and fluid, the mother's innate desire to nurture her calf was a beautiful and amazing sight. He waited for both mother and baby to stand, and for the baby to begin to nurse, and for the first time, watching these moments, spurred thoughts in him about his own future. About having children with Elisabeth someday and watching her take their baby to her breast.

Once he was certain the baby was nursing well, he knew they were in the clear and breathed a much-needed sigh of relief.

He needed to go home and shower before seeing Elisabeth, though he wanted nothing more than to go to her house, take her in his arms—and never let her go. He called her, and his call went to voicemail after the third ring. He left a message.

"Hey, babe. I'm heading home to shower and then I'll come over with the boys. Sorry it's so late. Miss you."

He called Wes on his way home.

"Hey, bro. How's the calf?" Wes sounded like he was in a good mood.

"Fine. Long night, but mother and calf are both fine. Just wanted to thank you for helping Lis tonight.

Sorry to leave you hanging." He could always count on his brothers, just as they could always count on him.

"No worries. Besides, I owed you for the day I called and had you drop everything to come take the quills out of Sweets, remember?"

Ross laughed under his breath. "That's a day I'll never forget. That was the day I found out about you and Callie. I remember thinking that you'd been roped and I'd never be in that position." He shook his head as he pulled into his driveway.

"Yeah, I remember that look in your eyes, and now?"

He pictured the smirk on Wes's face and was tempted to give him a smart-ass answer, but when Elisabeth's beautiful face and red-rimmed eyes flashed in his mind, he couldn't muster the lie.

"Honestly, Wes. I can't imagine my life without her."

THE FIRST THING Elisabeth did when she got home was call her mother and give her hell for telling Robbie where she was. After an uncomfortable, albeit necessary, conversation, she ended the call, then contemplated calling Robbie for so long that she thought she was going to lose her mind if she didn't just do it. She didn't even know why he'd given her the stupid card for the lodge. She had his cell phone number in her phone. Some couples were venomous when they broke up. She and Robbie hadn't been like that. They'd dated for more than a year, and Elisabeth had been happy. For the first time in all the years that she'd been craving returning to Trusty, she thought that her hopes and dreams must have been wrong. That there wasn't really a stronger love. She thought that she'd somehow believed in a myth and that what she and Robbie had was what relationships were. Even-keeled and happy to see each other. And although she had longed to live in Trusty, and she longed for a stronger, deeper love, she was loyal to Robbie and accepted their relationship as her fate. Then one night when she'd least expected it, Robbie came over and they watched a little television, and the next thing she knew, Robbie was telling her that he needed to focus on getting his PhD. And just like that, as if it were as simple as changing his clothes, he'd ended the relationship. There was no yelling, and that night, there were no tears. The tears came later. The yelling never did.

Fate—*the real fate*—had played its hand. And she'd never again doubted fate, love, or that she'd find both in Trusty. And now it was time to deal with fate head-on.

She went to the closet and slid the box out. She pushed her aunt's letters to the side, pausing briefly to glance at them one more time, and withdrew Robbie's T-shirt and the framed photograph of them. She ran her fingers over the picture and could hardly believe he was there in Trusty. That he'd come all that way to try to win her back.

She closed the box and pushed it back into the closet, then leaned her back against the closet door as she called his number. He answered on the first ring.

"You called." He sounded so hopeful, it tugged at her heart.

"Yeah. Can you come over so we can talk?" She glanced at his T-shirt, folded neatly on the couch beside the framed photograph of the two of them.

"Sure. Just give me directions and I'll be there as soon as I can."

She gave him directions and then sat on the couch and buried her face in her hands. She'd told Emily, Callie, and Daisy about Robbie and that she wasn't interested in getting back together with him. They'd rallied around her, offering to spend the evening with her and to take her out for a cocktail. She'd had enough cocktails for a while. All she wanted was the life she'd always dreamed of, with the man she adored.

Fifteen minutes later there was a knock at the door, and she froze in the middle of the living room. Her legs wouldn't move. Her heart thundered against her ribs.

I can do this.

She took a deep breath and blew it out slowly, then breathed deeply several more times before answering the door with the shirt and frame clutched to her chest. Robbie stood before her with a kind smile and a soft gaze. He was the man she'd thought she wanted for a long time, and now here he was. Ready, willing, and offering to make things work. One of Aunt Cora's pearls of wisdom flashed through her mind. *You'll know when you let the one that matters get away, because when you look into his eyes that last time, your heart falls to your feet and you can barely breathe.*

She stepped out on the front porch and without a word, sat down on the top step. Robbie sat beside her, and she felt her heart squeeze. *That's Ross's seat.*

"I'm glad you called." Robbie leaned his elbows on his knees in the familiar way he had and clasped his hands together. "I know it took you by surprise when I showed up."

"Yes, it did." He was so sure, effortlessly comfortable. It would be easy to fall into that friendship again, which, she realized again, was exactly what they'd had. A really great friendship that had found its way into the bedroom. They could have been called friends with benefits, although she hadn't seen it that way at the time. Only since being with Ross did she understand how deeply her heart was capable of loving, how alive her body was capable of feeling.

Robbie reached for her hand, and she let him take it. There was no need to fight the friendly notion. She was ready to say her piece, and then, like the last time they'd ended things, he'd walk away, seemingly unperturbed. And unlike last time, she'd go back to Ross.

Passion. That's what was missing in Robbie. Passion for life, for others, for someone he loved. Robbie was a nice guy, a good man even, but not a passionate man. His passion was fleeting, based on what it would earn him in his career, or based on what was expected of him. Ross had passion for everything he did and for those he loved. Ross's passion was as real and true as the air that he breathed.

Robbie looked into her eyes with another hopeful

gaze. "Elisabeth, I want to be with you. Please give me another chance."

"Robbie." Her chest tightened and her throat swelled with emotion. This was more difficult than she'd imagined it would be. Not for what she had to say, but for hurting him. She forced herself to remember that he'd hurt her, and to harness that hurt and use it to move forward. But as she looked into his magnetic blue eyes, it wasn't hurt she felt. It was gratitude. If he hadn't set her free, she never would have met Ross, and Ross was her destiny. She couldn't drum up anger or resentment toward Robbie. Their breakup, like everything else in Elisabeth's life—even this uncomfortable night—was meant to be.

"Robbie, there will always be a part of me that loves you for the friendship we've shared, but that's what it was. A very strong, deep, caring friendship. I never quite made it over the edge from comfortable to lose-myself-in-you love." She paused, letting her admission sink in—for both of them. "I have that now. With Ross. I look at him and everything in my world is brighter, and somehow, it also falls away. There's only the two of us. I know you don't want to hear this, Robbie, but Ross is my forever love. He's the man I want to spend my life with."

He pressed his lips together, and she watched his Adam's apple move up, then slide down as he swallowed that heavy pill of honesty. She set the framed photograph and shirt in his lap.

"These are good memories, but they're your memories, Robbie. I cried them away long ago, and I have new memories to make. You're a good man, and you'll find the right woman for you. I know you will." She rose to her feet, and he rose with her.

"Elisabeth, I came all this way. Doesn't that mean anything to you? I'm moving in all the right directions. You can have anything you want, anything you need. You can have a house here and a house in LA." His brows knitted together, and the pleading in his voice was so foreign that it sounded surreal.

As bad as she felt being the cause of his hurt, it also made her stronger. There wasn't an iota of doubt in her mind or in her heart about the man she wanted to be with. The man she was meant to be with.

"I have everything I want right here, and he's going to be here soon."

Robbie nodded, defeat in his eyes. "You always said your heart was in Trusty. I just never imagined that I couldn't find my way back into it. I took that for granted."

Yeah, you did. She still didn't feel resentment, not even knowing that he'd taken her love for granted back then or now. The love she had for Ross was bubbling up inside of her, filling all the spaces that might have otherwise been reserved for those harsher feelings toward Robbie. It softened her heart and made it strong at the same time, and when she reached up to give Robbie a final goodbye hug, it was that love for Ross that brought a sigh.

ROSS SETTLED THE dogs into the cab of the truck and drove to Elisabeth's. Knight must have recognized the slowing of the truck and the view of Elisabeth's house from the road. He panted with anticipation. The truck's headlights flashed on a BMW in the driveway. Ross slowed to nearly a stop instead of turning in. His eyes locked on Elisabeth encircled in Robbie's arms, illuminated by the porch light. Jealousy and anger clawed at him, dragging deep and fast along every nerve in his body. He narrowed his eyes, following the line of Robbie's thick arms around Elisabeth's waist. Trout's words came rushing back to him. *You gotta let go of what you love so you can move forward knowing that despite it all, you helped someone else live the life they were meant to live.*

Fuck. Was she meant to be with Robbie? Sarge barked out the window, startling Ross out of his stupor. He lead-footed the gas and took off, cursing under his breath.

At home, he slammed the truck into park and stalked across the yard. The dogs followed on his heels. What the fuck was going on? He thought he knew Elisabeth so well. He thought he'd heard the strength of their relationship in her voice when he'd called. Then why the hell was she draped all over that asshole?

His cell vibrated and he knew without looking that it was her, but if he took it from his pocket, he feared he'd hurl the damn thing across the yard. How could he have been so wrong? How could every emotion he felt coming from her have been a lie?

No. Fucking. Way.

He stalked back toward his truck. Like hell if he

was going to let this whole thing fall apart, regardless of what he'd told Wes about it being her decision. He stopped halfway to the car, realizing this *was* her decision.

Fuck.

Fuck.

Fuck.

The dogs watched in limbo as he took a step forward, then back, then toward the truck again.

Aw, hell. He loved her and that was that. Fuck what Trout said. Fuck what he told Wes. He opened the passenger door of the truck.

"In," he commanded.

The dogs jumped inside. "Down." Knight lay flat along the floor. Ranger and Sarge lay on the bench seat. He needed a goddamn bigger truck.

The truck roared to life, and he gunned the engine around the circular drive—then slammed on his brakes at the sight of approaching headlights. *Christ Almighty. What now?*

Elisabeth's car came into view. He cut the engine again as she screeched to a stop and raced toward the truck. Her long hair flowed behind her, and she looked goddamn beautiful, stealing the starch from his gut. He climbed from the truck. The dogs barreled toward Elisabeth, blocking her way as they lifted off their front legs, vying for her attention, noses high, whining loudly.

"Ross!"

He heard tears in her voice and he closed the distance between them and swept her into his arms.

"Lissa. I can't play games. Not with you. You're either with me or you're not."

"I'm with you, Rossie. When I saw you leave, my heart fell to my feet. It fell, Ross, just like Aunt Cora said it would." Her legs dangled above the ground; her damp eyes were full of so much emotion Ross's eyes grew damp, too. "Now I can breathe again."

Having no idea of what the hell she meant, he sealed his lips over hers, and the day's confusion and the evening's anger fell away. She was in his arms, and that's all that mattered.

"Lissa," he whispered against her lips. "I'll stand by you and support you in everything you do, but I can't be expected to stand by while you're in the arms of another man. I wanted to tear his head off."

She kissed him again, then drew back and smiled. "Maybe I was wrong and you're a killer after all." She touched her forehead to his. "I was saying goodbye. For good. There's only you and me, Ross." She glanced down at the feel of Knight's tongue on her leg. "And the boys. And the pigs. And Dolly, and the goats, but that's it. Oh, and Rocky, but that's it. I promise."

"For now." He pressed his lips to hers. "But I'm not taking any chances. One day soon I'm going to put a ring on your finger, and we'll have babies to add to that list. As many as you want."

His words brought her legs around his middle and fresh tears to her eyes. For the first time in his life, tears didn't render him befuddled. They confirmed everything he'd known since their very first date.

With a tender kiss, he carried her inside.

Chapter Twenty-Three

SATURDAY MORNING FOUND Ross and Elisabeth on the back deck of Ross's house, tangled together like spiders beneath a blanket. They'd been snuggled together on the lounge chair since five thirty, when Storm woke up to the sounds of their lovemaking. Storm had whined to go outside, and he'd woken the other dogs. Ross had bundled a blanket under his arm and suggested they watch the sunrise from the deck. Rocky called from the other side of the trees. The dogs lifted their heads in response. Swallows sang their morning melody as dawn rose over the pasture.

Elisabeth opened her eyes and breathed deeply. "Add the chickens to my list of animals that are part of our lives."

He squeezed her tighter.

"We should really get going," she said softly against his neck. "I want to make muffins before we leave for your mom's and I have to feed the animals."

"One more minute?" His voice was groggy, thick with the familiar sound of desire as his hand traveled down her bare hip.

She closed her eyes and settled in for another few minutes.

"Your heart is beating faster. Is that a signal that you're getting anxious about being late and we should get up?" Ross opened his eyes and kissed her. "Or is it a signal that you can't resist me for another second and I should take you right here and right now?"

"God, whatever you do, please don't do *that*." Jake came around the side of the house, wearing the same clothes he'd had on last night and looking like he hadn't slept a wink.

"What the hell are you doing here?" Ross drew the blanket up and tucked it beneath Elisabeth's arms. She loved that he took care of her before sitting up and facing his brother with a frustrated sigh. "What time is it?"

"Half-past a monkey's ass and time for you to get your scrawny ass up." Jake flopped into a chair and sighed. "Elisabeth, right? Nice to meet you."

"Hi." *Oh. My. God. I'm naked.*

"I might get up if I had a stitch of clothing on." Ross's lips spread into a smile.

"Shit." Jake went inside mumbling about coffee. Elisabeth heard him take the stairs two at a time, then bound back down and return with a pair of Ross's shorts. He tossed them at him, and Ross caught them in one hand. "I guess this means the ex is out of the picture?"

Elisabeth felt her cheeks flush. "He was never in the picture."

"There was good money being bet about the outcome of that," Jake said. "Good thing I bet on the right side of the fence."

"Christ." Ross pulled Elisabeth against his side and kissed her temple. "Where have you been all night?"

Jake's lips quirked up. "You want all the juicy details?"

"Oh, hell no."

"Tate had somewhere to be today, so he asked me to help you with your...*thing*," Jake said.

"My *thing*?" Ross wrinkled his forehead.

"Something he was supposed to bring to Mom's this morning? I brought it here. I figured you guys would be asleep and it would be a nice surprise. It's up by the road. I didn't want to wake you, which is why I came creeping around your house."

"What thing?" Elisabeth was totally confused.

Ross stepped into his shorts and reached for her hand. He held the blanket tight against her body and slid Jake a look that could only be read as, *Don't even think about looking at my girlfriend's naked body.* That look was new, and she loved it.

"I had a little something fixed up for you," Ross explained.

"You did? Ross, you didn't have to do that."

He tucked her hair behind her ear. "It's barely a token of what you deserve for how hard you work."

"All this lovey-dovey stuff is cool and all, but do you mind if I make coffee?" Jake asked.

"I should get dressed anyway." Elisabeth gathered the blanket around her and hurried inside.

"Nice tat," Jake said as his eyes rolled down Elisabeth's back.

"Shut the fuck up." Ross kissed Elisabeth and pulled the blanket up higher on her back.

"Probably a good idea since we switched breakfast to your house, and everyone will be here any minute." Jake headed for the kitchen.

"What? Why? And how come nobody told me?" Ross brought the dogs in and closed the door, then followed Elisabeth and Jake into the kitchen.

"It wasn't planned. I texted Em to see if I could crash at her place for a few hours so I didn't wake Mom, and she said Mom's up because she was baking for the fair. She asked me if I did...*the thing*...and when I said I was about to, she said she'd get everyone and meet here." Jake shrugged.

"At six in the morning?"

"Well, I told them to come closer to six thirty in case you weren't here and I had to, I don't know, break into Elisabeth's or something because you didn't hear me knock at the door. I needed a little leeway."

"You're unbelievable." Ross turned to Elisabeth. "I guess you should shower, babe. I'll be up in a sec."

On her way upstairs, she heard Jake's voice. "Bro, go with her. I'm a big boy."

She stood on the stairs listening to them for a minute. Maybe she should be bothered by Jake showing up unannounced at the crack of dawn, but Elisabeth grew up without brothers and sisters, and with a mother who was more interested in being pampered than taking part in family-oriented activities. She loved the way Ross and his brothers pitched in and took care of one another and helped out with those they loved. She even enjoyed their gruff brotherly banter. Jake's showing up just proved how close they were.

By seven o'clock there was so much testosterone in the house that Elisabeth, Daisy, Callie, Emily, and Catherine escaped to the back deck. Knight lay at Elisabeth's feet as the girls sipped coffee and talked. It was a brisk, sunny morning. The birds chirped, and the dogs played with Sweets in the yard.

"I heard Jake was looking for Fiona last night," Emily said just above a whisper.

"Oh, no." Catherine leaned in closer. "Is that why he didn't come home last night?"

"No, he was with someone else," Emily said. "But I know he was looking for her because I stopped at the diner this morning and Margie asked me if Jake caught up with Fiona."

"Well, from what I've heard from Luke, she would have been just another conquest if he had, even if she was his long-lost love. Luke seems to think Jake will never find that part of himself again. That he'll never allow himself to fall in love again," Daisy said. "So it's probably a good thing. Rumors around here. Sheesh. Can you imagine?"

"I don't know. Braden love runs deep, and he never did get over her," Emily said.

Silence settled in around them, and Elisabeth tried

to break the tension.

"So, who was your money on last night? Ross or...?" Elisabeth asked Emily.

"What money?" Emily furrowed her brow, but Elisabeth saw the way her fingers tightened on her coffee mug.

"Mine was on you and Ross," Daisy answered.

"Mine, too," Callie said.

"I refused to feed into it," Catherine said. "But if I had, my money would have been on you and Ross."

"Oh, that money." Emily shrugged and shifted her eyes away.

Elisabeth gasped. "You thought I'd leave Ross? After I told you how I felt about him?"

"Actually, I bet double or nothing on you and Ross."

Elisabeth swatted her arm. "You...That was so unfair."

"If you're going to be in this family, you'd better grow thicker skin," Daisy said with a little nudge.

Luke and Jake came flying out the door. They were a tangle of arms and big, burly bodies as they pushed past Elisabeth, weaved around Daisy and Emily, and leaped off the deck. Jake tackled Luke as Wes ran out the doors, past Elisabeth and Daisy—stopping for half a second to kiss Callie—dove off the deck, and piled on. Ross walked leisurely out of the house and handed Elisabeth his coffee mug. He kissed her lips and sighed.

"It's that time, I suppose." Within seconds he was rolling around on the grass with his brothers as they wrestled and laughed and pinned one another down.

Callie turned her back and covered her eyes. "I can't watch. I'm always afraid someone's going to break a bone."

"That's what I'm here for," Daisy assured her. "My medical degree will be put to good use with these guys around."

Elisabeth watched Ross wrestle with Jake. They stopped, midtackle, and stared each other down. It lasted only a second or two, and then they were mangling each other once again. She smiled at them. Ross looked so happy, and she loved seeing this playful side of him.

"This is what family's all about." Elisabeth sipped Ross's coffee, happy as could be. She had a man she adored and she was surrounded by the nicest friends a girl could ever ask for.

"Okay, boys, time to stop." Catherine marched off the porch in a pair of blue capris and a white blousy shirt and stood over the pile of men, hands firmly planted on her hips.

All four men stopped cold and shared a knowing look. In the next breath, they had Catherine up in the air, her butt on Luke's and Wes's shoulders. The dogs barked at them.

"Put. Me. Down!" Catherine's smile was priceless.

Elisabeth couldn't imagine her mother ever looking so carefree and happy, and she felt sad. Not as much for herself as for her mother. She wished her mother were happier, but she knew that wasn't something she could do anything about. Happiness, she knew, came from within first; others only enlivened the feelings that were already present.

"To the driveway!" Emily hollered.

They carried Catherine out to the driveway, and when they set her on the ground, she hugged each one of them, then immediately swatted their backsides with a loving hand.

"I'm too old for that. I could have broken a hip," Catherine said through her laughter.

Daisy raised her hand. "That's what I'm here for."

Ross laced his fingers in Elisabeth's and pressed a kiss to them.

"My money was on us, too." Ross reached into his pocket and pulled out her aunt's key chain.

She looked at the keys, then back up at Ross. "I don't understand."

"Come on." He led her down the driveway, and like the Pied Piper leading mice, the others followed along.

"I never got rid of the van. I knew how much it meant to you, and my intention was just to fix it up for your pie deliveries, but then you started the pet business." He shrugged and pointed behind the berm of trees.

There, on the other side of the trees, sat her aunt's van, repainted bright pink. It had bold black lettering on the side that read, TRUSTY PIES & PET PAMPERING, along with a picture of a dog—complete with bows on her collar—sitting on its hind legs, holding a pie in one paw.

"That's why I was with Tate. Inside, there's a refrigeration unit for your pies and cabinets for your grooming supplies." Emily pressed her lips together and lifted her brows at Daisy and Callie. "Not dating, just coordinating. I cannot wait to go to Italy."

Elisabeth covered her mouth as tears streamed down her cheeks. "You did this for me?"

"I'd do anything for you." Ross took her in a passionate kiss that had all the girls *aww*ing, and Elisabeth melting in his arms. Exactly where she was meant to be.

The End

Please enjoy a preview of the next
Love in Bloom novel

Dreaming of Love

The Bradens

Love in Bloom Series

Melissa Foster

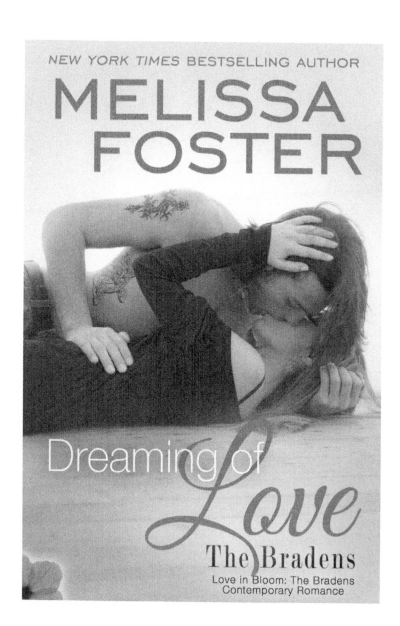

NEW YORK TIMES BESTSELLING AUTHOR

MELISSA FOSTER

Dreaming of Love

The Bradens

Love in Bloom: The Bradens
Contemporary Romance

Chapter One

LUSH. VERDANT. HILLY...Amazing. Emily stood on the covered balcony of the villa where she'd rented a room just outside of Florence, Italy, overlooking rolling countryside and the spectacular city below. The sun was kissing the last light of day goodbye, leaving chilled air in its wake. She sighed at the magnificent view, wrapped her arms around her body, and gave herself a big hug. She couldn't believe she was finally here, staying at the villa that her favorite architect, Gabriela Bocelli, built.

Gabriela Bocelli wasn't a very well-known architect, but her designs exuded simplicity and grace, which Emily had admired ever since she'd first come across this villa during her architecture studies. That felt like a hundred years ago. She'd dreamed of visiting Tuscany throughout school, but in the years since she'd been too busy building her architecture business, which specialized in passive house design, to take time off. If it weren't for one of her older brothers, she might still be back in Trusty, Colorado, dreaming of Tuscany instead of standing on this loggia losing her breath to the hilly terrain below.

She pulled her cell phone from the back pocket of her jeans and texted Wes.

You're the best brother EVER! So happy to be here. Thank you! Xox.

Emily had five brothers, each of whom had hounded her about her safety while she was traveling. Or really, *whenever* they didn't have their eyes on her. Pierce, her eldest brother, had wanted to use his own phone plan to buy her a second cell phone with international access. *Just in case.* She'd put her foot down. At thirty-one years old, she could handle a ten-day trip without needing her brothers to rescue her. It wasn't like she ever needed saving, but her brothers had a thing about scrutinizing every man who came near her. Yet another reason why she didn't date very often.

Still, she was glad they cared, because she adored each and every one of their overprotective asses.

Adelina Ambrosi appeared at the entrance to the balcony with a slightly less energetic smile than had been present throughout the day. Adelina had run the resort villa with her husband, Marcello, for more than twenty years. She was a short, stout woman with a friendly smile, eyes as blue-gray as a winter's storm, and wiry gray hair that was currently pinned up in a messy bun. She must have mastered the art of walking quietly to keep from disturbing the guests.

"Good evening, Emily." Adelina brushed lint from the curtains hanging beside the glass doors. Emily was glad they loved the property as much as she did. They rented out only two rooms of the six-bedroom villa in order to always have space available for family and friends. The villa was a home to them, not just a resort or a business, as was evident in the warm guest rooms.

"Good evening, Adelina. Any news on Serafina's husband?"

Serafina was Adelina and Marcello's daughter. She and her eight-month-old son had been living in the States when her husband, Dante, a United States Marine, had gone missing in Afghanistan while out on tour almost three months ago. Adelina had told Emily that she'd begged Serafina to come home and let her take care of her and baby Luca until her husband returned—and Adelina was adamant that he *would* return. Emily, on the other hand, wasn't quite so sure.

"Not yet, but I have faith." Adelina lowered her eyes, and with a friendly nod, she disappeared down the hall in the direction of her bedroom.

Emily turned back toward the evening sky, sending a silent prayer that Serafina's husband would return unharmed.

"It's a beautiful view, isn't it?"

The rich, deep voice sent a shiver down Emily's spine. She turned, and—*holy smokes.* Standing before her was more than six feet of deeply tanned, deliciously muscled male. His hair was the color of warm mocha and spilled over his eyes, hanging just an inch above the collar of his tight black T-shirt. She opened her mouth to greet him, but her mouth went dry and no words came. She reached for the stone rail of the archway she'd been gazing through and managed a smile.

His full lips quirked up, filling his deep brown eyes with amusement as he stepped closer.

"The view," he repeated as his eyes swept over her, causing her insides to do a nervous dance. The amusement in his eyes gave way to something dark and sensual.

It had been so long since Emily had seen that look directed at her that it took her by surprise. She cleared her throat and reluctantly dragged her gaze back to the view below, which paled in comparison to the one right next to her. The one who brought with him the scent of something hot and sexual.

Alluring.

How delicious are your lips?

Holy crap. Get a grip. It must be the Italian air or the evening sky that had her heart racing like she'd just run a marathon.

Or the fact that I haven't had sex in...

"Awestruck. I hear Italy has that effect on people." He leaned his forearms on the thick stone rail and bent over, clasping his large hands together.

"Yeah, right. Italy." Emily's eyes widened at the sarcasm in her voice. She clenched her mouth shut. She hadn't meant to say that out loud. He probably had this crazy effect on all women, and here she was gushing over him. She didn't gush. *Ever.* What the hell?

He cocked his head to the side and smiled up at

her. Emily drank in his slightly wide-set nose, the sexy peppering of whiskers along his square jawline, and the spark of playfulness in his eyes. A low laugh rumbled from his chest as he arched a brow.

Oh God. She felt her chest and face flush with heat and crossed her arms. A barrier between them. Yes, that's what she needed, since apparently she couldn't control her own freaking hormones.

"I'm sorry. I just got in this evening and it was a long trip. Eye fatigue." *Eye fatigue?* She held her breath, hoping he'd pretend, as she was, that that was the real reason she was ogling him.

"I just arrived myself." He held a hand out. "Dae Bray. Nice to meet you."

Emily felt the tension in her neck ease as he accepted her explanation. "Emily Braden. Day? That's an interesting name." She shook his strong, warm hand, and he held hers a beat too long, bringing that tension right back to her body—and an entirely different type of tension to her lower belly.

"Maybe I'm an interesting guy. Dae. D A E," he said, as if he had to spell it often, which she imagined he did. "Is this your first time in Tuscany?"

How could he be so casual, speak so easily, when her heart was doing flips in her chest? He didn't have an ounce of tension anywhere in his body. He was all ease and comfort, his body moving fluidly as he shifted his position and leaned his sexy, low-slung-jeans-clad hip against the rail. When he crossed one ankle over the other and set his palms on the stone, his T-shirt clung to his wide chest, then followed his rippled abs in a sexy vee and disappeared beneath the waist of his jeans. Her eyes lingered there, desperately fighting to drop a little lower. It took all of her focus to ignore the heat spreading through her limbs and drag her eyes away.

"Yes." *Why does my voice sound breathy?* She drew her shoulders back and met his gaze, forcing a modicum of control into her voice. "How about you?"

He shook his head, and his hair fell in front of his eyes. Could he be any sexier? One quick flick of his chin sent his long, shiny hair off his face, giving her a brief look at his deep-set eyes and chiseled, rugged features. *Holy cow. Hold it together.*

"It's the first for me, too."

Emily's phone vibrated and Wes's name flashed on the screen. She reached for it and read Wes's message, desperately needing a distraction.

So glad. Be safe and have fun. You deserve it.

"Probably your husband wondering what you're doing talking to some dude instead of taking a romantic stroll through the vineyards with him." His eyes narrowed a hair, but that easy smile remained on his lips.

Emily met his gaze. "That would be a feat, considering I'm not married." Not that she wouldn't like to be. Recently, she'd watched four of her brothers fall head over heels in love. They hadn't even been looking for love, and there she was, waiting to love and be loved and trying to keep the green-eyed monster inside her at bay. She was happy for them. She really was. But she couldn't deny her desire to find that special someone who would cherish her for more than the Braden wealth. She'd come to accept that she wouldn't find that in her small hometown. She'd buried herself in building a successful business to fill those lonely hours.

"Well, in that case, would you care to join me for a glass of wine?"

Before Emily could answer, another text came through from Wes.

Not TOO much fun! I'd hate to have to come all the way to Tuscany to pound some guy for taking advantage of my little sister.

Emily laughed, taking comfort in Wes's overprotective nature. Somehow, it put her at ease. She slid her phone into her jeans pocket and smiled up at the gorgeous man beside her. She was a million miles from home in the most romantic place on earth. Why shouldn't she have *too much* fun? She wondered what Wes considered too much fun and decided that, knowing her brother, holding hands with a guy was too much fun for his little sister. Maybe, just maybe, it was her turn to have fun.

Feeling emboldened, and a little rebellious, she lifted her chin and gave her best narrow-eyed gaze, which she hoped looked seductive, but she was sure it fell short. She didn't have much practice at being a temptress. But a girl could try, couldn't she?

"Sure. That sounds great."

Dae pushed from the rail and reached for her hand. "Shall we?"

"Um..." Was that too familiar of a gesture? Had she

given him too good of a look?

"I'm harmless. Just ask my sisters. But I'm also affectionate, so it's a hand or an arm. Take your pick."

"You have sisters?" Why did that make him seem safer? He reached for her hand, and damn if their palms didn't fit together perfectly. His hand was warm and big, a little rough and calloused.

"Two. And two brothers. You?" He led her through the villa toward the kitchen. She was glad he didn't release her hand when they reached the high-ceilinged kitchen, which smelled of fresh-baked bread. He surveyed the bottles in the built-in wine rack that was artfully nestled into the wall, pulling out one bottle after another and scrutinizing the labels until he found one he approved of.

"Five brothers. Um...Are we allowed to just take a bottle of wine?" Emily looked around the pristine kitchen. Colorful bricks formed an arch over recessed ovens and cooktops. A copper kettle sat atop one burner, and on either side of the ovens were built-in pantries in deep mahogany.

"They said to make myself at home." Dae handed her a bottle, then led her past the large table that seated eight and an island equally as large. He reached into a glass cabinet on the far wall and retrieved two wineglasses.

He smiled a mischievous smile. "So...You're a rule follower?" He narrowed his eyes as he opened the bottle of wine.

A rule follower? Am I? She had no idea if she was or wasn't. She liked to joke and tease. Did that make her a rule breaker? Were there rules for thirtysomethings? A fleeting worry rose in her chest. What if he was a *major* rule breaker? What if he wanted her to do things she shouldn't? She was a Braden, and her family was very well respected, and no matter where she was, she had a reputation to uphold, which somehow made the whole situation a little more tempting.

"Emily?"

Oh no. What if—

His hands on her upper arms pulled her from her thoughts, which were quickly spiraling out of control.

"Emily. Relax." His hair curtained his eyes, but she caught a glimpse of his smile. "I was kidding."

Now I look like a boring Goody-Two shoes. She rolled her eyes—more at herself than at him. Wes's text must have subconsciously made her worry. *Or maybe I really am a Goody-Two shoes who can take banter but not rule breaking. Boring with a capital B.*

"Adelina told me to help myself to anything in the kitchen, including the wine. Day or night."

He snatched her hand again and led her out a heavy wooden door and across the lawn.

"I'm sorry, Dae. I didn't mean to seem like a buzzkill."

"It's okay. If you were my sister, I'd have hoped for that same careful reaction. You had the am-I-with-a-serial-killer look in your eyes." He glanced at her and smiled.

"Yikes. That's not very nice, is it?" She walked quickly in her heeled boots to keep up. Her eyes remained trained on the thick grass to keep from ogling Dae.

"I'm guessing that it has less to do with *nice* than to do with *safety*. Safety's always a good thing." He stopped short, and Emily bumped right into his side.

Their hips collided. Her hand instinctively rose to brace herself from falling, and the bottle of wine smacked against his chest, splashing wine on his T-shirt. He wrapped an arm around her back, bracing her against him.

"Oh my gosh. I'm so sorry." *Crap, crap, crap.* She swiped at the wine on his shirt as she tried to ignore how good his impressive muscles felt.

"I've been impaled by worse." He flashed that easy smile again, but his eyes darkened and filled with heat, and just like that, her knees weakened.

Damned knees. He tightened his grip on her. *Damned smart knees.*

Just when Emily was sure she'd stop breathing, he dropped his eyes to her boots. "Heels and grass don't mix."

She was still stuck on the feel of his arm around her and the quickening of her pulse.

"You okay?" he asked.

I don't know. "Yes. Fine. Yes."

He ran his thumb along her cheek, then licked a dash of wine that he'd wiped off with his thumb. "Mm. Good year."

Holy crap.

His eyes went smoky and dark. She liked smoky and dark. A lot.

"Let's sit. It's safer." He nodded toward his right.

Emily blinked away the crazy unfamiliar desire that had butterflies nesting in her belly and followed his eyes to an intimate stone patio built at the edge of the hill. Her eyes danced over the wisteria-laced trellis. Purple tendrils of flowers hung over the edges, and leaf-laden vines snaked up the columns.

"This is incredible." Tree branches reached like long, arthritic fingers from the far side of a path at the top of the hill to the wisteria, creating a natural archway. Rustic planters spilled over with lush flowers, lining a low stone wall that bordered the patio.

Holding the wine and the glasses, Dae crooked out his elbow. "Hold on tight. Wouldn't want you to stumble."

She had the strange desire to press her body against his and let him wrap his safe, strong arm around her. Instead, she slipped her hand into the crook of his elbow and wrapped it around his muscular forearm, wondering how a man could make her hot all over after only a few minutes.

DAE COULD PRACTICALLY see the gears turning in Emily's head, and even in her befuddled state, she was sexier than any woman he'd ever met. She was slender, with gentle curves accentuated by her designer jeans and the tight white V-neck she wore under an open black cardigan. He stole a glance at her profile as she took in the patio. She had a cute upturned nose, high cheekbones, and long hair the same dark color as his, which he'd like to feel brushing his bare chest. She wore nearly no makeup, and as his eyes lingered on the sweet bow of her lips, the word *stunning* sailed into his mind. He had a feeling that when Emily Braden wasn't caught off guard by an aggressive demolition expert who rarely gave people time to think things through, she was probably feisty as hell.

He'd felt her body tense when she'd run into him, and unstoppable heat had flared between them. She'd melted a little right there in his arms. *Melted.* That was the only way to describe the way the tension drained from her shoulders and back and brought all her soft curves against him. If he were the type of guy who was into casual sex, she'd be ripe for the taking. But Dae had left casual sex behind and had grown a conscience a few years back.

As he poured them each a glass of wine, he wondered who had texted her earlier and caused her to laugh.

Dae handed her a glass of wine and held it up in a toast. "To Tuscany."

Emily smiled as they clinked glasses, then took a sip of her wine. "Oh, that's really good. It's just what I needed."

Dae watched her as she forwent the long wooden bench and sat atop the wide table.

"I can see better from here," she explained. "I don't want to miss a second of this incredible view."

She could have no way of knowing that Dae almost always preferred to sit atop tables rather than on benches or chairs. Always had.

"A woman after my own heart. I always prefer tabletops to chairs." He sat beside her and rested his elbows on his knees. "So, Emily Braden, what brings you to Tuscany?"

"My brother gave me this trip as a gift for helping him arrange a special night for his girlfriend." She smiled as she spoke of her brother, and he liked that she seemed to like her family. Family was important to Dae. He'd found that he could tell a lot about the generosity and loyalty of a person by how they spoke of and treated their family.

"That's a hell of a gift." Her thigh brushed his, and when their eyes met and she didn't move hers away, he realized she'd done it on purpose, causing a stirring in his groin. *Down, boy.* Emily was just beginning to relax, and the last thing he wanted to do was to scare her off.

"Yes. It was. He knew I've been dying to see Tuscany, and this villa in particular. Gabriela Bocelli is one of my favorite architects. But if it had been left up to me, I'd never have made it here. Between work and my family, well, I'm not really good about taking time for myself." She finished her wine, and Dae refilled their glasses.

"Life's too short to miss out on the things you really want to do. I'm glad your brothers are looking out for you." Dae was a self-made man with enough money that he could buy all of his siblings trips to Tuscany, but while he and his sisters were close, buying them a trip to Tuscany was so far out of the realm of their relationships that he could barely comprehend the gesture. Leanna never planned a damn thing in her life, and Bailey, his youngest sister, was a musician with a concert schedule that rivaled the busiest of them. Even coordinating dinner with her was a massive undertaking. If he ever purchased a trip for them, Leanna would miss the flight and Bailey would probably have to cancel it. Their gifts to one another were typically as simple as making time to get together and enjoy one another's company.

"My brothers are good at taking care of me. Maybe a little too good." She sighed.

"Overprotective?" Why did he enjoy knowing that?

"Oh, you could say that. They're great, really. I adore them, but...yeah. They're overprotective." She met his gaze, and the air around them sizzled again. She looked away, pink-cheeked, and pressed her hands to her thighs. "To be honest, I don't hate the way they are. I mean, it probably sounds childish, but I feel the same way about them."

"Overprotective?" She couldn't weigh more than a buck twenty. What could she possibly do to protect a man?

She smiled, and it lit up her beautiful, dark eyes. Her voice softened, and she sat up a little straighter. "Yeah. I know it's weird, but like, when they started dating their girlfriends, I watched out for them. Made sure the girls weren't going to treat them badly, or...well...My brothers are the catch of our town, and girls can be fickle. I didn't want them to get hurt. But now the ones who live in town are all in relationships, so..." She shrugged.

Loyal. He liked that. He wondered if she was the catch of their town, too. "Do you live in the town where you grew up?"

"Yeah, in Trusty, Colorado. It's about as big as your fist. All of us live there except my oldest brother, Pierce, and one of my other brothers, Jake. Pierce is in Reno, and Jake is in LA. But they visit a lot. We're all really close. I can't imagine living anywhere else—or living far away from my family. Being away for college was enough. I'm glad to be back in my hometown." She finished her wine and set the glass beside her.

Dae held up the bottle. "More?"

"In a few minutes. I'm a lightweight. I wouldn't want you to have to carry me back up to my room."

Now, there's an idea. "Fair enough." He paused, pushing the thought of Emily in his arms to the back of his mind. "So, what do you do for a living?"

"I'm an architect. I specialize in passive houses, green building." She gazed out over the hillside, and her features softened again.

"Really? The passive-house movement is a good one, but it seems like builders don't understand it well enough to make headway."

Her eyes widened, and he felt the press of her leg against his. "You know about passive houses? Usually when I bring it up, people look all deer in the headlights at me."

"That doesn't surprise me. Most people don't understand heating by passive solar gain and energy gains from people and appliances. It's a concept they just aren't familiar with, so it sounds space-agey to them." Passive houses were the way of the future, as far as Dae was concerned, and not just houses, but schools and office buildings, too. The technology may seem space-agey, but then again, so did electric cars and cell phones twenty years ago.

"Exactly." She smacked his thigh, and both of their eyes dropped to her hand.

He lifted his eyes to hers, and she swallowed hard. In the short time they'd been talking, he'd seen a handful of looks pass through her eyes: embarrassment, arousal, worry. She had to feel the way the air zapped between them. Her eyes darkened, and her lips parted.

Oh yeah, she feels it.

She licked her lips, and it just about killed him.

"What about you?" she asked, visibly more relaxed now as she leaned back on one hand and turned her body toward him. "Where do you live? What do you do?"

Her question made him think a little deeper about the two of them. *A sexy architect into green building. Figures.* It had been his experience that tree huggers rarely held much respect for demolition experts. He sucked down his wine and went with an evasive answer in hopes of postponing any negative discussion.

"Depends on the week. I don't like to be tied to one place for too long. I get itchy." He'd always been that way. Spending too much time alone in any one of the houses he owned made him edgy. He'd never met anyone he'd liked enough to spend a few weeks with, much less settle down with.

Emily's finely manicured brows furrowed. Clearly he wasn't going to get off that easily.

"So..."

"I'm into construction. I go where the jobs take me."

"Oh. I thought construction workers usually worked around where they lived."

"Some do. I work with larger projects, which means that I travel a lot." He didn't want to talk about his job. Especially not the demolition job he was assessing there in Tuscany. He was enjoying spending time with Emily, and the last thing he wanted to do was talk about why he blew up buildings for a living.

"How long are you here?" His feeble attempt at changing the subject.

"Ten days, and I have every day planned so I don't miss a thing." She held up her empty glass.

"No longer worried about me carrying you to your bedroom?" Their eyes locked, and he couldn't help but think, *Or mine*, as he filled her glass. Although he knew it was just his ego talking. He'd stopped having flings a few years ago—but they were still fun to think about.

"I can think of worse things." Her voice was quiet, seductive. She mindlessly twirled her finger in her hair and lowered her eyes. When she raised them again, she said more confidently, "Besides, you have sisters. I think you'll take care of me."

"That's a lot of trust in a guy you've known for only a little while." He refilled their glasses.

"If you were a serial killer, you'd have stabbed me and hidden my body by now. And if you were going to make a move, I think you'd have done more than talk about family." She moved her fingers over so they were touching his. "Like I said, you have sisters. I think the big brother in you will keep me safe."

Damn. Talk about conflicting signals. The hand. The brother talk. A guy could get whiplash trying to keep up.

An hour and an empty bottle of wine later, they were standing in front of the door to Emily's room. She was tucked beneath his arm, her cheeks flushed, her eyes glassy, and her head nestled against his chest.

Lightweight indeed. Cute-as-hell lightweight. Dae took a step back and leaned his hip against the doorframe and crossed his arms. Debating. He wanted to kiss her, to feel the soft press of her lips against his and taste the sweet wine on that sassy tongue of hers. *I think the big brother in you will keep me safe.*

"These five overprotective brothers of yours, would they mind if we spent tomorrow together?"

She took a step back and raked her eyes down his body. "That depends. Do serial killers ask women on dates?"

He laughed. "I don't have enough experience with serial killers to answer that."

Emily's phone vibrated in her pocket.

"Maybe that's one of them. You can ask."

Emily pulled her phone out of her pocket and read a text. She trapped her lower lip between her teeth and raised her eyes to his, then held up her index finger before responding.

"Christ, you're not really asking your brother—are you?"

She shook her head, and her hair tumbled forward. "Soon-to-be sister-in-law. Daisy. She's marrying my brother Luke the weekend after I go home."

Dae scrubbed his hand down his face at the prospect of her asking her soon-to-be sister-in-law about going on a date with him. "Great." He didn't even try to mask his sarcasm.

Her phone vibrated again, and her long lashes fluttered as she read the text.

"Well? What does Daisy say?"

"Um..." She lowered the phone and held it behind her back with a coy smile.

Dae rolled his eyes. So much for their date. The words *stranger danger* came to mind. "It was nice getting to know you tonight, Emily."

Her smile was replaced with tight lips and a wrinkled brow as he took a step away. "What? That's it? I haven't answered you yet."

He closed the distance between them, so their thighs touched. Their lips were a breath apart, and her eyes held a seductive challenge. It took all of his focus for him not to lean down and wipe that smug look off her face with a kiss.

"I assumed..."

"Assumed?" Her voice turned low and sexy. "What happened to Mr. Hand or Arm? Wow, you're not quite the man I thought you were if you give up that easy."

She touched his chest, nearly doing him in.

Dae clenched his jaw at the challenge. "I'm trying to be respectful. You're the one who gave me the big-brother lecture earlier."

"Oh, yeah." She wrinkled her nose, and her eyes held a hint of regret.

She was so damn cute that he wanted to take care of her as much as he wanted to kiss her. "Yeah." He leaned down and pressed his cheek to hers, then wrapped an arm around her waist, holding her against him. "I honestly don't give a rat's ass what Daisy said," he whispered.

Emily nibbled on her lower lip.

Their bedrooms were located on more of a balcony than a hallway, with wrought-iron railings overlooking the great room below. The villa was silent, save for the sound of their heavy breathing.

"It's your answer I want, not hers."

He leaned back and gazed into her eyes, hoping she'd take a chance on the desire he could see lingering in them.

"Okay," she whispered.

"Great, and just for the record, I'd have kept you safe even if I didn't have sisters, but I can assure you that my feelings toward you are not brotherly."

Emily's eyes widened.

"And I wouldn't mind if you didn't act sisterly toward me, either."

"I—"

"Good night, Emily."

(End of Sneak Peek)
To continue reading, be sure to pick up the next
LOVE IN BLOOM release:

DREAMING OF LOVE, *The Bradens*

Please enjoy a preview of the next
Love in Bloom novel

seaside
Sunsets

Seaside Summers, Book Three

Love in Bloom Series

Melissa Foster

NEW YORK TIMES BESTSELLING AUTHOR

MELISSA FOSTER

seaside
Sunsets

Love in Bloom: Seaside Summers
Contemporary Romance

Chapter One

JESSICA AYERS COULD hold a note on her cello for thirty-eight seconds without ever breaking a sweat, but staring at the eBay auction on her iPhone as the last forty seconds ticked away had her hands sweating and her heart racing. She never knew seconds could pass so slowly. She'd been pacing the deck of her rented apartment in the Seaside cottage community in Wellfleet, Massachusetts, for forty-five minutes. This was her first time—and she was certain her last time—using the online auction site. She was the high bidder on a baseball that she was fairly certain was her father's from when he was a boy.

"Come on. Come on. Come on." *Fifteen seconds.* She clenched her eyes shut and squeezed the phone, as if she could will the win. It was only seven thirty in the morning, and already the sun had blazed a path through the trees. She was hot and frustrated, and after fighting with her orchestra manager for two weeks about taking a hiatus, and her mother for even longer about everything under the sun, she was ready to blow. She'd come to the Cape for a respite from playing in the Boston Symphony Orchestra, hoping to figure out if she was living her life to the fullest, or missing out on it altogether. Finding her father's baseball autographed by Mickey Mantle was her self-imposed distraction to keep her mind off picking up the cello. She'd never imagined she'd find it a week into her vacation.

She opened her eyes and stared at the phone.

Five seconds. Four. Three.

A message flashed on the screen. *You have been outbid by another bidder.*

"What? No. No, no, no." She pressed the bid icon, and nothing happened. She pressed it again, and again, her muscles tightening with each attempt. Another message flashed on the screen. *Bidding for this item has ended.*

No!

She stared at the phone, unable to believe she'd been seconds away from winning what she was sure was her father's baseball and had lost it. She hated phones. She hated eBay. She hated bidding against nonexistent people in tiny little stupid phones. She hated the whole thing so much she turned and hurled the phone over the deck.

Wow.

That felt really, really good.

"Ouch! What the..." A deep male voice rose up to her.

Jessica crouched and peered between the balusters. Standing on the gravel road just a few feet from her building, in a pair of black running shorts and no shirt, was the nicest butt she'd ever seen, attached to a tanned back that was glistening with sweat and rippled with muscles. Holy moly, they didn't make orchestra musicians with bodies like that. Not that she'd know, considering that they were always properly covered in black suits and white shirts, but could a body like that even *be* hidden?

He turned, one hand rubbing his unruly black hair as he looked up at the pitch pine trees.

Yeah, you won't find the culprit there.

His eyes passed by her deck, and she cringed. At least he hadn't seen her phone, which she spotted a few feet away, where it must have fallen after conking him on the head. His eyes dropped to the ground...and traveled directly to it.

Jessica ducked lower, watching his brows knit together, giving him a brooding, sexy look.

Please don't see me. Please don't see me.

He looked at the cottages to his left, then to the pool off to his right, and just as Jessica sighed with relief, he crossed the road toward the steps to her apartment. His eyes locked on her. He shaded them with his hand and looked back down at the phone, then back up at her, and lifted the phone in the air.

"Is this yours?"

She debated staying there, crouched and peering between the railings like a child playing hide-and-seek, hoping he really couldn't see her.

I've been seen.

Darn it! She rose slowly to her feet. "My what?" She had no idea what she was going to say or do as the words flew from her mouth.

He laughed. God, he had a sexy laugh. "Your phone?"

He stood there looking amused and so damn sexy that Jessica couldn't take her eyes off of him. "Why would that be mine? I don't even have a phone." *Great. Now I'm a phone assaulter and a liar.* She had no idea that being incredibly attracted to a man could couple with embarrassment and make her spew lies, as if she lied every day.

He looked back down at the phone and scratched his head. She wondered what he was thinking. That it fell from the sky? No one was that stupid, but she couldn't own up to it now. She was in too deep. As he mounted the stairs, she got a good look at his chest, covered with a light dusting of hair, over muscles that bunched and rippled down his stomach, forming a V between his hips.

He stepped onto the deck and raked his hazel eyes down her body with the kind of smile that should have made her feel at ease and instead made her feel very naked. And hot. Definitely hot. Oh wait, he was hot. She was just bothered. Hot and bothered. Jesus, up close he was even more handsome than she imagined, with at least three days' scruff peppering his strong chin and eyes that played hues of green and brown like a melody.

"Hi. I'm Jamie Reed."

"Hi. Jessica...Ayers."

"How long are you renting?" He used his forearm to wipe his brow. She never knew sweating could look so sexy.

"For the summer." She shifted her eyes to her phone. "What will you do with that phone?"

He looked down at it. "I guess that depends, doesn't it?" The side of his mouth quirked up, making his handsome, rugged face look playful and sending her stomach into a tailspin.

Jessica needed and wanted playful in her too prim and proper life, but she needed her phone even more, in case her orchestra manager called.

"Let's say it was my phone. Let's say it slipped from my hand and fell over the deck, purely by accident."

He stepped closer, and suddenly playful turned serious. His eyes went dark and seductive, in a way that bored right through her, both turning her on and calling her on her shit. He placed one big hand on the railing beside her and peered over the side. His brows lifted, and he stepped closer again. She inched backward until her back met the wooden rail. He smelled of power and sweat and something musky that made her insides quiver.

"That's a hell of an accident." His voice whispered over her skin.

Jessica could barely breathe, barely think with his eyes looking through her, and his crazy, sexy body so close made her sweat even more. The truth poured out like water from a faucet.

"Okay. I'm sorry. I did throw it, but it's not my fault. Not really. It's that stupid eBay site." Her voice rose, and her frustration bubbled forth. "I don't know how I could lose an auction in the last ten seconds. My bid held strong for forty-five minutes, and then out of the blue I lost it for five lousy dollars? And it was all because the stupid bid button was broken." She sank down to a chair. "I'm sorry. I'm just upset."

"So, let me get this straight. You lost a bid on eBay, so you threw your phone?" He lowered himself to the chair beside her, brow wrinkled in confusion, or maybe amusement. She couldn't tell which.

"Yeah, I know. I know. I threw my phone. But it must be broken. I hate technology."

"Technology is awesome. It's not the phone's fault you lost your bid. It's called sniping, and lots of people do it."

"Sniping?" She sighed. "I'm sorry. I know I sound whiny and bitchy, but I'm really not like this normally."

He arched a brow and smiled, which made her smile, because of course he didn't believe her. Who would? He didn't know she was usually Miss Prim and Proper. He couldn't know she never used words like *stupid* or even visited the eBay website until today.

"I swear I'm not. I'm just frustrated. I've been trying to find the baseball my father had as a kid. It was signed by Mickey Mantle, and somewhere along the line, his parents lost it. His sister had colored in the autograph with red ink, and I think I finally found it...and then lost it."

"That's a bummer. I can see why you're upset. I'm sorry."

"How can you be so nice after I beaned you with my phone?"

He shrugged. "I've been hit by worse. Here, let me show you some eBay tricks." He scrolled through her apps, of which she had none other than what came with the phone. He drew his brows together. "Do you want me to download the eBay app?"

"The eBay app? I guess."

He fiddled with her phone, then moved his chair closer to hers. "When you're bidding on eBay, and other people are bidding at the same time, you need to refresh your screen because bids don't refresh quickly on all phones." He continued explaining and showing her how to refresh her screen.

She only half listened. She simply didn't get technology, and she was used to sitting next to men in suits and tuxedos, not half-naked men with Adonis-like bodies wearing nothing but a pair of shorts with all their masculinity on display. She could barely concentrate.

JAMIE COULD TELL by the look in Jessica's eyes that she wasn't paying attention. As the developer of OneClick, the second-largest search engine rivaling Google, he'd been in his fair share of meetings with foggy-eyed people who zoned out when he started with technical talk. But refreshing a screen was hardly technical, which meant that either beautiful Jessica was really a novice and had lived in a cave for the past ten years or she was playing him like a cheap guitar. She sure as hell didn't look like she'd been living in a cave. She was about the hottest chick he'd seen in forever, sitting beside him in a canary-yellow bikini like it was the most comfortable thing in the world. Maybe she was a fashion model with handlers that did these kinds of things for her.

Her light brown hair brushed her thighs when she leaned forward, and her bright blue eyes, although looking a little lost at the moment, were strikingly sexy. She had a hot bod, with perfect, perky breasts, a trim waist, curvaceous hips, and legs that went on forever, but that didn't change the fact that she'd tried to avoid admitting that the phone was hers. The last thing Jamie needed this summer was to be played, even by a beautiful woman like Jessica. This was his first summer off in eight years, and he intended to relax and spend time with his grandmother, Vera, who was in her mideighties and wasn't getting any younger. If the right woman came along, and he had the time and interest, he'd enjoy her company, but he had no patience for games.

"Either your phone is new, or you don't use many apps."

"No. To be honest, I don't even text very often. I've been kind of out of the swing of things in that arena for a while. And after this I'm not sure that I really want to dive in."

He handed her the phone. "You can do this on your computer. Some people find that easier."

She closed her eyes for a beat and cringed. "I get

along with my computer even worse than I get along with my phone."

He still couldn't decide if she was playing him or not. She sounded sincere, and the look in her beautiful baby blues was as honest as he'd ever seen. Oh hell, he might as well offer to help.

"Then you've met just the right guy. I can give you a crash course in computers and phones."

"I've taken up so much of your time already. I would feel guilty taking up any more on a beautiful day like today. But I really appreciate your offer."

Are you blowing me off?

Jamie rose to his feet. "Okay, well, if you need any help, I'm in the cottage on the end with the deck out front and back. Stop by anytime." He hesitated, knowing he should leave but wanting to stay and get to know her a little better. If she was playing him, she would've taken him up on his offer for sure.

Jessica rose to her feet, grabbed a towel from the back of her chair, and picked up a tote bag from beneath the table. "I'm heading to the pool, so I'll walk down with you."

They walked down to the pool together in silence, giving Jamie a chance to notice how nice she smelled. It took all of his focus not to run his eyes down her backside—he was dying to see her ass, but why rush things and make her uncomfortable? She'd walk into the pool and he'd have his chance.

Jessica dug through her tote bag. She placed a slender hand on her hip and sighed. "I forgot my key. Why do they keep the pool locked, anyway?"

He had no idea why, but she looked so curious that he made up a reason. "To keep the derelicts out."

"Derelicts? Really? My friend suggested that I rent here. He said there was almost no crime on the Cape."

Jamie wondered who her *friend* was. "We had some trouble with teenagers two summers ago, but other than that, your friend was right. There are no derelicts lurking about."

"Oh, thank goodness. I didn't think my coworker would lead me astray. I guess I'll go get my key."

She turned to leave and—*holy hell*—her bikini bottom was a thong. A thin piece of floss between two perfect ass cheeks. How had he missed that?

It was all he could do not to drool. "Nice suit," he mumbled.

She looked over her shoulder. "Thanks! I saw the Thong Thursday flyer and thought, why not? I bought this suit when we were overseas and wore it there once. I brought it with me, but I never would have had the guts to wear it here, until I saw that you guys had an actual *day* for one." She waved and disappeared up the steps to her apartment.

Jamie spun around and scanned the bulletin board where the pool rules were posted. A blue flyer had been tacked front and center: JOIN US FOR THONG THURSDAY!

Thank you, Bella.

Jamie jogged up to Bella's cottage. The screen door was open.

"Bella?" Bella Abbascia owned the cottage across from the apartment Jessica was renting. Bella was the

378

resident prankster. Her favorite person to play tricks on was Theresa Ottoline, the Seaside property manager. Theresa oversaw the homeowner association guidelines for the community—including the pool rules, which included a rule that clearly stated, *No thongs on women or Speedos on men.*

Her fiancé, Caden Grant, walked out of the bedroom in his police officer uniform. "Hey, Jamie. Come on in."

Jamie stepped inside. "Hi. I wanted to thank your fiancée for Thong Thursday."

Caden shook his head. "She did it, huh?"

"Hell, yes, she did it, and..." Jamie looked out the window at the *big house* where Jessica was renting. The house was owned by Theresa Ottoline, the property manager for Seaside. The apartment Jessica rented had a separate entrance on the second floor.

"Did you see the new tenant? Jessica Ayers?" He whistled. "Hotter than hell."

"I saw her sitting on her deck the other night when I pulled in, but I haven't met her. Bella's over at Amy's with the girls."

Evan, Caden's mini-me teenage son, walked out of his bedroom. Evan was almost seventeen, and this year he'd cropped his chestnut hair short, like his father's. Over the year he'd grown to six two. His square jaw and cleft chin, also like Caden's, had lost all but the faintest trace of the boy he'd been two years earlier.

"Dude. You went running without me?" Evan, Caden, and their other buddy, Kurt Remington, whose fiancée, Leanna Bray, owned the cottage behind Bella and Caden, sometimes ran with Jamie in the mornings.

"Sorry, Ev. Vera wanted to get a jump on the day, so I went early."

"That's okay." Evan glanced out the window in the kitchen and looked down by the pool, where Jessica was spreading a towel out on a lounge chair. "I was gonna go for a run, but if it's Thong Thursday, I think I'll go for a swim instead, then head over to TGG for the afternoon." Evan had worked with Jamie for one summer, learning how to program computers, and he'd been working part-time at TGG, The Geeky Guys, ever since.

Jamie set a narrow-eyed stare on Evan.

"What?" Evan laughed.

"Behave," Jamie said, before walking out the door and across the gravel road to Amy's cottage. *Christ, now I'm jealous of a kid?*

He glanced at the pool, tempted to put on his own suit and head down for a gawk and a swim. Instead, he headed across the gravel road to Amy Maples's cottage.

"Hi, Jamie. Just in time for coffee." Amy handed him a mug over the railing of her deck.

"Thanks."

Jenna Ward, a big-busted brunette, and Bella, a tall, mouthy blonde, followed Amy out of her cottage. They wore sundresses over their bathing suits, their typical Cape attire. The Seaside cottages had been in their families for years, and Jamie had grown up spending summers with the girls and Leanna Bray, who owned the cottage beside Vera's, and Tony Black, who owned the cottage on the other side of Leanna's.

"Come on up here, big boy." Bella waved him onto the deck and pulled out a chair.

"I owe you big-time, Bella." He sat beside her and set his coffee on the glass table.

"Most people do," she teased.

"I know I do." Jenna had recently gotten engaged to Pete Lacroux, a local boat craftsman, who also handled maintenance for Seaside—and had been the object of Jenna's secret crush for years. Bella and Amy had secretly broken things in Jenna's cottage for several summers without Jenna knowing, to ensure that she and Pete would have reasons to be thrown together.

"Thong Thursday?" Jamie shook his head. "You are a goddess, Bella."

She patted her thick blond hair. "Thank you for noticing."

"Leanna is going to be so mad at you for doing that," Jenna said. "She doesn't think our men need to see butt floss on any of us." Leanna ran a jam-making business out of Kurt's bay-side property.

Bella swatted the air. "She's staying at their bay house for a few days. She'll miss it completely." The lower Cape was a narrow peninsula that sprawled between Cape Cod Bay and the Atlantic Ocean. The cottages were located between the two bodies of water, and both Kurt and Pete owned property on the bay. Caden and Bella had a house on a street around the corner from the bay, and all three couples spent most of their summers at Seaside and the rest of the year at their other homes.

Luscious Leanna's Sweet Treats had really taken off in the last two years, and since her business was run from a cottage on their bay property, she was spending more and more time there.

"I'm sure Tony won't complain," Amy said with an eye roll that could have rocked the deck. Tony Black was a professional surfer and a motivational speaker, and Amy had been hot for him for about as long as Jenna had been lusting after Pete, but Tony had never made a move toward taking their relationship to the next level. Jamie didn't get it. He'd seen Tony eyeing Amy, and Tony took care of her like she was his girlfriend. Amy was hot, smart, and obviously interested—Tony was a big, burly guy with a good head on his shoulders. They'd make a great pair.

"Speaking of Tony, I saw him leave early this morning. He's spending the day at the ocean." Jamie sipped his coffee.

"Good, then maybe he'll miss the thong show, too." Amy leaned over the table and lowered her voice. "Did you guys see the chick renting Theresa's condo?"

"All I know is that she's smokin' hot and she doesn't talk much." Jenna was busy resituating the top of her sundress, pulled tightly across her enormous breasts.

"I don't know what her deal is," Bella said. "But she was yelling at her phone the other day."

"You mean yelling on her phone," Jenna corrected her.

"No, I mean at. She was staring at it, smacking it, and yelling at it." Bella made a cuckoo motion with her finger beside her head.

Nothing new here from the girls. A little jealousy over the new hot chick. Jamie picked up his coffee mug. "Mind if I bring this back later? I have to get going. I'm running into Hyannis to pick up a few things. You guys need anything?"

The girls shook their heads.

"You're willingly going to miss Thong Thursday?" Bella put her hand to his forehead. "You must be ill."

No shit. "One look at my ass in a thong and she'll be chasing me around the complex. I wouldn't want to subject you three ladies to that. It could get ugly." He smiled with the tease.

"Ha! Yeah, right. Like you'd ever wear a thong." Jenna threw her head back with a loud laugh. "You're just worried about sporting a woody down by the pool."

She had him there.

"You've got woodies on the brain," Jamie said. "Are you guys coming to Vera's concert tonight?" Vera had played the violin professionally when she was younger, and this summer a group of older Wellfleet residents had put together a string quartet and invited Vera to play. They never saw much of a crowd, but it got her out of the house and playing for an audience again, which she enjoyed.

"I wouldn't miss Vera's concert," Amy said.

"Bella and I are going over together because Caden's taking someone's shift and Pete's hanging with his father tonight, working on a boat. I'll ask Sky if she wants to come, too." Sky was Pete's sister. She'd come to the Cape last summer to run their father's hardware store while he was in rehab, and she'd never gone back to New York other than to pack up her things. Now sober for almost a year, their father helped Pete with his boat-refinishing business.

"Vera will be glad to hear it, and she loves Pete's sister." He glanced down at the pool, then headed for his cottage.

"Wanna bet who's gonna bang the new chick? Tony or Jamie?" Jenna's voice trailed behind him.

Jamie slowed to hear the answer.

A crack of hand on skin told him that Amy had shut Jenna up with a friendly swat.

(End of Sneak Peek)
To continue reading, be sure to pick up the next
LOVE IN BLOOM release:

SEASIDE SUNSETS, *Seaside Summers*
Love in Bloom series

Full LOVE IN BLOOM SERIES order

Love in Bloom books may be read as stand alones. For more enjoyment, read them in series order. Characters from each series carry forward to the next.

SNOW SISTERS

Sisters in Love (Book 1)
Sisters in Bloom (Book 2)
Sisters in White (Book 3)

THE BRADENS

Lovers at Heart (Book 4)
Destined for Love (Book 5)
Friendship on Fire (Book 6)
Sea of Love (Book 7)
Bursting with Love (Book 8)
Hearts at Play (Book 9)

THE REMINGTONS

Game of Love (Book 10)
Stroke of Love (Book 11)
Flames of Love (Book 12)
Slope of Love (Book 13)
Read, Write, Love (Book 14)

THE BRADENS

Taken by Love (Book 15)
Fated for Love (Book 16)
Romancing my Love (Book 17)

Flirting with Love (Book 18)
Dreaming of Love (Book 19)
Crashing into Love (Book 20)

SEASIDE SUMMERS

Seaside Dreams
Seaside Hearts
Seaside Sunsets
Seaside Secrets

THE RYDERS (coming soon)

Seized by Love
Claimed by Love
Swept into Love
Chased by Love
Rescued by Love

Acknowledgments

I didn't think anything could bring me quite as much joy as writing about the Bradens, but hearing from my readers as you demand more of our sexy heroes and sassy heroines is equally as exciting. I love receiving your emails and messages on social media, so please keep them coming. You inspire me to be a better writer and to continue the bloodline. Thank you!

A hearty thank-you goes out to Giacomo (Jim) Giammatteo, who was kind enough to share his stories of his beloved Gracie with me. I hope I did her justice. Jim was also kind enough to fill me in on all things pig related, and Shanyn Silinski offered an education on calving and large farm animals. Thank you both for your time and for sharing your knowledge. Any and all errors are my own. Elisabeth Nash is named for a reader whom I chat with often on Facebook, Elisabeth Occhipinti. I hope you enjoy your namesake. I'd like to thank Russell Blake for naming Aunt Cora. The name suits her perfectly. And much gratitude goes to all of my supportive friends and family for their endless patience and encouragement. You're an inspiration to me on a daily basis, and I appreciate your efforts.

My editorial team and proofreaders make my work shine with their superb skills. Thank you: Kristen Weber, Penina Lopez, Jenna Bagnini, Juliette Hill, Marlene Engel, and Lynn Mullan. Thank you, Natasha Brown, for the gorgeous cover, and Clare Ayala, for formatting my work.

Last but never least, thank you to my husband,

Les, and my youngest children, Jess and Jake, who graciously allow me to live in my fictional worlds for far too many hours each day.

Melissa Foster is a *New York Times* and *USA Today* bestselling and award-winning author. Her books have been recommended by *USA Today's* book blog, *Hagerstown* magazine, *The Patriot*, and several other print venues. She is the founder of the World Literary Café, and when she's not writing, Melissa helps authors navigate the publishing industry through her author training programs on Fostering Success. Melissa also hosts Aspiring Authors contests for children and has painted and donated several murals to the Hospital for Sick Children in Washington, DC.

Visit Melissa on her website or chat with her on social media. Melissa enjoys discussing her books with book clubs and reader groups and welcomes an invitation to your event.

Melissa's books are available through most online retailers in paperback and digital formats.

CPSIA information can be obtained at www.ICGtesting.com
Printed in the USA
BVOW08s2152221215

430848BV00001B/9/P